No trumpets sound when the important decisions of our life are made. Destiny is made known silently.

—Agnes DeMille

Destiny's Dowry

by
Rosemary Gard

Booklocker.com, Inc.
2008

This book was written for:

Kristina Gard Browne
&
Michael Gard

So that they may better understand
their colorful Croatian heritage.

Dedicated to Bob Gard
&
The memory of Janice Thrall
Beloved Patron of the Arts

Part I, Chapter 1

October 1892 - Croatia

*I should have kept on going...*thought Mato, *just kept on going.*

About a three hour buggy ride, east of Zagreb, nestled among the green hills in Croatia, was the little village of Selna. Seven simple small log houses, each framed with a wooden fence, sheltered the total population, which at that time were 26. The inhabitants of Selna, each in some way related to one another, were simple, superstitious peasants who worked hard to survive the unpredictability of nature and the oppressive rule of the Austro-Hungarian government. Between the years of 1880 and 1914, some 600,000 Croatians left Croatia-Slavonia seeking a better life elsewhere.

Mato Balich lived in the very first house with Mila, his wife of ten years, along with their ten-year-old daughter, Anka. Anka inherited her mother's light brown hair, pale skin and pretty brown eyes.

On this particular afternoon, somewhere around 5 o'clock, Mato was sitting on the cool ground, his thin legs stretched out before him on the bare earth. His bony back rested on the trunk of a dying apple tree, its few leaves rustling now and then, whenever a breeze past through the yard stirring dust.

Within this yard was a small one-room log dwelling. It was simply constructed, rectangular with one door and two windows.

The barn was little more than a narrow shed. What looked to be the remains of a garden was overgrown with weeds, but some cabbages were visible along with a few onions.

The well, made of stacked rocks, stood as a lonely sentinel in the middle of the yard. There was no movement here...all was still, except for the breeze.

Mato's brooding face was dark and leathery. Even with a full head of dark hair he looked much older than his 30 years. Beside him was an empty jug of slivovic, a brandy made of plums. The brandy had been his companion for the afternoon. The man looked like so much rumpled laundry sitting there on the ground in his pants and shirt of homespun cloth. The legs were cut full...like pajamas. It was the style worn by most of the Croatian men of the villages. He shivered feeling the autumn chill.

This was the time of the strangling rule of the Hapsburgs when thousands upon thousands of Croatian peasants, with their possessions tied in bundles, fled to a new life in America. Even though the peasants were no longer serfs and able to buy land, the taxes were high and the payments for land were hard to meet, so the debts mounted. To make matters worse, the government encouraged the ambitious Germans to settle in the Northern regions, squeezing out the Croatian population.

Mato lusted for America! It was all he thought about. It seemed that every village and city lost men and families to America. How he longed to be one of them.

AMERICA...he loved the sound of it. He had to go there! He would go there! Secretly, he had been planning his escape. Ever since his younger brother, Franko, left for America evading military service, Mato thought of nothing else. Agents from foreign steamship companies came through the villages explaining how travel arrangements could be made. It was easy to be seduced with promises of work and wealth. Sponsors would pay for the passage in exchange for labor.

Mato had been hiding money for nearly a year. There seemed no good reason to stay in Selna. Mila and Anka would stay here, of course. They'd get by. They were both good workers. Besides, their friends in the village wouldn't let them starve. He would send them money, he reasoned. He might even send for them...but he doubted it. He sighed, *No good reason to stay. Why, we don't even have good wine!* Ever since the phylloxera disease ravaged the vineyards, no one had any good grapes. It would take a long while for the grapes to come back.

The sweet plum slivovic seemed to be working on him, its heat warming him as he swallowed. His thoughts drifted from one thing to another. Everything went to the Hungarians! Hell, he was no better off than his father, who had been a serf. Mato shook the empty brandy jug...nothing...he threw it down, watching as it slowly rolled across the dirt.

There was nothing for him here. They only had a couple of scrawny chickens and one skinny cow. No horses...no pigs...no ducks. *Well*...he thought with a touch of guilt, *I could have bought a pig, but then I would have spent some of my 'America' money.*

Mato moved his back against the bark of the tree relieving an itch. He glanced at the house. It had been quiet in there for some time now. Mila was having a long labor. He wasn't happy about the baby. Baby or not...he was going to America! His eyes searched the doorway of the log house. This was a long labor...eighteen hours. He shaded his eyes with his work roughened hand and looked at the sun to verify the time. It shouldn't be long now...it had been so quiet.

Mato's dark eyes stared ahead, unseeing. His calloused fingers played with a letter he held in his hand. It was a letter from his brother Franko, now in Chicago. Franko was five years younger, a handsomer version of Mato, always quick to laugh and joke.

Mato had been very sad the night Franko came to say good-bye, that night before he left for America. Mato knew he would miss his brother and wished with all his heart that he could go with him on his adventure to America. Franko hadn't noticed his older brother's mood that night, for the younger man was giddy with the excitement of leaving. The brothers had spent the night talking, drinking, singing and crying.

Mato toyed with the letter...a letter he couldn't read. Whenever a letter arrived, he had to find someone to read it to him. In America, Franko had to find someone to write his letters, since he also couldn't read or write. Sometimes the clerk at the post office in Petrina would read the letters, however he refused the last time Mato asked. It seemed the civil servant felt put upon by all the ignorant people getting letters from America.

Then Mato asked the priest to read the letters. Mato wanted to hear the letters read more than once, but after one reading, Father Lahdra didn't offer to read it again. So Mato tried to memorize what he had heard. He ran what he remembered through his mind, over and over again. From the most recent letter Mato remembered:

'I have so many friends here. We gather together for weddings, christenings, funerals or just to dance.'

In his mind, Mato could envision himself part of this new life. He even saw himself in a dark wool suit, the kind he had seen doctors and professors wear in Zagreb. His mind went back to the letter.

'We call each other Kum (godfather or close friend). It is as if we are all related. While on the ship, I learned how to write my name. It wasn't necessary because we can just make a cross. When we got to New York, we had to tell our names to get our documents. Instead of Franko Balich, the man in the uniform wrote Frank Ball. I protested when I didn't hear Balich. So, now in America I am Frank, not Franko, but my last name is still Balich.'

Milan Obradovich is now Mike O'Brady and Andra Ivanovic is Andrew Evans. Andra likes his new American name, so we have to remember to call him Andrew or Andy.

Reluctantly Mato's thoughts returned to the present. He frowned as he looked at the house. Why hadn't he heard the baby cry? Mila's birthing moans had stopped some time ago. Even if it was to be a son, Mato was going to America! He didn't want another child. Hell, he hadn't wanted the first one. For that matter, he hadn't wanted to marry Mila when she got pregnant.

He should have kept going...ten years ago...he should have kept going.

Ten years ago his plan had been to work for Mila's father only for the season. He slept in the barn and was given meals. When the crop was to be sold, Joso Perpich, Mila's father, was to pay Mato. Mato had planned to move on.

Mato hated the old, white haired Perpich. His bushy white brows shaded those mean cold as ice, blue eyes and his handlebar mustache hid his thin bitter line of a mouth. Mato worked long, hard, fourteen-hour days for the old man.

Mato had not loved Mila. She was just there with a sweet smile, light-brown braids and always barefoot which was common. Shoes, if one had them, wore out too quickly.

Mila's mother had died when the girl was five years old, leaving her an only child. At fourteen, still unmarried, Mila did everything expected of the woman of the house. She did the cooking. She gardened, spun flax and wove cloth in the winter.

Mato had been a young man with sexual needs and he saw how Mila watched him. How she brought him cold water when the day was hot. The secret lovemaking had given Mato great pleasure. In a way he was getting even with his mean boss. He had smiled to himself and thought...*If you only knew you old fool...if you only knew!*

The old man's face went purple with rage when he caught Mila and Mato, both naked in the barn stall. Incensed with fatherly fury, Joso grabbed a near-by pitchfork meaning to do as much damage to Mato's body, as Mato had done to Mila's virginity.

"Bastard!" The old man yelled, as he aimed the fork at Mato, who was now desperately tugging and pulling up his pants.

"No, Tata, no!" With tears streaming down her reddened cheeks, Mila had thrown herself across Mato, protecting him from her father.

Joso froze seeing his daughter's naked body shielding Mato who had stopped struggling, while Mila sprawled herself against him. Mila was crying incoherently. Neither man could understand her. It was a while before both men realized she was sobbing, "I am pregnant."

If only he had kept going...

A shadow falling across his face brought him out of his inebriated reverie. A tall figure all in black stood before him and clumsily he scrambled to his feet.

"Kuma Julia." he said in the way of a greeting. Julia was one of the few people Mato respected. She was an imposing figure, almost six feet tall. She was doctor, friend and sorceress to everyone in the village. No one knew how old Julia was. As always, Julia wore her widow's wear of a black babushka, black blouse and skirt. Her face was lined and her eyes were a watery gray now, but once they were sharp and bright blue.

Julia spoke softly. "She's going to die." She said it simply, sadly.

Mato just stood there for a moment. The alcohol had dulled his comprehension. It seemed a minute or so had passed before he said, "This can't be true." His eyes went to the log house and then back to Julia's somber face. Her eyes were watery with grief or age or both.

"Kuma Julia..."

He searched those eyes for some encouragement, "Surely, you can do something." His voice was hoarse. "You always know what to do." This isn't what he wanted, not for Mila to die.

Julia touched his arm sympathetically. Her hand was gnarled from work. Her veins showed through her aging transparent skin. "Mato," she said, almost apologetically, "she is just too weak." The old woman took a deep breath and continued, "Mila has been frail for a long time. She shouldn't have tried to have this baby." She spread her hands out and then dropped them to her sides in resignation. "The baby is in wrong."

Her voice faltered, "I can't turn it...I've been trying...I can't." Tears welled in her almost colorless eyes.

Fear crept into Mato's heart. He had to see Mila. He had been such a bastard and it bothered him...oh, how it bothered him now. She couldn't die. Not until he could make it up to her! Mato turned from Julia and ran towards the open door of the house.

The room was rectangular with a dirt floor and sparsely furnished. In front of a window was a square table. On each side of the table were narrow beds. One neatly made up with huge down pillows while the other bed held the perspiring figure of Mila, her abdomen large with the baby.

Young Anka, stood at the foot of her mother's bed still as a statue. The fear etched in her eyes, her hand clutching the footboard. Anka was very plain with sandy colored hair hanging in braids. She had her mother's brown eyes, but not the pretty smile. There were times when his daughter's sober face unnerved Mato. He thought she might be a witch. The girl had never shown affection to anyone, but her mother.

Seeing Mila's colorless face made Mato fall to his knees beside the bed. Her face was damp with perspiration and her hair was matted. Mila rested against several down pillows, so that she was almost seated, which was the usual birthing position.

Clumsily, Mato sought her clammy hand and felt sick. Deep inside of him spreading like a flame was the fear that he would somehow have to pay for Mila's pain. He had heard about retribution in church. The words of Father Lahdra rang in his head. 'God keeps a book for every one of us! In it he records what good we have done...and the bad. Be sure that your bad list is shorter that your good list.'

Mato knew his bad list wasn't shorter.

"Mila..." he said it softly. "Mila...oh God...Mila."

She heard him through some hazy, far away place. She heard him and smiled. That smile! It was always there for him.

"I'm having...a...bad time." The words came out in soft, labored breaths.

"You'll be fine." He thought he could hear the fear in his voice. "Julia knows what to do." He tried to smile as he clumsily tried to smooth the damp hair from her forehead. As he looked at her, he thought, My God, what have I done to her? She was so pretty ten years ago. He looked down at her face wrinkled from years of working in the sun and the result of poor nutrition.

Her voice was hoarse and low. "I know you..." she hesitated, caught her breath and went on, "want to go to...America."

Embarrassed that she knew, Mato started to protest. She sighed and gently shook her head indicating for him to be still. She was summoning her strength. There were things she had to tell him. "I know you...want...to leave...us." She spoke haltingly. Mila glanced to the foot of the bed where her tearful daughter stood. Anka's knuckles were white from clutching the bed frame. She watched her father's face grow paler with the fear of losing Mila. "I'm ...going to…" she coughed, "give you a son."

Mato gave Kuma Julia a quick glance. Tears filled the old mid-wife's eyes as she shook her head indicating 'No.'

"I know...it's...a boy." Mila tried to smile, but a stab of pain stopped her.

Mato looked to Julia, who was now standing behind his daughter, her hands resting on the girl's shoulders. This time the woman turned away from his imploring eyes.

"I don't..." Mila tried to speak, but the words trailed off in a sigh. Another deep breath and she continued, "Don't think...I...I...will live."

Hearing her mother's words, Anka made an animal-like cry. She ground her fist against her mouth trying not to make disturbing sounds, her eyes filling with panic.

Mila turned her gaze toward her frightened child, her tongue tracing her dry lips before she spoke, "Come...here, Ankitza."

Hesitantly, the girl let go her iron grip of the bed and slowly slid to where her father was kneeling. He moved to make room for her. The girl laid her head on the bed next to her mother's body and Mila lovingly whispered, "My...little Ankitza." Then a spasm of coughs wracked her already worn out body. Julia was instantly there with a damp cloth, dabbing the dying woman's dry lips. Anka stayed at her mother's side, still as stone, except for the movement of one finger idly tracing a pattern on the coverlet.

In a barely audible whisper, Mila said, "I won't die...yet...I ...I must hold...my...son."

Mato couldn't breath! He gasped as if the wind had been knocked out of him. "Oh, Mila," he whispered hoarsely. "What have I done?"

Guilty thoughts raced through his foggy brain. He could have used his secret hoard to buy a pig. Yes! A pig would have been meat for Mila...it would have made her strong. And a horse! Oh, God...yes, a horse! He should have bought a horse instead of having Mila pull the plow. She never complained as she pulled on the straps under the hot sun, while Mato guided her. He knew when she had become tired, because the rows would be crooked. Pulling the plow was just one of the many ways Mato punished Mila for becoming pregnant and keeping him in Selna. He used every opportunity to make her life as miserable as he had believed his own life to be.

Now he feared the money had become evil. He felt like Judas. He had sold Mila's life for his dream of America and in his drunken reasoning, he was sure God was already starting to punish him for his mean, selfish ways. First, God was going to take away this wonderful woman and then he was going to drive Mato mad with guilt. He knew how God worked. It was starting...his limbs felt heavy. He was being ground down with guilt!

He looked down at his daughter with her head still resting next to her mother, and then he looked to Julia, who stood like a sentinel at the foot of the bed. In his head he heard Mila's words: I want to hold my son. I want to hold my son. The words were ringing in his head. I WANT TO HOLD MY SON! He put his hands to his ears, trying to shut out the words that echoed there.

He knew what he could do to make it all up to Mila. He knew how to stop the noise in his head. He turned and stumbled towards the door. Old Julia, who was startled by his actions, called out to his disappearing form, "For God's sake. Where are you going? Mato! Mato!"

He was running through the rough-hewn wooden gate, down the road and away from the village, into the last golden traces of the sunset. Pounding in his head was the litany:

I want to hold my son...I want to hold my son.

Part I, Chapter 2

Julia sat wearily at the table. She had no idea what time it was. Anka had fallen asleep kneeling beside her mother's bed, her head resting on the straw-filled mattress. Julia was drinking a tea made of dried mint. She would have preferred chamomile. She had some at home, but didn't want to leave, not even for the short time it would take to cross the dirt road and get her favorite tea.

The night was only illuminated by the moon, for no lanterns hung along the road for light. Most of the houses were dark. No one wanted to waste the scarce oil or even the fat they sometimes used as fuel. Julia had lit a lamp, along with some stubs of candles she found. She needed the comfort of light just now. She pulled her shawl around her chilled shoulders. Maybe she should build a fire. She decided against it, as she was already using wood for the clay stove. She was glad none of the village women were there. Tomorrow would be soon enough to make explanations. Mato had run them off when they had come to help with the birthing. He told them he didn't need gossips poking around his house. Well, thought Julia, there was little enough entertainment in Selna, so gossiping was a welcomed pastime. Julia was one of those rare persons who never gossiped or had anything bad to say about anyone. She kept all her opinions to herself. Julia knew everyone in the village, for she had delivered most of them and was easily the oldest person in Selna. She knew everyone's secrets.

Julia thought Mato was an ass. She thought it when he first came to work for Mila's father 10 years ago and that opinion had remained constant. Mila's father had been an ass, too. Joso Perpich never forgave his wife because their first-born had been the girl, Mila. When his wife died before giving him a son, his young daughter tried so hard to please him. She always smiled and waited on him like a servant, perhaps hoping he would forgive her for having been born a female. What an ass. Julia thought again. It was that damn dowry business, all that haggling by the fathers of the intended, each one trying to profit. Joso was poor, so he was in no real position to make demands. Then, Mato got Mila pregnant and Joso lost what little bargaining power he might have had.

Mila didn't have to worry about pleasing anyone anymore. The exhausted woman with all her energy spent, had died shortly after Mato ran out the door. Julia didn't bother to wake Anka. Time enough for bad news.

Her tea was cold. Quietly she rose from the table and moved to the far side of the room to the clay stove. The water in the iron pot was still hot. She didn't need to add more wood to the fire. She took a pinch of the dried mint from a jar and crushed it between her fingers, letting the flakes drop into the cup then pouring the steaming water over them.

Watching the hot water spill into the cup, Julia remembered Mila's weekly visits for the herbal mixtures to help her become pregnant. Mila had been so determined. "A son for Mato...it will make him happy," she had said it often.

On her way back to the table, Julia glanced at the calendar on the wall. It was a religious picture of the Holy Family, faded and flyspecked. October 4, 1892...I'll never forget this day thought Julia. With a weary voice, she said softly, "I'll always remember October 4th."

She turned back to the table. A dog barked somewhere. Soon another one joined in. Julia looked out the open window. She saw nothing in the night. She glanced at the bright moon just as a filmy, thin cloud passed in front of it. It must be well past midnight, she thought.

She heard the gate creak and stumbling footsteps. Before she could move her weary body from the window, Mato burst through the door. Julia was ready to say, "Thank God, you're here." But his dazed look and reddened face stopped her. In his arms was a bundle and from it came mewling sounds.

"Holy Mother of God!" she exclaimed, guessing what was in the bundle.

Without a look at Julia, Mato ran across the room and placed the bundle in the crook of Mila's lifeless arm. He was tremendously pleased with himself. A stupid grin was frozen on his face. There! He had shown Julia, Mila, Anka and God, what a good husband he could be. All his sins were now forgiven.

"Mila," his voice was soft and gentle. "Mila..."

Anka, waking raised her head. Her father was bouncing up and down in his excitement calling out a little more urgently, "Mila!"

Anka looked to her mother and seeing the bundle cried out, "The baby, the baby!" Her face glowed with happiness.

Julia had moved from the window and was grasping Mato's arm while he was still making little up and down bounces. *He has gone mad.*

"Listen to me!" Julia demanded in a hushed tone. "Mila died right after you left, with the baby inside of her."

He didn't understand. Mato looked from Julia to Mila and back to Old Julia. He looked down at the lifeless pale form in the bed. Slowly the words soaked into his brain and he let out a dog-like howl. He bent over clutching his body and let out a horrible moan. SHE WAS DEAD! Now he would never find peace. She had died before he could give her the baby and it meant her soul would never forgive him.

Mato straightened. He quickly pushed past Julia running into the darkness. Julia stood calling after him, "Mato, Mato! For God's sake come back here." She called until she could no longer hear his steps. A dog barked again somewhere in the distance breaking the stillness. Julia turned toward Anka feeling every bit the old woman she was.

Anka held the crying bundle in her arms as Julia hurried to the girl. The young girl's head was bent down as she cooed to the baby. When Anka looked up at Julia, for the first time in her life, the young girl had her mother's sweet smile.

Julia put her arm around the girl and led her, with the baby still cradled in her arms, to the empty bed on the other side of the table. Julia sat at the table and watched as Anka placed the bundle on the bed. "Come here, girl," she said taking the girl's work-roughened hands into her own. Julia took a deep breath, let it out slowly and said, "Ankitza...your mother left us while you were sleeping."

Anka smiled through tears, "Yes, I know...Mama said good-bye to me. And, that she was leaving the baby for me, so that I could have something to love and take care of."

Julia said nothing. She looked at the little girl for a long time. In the old woman's lifetime she had seen many deaths and just as many ways of coping with grief. "Boze Moj...My God," she sighed.

Anka turned from Julia going back to the baby, picking it up to rock it. Julia studied the bundle in Anka's arms. Where had Mato gone she wondered? He had been gone several hours. Had he stolen the infant? Did he buy the baby from Gypsies? Or, had he gone to the convent? Occassionally the convent had orphaned babies.

Julia shook her head sadly. No matter how long a person lived there could still be surprises. "What a day," she murmured to herself. "October 4, this is certainly a day to remember."

She pressed the palms of both hands hard against her eyes, as if the pressure could clear her mind and give her more strength. She let out another deep sigh and then said aloud to no one in particular, "So...life goes on. We have things to do." The old woman looked at Anka rocking one of the tiniest babies Julia had ever seen. Julia felt every one of her arthritic bones as she rose and went to where the young girl played with the baby.

"Come," she said, "let's see if the baby is wet, then we will wake Eva Kosich. She is still nursing her baby, so she can feed this little one, too."

The two women, one a child, the other who felt as old as a rock, bent over the baby. Julia guessed the baby could be only a few hours old for it was so tiny with pink skin. She wondered if it would live through the night. Anka removed the thin fabric covering the baby and let out an uncontrollable giggle.

From a surprised Julia came, "Oh, My God!" They were looking at a baby girl.

Part I, Chapter 3

Ten-year-old Anka, left with a newborn sister so tiny that it might not live, along with Mato's disappearance, created a stir in the quiet village. The morning was unusually warm for October, yet it was cool enough for a jacket or shawl.

The shock, questions, gossip and information flew like arrows between the seven little dwellings.

"Did you know there was another baby? Maybe two more! Did you see how big her belly is? There must be another one in there. Poor thing, no wonder Mila died."

"Where's Mato? Has anyone seen Mato?"

"Will the baby live?"

"Poor, Anka! How will she manage?"

"Did you see the baby? I don't think it will live."

"What if Mato doesn't come back?"

"There is the uncle in America. He could be rich by now. Maybe he will send money to Anka."

"Do you think Eva will have enough milk for her own baby and this one?"

"If this were Zagreb, Eva would get paid for her milk."

"Where's Mato? Mila should be buried."

"Has anyone gone for the Priest?"

As always, Old Julia had little to say. She offered no information and her silence caused much frustration among her neighbors.

By noon Mato had not returned and Mila had been dead about sixteen hours.

Julia sent one of the children passing by the house to fetch Milan Kosich, the husband of the woman who was supplying breast milk for the baby.

Milan was eighteen years old, newly married and also a new father. Old Julia took Anka and the baby to the Kosich house late in the night, where they remained under the care of Milan and Eva. The curious villagers stayed near their homes. This was a sad time for them and also an exciting one. Reluctant children were sent to tend the flocks or take the cattle to pasture, while the adults reacted to these startling events with morbid fascination.

Realizing that Julia had summoned Milan, a couple of babushka wearing women walked a respectful, but curious distance behind Milan as he hurried to Julia.

When Milan went into the yard and through the open doorway, a small gathering of men and women stood on the road just outside the window, which was no more than five feet away from them. They were hoping to look inside or to overhear any news they could carry back to anxiously waiting friends.

When he stepped through the doorway Milan's dark eyes fell where Mila's body lay. Old Julia had tied a scarf under Mila's chin and up over the head, something like a strap to keep the mouth from falling open. This was a common practice, as was tying the hands together.

Milan made the sign of the cross and turned away from the sight of death. Seeing the protruding belly, knowing a baby was dead inside the corpse disturbed him very much.

"I'm here," he said, nervously running his fingers through his dark hair. "What do you need of me?"

Julia looked at him and couldn't help smiling. He was such a good boy. She had helped with his birth and remembered it as if it were a week ago and not eighteen years. So tall and strong she thought, like his mother's family from the village of Sibic.

She gave her head a shake. Her mind was drifting. *Tired, just too tired.* She thought.

"Mato ran out of here last night like a crazy man," she told him. Then she motioned her hand toward the bed and Mila. "We must bury her. I don't think we should wait very much longer. The sooner we get it over with the better."

Milan nodded in agreement, aware that soon there would be the death odor.

"With my brother's help, we can have a coffin made by morning," he said.

Old Julia shook her head, disagreeing.

"Come with me," she said, and led him out the door.

She was guiding him to her yard which was just across the road. Passing the curious onlookers, she called out to a man with a full, flowing brown mustache, "Come with us, Stevo. We need you."

With a look of surprise, the slight man, standing amidst the group of curious neighbors followed Milan and Julia. He turned back to the people on the road and gave a shrug of his shoulders, as if to say, 'I don't know why she called me.'

"In the barn," said Julia, "covered with blankets is a coffin. Take it to the house."

A look of mild surprise passed between Milan and Stevo. It seemed Old Julia had prepared for her own passing.

Not waiting for the men, Old Julia turned and went back across the road.

As she passed the cluster of people again, she announced, "All right Yaga, Mara., I'll need you both to prepare the body."

It would not have occurred to either woman to refuse. This was how things were done in the village. Grudgingly or not, they helped each other. In this case the women were pleased to have been chosen, for their temporary popularity was assured. Now they would have first hand information to pass on to their neighbors.

The resemblance between Yaga and Mara was remarkable, for facial similarities were common in this area. They could have passed for sisters, though they were not. Both women were only about five feet tall and pale, with light brown eyes and skin that looked older than it should have. Leathery weather worn complexions from working in the fields or tending sheep, robbed them too quickly of their youth. Being married, both women had their heads covered, so that one could only guess at the color of their hair.

With respectful silence the pair entered the house. Upon seeing Mila's corpse they made the sign of the cross almost in unison.

No one spoke a word. Yaga went to a small wooden chest which stood against a wall. The house had no closets or dressers, just this small chest and some hooks on the wall for the clothing. The room was monastic in its simplicity. A table with benches, a bed on each side of the table and on the far side of the room, was the clay stove.

With Yaga busy at the chest, Mara headed out to the well for water with which to wash the body.

No instructions needed to be given. This ritual was known to them. They took care of their own from birth to death. They knew what to do.

Seeing the coffin carried across the road and into the Balich house caused a stir among the onlookers. Finished with his task of helping carry the coffin, Stevo announced to the waiting neighbors, "We are going to bury her." As one, the group started to move towards their houses. They all had things to do. The grave had to be dug, pallbearers appointed and prayers to be said.

Someone brought a black cloth and hung it across the window to signify that this was a house of mourning.

The shocked silence was replaced by open weeping. The weeping was not just for Mila, but also for the young Anka and the tiny baby, which would surely not live long. They wept because Mato wasn't there, leaving others to make decisions that should be his to make. And they wept because life was so fragile and uncertain.

Old Julia hadn't slept much through the night. After taking Anka to the Kosich house, she kept the death vigil alone. She had dozed now and then. She was sure of that, though it seemed she spent most of the night straining to hear Mato's return or talking to Mila's still form.

"So, Mila," she said, "you go before I do."

"What plan does God have for Anka and that innocent baby?" she had asked the still form. "What am I to say about the baby?"

Now very tired, Julia sipped tea fortified with homemade brandy and watched the capable Yaga and Mara making preparations.

The two women cut loose from Mila's body the long blouse that covered her swollen belly, pulled the soiled straw mattress from under her and carried it outdoors to be burned.

With heavy hearts they washed their childhood friend's body. They found a simple blouse and skirt, which they put on Mila with some difficulty, for her joints had stiffened. Then, they covered her light brown hair with a colorful babushka.

In the chest was a richly embroidered outfit with roses of silk thread and heavy lace. It was left for Anka to someday wear as a wedding dress.

When finished, Yaga said to Julia, "It looks as if we are ready."

She went to the door and signaled to Milan and Stevo, who had been waiting in the yard.

"We are ready for you," she told the men.

Two chairs had been borrowed and were placed in front of the table to hold the casket.

Milan was young and strong. Stevo, a handsome man, looked much older than his 28 years. His large mustache and creased skin added years to his face.

Milan and Stevo carried the casket in and set it on the chairs. It was a simple wooden box, looking more like a crate. There was no cloth lining, but someone had brought a length of shiny blue fabric for the bottom of the box. Yaga recognized the material. It belonged to her cousin, Bara. This was another act of unselfishness, a last gift from a loving friend.

Milan picked up the body of Mila and placed her in the coffin on the fabric. Yaga stepped up and arranged the clothing and made sure all was in proper order.

"When do you think the priest will be here?" asked Yaga, wondering how much time she had to change into proper mourning clothes.

"It should be soon," answered Old Julia.

Milan glanced about the room aimlessly, wondering what more he needed to do. After a few moments, feeling useless he said, "I had better go home and tell Anka what we have done."

Old Julia nodded, "Perhaps she can prepare herself at your house. She might become too upset if she sees her mother."

Milan agreed. He nodded good-bye to Mara and Yaga as he left.

Mara walked to the table, which was behind the casket, "Julia...would you like some more tea."

"No." She waived the young woman off. "Go home. You've done all you can."

Each woman made the sign of the cross as they passed the coffin, leaving to ready themselves for the funeral.

Julia was too tired to change clothes. She sat with her elbows on the table and rested her chin on the palm of her hand.

Stevo, who helped carry the coffin, was alone in the yard watching the fire made by the burning straw mattress. It pleased him to have something to do, to help in some small way.

Staring into the dancing flames, he remembered the dead Mila as a sweet young girl in braids. He would have married her, but he was too frightened to ask Joso for her hand. Stevo covered his tearing eyes with his trembling hand and thought how different it might have been if Mato Balich had never come to Selna.

Some time had passed when Stevo, lost in his thoughts of Mila, walked to the gate and looked up the road towards the cemetery. Three men were coming down the hill with shovels slung across their shoulders. He went to the open door and said to Old Julia, "The men have finished digging the grave."

The appearance of the gravediggers seemed to be a sign. Figures started to appear in twos and threes, dressed in clean suitable clothes. Sounds of weeping could be heard. One by one they entered the house. They had all dressed almost at the same time. Soon the room was full of black clothed figures, wailing and weeping.

It nearly broke everyone's heart when little Anka, accompanied by Milan and his wife, Eva, entered the crowded room. In Anka's small arms was the baby. One of the women took the baby from Anka as she walked toward the casket. Her steps were short, hesitant. At the casket she fell to her knees and threw an arm over the coffin. Her heartbreaking sobs caused the others in the room to cry, starting the wailing of, "Ah yoy...Ah yoy!" Some of the men said, "Boze moy!"

Old Julia was still seated at the table near the open window, watching Anka with a heavy heart.

Stevo, with nothing more to do after burning the mattress, had taken it upon himself to be the lookout for Old Julia. Seeing that he couldn't get near to her because of all the mourners, he spoke to the old woman from the road through the open window.

"Kuma Julia," he said, "I've gone to the hill and I still don't see the priest coming." Then, he added, "And, I don't see Mato, either."

Old Julia sighed one of her deep sighs and said, "Then we'll do it without them."

From under her apron she pulled out her ever-present rosary and started to pray aloud.

Looks of concern registered on several faces. No priest? No husband? Were they really going to go on with the burial?

Soon the room echoed with a chorus of, "Sveta Maria, Majka Boza..." On it went sounding like a mantra.

When the prayers were concluded, Julia rose and moved away from the table. It was a signal that it was time to go.

There was some uneasiness among the mourners. Weren't they going to wait for Father Lahdra?

When Anka saw the coffin lid put in place concealing her mother, she cried out anxiously, "Mamitza ...Mamitza!" It seemed to Anka things were happening too quickly.

From the back of the small crowded room four men came forward and picked up the casket. As they carried it through the door Anka gave a cry of utter anguish.

Milan wrapped a comforting arm around her as he guided her behind the casket for the procession to the cemetery. Tears blurred his vision.

The wailing of stringed instruments accompanied the mourners on their sad journey. Musicians played their braches, primas and violins.

The cemetery was at the very end of the village on a hilltop where an unpainted wooden fence enclosed it. Most of the grave markers were wooden crosses, but here and there a proper stone monument could be seen.

The road in the cemetery was just wide enough for a wagon when the occasion called for it.

A freshly dug grave awaited Mila. The graves of her mother and father were next to the newly dug hole. The casket was placed alongside the opening on two long, well-worn leather straps.

It was early fall and the flowers had lost their freshness. Those flowers that were not dry looked faded and sad, equal to the occasion.

The entire population of Selna was gathered there, except for the few children left to tend the cattle in the pasture. The mourners clustered about the open grave, each knowing how close to the casket they should stand, according to an unspoken etiquette.

The men removed their hats or caps and the women held on to their rosaries.

Again they prayed The Lord's Prayer, "Oche Nas..."

Anka's lips moved in prayer, tears streaming down her cheeks.

When the prayers were finished, Anka knelt beside the grave and said aloud, "Oh, Mamitza. I'm so afraid." She kept repeating it, until Milan lifted her gently drawing her away from the coffin.

Old Julia made the sign of the cross over the casket and Stevo, who never married because of his unspoken love for Mila, wiped his mustache, wet with tears on the sleeve of his shirt. Then he and several men took hold of the straps lowering the casket into the grave.

The sound of Anka's heart-breaking sobs brought on by the sight of the coffin being put into the ground, caused even some men to cry openly.

As the mourners passed the grave to say a last good-bye, each threw a handful of earth on top of the casket. Then they turned and headed down to the road planning to go back to Anka's house.

It was now the time to comfort Anka and each other. Time to eat a little something, drink a little something, and there would be music. There was always music. It was in their souls. They would cry and sing, tell stories and laugh and then cry and sing again throughout the night.

The mourners weren't halfway to Anka's house when they could see a wagon approaching.

Stevo was the first to recognize the driver. Excited he called to the others, "It's Father Lahdra."

The wagon stopped when it reached the first cluster of people. The young priest was smooth faced, fair skinned, with light blue eyes that became darker when he was upset. Now they seemed almost black.

Over his dark hair was a wide-brimmed black hat and he wore a black cassock. He looked annoyed or angry. The villagers couldn't decide which it was.

"What's going on?" His voice sounded harsh.

"We just buried Mila Balich." Someone answered. "We didn't think you were coming."

The young priest's eyes blinked in surprise as he looked toward the cemetery. He shook his head as if disgusted and flicked the reins urging the horse onward.

The neighbors who were already on the road turned and followed the wagon back to the cemetery, fearful they had angered the priest by not waiting for his arrival before lowering Mila into the ground.

Father Lahdra urged the horse on and up, right onto the trail that went through the cemetery coming as close as he could to the open grave.

He had been away for the night and had no idea that Mila Balich had died.

All eyes were on the priest as he got down from the wagon. There was no mistaking his anger as he approached the grave.

Seeing the priest, Julia nodded approvingly. "Ah, you are here at last."

Father Lahdra gave her a quizzical look. What was she talking about? No one summoned him. But before he could reply, she said, "Say your prayers and bless the grave."

Julia looked at the priest, as if he were a simple child.

The young priest seemed distracted. Old Julia was disrespectful as ever. Her reputation as a healer or witch always made him uneasy. Nevertheless, he made the sign of the cross and proceeded to pray.

The villagers bowed their heads and were relieved that the priest had finally come to give Mila a proper funeral.

Not everyone bowed his head in prayer. Stevo was near the wagon and was curious to see what Father Lahdra had in there, for the priest usually came to the village on horseback.

While his friends prayed, Stevo reached a veined hand into the wagon and pulled back a woven coverlet.

A startled Stevo looked down into the unseeing, dead eyes of Mila's husband, Mato.

Part II, Chapter 1

Late spring - 1907

She was out of breath and tired from running across the newly plowed fields. The overturned ground had the mingled odor of earth and manure.

Katya Balich stopped to rest, her chest aching as she took in great gasps of air. Perspiration glistened on her flawless cheeks and forehead. She was fifteen years old, slender and delicate, with long red hair wild with curls. Her green eyes were set off by finely arched brows and her full lips were a bit large for the proportions of her face, yet she was the most beautiful girl to ever be seen in Selna.

Exhausted, she dropped her hastily thrown together bundle of possessions and used it as a seat. The bundle was made up of a tablecloth tied corner to corner. In it was a blouse and skirt made of homespun flax, a small wooden crucifix, a hand crochet black shawl, some hard cheese and some equally hard bread and a wooden mortar and pestle.

With her hand shading her eyes, she surveyed the terrain searching for her pursuers. Her full skirt of heavy linen fabric was soiled and stained because of her escape. She wore a simple long-sleeved blouse embroidered with flowers at the neck and also down the length of the sleeves.

Katya was running away from her brother-in-law, Elia. This time she had to go where he wouldn't find her.

The hilltop provided her a panoramic view of the countryside and probably her last look at Selna.

This part of Croatia was a lush green. Katya could see patchworks of crops and a small church on a distant hill. A few long-horned milking cows were grazing about lazily. The bells around their necks sent musical sounds long distances. Some sheep were scattered on the side of a hill. The river Sava, with its clean fresh water, snaked its way through the landscape, and there to the East, she could see the small wooden cabins of her village.

Her eyes filled with tears. The village had been her home all of her life and now she must leave. Would she ever see those sweet people again? If only her sister had not married that horrid man! The thought of Elia made her shiver.

Lost in her thoughts, she almost didn't hear the approaching horses. The sun shining directly into her eyes blinded her. She didn't have time to wait and see who was coming.

Cursing herself for stopping, she half-ran half-fell down the side of the hill and took cover in a clump of wild berry bushes. Dropping to her knees, she shoved her bundle under the leafy branches. With her heart pounding she flattened herself to the ground, praying that she had made herself invisible. "Mother of God, don't let him find me," she begged.

The sounds of the team and wagon grew louder as it rattled near. Then it stopped. *He saw me!* The thought was a silent scream in her head.

The pounding of her heart was echoing in her ears. She held her breath and felt herself trembling.

Katya could picture Elia Sokach with his thinning hair and tiny dark eyes. The eyes seemed perfectly suited to his rodent-like face and his pointed nose. His mouth was a thin line that seemed to be smirking even when he smiled. She thought everything about him was low and sneaky.

When Katya was a small child Elia had been cruel to her. He had slapped her, kicked her...ridiculed her.

"You're a freak," he had told her. "Where'd you get that red hair, from a witch?"

Her flaming hair totally set her apart from the inter-related villagers. Throughout the years comments were made about the color of her hair. Annoyed because of all the dubious comments and the fact that she had no control over what nature had given her, she refused the traditional braids. Instead, she wore her copper tresses wild and loose.

"Just like a Gypsy." The older women would say, shaking their heads in disapproval.

As she grew older, prettier, Elia tried to touch her or caress her. He would hide outside the window and watch her bathe in the wooden tub, which had to be brought into the house from the barn.

One day, when she was ten years old, while her sister, Anka, was nowhere near, Elia came into the house and watched her bathe. He didn't touch her or attempt to. He just watched waiting for Katya's reaction.

"Get away from me you ugly man," she demanded. "Get out of this house!" Everything about Elia repelled her.

From the house across the road Old Julia heard the yelling, a common occurrence from the time Elia had married Anka. But this time it wasn't Elia screaming invectives. It was Katya's voice the old woman heard. "Get out! Get out! Stop looking at me!"

As fast as her old aching legs could carry her Julia hurried across the road and through the open door of the cabin. She saw Katya naked in the wooden tub with Elia standing above her.

"Holy Mary!" said the old woman. "Save us from the men in this family." Grabbing a straw broom leaning against the wall, Julia beat Elia over the head several times, sending him running from the house.

It was after that episode Katya moved across the road into the house with Old Julia.

Now, Katya didn't hear the dog sniffing around the bushes where she was hiding. When it started barking excitedly, she thought she would faint. She felt two arms lifting her from the ground. Instinctively she started kicking and hitting. The tears were rolling down her cheeks as she cried, "Leave me alone! I won't go with you...I won't!"

Her tracker was a large, strong man.

With blind hysteria, Katya fought him. He grabbed both her flailing arms with ease and pinned them to her side.

"Stop it!" he demanded, giving her a good shaking.

Startled, Katya opened her eyes and looked into the bearded face of her godfather, Milan Kosich. It was his wife who had wet-nursed her when Katya had been a baby and it was he who had gently placed her dead mother in the casket those many years ago.

She smiled, relief pouring over her like spring rain. She wrapped her arms around the six-foot Milan and clung to him, her legs going weak.

Milan held her. "You're safe," he whispered. The tall man bent his head of curly black hair to rest on Katya's flaming curls. His dark brown eyes were closed as he gently rocked her, soothing her as he had done when she had been a child with a scraped knee, cut foot, or after a beating administered by Elia. Milan loved this girl as if she were one of his own daughters. After all, with her ample supply of breast milk, his wife Eva had kept the tiny baby Katya alive.

Milan was easily the tallest and strongest man in Selna. But, with children and those he loved, he could be very gentle.

"How did you know I was gone?" Katya asked holding on to him.

"Elia came to the house looking for you. He told Eva you ran away."

He released her slowly. "Come, we must go. Elia and that man from Petrinja are looking for you," he said.

"Do you know what he did?" demanded Katya, feeling brave as she stood next to Milan. "Do you know he sold me?" She was shaking with anger. "He sold me! He sold me as if I were a horse or cow."

"I thought that it might be something like that," he said, the anger building in him, wanting to kill Elia. "Hurry we can't stay here."

"My things," she said. "I need my things." Katya reached under the bushes for her meager belongings, while Vuk the dog gave the tablecloth wrapping an approving sniff.

Vuk was a large gray animal with thick fur around his neck. He resembled a wolf, which was his name. Finished with his inspection of the bundle, Vuk nuzzled Katya's hand hoping to be petted, but her attention was elsewhere.

Milan took the bundle in one hand and holding Katya's arm with the other, helped her up the steep incline to the road where the horses and wagon waited.

The wooden wagon was made for hauling and didn't provide the comforts necessary for transporting passengers. There were no springs to ease the jolts felt from every rock and rut in the dirt roads.

The horses were a mismatched pair. Leena, the larger and older horse, was Milan's. The smaller black and gray belonged to his brother and was mainly used as a plow horse. So, when hitched together they made an odd-looking team.

Katya stood next to the wagon reluctant to get in. "I don't want to go back," she said sadly, avoiding Milan's eyes. "I won't marry anyone until I'm ready."

"I know. You won't have to marry anyone," he said, remembering the disappointment he had felt when she had refused his son, young Milan. He remembered how happy he had been at the prospect of having Katya as another daughter and to know that Elia couldn't come near her, once she was married and protected.

He easily lifted her into the wagon which had been prepared for her with a goose down comforter and some blankets. Then he placed her bundle next to her.

He swung himself up into the driver's seat. "Now get under the blankets and don't talk to me or get out from under them unless I say you can."

Milan watched her get comfortable on the goose down padding. Adjusting a blanket, he concealed her. A few sacks of grain were at the back of the wagon to make it look as if Milan was going to the open-air market.

Vuk jumped up and over the wagon seat, finding himself a place on the blanket next to the hidden Katya. He nuzzled the blanket just to let her know he was there.

Milan took one last glance at the wagon to make sure its contents didn't look suspicious. Then he made a clicking sound with his tongue and called out, "Aide!" The horses grudgingly moved, not quite in unison, as they weren't used to working together.

The day was warm with clear skies and the pleasant spring breeze felt good on Milan's face. He was grateful for the good weather. It would make their journey more pleasant.

It wasn't long before Milan could make out two riders on horseback coming towards him.

"Riders coming," warned Milan.

As they neared, Milan recognized Elia Sokach, Katya's brother-in-law and another rider, a stranger. Elia was a small man, about 5'6". He had on a pair of loose fitting black trousers and a linen shirt, which was worn loose over the trousers. He wore a cap of black felt with a small visor. The cap seemed to sharpen his already pointed features.

The other rider Milan presumed to be the man from Petrinja. The stranger was an older man with a round face and little round eyes that seemed almost hidden by his fleshy cheeks. He wore a black fez and Milan could see the man was bald. His form was short and bulky. Everything about him was soft looking, like a full pillow. His pants were black and not homespun. Over his white shirt he wore an elaborately embroidered vest and the heavy pouch hanging at his waist suggested wealth.

His fat, perspiring face was red, as if he were angry.

So...thought Milan, this is the man to whom Elia wanted to sell Katya.

No sign of recognition was exchanged between Milan and his longtime enemy as the riders and wagon passed each other. Any pretense of friendship between the two men had disappeared long ago.

The man from Petrinja courteously nodded his head, but was ignored by Milan.

Vuk sat up when he recognized Elia emitting a low, threatening growl. Even though Katya was hidden under the blanket and could not see the riders, she knew Elia was there. She had heard that familiar growl many times before, always when Elia was near.

Milan drove the horses slowly, as they had a long way to go and he didn't want to tire them.

He would miss Katya, but he knew this was the best that could be done for her. Milan and his wife, Eva, were sure their plan to get her away from Elia was a good one. He smiled to himself when he thought of Elia's anguish when he would have to return the money paid for Katya. Milan wondered how much the stranger had been willing to pay for the beautiful, strong-willed girl.

He looked over his shoulder at the wagon bed. Vuk was lying on top of the blanket, next to the hidden form of Katya.

"How are you doing?" He asked.

"Have they gone?" She asked, feeling warm under the cover.

"Yes, they're gone," he said. "You can come out. I don't think they can see us now."

"Milan, where are you taking me?" Her green eyes looked at him searchingly and her hair was a mass of loose curls. He wondered for the hundredth time how Mato and Mila (God rest their souls) could have produced this beautiful child.

"To a place where I hope you will be safe and happy," he answered.

Milan didn't know it then, but soon she would be gone from their lives forever.

Part II, Chapter 2

All his life, Elia Sokach had bad luck. It started the day he was born. He was the fourth son, which meant he would inherit nothing. His oldest brother, Bronko, was to inherit the modest house and small piece of land.

When Elia had married the young girl, Anka, he thought his luck had changed, but it wasn't so. Ten years into the marriage, Anka, just as her mother Mila had done, died in childbirth along with the baby. As Anka's husband he had a right to stay in the house, but the land had to be shared with a blood relative. Katya was the only recognized blood relation of Anka's so the land was hers, as much as his.

Elia's relationship with Katya was an extremely poor one. She loathed him and avoided him.

It drove Elia wild whenever he thought about the land. Not only did Katya have rights to the land he lived on, but she owned the little house and land Old Julia left to her upon the old woman's passing. *It wasn't fair.* These words were on the tip of his tongue and in his head all the time. *It wasn't fair that Katya had rights to the land and he had very little to call his own.*

When Elia's neighbors asked about Katya's absence, he lied and told them that she ran off with a tavern keeper in Petrinja. He couldn't tell them about the stranger he met there at the tavern.

It hadn't been a grand plan of Elia's to rid himself of Katya by selling her to the stranger, it just happened. At the time he hadn't considered whether it was legal or not, since he was only an in-law and not her father or brother.

Meeting the stranger in Petrinja was like a spark that caused an explosion, altering Katya and Elia's lives forever.

Every Thursday people came to Petrinja from all the nearby villages to buy and sell things. Women spread blankets on the ground and on them placed whatever they had to sell. Usually it was homemade cheeses, freshly baked bread, jugs of milk, some eggs or needlework. The men brought seed or pigs or other farm animals.

The open field where the market took place came alive with the sounds of music, talking, laughing and haggling over prices. Children played or watched the livestock, and the smells of civapcici sausages, along with the aroma of roasting lambs, made the day festive.

It was the market that lured the stranger. He was on his way to Zagreb always in the pursuit of something he could buy and later sell at a profit.

All eyes were on the heavy-set stranger as he strolled casually through the throng of people, who respectfully moved out of his way. He was an unusual sight in his richly embroidered vest over a full-sleeved white shirt. His black trousers were tucked into soft leather boots and atop his bald head was a black fez. He was never without the fez. Around his thick waist was a red sash and from it hung a money pouch, which jingled as he walked from blanket to blanket, surveying what was being offered for sale.

Nothing interested him very much. He had considered some lace, but thought the threads too coarse.

The Turk had not planned to stop this soon to rest, but seeing the tavern or gostiona, as it was called, he went in for some breakfast.

The tavern was no more than a room with eight wooden tables and some crude benches. A large window overlooked the market. One door served as an entrance and another, in back with a crucifix above it, led to the owner's living quarters.

A faded picture of St. George on horseback slaying a dragon was the only decoration in the simple room.

When the Turk entered the tavern he saw that it was already crowded. Looking for somewhere to sit he noticed a skinny, sharp-faced man sitting alone.

He approached Elia and asked in fluent Croatian, "If no one is joining you, may I share this table?"

"Of course," said Elia, extending his hand towards the empty bench, all the while taking in the rich clothes and the money pouch. He felt important, because all eyes were on him and the stranger.

Settling himself on the bench the Turk said, "May I buy you some refreshment?"

"Thank you," said Elia smiling, hoping a friendship with this wealthy person was possible. "I am named Elia." He extended his hand.

Ignoring the extended hand, the stranger said, "And I am called Abuh."

He saw a girl with a tray and motioned for her to come to them.

The full figured girl nodded, smiling as she made her way towards them. Her blond hair was braided and wound into a crown on top of her head forming a halo around her face. She was pink cheeked with lively brown eyes and had a healthy glow to her skin.

The Turk indicated Elia should order first. "I'll have a Krushkovac." It wasn't unusual for the men to drink early in the day and Elia seldom had money for the sweet Pear Brandy.

The Turk ordered Turkish coffee, bread and fruit. He smiled at the girl and studied her closely as she walked away.

"A beautiful girl," he said to Elia. "In my country a man would pay much for such a woman."

Elia glanced at the girl he knew as, Seka, and shrugged his shoulders indifferently. Wanting to impress Abuh, he said, "She's alright, but I know of a much greater beauty." Seeing the Turk's look of interest he continued, "The girl has hair of bright copper, long with loose curls and her eyes are as green as the grass."

Elia had the Turk's full attention.

Elia went on, "Her form isn't like those you see out there." He waived to the open window indicating the women at the market. "She is delicate...small. Her hands and fingers are slender."

"How old is this girl?" asked theTurk, leaning back so Seka could place the drinks and food on the table.

"She's fifteen," said Elia, raising his glass in a toast to Abuh with the pear brandy.

"Ah...and married," said the Turk, breaking the bread with his fingers. By the age of fifteen, he assumed she was surely married with babies.

"No," said Elia, "she has refused all proposals."

Disbelief flickered in the Turk's eyes for a moment. "What does her family say?"

"She has no family...she lives alone...an orphan." Elia watched Abuh's eyes.

The Turk looked up, his interest growing. "So..." he asked, "How is it you know this girl?"

Elia's smile was sly, "I am her brother-in-law."

"You said she was an orphan, I don't understand."

"I am a widower," said Elia trying to look sad. "The girl was my wife's sister."

"You didn't marry her? Where I come from, we take over the responsibility of unwed women in the family." Abuh studied Elia waiting for a reply.

"I need a stronger woman," Elia lied. "Such a small girl is of no help to me."

The Turk looked thoughtful as he split a ripe plum, the juice running down his fingers. He gazed out the window, not looking at anything in particular, lost in thought. He doubted Elia's story of why he had not married her. It didn't matter. He didn't care much why the girl wasn't married. He only cared that she be as beautiful as this foolish man claimed.

"No relatives," he said, thinking out loud. Looking at Elia, he asked, "You can arrange a meeting?"

Elia smiled broadly and tried not to look too eager. "We can go there today...for a price," said, Elia. *He felt his luck changing.*

The Turk studied Elia for a moment. Then in a low voice, so as not to be overheard, he asked, "Will there be anyone around to try and stop us...if I decide I want her?"

"Almost everyone is here at the market," said, Elia. Now Elia leaned forward and whispered, "I am new to this." His eyes glistened with excitement, "How do we do this, say...if the girl doesn't co-operate."

"Not to worry," said Abuh, "if she is as beautiful as you say..." He paused — his smile was sinister. "I can manage it...with some help."

Elia was elated. Katya would be gone and after a length of time, he would go to the magistrate and petition for her land, including what Old Julia left to Katya. He fairly beamed as he pretended to spit into the palm of his right hand which he extended palm up to the Turk. Abuh also pretended to spit into his right hand and then he slapped his palm hard against Elia's, for this was how men closed their deals at the market.

Some heads turned toward them, hearing the slap of hands, only a little curious as to what sort of bargain was made at that table.

It was only 11:30 when Elia and the Turk reached Selna. No one was out and about. It was as deserted as Elia had predicted.

Old Julia's house was the same as all the others, made of logs with a dirt floor, which had to be packed with fresh earth every spring. Sitting in the corner was the usual clay stove. A table stood before the open window with a bed on each side of it.

There was one major difference in this house from all the others. Against a wall, opposite the window, were many shelves. Here were jars and bowls of assorted roots and herbs. There were even some flowers used in the medicines once prepared by Old Julia, but now used by Katya. A cord ran from one wall to the other in front of the shelves with flowers and herbs hanging there to dry.

While Julia was alive she tried to teach Katya all she knew about herbal healing. Katya had absorbed Old Julia's knowledge with eager fascination.

It was Katya's knowledge of medicine that Elia hoped would get him and the Turk into the house.

Approaching Katya's house, Elia felt anxious. He hoped the Turk could steal Katya away without too much trouble, for he knew she would not go willingly.

Elia's knock at the open door surprised Katya. He hadn't crossed this threshold since she left her childhood home on the day Julia assaulted him with the broom. Katya's look of surprise became astonishment when she saw the stranger.

Katya was openly suspicious and her dislike of Elia was evident.

"What do you want, Elia?" her voice was cold.

"My friend here," he nodded toward Abuh, "is traveling and the changes of food and water are distressing his stomach," Elia lied. "I told him you could make a tea that would make him feel better."

Katya eyed them both. The stranger didn't look ill. He was openly staring at Katya with approval, satisfied that Elia had not exaggerated the girl's beauty.

The Turk envisioned her in skirts of soft filmy fabric gathered at each ankle. He could see her bare arms with gold bracelets above the elbows and gold threaded vests, and around her neck, chains with gold coins.

He found himself aroused by the picture he had of her in his mind. She would be exquisite.

Katya's icy stare halted his thoughts. When he spoke, it was an educated Croatian, not the local dialect.

He bowed courteously to Katya and said, "It is true...I am not well. My stomach hurts and I cannot ride comfortably with this pain." He smiled trying to convey a trusting manner. "When this kind man," he pointed to Elia, "told me there was someone of your talent who could make an infusion for me to drink. I begged him to bring me to you."

Elia was greatly impressed by this speech and nodded in agreement, hoping Katya believed it.

Katya looked from Elia to Abuh and then back to Elia again. She didn't trust Elia. However, it would be just like him to take money from this man on the promise that Katya could make the stranger feel better.

She didn't like Elia and she didn't like the foreigner. Against her better judgment, she moved aside to let them in.

A momentary triumphant glance passed between Elia and the stranger.

Katya saw the glance and immediately knew she had made a mistake letting them in, but it was too late. They were in her home and she was frightened of them.

As the men came in, Katya glanced quickly out the door, hoping to see someone, anyone. The road was deserted.

"Please sit down." She motioned to the table and hoped her voice sounded normal. "Is the pain sharp or tender?" She stood away from the table.

Abuh was totally entranced by Katya. Even in her bulky skirts and thick linen blouse, it appeared she had a beautiful figure. Her red hair glistened as the light played on it. He was so caught up in his assessment of her, that he didn't answer her question.

Elia nudged the Turk to make a reply.

"Oh, a sharp pain," he said. "It is not constant, just every now and then. After the attack, it feels tender." He pointed to the supposed pain in his round belly beneath the sash.

Had this been one of her neighbors, Katya would have felt the area of pain with her hand, but she wouldn't go near this man.

"I'll make something for you." She hoped the tremor in her voice didn't betray her fear.

As Katya surveyed her assortment of herbs, she knew she never should have answered the knock at her door. She was very aware how quiet it was outside. Market day! Almost everyone was gone.

Standing in front of the shelf of herbs, her back to the men, she dropped various leaves into a bowl with trembling hands and ground them with the pestle.

I want to run...do I dare?

Sitting at the table, Elia looked at Abuh, for some sign of what he planned to do. The Turk was watching Katya.

When she was finished grinding, Katya brought the cup of herbs to the table and poured boiling water over them. After a minute she strained the mixture through a cloth into another cup. When she felt it was ready to drink, Katya placed it in front of Abuh.

"Ah, thank you," he said, letting his fingers brush against Katya's hand as he took the cup.

His touch sent another shiver through her. She glanced at Elia for some clue as to what was going on, but he was looking at the stranger, watching him taste the tea.

Katya turned away and walked back to the shelves of herbs wondering, "What *is going on?*"

The sound of coughing broke into her thoughts.

"Is this supposed to be so bitter?" Abuh coughed in a strangled voice.

"No," she said, alarmed by his reaction to her tea. "This is a very mild mixture. It is meant to soothe your stomach."

"Well then," he said, sounding annoyed, "you must have mixed something incorrectly." He said it accusingly, "It is too bitter, so that I cannot drink it."

A puzzled frown creased Katya's forehead.

"That can't be." Her voice was almost a whisper.

"Taste it then," he said. "It's awful! I thought you were a healer."

Katya looked from Elia to the stranger and then to the cup, which he pushed towards her.

She was confused. She had never made such a mistake before. Perhaps her nervousness caused her to pick the wrong herb. She lifted the cup and almost took a sip. Katya detected a faint, unknown odor, an odor that should not have been in the tea. It took all her nerve not to betray her discovery. She pretended to take a sip. With the cup under her nose, she was sure something had been added to it.

In an instant Abuh stood up, grabbed her hair, pulled her head back, and tried to pour the remaining liquid down her throat. She gagged and struggled, finally, she let herself go still, slowly sinking to the floor.

"You see," she heard Abuh say. "I told you there would be no trouble. Now help me get her on the bed."

Katya kept her body limp, as if she were fully drugged. She hoped she had not swallowed any of the tainted tea. When they picked her up, she let her feet drag and her head rolled from side to side.

She felt herself being lifted and carried to the narrow bed.

Elia whispered hoarsely, as if afraid of waking her, "How much will you pay me for her? I told you she was a beauty."

Abuh didn't answer Elia. He was lifting Katya's hand smelling her fingers. He bent down and smelled her hair and neck. She didn't smell of sweat the way the other village women did. She smelled of clean herbs and fresh flowers.

He took her hand and looked at the slender fingers. He raised her hand to his mouth and ran his tongue over one of her fingers.

A wave of revulsion flushed through Katya. Through sheer will power she kept her face immobile.

She felt her skirt being lifted up and he ran his hand along her calf. Then the skirt was dropped. Next, her blouse was being pulled free of her skirt and lifted.

Abuh looked approvingly at the firm full breast. He placed his hand on it and ran his thumb over the pink, erect nipple.

Katya felt panic rising within her, still she didn't move.

Elia stared in silent fascination, now more than ever sorry that his fear of Julia and Milan had kept him from forcing himself on Katya.

When Abuh dropped the blouse, he smiled at Elia and said, "I want your horse and wagon. You have a horse and wagon, don't you?"

"Of course," said Elia, trembling with excitement. "Yes, come across the way to my house. I'll show you." Then he added, "It will cost extra."

The Turk turned to Katya who seemed asleep. He ran his finger across her cheek and down her throat.

"She'll be asleep for awhile. Let's be quick, though. I don't want anyone to see us."

Katya heard them leave. She waited for what seemed to be an eternity.

When it was silent and Katya was sure they were gone, she slowly, quietly, rose from the bed.

She felt weak with fear. Her skin was moist with perspiration. Forcing herself to be strong, she picked up a tablecloth and threw into it a few belongings and then tied it corner to corner. Feeling weak and a little light headed, she made her way to the open doorway. Carefully she peered out. She didn't see them.

The land directly behind her house sloped down into a ravine. She felt as if she was moving in slow motion. Soon her fear gave her strength and she was running and she kept running until Milan found her hiding under the berry bush.

Elia felt sick every time he thought of finding the house empty and Katya gone.

He had just become the richest man in Selna. Abuh had given him the money pouch from his waist. Elia planned to go to Zagreb and make a new life for himself. He would hire a good Zagreb advocate to have Katya's land put into his name.

The fat, short Turk did not look strong. Elia was surprised when Abuh grabbed Elia by the throat.

"Do you think you and a peasant girl can make a fool of me?" He screamed. "What trick is this to get my money? You must think you and your sister-in-law, if that is who she is, have a clever game."

Elia had somehow managed to pull free. "No. Please!" he gasped. "We will find her. She is yours, I swear it."

The rest of the day was spent riding through the countryside looking for her. They asked everyone they met, if they had seen Katya, everyone that is, but Milan Kosich. Elia wondered about Milan, but he didn't want to tangle with him and that dog, Vuk. Some night Elia was going to kill that dog. He thought about it often, but his fear of the wolf-like dog kept him from doing the animal any harm.

Abuh rode with Elia in angry silence, his face red and his features hard, becoming angrier as the hours passed with no sign of Katya.

Elia tried to make conversation, tried to convince the man they would find Katya.

By late evening they were miles from Selna on the road that lead to Karlovac and Abuh was tired of the fruitless search. When Abuh dismounted, Elia did also, thinking they were going to rest a bit.

"Give me the money," demanded Abuh, his eyes narrowing.

Elia couldn't part with the money. It was his! He was rich now!

"You let her get away," Elia whined accusingly. "You didn't make a strong enough potion. You can't blame me."

"I do blame you, you stupid fool," Abuh said evenly. "You have made me waste an entire day. A day I could have used in better ways to profit myself."

Elia was defiant, "I won't give you the money. It is mine!"

Elia never saw the knife. He didn't even know Abuh had it. He only saw the glint of the blade as it slashed across his face, from his ear down to his chin.

He felt the money pulled from his pocket, and then, he felt the warm blood seeping from the gash on his face.

Abuh mounted his black stallion, leaving a stunned Elia holding a hand to the bleeding wound on his cheek. The Turk rode away swearing to himself that if he ever saw the beautiful, red haired accomplice, he would leave her with a scarred face. No one tricks Abuh and gets away with it.

Part II, Chapter 3

Katya was running as fast as she could, the blood pounding in her ears. She tripped on the ruts in the uneven ground and fell. Old Julia was lifting her up, gently smoothing the tangled red hair away from Katya's frightened face. The wrinkled old face with the watery eyes came close and kissed Katya's cheeks repeatedly. The kisses were hard and wet and Katya tried to push Old Julia away.

It was Vuk…the dog, not the ghost of Julia slathering Katya's face with wet kisses as she awoke. It took her only a moment to realize she had been dreaming and that the running was over. She was in the wagon under a dewy bright morning sky, fresh with the scent of a nearby orchard.

With sheer glee, Katya let out a hearty laugh and hugged Vuk, who wagged his tail in appreciation.

Katya ran her fingers through her red tangles realizing she didn't have a comb. She stretched the kinks out of her back, smoothed the wrinkles in her skirt and playfully pushed Vuk away. She looked around the green clearing for Milan.

She felt a new sensation and realized that she was feeling excitement. Katya had never traveled any further than Petrinja. She trembled with the thrill of her adventure.

"Come on, Vuk," she said, climbing over the wooden seat down onto the soft velvety grass.

Feeling completely serene and heady with the near overpowering scent of blossoms, Katya and Vuk wandered through the orchard. She could hardly believe that it was only yesterday that she had escaped from Elia and the disgusting man in the fez.

Lost in her thoughts, Katya didn't notice that Vuk had stopped walking. He was staring straight ahead. She looked up, but only saw more plum trees.

"Oh, come on," she urged. "Let's see what's beyond those trees." With a gentle nudge, Katya encouraged Vuk to walk with her. He pressed his body protectively against her leg. As they neared the edge of the orchard, he emitted a low cautioning growl. Katya stopped walking, wondering what sort of animal Vuk had discovered.

Hearing the crunch of approaching footsteps Katya almost called to Milan, but Vuk's low warning growl stopped her. It wasn't Milan.

Two small, young boys, dark-skinned with shiny black hair, their dark eyes huge, stood before Katya, firewood stacked in their arms. They looked like brothers, one slightly taller than the other, both barefoot and wearing rumpled, dirty clothes.

The older, taller boy said something to his companion in a language Katya didn't understand. The boys didn't show fear, but were wary and cautious. With their eyes on Katya and Vuk, they slowly backed away, not turning.

"Zolton!" One of the boys called out, still keeping his eyes on Katya.

Vuk moved protectively in front of Katya, his head down low, his ears laid back, ready for anything.

Vuk started barking aggressively when he saw a tall figure appear behind the boys. A dark-skinned young man, with black shiny hair, wearing one gold earring, put a protective hand on each boy's shoulder. He wore black straight-leg pants tucked into black boots. Over his slightly soiled red shirt was a brown leather vest. He was handsome with the blackest eyes Katya had ever seen.

For a long moment Katya and the young man stared at one another. He stared at her beauty. She stared because she had never seen a man with an earring.

Vuk growled long and low.

"Hush, Vuk." She placed her hand over his muzzle to still him. The dog looked up at her with disgust, as if to ask, *Don't you know these are strangers?* He sat back on his haunches, quiet, but watchful.

The young man looked relieved that Katya stayed Vuk. Smiling nervously he said in Croatian, "We are camping in the clearing just ahead."

"Oh!" exclaimed Katya, relieved that he spoke Croatian. "We are at the other clearing...on the other side of the orchard." She indicated the direction with a wave of her hand.

Katya felt excited and flustered in a way she had never experienced before. She had always been aloof and cool, a form of protection, perhaps. But, now she felt this handsome stranger's approving gaze and enjoyed it. For the first time in her life, she enjoyed being admired by a man. A handsome man at that!

"My name is Zolton," he said, extending his hand. His smile showed straight white teeth.

"My brothers," he patted them on their heads, as he said their names. "This one is Varol and this one Rosh."

Katya smiled back feeling no fear with this trio.

"My name is Katya," she said, "and this is Vuk." Vuk ignored the introduction, keeping his eyes on the strangers, ready for anything.

"How many are in your caravan?" Asked Zolton, pleased to make conversation with this beautiful girl, who didn't seem to be afraid of him or to dislike him.

"Caravan?" Katya didn't understand.

"In your group, how many of you are traveling?" asked Zolton.

"Just three of us." She found herself smiling warmly to this handsome stranger. Katya was surprised that she felt no fear, especially after her frightful experience with Elia and the stranger. "Just Vuk," she pointed to the dog, "and my uncle and myself."

Why did she say Uncle? What did it matter she thought...Uncle, Father, Brother...Milan was all these things to her.

He laughed when he heard there were only three. She liked his laugh.

"We are seventeen in our caravan." He said, "We are a tribe." Katya's expression showed that she didn't understand.

Zolton laughed a deep, warm laugh again and said, "We are a tribe of Gypsies."

The look of disbelief on Katya's face erased Zolton's smile. There it was he thought...the fear and distrust of Gypsies. They seemed to be doing fine until he told her he was a Gypsy.

For a moment, Katya stared in silence. What she had heard all her life couldn't be true. This wonderful, beautiful person couldn't possibly steal babies or kill people in their beds at night. Weren't Gypsies supposed to steal anything and everything in their path? It couldn't be true. She refused to believe it.

Katya saw that wary look on Zolton's face that replaced the one of open friendliness just the moment before. She was embarrassed. She couldn't tell him what she had been thinking. It would be rude and unkind. Katya could tell she had already hurt him and didn't want to add to it.

"Forgive me," she said hastily, trying to regain the mood that had been before. "I don't know what a Gypsy is." She lied, smiling warmly once more.

Zolton wasn't sure if Katya was telling the truth or not, but her smile thawed his reserve. If she was lying he was appreciative of the gesture. He wanted to be friends with Katya. How tired he was of being distrusted and feared...yes, and hated, because he was a Gypsy.

"You have never met a Gypsy?"

"No, never," she said, and he felt she was telling the truth.

He wanted to take her hand and lead her to their camp, but Vuk couldn't be trusted.

"Come with us. Let us show you our camp and share some breakfast."

Katya never hesitated a moment. She never gave a thought that Milan would be worried when he found the wagon empty. She was surprised that she wasn't concerned with Milan's absence.

Her eyes glistened with excitement and the sun made the coppery color of her hair sparkle. Katya was drunk with freedom and adventure.

"I would love to see your camp." She brushed past a disgusted Vuk, who got a gentle smack from Katya for growling. Katya happily walked alongside Zolton, noticing that the young man was taller than she.

The young Gyspy brothers, Varol and Rosh, seemed to be as doubtful as Vuk. They gave Zolton a questioning glance, which he ignored. The two young boys, arms loaded with firewood, ran on ahead to warn the camp of the approaching stranger.

This was a new sensation for Katya, this delight at being admired by a man that didn't disgust her. She was enjoying it very much.

"Is the camp very far?" Katya could only see an open field ahead and the orchard behind her.

"It is on the other side of those trees." He pointed to a grove that clustered at the end of the field. "There is a river there. We always try to camp near water."

Katya nodded, being alongside the river sounded sensible.

Zolton liked the nearness of Katya. Their shoulders touched as they walked side by side and no move was made to widen the space between them. Vuk walked alongside Katya, glancing frequently at Zolton.

"The first person I must present you to is my grandmother." said Zolton.

Again Katya nodded, it was only respectful that she first pay her respect to the oldest member of the family. They weren't so different, thought Katya, we do the same in the village.

Zolton took Katya's arm to help her navigate some holes in the ground.

"My Grandmother is Valina, the Queen of the Gypsies."

Four brightly colored little houses on wheels were spaced so that they formed a semi-circle. In the center of the half circle was a campfire, with kettles hanging from iron braces.

A couple of skinny dogs were tied to wagon wheels and they barked an alarm as Katya, Vuk and Zolton came near. Sensing he was outnumbered and not on his own turf, Vuk could only look displeased as he pressed closer to Katya.

Katya smelled the campfire. She saw several children all dressed in ragged clothing. Men stood about, smoking and openly staring at Katya. She had never seen such women with their hair loose and uncovered. Now she understood why the old women in the village called her a Gypsy, as none of these women wore their shiny black hair in braids. Their hair hung loose and wild in the style she preferred. Their clothes were of a shiny fabric, not home spun like her own. The skirts and blouses were brightly colored, though a bit soiled. Young women and old wore earrings, bracelets and many necklaces of gold and silver. The women of the Croatian villages only wore what little jewelry they had at festivals, not every day, as did these exotic-looking creatures with their smoky, wary eyes.

Katya was speechless. She looked around in wonder. They looked *so* poor and yet, all that gold and silver! She had never seen one person wear so much jewelry. Each girl and woman she saw had gold earrings and bracelets.

Zolton led Katya to the first caravan, painted red and blue and yellow. It had a window on each side and a door with steps leading to the ground. On the floor inside, could be seen pillows and blankets. Katya didn't think there was a bed.

Seated on a small stool next to the caravan was an old woman. Her black hair hung loose. She was small, but had an aura of strength. Her dark eyes were clear and bright, not milky like Old Julia's eyes had been. She wore a skirt and blouse of faded purple velvet. The blouse was gathered at the neck and had long sleeves. From her stretched ear lobs dangled long gold earrings with red stones in them. Her necklace was made up of several rows of gold coins. On each arm were several gold bracelets, some etched with designs, and others set with colored stones.

Katya had never seen anything like this in her life. This woman wore more jewelry than could be found in the entire village of Selna.

Zolton approached his grandmother and kissed her cheek. She didn't acknowledge the kiss, but kept her gaze on Katya. If the Gypsy Queen looked unusual to Katya, so did Katya look unusual to Old Valina. Katya's flaming hair and green eyes and fair skin were an uncommon sight to her.

When Zolton spoke to his Grandmother, it was in the language Katya heard Rosh and Varol speaking earlier. The old woman answered Zolton in the same language.

Standing behind the old woman was a slender, dark haired woman. She too had gold shining from her ears, neck and wrists. Her face was expressionless.

Katya heard Zolton say in Croatian, "Grandmother, this is Katya. She is camped nearby." Then, proudly he said, "Katya, this is my Grandmother, Queen Valina."

"I am honored to meet you, but I don't know the proper way to greet you," said Katya, hesitantly.

Queen Valina stood up. She was small, but gave the impression of being larger, stronger. "A polite greeting is always a correct one." She acknowledged, responding in Croatian. "I welcome you to our camp."

"Bring a stool," she said to no one in particular. A young girl quickly returned with a crude seat made of rough tree limbs, her bracelets making a jingling sound as she dropped the stool unceremoniously. She stood glaring at Katya.

"This rude girl is Roha. She is to marry my grandson, Zolton."

Katya thought she saw a momentary flicker of triumph in the girl's black eyes and Katya was surprised to realize she felt a small disappointment at hearing the news that Zolton was engaged.

"Kaja is Zolton's mother and my only daughter," she said, motioning toward the woman who stood behind her. Katya could see that Zolton looked like Kaja. Zolton's mother gave a silent nod to Katya.

"Sit, my child," said Valina. "Let us talk and find out why you have been brought to me."

What Valina was saying seemed strange to Katya. She said, "Zolton brought me here to meet you. That is all."

"It is never all," said the Old Woman, emphasizing the 'all.' She motioned for Katya to be seated and she also sat down. "There is always more. There is always a reason for every happening. I must find the reason for our meeting."

Katya was confused. "This was just a chance meeting. I am traveling and so are you. We just happened to stop at the same place." She paused, looked around for some agreement. Seeing none from Zolton and his mother, she shrugged her shoulders. This was too much thinking for God's Sake! She just came to meet Zolton's grandmother and see the camp.

Around them women were sweeping the earth with branches, using them like brooms.

In the distance, Katya could see some young men at the river. They were lying on their stomachs and dangling their hands in the water. She saw a hand pull upward with a live fish in it. She had heard of hand fishing but never knew anyone who could 'tickle the fish's belly.'

Zolton dropped on the ground next to his grandmother. Obvious pride shone on his face. Katya sat on the stool facing Valina. Vuk lay obediently at Katya's feet. No longer sensing danger he was ready to nap. Valina's daughter Kaja stood by, always in attendance. It was Roha, the belligerent fiancé, who brought steaming cups to the three of them. Katya smelled the brew and didn't recognize it.

As if reading her mind, Valina said, "You smell cinnamon. It comes from a far away place called Ceylon."

Katya had never heard of Ceylon.

Katya tasted the drink. There was chocolate in it. It was so unusual, but she loved it.

After a moment Queen Valina said, "To where are you traveling?"

"I don't know." For the first time Katya's eyes looked troubled. "I'm going as far as I can away from my brother-in-law."

She could see they were watching her, waiting for more, so she blurted out, "He tried to sell me to a man with a fez. I pretended to be asleep, and when they left the room I ran away."

"Where was your uncle that he let such a thing happen?" Zolton asked, for he would protect anyone in his tribe and expected as much from the villagers.

"He's not really my uncle." Katya realized what she said earlier made her seem a liar. "I have no one. Milan is my only friend. He has known me since I was born. He always takes care of me." Glancing at Vuk she said, "He and Vuk take care of me."

Queen Valina leaned forward and took both of Katya's hands in her own. She turned them palm up and studied the lines. Katya had no idea what Valina was looking for.

It seemed to Katya that it became very quiet. The Gypsies, who were near, now were silently watching the Queen read Katya's palm.

For several minutes Valina stared at Katya's hand. She turned the palms from sided to side for a better view. At one point, she took her skirt and rubbed some grime from Katya's hand, so she could 'read' better.

Everyone watched while Katya became increasingly embarrassed by this attention. Katya wanted to speak, to say something to break the silence, but didn't dare. Valina turned to Zolton and spoke to him. "She is in danger. I can't make out the time. It could be today, tomorrow or next month." Valina dropped Katya's hands and started to think out loud. "She is here and she is in danger. Then it must mean we are to help. How? Is she to stay with us?" At this remark, Roha, Zolton's fiancé's face reddened and her eyes grew darker. She didn't want Katya anywhere near Zolton. Roha knew that Zolton would marry her when Valina said it was time. It had been decided and he would not refuse, but Roha didn't want any temptation near-by.

Roha wanted to speak. She wanted to say this girl couldn't travel with the tribe. What did Katya know of living the way they did? And what could she do to earn money? Could she tell fortunes, or cast spells for city women? Could she make love potions or good-luck charms to sell? Roha didn't say any of these things, but she wanted to. In the end, she would have to do what Queen Valina decided.

Roha sat on the ground next to Zolton and put her arm possessively through his.

Katya's mind was reeling. What danger? Were Elia and the stranger following them?

"This is not a small danger..." Valina was still working on the problem. "This is bad. It could put our people in danger, too."

Roha started to relax. This meant Katya wouldn't travel with them.

"The brother-in-law is the problem," said Zolton. "So we find him...and," he didn't want to say 'and what' in front of Katya. It didn't matter for Katya was in such a dazed state she didn't catch his meaning.

Valina stood up and began to pace, her hands on her hips. The bracelets jangled each time she moved her hands. She was muttering to herself and shaking her head. At last she demanded, "Get me the crystal."

Zolton's mother Kaja disappeared into the brightly painted caravan. She emerged quickly with a piece of red cloth in her hands. She handed the cloth respectfully to her mother. Valina removed the cloth producing a large crystal ball. She plopped herself on the ground, like an agile child instead of the old woman she was, and placed the crystal on the stool.

No one spoke as she peered into the ball. Her eyes moved across the ball as if she was watching something. "That's it. I see what we are to do." She nodded to her daughter, Kaja, who took the sparkling globe and re-wrapped it in the red cloth, disappearing with it into the caravan.

Valina got up from the ground, not bothering to brush off her skirt. She sat on the stool again and took Katya's hand in hers. "Don't be frightened. There are those who would harm you, but nothing bad will happen to you," she said.

"Those? Do you mean that more than one person wants to harm me? What is this? I am no one, I have nothing." Katya was numb. What had happened to her glorious morning of freedom? In Selna, she knew her enemy, but out here she didn't know who 'those' could be.

Valina pulled off one of the many bracelets she wore. It was a heavy gold bangle set with rubies and sapphires. The jewels were placed in various designs, each having a secret meaning known only to the Gypsies.

"Promise me," ordered Valina fiercely, "that you will wear this bracelet always. You will never take it off. I promise that it will protect you." She paused to see if Katya understood her. "Promise me!" she demanded, as she waived the bracelet in front of Katya's face.

"Yes, yes, I promise. I will wear it always," said Katya, confused and concerned by the old woman's declaration that she was still in danger.

"Good!" said Valina as she slipped the bracelet on Katya's wrist and snapped the clasp shut. The bracelet sparkled with swirls and shapes centuries old and full of secret meanings.

"Now, you must leave us," said Valina. "We will meet again in the future and then we shall spend more time together. Remember," she warned, "always wear the bracelet."

Valina turned to her grandson. "Walk her back to her camp. Try not to be seen. It is better that no one knows you are her friend." Everyone seemed to understand this logic, but Katya. Unnerved and bewildered, she rose to leave.

Queen Valina put her arm through Katya's and walked a short distance with her.

"I have never seen such a hand as yours." Valina paused. She wasn't sure how to explain what she saw in Katya's hand. "Don't be frightened," she said again. "The danger is in the path that will take you where you should have been in the first place. For some reason you were put where you did not belong. It will fall into place. You are finding your way."

Part II, Chapter 4

The Danube River flows down through Hungary into the Pannonian Plains, where its tributaries are the Drava, Sava, Morava and Tisa Rivers.

It was the Sava River Milan's wagon crossed, as he and Katya made their way through Zagreb.

Riding in back Katya had the urge to ask Milan to stop so that she could see something of the city, but ever since her return from the Gypsy camp they had traveled in cool silence.

The silence came after a furious argument.

Milan had gone for milk to a farmhouse they had passed the night before. The farmhouse was in the opposite direction of the Gypsy camp, so Milan didn't know of the camp. When he returned with bread and fresh milk he found Katya and Vuk gone.

His first thought was that she had gone to relieve herself, but when she didn't return, he became more concerned. Then the concern became fear that harm had come to her. Milan even imagined that Elia had somehow followed them and taken Katya.

With panic rising he went searching for her, heading across the field, when he saw Katya and Vuk emerge from the trees. They were with a dark-skinned man who Milan immediately recognized as a Gypsy. He saw Katya and Zolton exchange some words, then the Gypsy kissed Katya's hand, turned and disappeared into the trees.

Confused and angered by what he saw, Milan began running toward Katya. Seeing Milan, Katya gave a small wave. When he reached her the words came tumbling out. "Who was that? What happened? What's wrong?"

"Nothing, nothing is wrong." Her voice was low and embarrassed by Milan's attitude. Her eyes averted his.

Milan spotted the bracelet. "What's this?" He pulled at her arm.

"It's an amulet, a charm. It will keep me safe," she said.

"What do you mean *it will keep you safe?* I'm here to keep you safe." He was yelling, "Gypsies trick gullible girls like you. What did you have to trade for the bracelet?" Shocked at his accusation, Katya gave Milan the coldest look he had ever seen.

At her most furious, Milan's wife, Eva, had never given him such an icy stare as Katya gave him now.

"I did nothing!" protested Katya, hurt and confused by Milan's anger. "I had a cup of chocolate with the Queen of the Gypsies and she told my fortune."

Milan wanted to say something sarcastic about the Queen, but thought better of it. Instead he demanded, "What did you pay with?"

"I paid nothing." She was close to tears.

"Gypsies always get paid." He shouted back at her. "They never do anything without pay."

Katya looked straight into Milan's eyes. "I said I paid nothing!"

"Why did you let the Gypsy kiss your hand?"

She had felt safe with the Gypsies. Even though some watched her warily from a distance, she felt warm towards Queen Valina and Zolton.

She had barely felt Zolton's lips on the back of her hand, but she thought it was nice. Katya paused before answering, "Because I liked it."

Milan raised his hand to strike her. Katya's hands swiftly came up to protect her face, and Milan stopped himself. *What am I doing?* Instead, he gave Vuk a kick in the rump and shouted, "Ha, worthless watch-dog!"

So they had ridden in total silence for hours, neither one wanting or caring to make the first move towards a truce.

Milan was aware that he was behaving like a protective father. He had protected Katya since the night Old Julia put the tiny red baby in Eva's arms. No one thought the baby would live when baby Katya took milk from Eva's full breast. Milan didn't know how to behave any other way towards Katya.

It hurt him that she could be so cold. Katya's angry look was now replaced by one of indifference. He couldn't understand what had happened to change her so.

The Gypsies were clever, he thought. They had done something to change her.

The more time passed, the angrier Katya was with Milan. She had wanted to tell him about Queen Valina's prediction.

The Old Gypsy's words kept coming back to her. *You were put in a place you didn't belong.* Put where? The words meant nothing to Katya. *There is a big danger.* The memory of those words made her shiver. She never wanted to re-live anything as frightening as the experience with Elia and the Turk. Was that the kind of danger she had to watch for?

The dog, Vuk, sensing the strained mood wisely dozed in a remote corner of the wagon.

The streets of Zagreb were crowded with people on foot and in wagons or on horseback. There were all sorts of people. Some were dressed in the fashionable French garb of the sophisticated upper classes and many more were dressed in the ethnic costumes of the varied regions of the country.

A Serbian woman wore a full white skirt with a heavily woven fringed apron. It resembled an oriental rug of geometric design. Her white blouse was embroidered in repeated diamond shapes of red and black. Her cropped vest was also black and red. On her head was a flat-topped, round red hat. Silver coins were sewn on the hat and also on her blouse collar, with more coins dangling at her waist. Her leather opanke or shoes, curled upward at the toes.

Katya stared openly at a man from Dalmatia. He wore a simple white shirt. That was all that was simple about his dress. On his head was wound a red turban, emphasizing his bushy white brows and impressively full mustache. His red vest was heavily embroidered with white and gold threads. The pantaloons were blue velvet, full to the knee and then tight down to the ankle. His shoes also had the curled toes. An enormous paisley cummerbund circled his waist, into which was tucked an elaborately decorated silver-handled gun.

In the center of the city Katya could see an outdoor market with many stalls.

Beyond the square Katya saw a church with a brightly decorated roof. It was the church of Saint Marco built in 1256. Its colorful tiles depicted two large shields. One had the Croatian red and white squares next to a field of three fleur di lis. The other shield had a castle with three turrets.

Beyond the church was an archway where many flowers and crosses had been placed. Katya stood up in the wagon for a better view of Zagreb, for it was like nothing she had ever seen before.

Milan spoke his first words since their argument, "That is one of the four doors leading out of Old Zagreb." He was referring to the time when the city was walled for protection from the Turks.

When Katya didn't reply, Milan once again fell into a moody silence.

Katya's heart raced with excitement. This was so wonderful. So many people! So many different people! Her eyes couldn't take all of it in fast enough. All this was only hours from Selna.

A black carriage stood before a large stone building. Katya had no way of knowing it was a hotel. A footman was helping a beautiful woman descend from the open carriage. Katya saw the woman's dress and caught her breath. It was a dress of yellow silk, full skirted, tight at the waist. It showed the woman's white shoulders and the curve of her breasts. A black hat with curling yellow feathers was perched on her head, and above that the woman held a yellow silk ruffled parasol.

Katya slowly released her breath as she watched the woman walk elegantly into the large doors of the hotel.

I want to look like that! Thought Katya, *She is so beautiful.*

When it became late afternoon and the sun glowed red against the skyline of Zagreb, Katya thought it would take her breath away. Everything was so fascinating and new to her.

What if she kept moving, kept on seeing new places? Could she outrun her 'danger'? Valina's words were always in the back Katya's mind.

Katya absently fingered her bracelet and looked down at it. Two half-moons intersected a square, which overlapped a circle, then another half-moon and an ankh. More squares and circles were interlaced up to the clasp.

The rubies and sapphires sparkled protectively, reminding her of Valina's promise. Yes, she did feel safe wearing it.

As the wagon jostled leaving Zagreb behind, dusk settled about them.

Milan and Katya, life-long friends were still not speaking, each nursing their own hurts, not understanding the change that was taking place. It was a change beyond their control and beyond their imaginations.

Katya leaned back on her bundle resting her head. Vuk cautiously moved closer. When Katya scratched his ears, he moved alongside her and wagged his tail.

She thought about Queen Valina and hoped she would see the old Gypsy again. And she hoped she would also see Zolton.

Katya fell asleep thinking about the brightly painted houses with wheels and doors with steps at the back called caravans. She thought about chocolate drinks and crystal balls, about handsome dark men and women with gold earrings, and Zolton kissing her hand.

Part II, Chapter 5

A solidly built man, just under six feet tall, stood on the porch of his cottage watching with satisfaction the festive preparations for the wedding of his second son. In his yard were women in brightly embroidered skirts and blouses, hair covered if married, long braids and uncovered if single. Some were spreading heavily embroidered cloths over tables in anticipation of the wedding feast.

Wagons were starting to form a line in the pasture adjacent to Marko Balaban's cottage. Wagons arrived with friends carrying food, pastries and gifts. Children were noisy with excitement, while parents were admonishing them to quiet down. Everywhere the air was filled with happy greetings and joyous laughter.

Marko was bursting with happiness for everything was going well. The weather was perfect, a sunny day, not too hot. The pleasant breezes stirring every now and then sent the delicious aroma of roasting meat into the yard. Several men had come as dawn was breaking to tie and salt the pigs and lambs, which had been slaughtered the night before.

"So this is all you are going to do? Stand and watch everyone else work."

Smiling at the voice he knew and loved so well, Marko turned towards his pretty wife. Her eyes, on that round little face he loved so much, were playfully mocking him. Her head encircled by a thick golden-brown braid complimented her hazel eyes sparkling above her flushed cheeks.

Draping his big arm gently over her slender shoulder, he turned her so she could see the activity in their yard. "Look, Vera. Are you not proud?"

He didn't wait for her answer, but went on, "Aren't you proud that we can have such a wedding for Nikola?" He bent his head and kissed her on the cheek. "I wish we could have had such a wedding, not...not what we..." The words caught in his throat.

"Hush, Marko," said Vera softly, putting her finger to his lips. "I only wish that Nikola and Luba will find the happiness that we have." She paused and looked up at him, her eyes full of love,

"How we came together doesn't matter. I thank God every day that you were the one."

Marko gently wrapped his strong, blacksmith's arms around Vera and pressed her lovingly to his solid frame. "Oh, my little Veritza." he whispered into her hair.

"Hey, watch it." A voice called out from nearby. "Tonight is for the bride and groom, not you." Friendly laughter broke out and Marko let go of Vera, laughing along with their friends. Vera blushed, gave a dismissive wave of her hand and disappeared into the house.

Vera Balaban was very proud of her home. She and Marko had worked side by side, almost from the day they met, partners in everything.

The house was made of hewn logs, typical of the area. A shed was nearby and it doubled as Marko's forge, where he made tongues and wheels, and sometimes, artistic latches and pulls for doors. At the back of the large barn were stalls for several horses and a couple of cows. Behind the house, enclosed by a twig fence, were ducks, geese and chickens. In a meadow beyond the barn, sheep grazed lazily. Today three large pigs had to give up their usual run of the yard, for the safety of a pen far away from the guests and tempting food.

It was to a one-room house that Marko had brought Vera, when she needed a place to stay. He added a room on the side, just for Vera, a room where she could be alone. Marko made for her a handsome bed, a table and chair, but traded some blacksmithing work for the large loom that now stood with black and red thread, showing promise of becoming a beautiful bedspread. The bed was piled with feather mattresses and coverlets. Thick down pillows were covered with Vera's woven handwork of intricate geometric designs. Also from Vera's loom were the white curtains framing the windows overlooking a flower box filled with red geraniums.

Later a room had been added above, a second floor, so their two sons, Ivan and Nikola, could have a room of their own. This second room was a luxury since many families lived and slept in one room.

The back of the house had a small kitchen where the cooking was done on a clay stove. A doorway led out to the vegetable garden and chicken coop.

The main room of the house, which in the beginning was kitchen, living room, and bedroom all in one, now stood neatly only as a room for dining and sitting. It was simply furnished with a table, which could hold six for a meal. On each side were long benches and at the head and foot of the table were placed a chair for Marko and Vera. A wide bench along the wall offered comfortable seating.

On another wall, a shelf with spindles held the dishes, each slipped into its own slot, while the cups rested on a shelf above. A beautiful oil lamp hung from the ceiling, directly above the table. It had a shade made of red glass about fourteen inches round, covering the clear glass bowl, which held the oil. This treasured possession had been a wedding gift to Marko and Vera from Anton Vladislav, who owned almost all the land in the area except for the land he gave Marko as a gift many years ago.

Today Marko strode out into his yard happy with all the activities going on. He was pleased that he could entertain his friends so well. Peasants were never able to take vacations or days off, so weddings, funerals and festivals gave them a break from the drudgery of everyday survival. The anticipation of a wedding such as Nikola and Luba's brought much excitement, because it was sure to last for several days. There was no doubt in anyone's mind that there would be enough to eat and drink to keep the guests happily content.

Fourteen-year-old Luba Ruzich nervously stood outside the private chapel of Anton Vladislav. She felt uncomfortable in the wedding outfit that her mother and aunts labored over for months. The red and white blouse had a stiff pleated collar of lace that chaffed her chin. Her underskirts and dress skirt, which came just below the knee, had to weigh twenty pounds. On top of the heavily laced skirt was an equally heavy pleated apron profuse with colorfully embroidered flowers. Her flat-heeled shoes had tiny red flowers painted on the toes with green leaves trailing to the back near the heels.

She was a pretty young girl with brown eyes fringed with long dark lashes, rosy cheeks and nice straight teeth. She nervously pressed together her full lips. On her head was a halo of lace and flowers from which streamed yellow and red ribbons down her slender back.

The bride's mother Mara Ruzich stood near her daughter, pride shining through every part of her. She looked much older than her thirty years. Her face was pale, very wrinkled, with thin pale eyebrows and invisible lashes over colorless eyes. Her nervous smile revealed several missing teeth. Her embroidered clothing did nothing to hide a body, which seemed to be in poor health. Mara Ruzich wrung her hands nervously. She couldn't believe her daughter was to be honored by being married in Anton Vladislav's private chapel.

Luba's father, Andra, with a full brown mustache, blood-shot eyes under shaggy eyebrows, smelling strongly of spirits and garlic, was dressed in a white long shirt, topped with an embroidered vest, and full gaucho-like pants over shiny new black boots. He stood near the road overlooking the countryside watching for the wagon that was to bring the groom. He was nervous, but not for the reason his wife was. He feared something would go wrong. That Nikola would not show up and Andra would have to return the gifts Nikola had given him in payment for Luba. Nikola had paid ten pigs, some geese, a cow, and a nice new wooden wagon when the marriage was agreed upon.

Luba would have preferred her wedding to be in the local church, so that all the villagers could see her get married. When Anton Vladislav offered his private chapel for the wedding, no one dared refuse. No one understood the strong connection between Marko the blacksmith and Anton the landowner. They had been childhood friends and remained close as adults.

The chapel was small so that only the family and Kumovi (godparents) could attend the service. It didn't matter to Andra Ruzich if his friends and neighbors were not witness to the marriage. All that mattered to him was that his daughter was marrying well. Everyone could see how much easier Marko's life was compared to the rest of local people. Little Luba would have plenty to eat. Who knows? There might even be money. Luba could help her poor father and give him some money, he thought. Yes, Andra was a very happy man. He didn't need his poor neighbors crowding the Vladislav chapel, not when his daughter was the only girl in the village to be married there.

The young bride was not as happy as her parents. She stood outside the chapel feeling the perspiration trickle down the middle of her back and between her small breasts. She was wary of this union. Nikola was very nice and she liked him. Yes, she thought she even loved him. But, Luba felt she wouldn't fit into his family. Anton Vladislav was a personal friend of her future in-laws. She couldn't even bring herself to look at Mr. Vladislav when he had congratulated her. Instead she kept her eyes down and couldn't answer him when he spoke. Her lack of education made her feel inferior to Mr. Vladislav and even Nikola and Ivan. The boys' attic room was full of books and she couldn't even read.

Then there was Tata. He thought he would be rich because Luba was marrying Nikola. It was all making her sick. They were expecting too much of her. What could she give her father? She was going into this marriage with nothing. She had no dowry to speak of, just a few linens, which were nothing compared to what Nikola's mother had.

Yes, she was sure she loved Nikola. He was handsome and he seemed to have a loving nature.

"They are coming!" Luba's father shouted excitedly. "I see the wagon." He ran quickly toward the chapel and grabbed his daughter's arm. "You do what ever he wants. Do you understand me?" The old man was almost snarling. "I don't want him giving you back to me for any reason. I'm not giving back any of the dowry." Andra was hurting her arm, "You just spread your legs and give him sons."

With flaming cheeks and eyes brimming with tears, Luba walked into the chapel followed by her silent mother, who was so afraid of her husband, that she said nothing, only putting a comforting arm around her daughter's shoulders.

Luba walked directly to the altar, not seeing the beautiful flowers or the candles glowing in every corner of the lovely little chapel. She saw nothing, but the figure of Christ on the Cross in front of a large, arched window of blue and yellow glass.

Luba knelt and made the sign of the cross as a tear trailed down her cheek.

"Please, Dear God, don't let Nikola be like my father," she prayed.

Part II, Chapter 6

Long tables made of doors or planks, covered with brightly embroidered cloths, strained with the weight of the food offered on them. Jubilant people filled the seats enjoying the company of their friends and savoring the aroma of the roasting lambs and pigs. Standing in a wagon, above the wedding party, the Tamburashi played their stringed instruments for everyone's pleasure.

At the head table, nearest the house, sat the bride Luba with her handsome husband Nikola. He couldn't take his eyes from her pretty face. Her father and mother were at one end of the food-laden table, while Marko and Vera were seated at the other. Ivan, the groom's older brother, was seated next to his mother. Ivan raised his glass to toast the bride and groom.

"May Luba and Nikola have many happy years and many beautiful children."

"Nazdravlje, Good Health." The guests called out, raising their glasses.

After the toast when Ivan sat down, his mother smiled proudly patting his arm approvingly.

Marko smiled broadly at his handsome first-born son, who had inherited his mother's light brown hair and gold-flecked eyes.

"So, my other son, when will you marry?" His father asked, half joking. "You should have married before your brother."

"Find me a girl like Mama," he said, affectionately putting his arm around her shoulder, "and I'll marry tomorrow."

Marko looked at his wife admiringly, "Ah, my son, that will not be so easy."

Marko saw in Ivan's face the same fair skin and round face he loved so much in Vera. Hearing his other son's laugh, Marko turned toward Nikola, his other source of pride, taller than Ivan, darker hair, fuller face and body. Nikola strongly favored his father. His generous mouth was almost always in a smile, while Ivan was more serious. Nikola had a build like his father's, strong and muscular.

Marko started to raise his glass in another toast, when something caught his eye. Walking through the pasture past the wagons, Marko saw a tall, black-haired man with a bearded face. Alongside him was a small slender girl with wind-blown red hair.

Following Marko's gaze Vera saw them, too. "Who are they?"

"I don't know." He said, rising. "They aren't dressed for a wedding."

"Come Ta," said Ivan, "I'll go with you. Maybe they are lost."

"Yes, we'll go together," said Marko, hoping these strangers didn't mean trouble.

Heads turned to look at the tall man and slender girl approaching, a large wolf-like dog at their side. The crowd looked on curiously, as no one recognized them.

Katya was embarrassed, for she could tell these were people of some means. She and Milan were still being cool to one another, so she didn't ask what this place was, or why they were stopping to visit.

She saw a compactly built older man come towards them. He was a strong man, with concern showing on his face. With him was a younger man, with a nice face and kind eyes, eyes that were locked on Katya. His well-shaped lips broke into a smile and shyly Katya smiled back enjoying his obvious admiration.

"Friend, are you lost?" asked Marko extending his hand to Milan.

"I am looking for Marko Balaban," said Milan. Seeing the fine garments on the men made Milan embarrassed with his own shabby clothes.

"You have found him," said Marko, "I am Marko Balaban."

Milan was momentarily speechless. This man was too well-off to be his cousin. "Perhaps, I have found the wrong Marko Balaban."

"I am the only Marko Balaban in these parts." He said. "Suppose you tell me what this is about. I want to get back to my party."

Ivan had not taken his eyes off Katya and it sounded as if his father wanted to dismiss them, so he quickly said, "You look as if you have been traveling." With an anxious glance at his father, he added, "Perhaps you would like to have something to eat, while we talk."

Katya was disappointed to hear Milan say, "No, No thank you. I must find my cousin Marko."

"Who are you?" asked Marko, "I don't believe I know you."

"My name is Milan Kosich and I am from Selna."

A huge smile broke out on the older man's face. "Mali Milan!" he shouted, wrapping his huge arms around his cousin. "Little Milan. I have not seen you since we were children." Together the men hugged and kissed one another on each cheek, laughing and crying with happiness, while Katya and Ivan looked on smiling.

Noticing Katya, Marko said, "And then, this must be a cousin, too."

"Not by blood," said Milan," but, Eva and I have looked after Katya since the day she was born."

The curious wedding quests watched from the yard as Marko hugged Katya and said, "Welcome, my almost cousin. Welcome to my son's wedding party."

Seeing the lace and embroidered vest Ivan was wearing, Katya thought with some disappointment that he must be the groom. As if he were reading her mind, Ivan smiled and pointed a finger to himself while he shook his head "no". It made her blush.

"This is my oldest son, Ivan. Ivan, this is my favorite cousin from my childhood, Milan Kosich." Then laughing, he pointed to Katya, "And your almost cousin, Katya."

Milan and Ivan hugged, as was expected of relatives. When Ivan's lips brushed Katya on the cheek, she blushed again.

"The party is in the yard," said Vera, coming to see what was keeping Marko and Ivan. "All eyes are on you instead of on the bride and groom."

In his joy Marko scooped Vera in his arms, twirled her around and put her down in front of Milan and Katya. "My precious wife, Vera." He announced with pride. "Veritza, can you believe my cousin Milan from my childhood had appeared on this special day. It is an omen, a good omen."

"Mamitza," said Ivan, "this is Katya, not a cousin, but we'll hear all that later."

Vera saw the look on Ivan's face. A look she had never seen before.

"Come relatives," she said, "we must let you freshen yourselves and join our celebration. You must be hungry."

Milan hesitated. "Marko, I have come to ask something of you, but I see that I have not chosen a good day."

Marko slapped Milan on the shoulder affectionately and headed him towards the festivities, "You have chosen a good day. Should I bring my son, the groom, bad luck by refusing a favor to you on his wedding day? No, Mali Milan, this is a good day!"

Milan motioned for Vuk to stay near the wagon. The dog lay on the ground making sounds of disappointment, as he watched the group walk toward the roasting meat he smelled.

Vera put her arm through Katya's and took in the girl's beauty. Noticing the smile on her usually serious son's face she said, "Yes, this seems to be a *very* good day!"

With the sounds of the wedding celebration coming through the open windows, Katya was in Vera's room and Milan in the kitchen, each washing off the travel dirt. Excited to join the party, they quickly dressed in clothes put out for them by Vera.

Both Katya and Milan were awed by the house, its possessions, and what seemed to them to be wealth.

When Katya came into the living room, both Vera and Ivan were there to greet her with approving nods. "You look wonderful," said Vera. "I was hoping the dress suited you."

Katya looked down at the blouse, embroidered in gold threads and heavily laced, tucked into a skirt with hundreds of small flowers of every color and shape sewn into each pleat. Over this was an apron of more embroidered flowers. Katya was pleased the long sleeves covered her bracelet. She didn't want to explain about the Gypsy bracelet. If Milan had become upset seeing it, then his cousins might be upset also.

Ivan smiled approvingly. "It suits you very well." He said approvingly, noticing she seemed even prettier than before.

"I have never seen anything so beautiful," said Katya, running her hand over the design on the sleeve. "I'm afraid I may ruin it. Truly, I feel uncomfortable wearing it."

"Don't worry about such things," admonished Vera. "Eat, dance, enjoy yourself and do not worry about the dress."

Just then Milan came from the kitchen, dressed in a fresh white shirt and pants trimmed in lace, wearing a gold and black vest. Katya marveled at how handsome Milan looked.

Cousin Marko came into the room before anyone could comment on Milan's attire and said, "Come, meet my family and friends. We must eat. I make my own wine." To Milan, he said, "You must tell me if you like it." Marko took Milan's arm and guided him out into the yard where the kolo dancing had already begun.

Ivan was at Katya's side as he led her out into the bright sunlit yard. It was as if the angels had gifted the union with a glorious day. The day was not too hot. A gentle breeze wafted through the yard, not once stirring the dust. It was a perfect day for dancing. About ten men and women were in a circle arms linked, stepping in time to the music. The girls' heavy embroidered skirts flared out like fans as they twirled about.

"Sit here." Ivan made a place for Katya at the head table. Katya nodded and smiled at the shy bride. The young Luba was becoming increasingly embarrassed by her father's drunkenness.

Ivan ignored the bride's drunken father, Andra Ruzich, who was muttering something about 'how well his little Luba did by marrying Nikola.' Instead Ivan introduced Katya to Nikola and Luba. Nikola reached across the table, his dark eyes full of warmth, as he took Katya's hand. "I hear we are cousins. Welcome to our party." Turning with pride to his blushing Luba, he said, "This is my bride, Luba." Shyly Luba smiled and dropped her eyes. "Say something." Nikola urged Luba. "Welcome my cousin."

Before Luba could say anything, her father seated nearby, slammed his fist down on the table so hard that the dishes rattled. "I told you to do whatever Nikola says to do." He was drunk, bellowing, "He says talk, you talk!"

This was too much for the young Luba. It was bad enough all their friends knew what her father was like, but now in front of this beautiful stranger, Luba was humiliated. She got up and ran into the house.

Katya watched in silence as Nikola rose from his seat and went to stand before his father-in-law. There were only Ivan,

Katya, Nikola and the drunken Ruzich at the table. Nikola bent his
face close to Ruzich's.

"Listen to me, Old Man," he said coldly, "I know you think
you forced your daughter to marry me." He grabbed the man's
collar. "Understand this. She is my wife now. She doesn't have to
listen to you or be afraid of you anymore."

Heads within hearing distance turned to watch the encounter.

Ruzich blinked. What the hell was going on? How dare
Nikola speak to an elder in this manner? Ruzich stood up wanting
to say something, but the combination of plum brandy, hot sun and
excitements made his head spin. The ground was coming up at
him. Nikola caught Ruzich as he pitched forward. Nikola laughed
good-naturedly and waived triumphantly to those who were
watching, then he carried his father-in-law off to his wagon to
sleep. Nikola dumped Ruzich in the back of the open wagon, with
little care for the old man's comfort. Satisfied the drunken man
would be asleep for a while, Nikola headed for the house to soothe
his sweet little Luba. Friendly laughter followed him and the
moment was soon forgotten.

Katya and Ivan were now at the table alone. She looked
around for Milan and could see him smiling, glass in hand, being
introduced to people by the happy Marko.

"Please eat a little," urged Ivan. "My mother will beat me if I
let you go hungry." His voice was low and encouraging. It was a
nice voice.

Katya smiled. "I can't imagine your mother beating anyone."

"She is nice," admitted Ivan. "But, she will give me the devil
if she doesn't see you eat something." He took a clean plate and
put some roast pork on it, then placed it in front of her.

"I felt sorry for your sister-in-law," said Katya, thinking
about the shy bride. "I had a brother-in-law who was like her
father. When I was little he always yelled at me or insulted me."
She saw Ivan listening intently, so she went on, "There are parts of
my childhood I don't remember. I think I hid most of the time. I
seldom spoke, hoping he would forget I was around."

Ivan was overwhelmed by the sight and nearness of Katya.
He had the strong urge to find this man who made her childhood
unhappy and beat him. The sight of her hair was dazzling in the
sunlight. He was pleased she had not confined the coppery mass to

braids, for it set her apart from all the unmarried girls with their hair in braids.

Among the guests were many unhappy girls who, along with their parents, watched their prospects of marrying into the Balaban family fade as they witnessed Ivan's attraction to Katya.

Katya was too excited to eat. She picked at the pork, taking only a small piece. She felt self-conscious knowing everyone was looking at her, especially Ivan. However, she found that she liked his attention.

Katya watched Marko with Milan in tow, traveling from table to table. Pleasure radiated from Marko's face as he introduced his cousin to all his friends. Milan enjoyed the limelight. Whoops of happy laughter could be heard from Marko and his friends,

Guests passing near the table smiled shyly at Katya, and nodded to Ivan, not stopping to intrude. There was plenty of time to get to know the pretty stranger.

Ivan's steady gaze into Katya's face made her a little uncomfortable and she looked away towards the dancers, who were now doing a dance with ribbons, criss-crossing them, weaving them in and out, forming overhead patterns of color with their graceful movements.

Watching the dancers was a handsome man dressed in tan colored riding pants, with a matching tan form-fitting jacket. The only decoration on this outfit was some delicate black stitching on the collar of the jacket. His black leather boots gleamed, even though they were covered with the dust stirred by the dancers. He was of medium build, with a well-proportioned body, no thick leg or arm muscles here. His perfectly cut brown hair, graying slightly at the temples along with his elegantly trimmed mustache, gave him the air of a professor or scholar.

Katya couldn't make out the color of his eyes as they crinkled at the corners when he smiled, which he was doing now in response to something that was said.

"Who is that man?" Katya asked, "The one next to the priest."

"He's here!" exclaimed Ivan excitedly," He has been out of the country and wrote that he would try and be here for the wedding. Come." He took Katya's hand, "I want you to meet my godfather, Anton Vladislav."

Standing next to Anton Vladislav was Father Lahdra.

Part II, Chapter 7

It was nearly midnight when Father Lahdra left the wedding festivities, which would continue the next morning. His rooms were in the house next to the Church of Saint Joseph, which was sponsored and supported by the Vladislav family.

His rooms consisted of a parlor, a library and sleeping quarters. Very little of the furnishings belonged to Father Lahdra. Almost everything belonged to the church. But after fourteen years, Father Lahdra came to think of the beautiful furnishings as his. A beautiful glass lamp sat on a highly polished wooden desk that stood in front of windows covered by heavy velvet drapes. The drapes helped to keep out the cold drafts in the winter and block the heat of the sun in the summer. An ornate velvet-tufted settee and a matching chair were in the parlor, gifts of the Vladislav family. When the pieces were first delivered, Father Lahdra was gloriously happy thinking they were his to keep. With great relief, he was thankful he had concealed his embarrassment when he realized the occasional deliveries of furnishings or books were meant as possessions of the church. These were to be enjoyed and used by the priests who would follow Father Lahdra as pastors of Saint Joseph's. Father Lahdra always included in his prayers the wish that he not be needed elsewhere, for he enjoyed his position as pastor of the church and as the personal pastor of Anton Vladislav's family.

Over the years, Father Lahdra liked to think he was not only Anton Vladislav's spiritual advisor, but also a personal friend, a good friend. He felt this was true, for he was included in all the Vladislav social gatherings, though they were few. Also with some pride, he felt he held all the family secrets in his heart. Through the Sacrament of confession and many intimate conversations, Father Lahdra was sure he knew all there was to know about this honored and respected family.

In his clean, comfortable room, Father Lahdra removed his shoes and stockings, unbuttoned his black cassock placing it in the walnut wardrobe opposite his bed. Still in his underclothes, he went to the round lace covered table next to his bed, picked up a waiting bottle to pour himself some wine. He filled a crystal glass

while his mind was full of thoughts about Anton Vladislav, Ivan,
Marko and the tall man and girl from Selna.

Father Lahdra looked at the comfortable bed high with
pillows. He knew this would be a sleepless night as something
about that red haired girl from Selna gnawed at him. He opened
the wardrobe once more, took out a red dressing gown. This would
be the closest he would come to wearing the church's princely
colors, he thought ruefully, as he went into his library.

He liked this room. The brightly colored Persian rug was
threadbare, but that didn't matter to him. That it was a thing of
beauty pleased him. The oil lamp was still lit. Zlata, the
housekeeper, always left one light so that he would not come
home to a dark house. It gave the room a warm glow. All the
shelves of books pleased him. Most were ecclesiastical and many
were historical works. Some works of Shakespeare and his own
personal possession, a gift from Anton Vladislav, Dante's *La
Divina Commedia* with nearly a hundred full-page illustrations by
Gustave Dore. It was the first printing in the Italian language and
Father Lahdra had no trouble with the text. Over and over he
would look with fascination at the illustrations depicting hell.

Placing the wineglass he brought with him on the desk,
Father Lahdra proceeded to look through his desk for his personal
ledgers. He had kept a daily record of events from the time he was
sent away to school. At first his ledgers helped fight his loneliness,
it was something to look forward to doing. Also it ate up time, the
time when he was alone at night in his monastery cell. Soon the
daily writing became a habit. As he grew older and reread his
earlier ledgers, he found a certain comfort in his own history. The
entries in the ledgers became more interesting, once Lahdra left
Selna and came to Saint Joseph's.

There were many ledgers now. The earlier ones were written
in lined notebooks, but lately his daily events were recorded in
unlined paper bound in leather. Now it was the older lined
notebooks he was looking for. He was rummaging in the bottom of
a deep drawer, when he thought he heard a gentle knock. He
stopped and waited. He heard it again.

Walking to the door through the dimly lit entryway he let out
a long sigh. It was always bad when someone had to summon a

priest in the middle of the night. Probably he would have to dress and ride out to administer the last rites.

"Anton!" the priest said with surprise when he saw who was at the door. "What is it my friend?" He moved aside to let the wan-faced man enter. "Come into the parlor. You look so pale. Let me get you some wine."

Anton Vladislav was a very handsome man. Unusual gray eyes were on a face that might remind one of a silent movie star.

Lahdra watched as his friend entered the parlor. The priest hurried into the small kitchen, where he took from a shelf two etched glasses. He found another bottle of wine, placed the items on a tray and returned to his sitting room.

Anton Vladislav was sprawled on the velvet settee, one leg extended on the seat, his boot careful not to touch the velvet, while the other leg was on the floor. He covered his eyes wearily with one hand as if to shut out the light.

Lahdra was alarmed that his friend looked so desolate. Quickly the priest poured a glass of wine and offered it to his friend.

"Here Anton, please take this." When Anton didn't move, Lahdra gently removed Anton's hand that was covering his eyes.

"Anton!" the priest exclaimed upon seeing the tear-stained face and the gray eyes brimming with more tears.

"What has happened? You must tell me! I have never seen you look so devastated."

Anton responded by feebly waiving his hand, unable to speak.

"Here, take some wine," urged Lahdra. "Please."

Father Lahdra watched in silence as his friend slowly took the glass of wine and sipped. The priest's heart was breaking for he loved his friend as a brother and couldn't bear to see him so broken. He pulled a chair near Anton, waiting patiently until his friend could compose himself.

There was nothing he would not do for Anton. Lahdra would still be in the poor Village of Selna if Anton had not interceded with Bishop Benekovich to have him moved to the Novo Mesto region. He would still be dealing with peasants who believed in the custom of stealing a bride on the eve of her wedding. The result being, that if the bride's father and brothers or fiancé did not find her, she belonged to her captor. Sometimes the bride was part of the intrigue, especially if her father had arranged a marriage the girl didn't want.

During his stay in Selna, Lahdra thought he would die of unhappiness surrounded by uneducated peasants. No one could read, so no one could discuss philosophy, religion, the world, or great fiction. Lahdra believed Anton had saved his life. Yes, Lahdra was sure he would have died in Selna, or drunk himself into oblivion, had Anton not arranged for his transfer.

Lahdra watched as his friend became calm. Anton straightened himself into a seated position, still wearing the tan riding outfit he wore earlier to the Balaban wedding. He pulled out a linen handkerchief that was discretely tucked into his sleeve, wiped his eyes and turned his head to politely blow his nose.

"I'm sorry, Lahdra," he said, in a low voice, for he always spoke in a polite and dignified manner. "I see that I've alarmed you and I apologize."

His handsome face was distressed, but the color was coming back to his cheeks with the aid of the wine. His trim mustache was wet from the tears.

Nervously he ran a hand through his full, brown hair, the lamplight playing off of the gray at his temples. He looked at Lahdra's concerned face and gave a timid smile, embarrassed at his own behavior. He reached out and placed his hand on the priest's knee.

"I'm very ashamed that you see me this way." He leaned back, took another sip of wine. "It was the wedding today. Watching the happy Balabans and the festivities nearly broke my heart."

"But, why would such a joyous occasion make you feel this way?" Lahdra asked.

With silent compassion the priest watched and waited for his dear friend to speak.

"I love them all," Anton said simply. "Marko, Vera..." His voice trailed after he said 'Vera'. He continued "And the boys, such wonderful sons." His eyes glistened again, but no tears fell. He rose and went to the window. Pulling aside the velvet drapes he peered into the darkness.

"I have to let it out or I think I'll go mad." His words were full of anguish.

Still seated, Lahdra spoke to Anton's back as his friend stared out into the night.

"Do you want the Sacrament of Confession?" he asked.

"No." Lahdra heard the despair in his voice. "No, I confessed this many years ago. Absolution did not take away the pain, or the thought of what could have been." He turned looking at Lahdra and laughed derisively, "I was a good son."

Then as if talking to himself, he said, "I should have found a Gypsy to tell my fortune. Had I known the future...had I known...I could have made better choices."

Seeing the look of disapproval on the priest's face, Anton said, "Don't look that way. Everyone has his fortune told one time or another." Taking another sip of wine he said, "I wish I had known what was to become of my life. For I tell you, Lahdra, I would have made other decisions."

"I am your dear friend, Anton. Not only your priest," said Lahdra soothingly, "But hopefully I have become the brother you never had. Tell me anything, anything that will lessen this agitation. I can't bear to see you this way."

The handsome man, his features distorted in anguish opened his mouth, as if to speak.

"Yes?" Father Lahdra waited for the words that were not coming. "What do you want to tell me?"

Anton put his drink on the desk. "I must leave." He said.

Lahdra was alarmed.

"Wait. What is it? Tell me what is disturbing you."

But, before the priest could get to his feet, Anton was through the door, not taking the time to close it behind him.

Part II, Chapter 8

Anton Vladislav held the horse reins as he walking slowly under the cool moonlit sky. Memories he had pushed back, along with feelings he thought were conquered, overwhelmed him. It had been the wedding that had aroused these emotions and feelings. It was good he had not told Lahdra what was bothering him, for the fewer people who knew the better.

He had been a student in Zagreb at University. He smiled as he remembered those days. He almost told Lahdra that "She was the tavern keeper's daughter and we students were all in love with her. I was twenty years old and enjoyed living in Zagreb. Learning was my passion, especially the languages. History was wonderful, too. I enjoyed that, but the languages I loved most." It fascinated him that words could be so similar in several different languages. Such as shkola in the Croatian language is scuola in Italian and then school in English. He smiled at how absurd that thought was. Why would he think of that?

His thoughts went back to what he would have told Lahdra. "The tavern where we spent our evenings was near the street, Harmica, and hours flew as we discussed the medieval architecture built in the Roman times, or how the Hungarian-Croat King Bela IV fleeing from Genghis Khan in 1242 proclaimed Zagreb a sovereign royal town, and how Matija Gubec the peasant king was executed in 1573."

There was so much he wanted to tell Lahdra. To tell how exciting it was to be in a cultural city of 40,000 people. It was exhilarating to be in that atmosphere. He never allowed himself to discuss Zagreb with Lahdra for fear he would give himself away.

He stopped walking and said aloud, "I've never loved anyone the way I loved her." A filmy cloud drifted across the moon, making the night match Anton's gloom. He was thinking how she had worked in the tavern for her father. How she did everything. She could cook. She served tables. She even kept the accounts. His eyes softened as he remembered how he found himself going to the tavern to see her instead of for the friendly debates with his comrades. And he was proud when he had been the only student she would go out with. There was much teasing from the other young men who wanted to go out with her. Some of it was friendly, some not. The teasing didn't matter, for she was all he could think about.

She was beautiful with thick hair and wonderful golden eyes. Her smile was warm and sincere, and she was intelligent. She was educated, which was unusual for a barmaid, and she was well read. Anton paused again. He found a rock and used it as a seat, while his horse wandered off to find some dewy grass to nibble.

Anton remembered how her father forbade her to go out with students. So they did what many young lovers do in such circumstances, they hid it from him. Surprisingly none of the students who knew their secret gave them away. She came to his room at university several times where they lost themselves in each other's arms and time stood still. He thought he would die with the sheer joy of making love to her. When they were spent, they would lie in each other's arms, their bodies hot and wet with perspiration and he would tell her what their life together would be like.

His gray eyes darkened as he remembered the fateful day the letter came informing him that his father was ill and he must hurry home. He went to the tavern and told His Love that he had to leave and would be back as soon as possible. He gave her a quick kiss when her father wasn't looking, then left to be with his family.

When he arrived home, he found his father was ill with pneumonia.

"How bad is he?" He asked his sister Sophie, who was spreading ground horseradish and ground mustard seed on the sick man's chest, hoping the mixture would clear his lungs.

Sofie was pretty, small figured with straight light brown hair, braided and wound like a crown on her head. Her eyes were clear blue, not gray like her brother's. Her smile, which shone often from her round face, warmed everyone.

She smiled that warm smile now spreading her horseradish-mustard stained hands outward, so as not to soil Anton's clothes. She walked into his arms and let him hug her. He kissed his sister's forehead affectionately. Seeing how tired she appeared and hearing his father's raspy breathing, he said, "You should have sent for me sooner. Taking care of Tata alone is too much for you."

Leaving her brother's embrace, she reached for a towel, staining it yellow as she wiped away the homemade medication.

"Tata didn't want you to leave school. He told me not to let you know he was ill. I sent you the letter when he got worse. I've been a little frightened that we might lose him." Almost apologetically, she added, "I didn't want to be alone if he died."

Anton took his sister in his arms again and this time she wrapped her arms tightly around him. They held one another for a while, giving each other strength and comfort.

After a week of more horseradish-mustard plasters, along with layers of sliced onions wrapped in cloth on the sick man's chest and many cups of garlic and honey tea, their father improved.

With his father well, Anton was happily planning his return to Zagreb and to His Love.

Anton remembered the day he discovered he wasn't much of a man.

He had been quite pleased with himself up to that certain day when he was reading aloud to his father.

His once robust father seemed pale and shrunken in his bed. The old man's once thick white hair looked yellow and limp, as did his mustache. His full-fleshed, handsome face was now gaunt with the ravages of his illness and his skin was the color of parchment paper.

Anton was happy to see some of the alertness return to his father's eyes as he read to him. His father had a fine collection of books and Anton was reading from the French volume, *Memoires Historiques, Militaires et Politiques*, when his father reached out his hand and lowered the book Anton was holding.

"What is it Father?" He asked, concerned his father might be feeling ill.

What the sick old man said changed the course of Anton's life.

"I've arranged a very good match for you with the daughter of an old friend," his father said it as a matter of fact. As if he were saying the weather was fine. Anton was speechless. He never thought much about marriage before His Love. It didn't occur to him that his marriage would be decided for him. Such a thing was never discussed before. But, he should have known. His father had tried it with Sofie, arranging a marriage that is. His pretty little sister fought their father and Anton didn't want to do that to the sick man.

He remembered all the arguing and screaming that went on when Sofie had defied their father refusing to go through the arranged marriage.

She was in love with a young man in Trieste and she stuck to her guns. Their father was well then, a strong man, able to take on battle. Now, he looked so small, so weak and pale. Anton couldn't distress him. Anton had always loved Old Vladislav and was proud to be his son.

It became a tug of war for Anton, this love for his father and family duty or the love of a barmaid. Ashamed, Anton recalled how he had denounced her! Just by thinking of her as a barmaid, instead of His Love...he had denounced her.

Anton knew his father had made a choice for him that would add to the family wealth. Surely there would be more money, more land. Perhaps even another title, to add to the Vladislav name.

The men of the Vladislav family had been Lords for many generations and the land they lived on was given to some ancestor as a reward for doing well in battle.

Now, in the night, Anton pushed aside the painful thoughts. He got up from his seat on the rock and started walking in the damp night air. He reached into his jacket pocket and pulled out an Egyptian cigarette. He paused in his walking long enough to light it with a stick match and inhaled deeply. Instead of the sword to gain land, Anton married for it. In its own way it had been a form of battle.

He never returned to Zagreb to see His Love. His eyes became moist with the memory of that time. He became so engrossed with the plans for the wedding, the details of the dowry and the other arrangements, that he thought only occasionally of the girl who waited for him, the one into whose arms he had so often melted.

Anton was glad he had not stayed to tell Lahdra his story, for then he would have to tell his friend, his priest that he didn't believe what the priest said in the Sunday sermons. Anton had long believed that one didn't have to die to be in hell, for he was sure it was here for him...now.

Lahdra would want to pray. Yes, that was the priest's solution for every problem, a prayer. Anton was bitter. He had prayed. Oh, how he prayed. He even tried to bargain with God, but God chose to ignore him.

He wished Lahdra weren't a priest. He needed a friend, someone to listen so that Anton could release this...this shame and pain that was deep inside of him. Nikola and Luba's wedding with all the happiness and love Anton witnessed crazed him to the point of being jealous of the blacksmith and his family.

Anton realized how wretched he had become. That he could envy a man, who fifty years ago, he could have owned like a horse or a cow.

In fact, Anton's grandfather probably owned Marko's grandfather.

Anton knew what Father Lahdra would say if he knew how Anton felt...what he was thinking. "I cannot believe a good man such as yourself, and a generous man," he would say, "can be as jealous as you say you are."

Anton's face was pale with fatigue. Dark circles rimmed his sad gray eyes. He had grown up with Marko. They were like brothers. When Marko wasn't working the land the two, as boys played together, grew up together. When they were older they hunted together. Even when Anton went away to school, his visits home would always include a hunt with Marko.

Tears filled Anton's eyes. "I love him and I hate him." He said to his horse. "Of course, I hate him! He has spent twenty years with the greatest love of my life and he has raised my son as his own."

Book II, Chapter 9

The wedding celebration for Nikola and Luba was into its second day. Many of the guests had spent the night sleeping in the barn or in their wagons. Others who lived near enough went home to take care of chores planning a hasty return to the festivities

It was near eleven in the morning, the livestock had been fed, also the chickens, geese and ducks. Wagons filled with cheerful friends were already threading their way on the dirt road back to Vera and Marko's yard for more music, company and food.

Vera looked remarkably fresh and pretty, considering how little she had slept with the music and singing and dancing going on far into the night. Standing on her porch and looking out over the yard, watching the party gear up for its second round, gave her much pleasure. She smiled when she saw Marko with his cousin Milan. Marko was delighted to visit with the cousin he hadn't seen since childhood, especially on such a happy occasion as a wedding. The bride and groom, asleep in the room once shared by the brothers, had not made an appearance yet. Every now and then someone would point to the upstairs window and laughter or giggles would follow. *Poor little Luba*, thought Vera, thinking of the shy child-bride. She will die of embarrassment when they finally come down.

"Good Morning." Vera called a greeting to some friends who waved from across the yard to her. "How are you?"

Vera spotted copper hair glowing like a shiny coin in the sunlight. It was Katya walking from the row of wagons where she had spent the night. With her was Ivan, who had slept in a nearby wagon. When he heard that Milan was going to sleep in the barn, Ivan felt he should spend the night near Katya.

"As a protector," he had said in all seriousness, not knowing that Vuk was more than enough protection for Katya. In fact, today Vuk was allowed to come into the yard, which made the dog very happy. He had spent the previous day grumpily confined to the wagon.

Vera saw the look of love on her son's face. She smiled. She was pleased as she watched Katya and Ivan walk together. Seeing them smile at one another caused a little flutter in her stomach and brought up old memories. Memories better forgotten. In her son's face she saw the love that had once shone out of the once young Anton Vladislav's face. Vera closed her eyes tightly. No, no! She thought. I won't let those thoughts in. I'm being foolish. Anton means nothing to me!

When she opened her eyes, Marko was standing a few feet away in her line of vision. Automatically her face broke into a big smile. Yes, she thought, there is the man I really love. And love him she did! He was not rich, nor handsome. He was strong and caring. He was the solid rock she had built her life on. Their years together had proven to her that she was first and foremost in Marko's life. He had never questioned, not once, how it was that Ivan was born seven and half months after they married. Also, he had never asked her where her home had been. It was as if she had been re-born on the day she had met Marko, and in a way it was true. It had amazed her that she could cut Anton out of her heart as cleanly as she had. It was when she saw Katya with Ivan, and his resemblance to Anton, which had stirred repressed memories.

Back in Zagreb, twenty years ago when Vera had missed her second period, she knew she had to leave. Vera never knew her mother and had no woman with whom she could confide. She knew it would be a matter of time before her father turned her out or killed her. So without telling anyone about her pregnancy, she set out to find Anton.

Vera had walked most the way from Zagreb, occasionally getting a ride in the back of wagons.

She was weary and hungry when she knocked on the side door of the large house atop a hill, within its gated wall. Vera knew that Anton's family was prosperous for he was a student at University. However, she was not prepared for the house she wanted to enter.

After several knocks at the back door, a plump, pleasant-looking girl somewhere in her late teens opened it. The girl wore a white homespun peasant blouse with a large lace edged apron over a white ankle length skirt. Her sandy colored hair was in two braids, criss-crossed at the back of her head. Her brown eyes looked the stranger up and down.

"Yes," she said. "What do you want?"

Feeling suddenly shy, Vera asked, "Is this the house of Anton Vladislav?"

Vera saw the disturbed look on the servant's face.

"Why do you want Anton?" The girl asked.

"I…I am a friend of his from Zagreb. I wish to speak to him."

Looking over her shoulder nervously, the girl stepped out onto the stoop, closing the door behind her.

"My name is Klara," the servant said. "This isn't a good time to see Anton."

"He will want to see me," said Vera. "Tell him that Vera is here."

"This isn't a good time," Klara repeated softly. "Perhaps you can come back another time."

"No! I can't come back another time," said Vera. "I am tired. I am hungry and I want to see Anton. I walked almost the whole way here from Zagreb. I have slept in wagons and along the road. I am tired." Tears were welling in her eyes.

Klara put her arm around the sad girl. What could she do? There was no way Klara could go into the main room of the house and ask Anton to come to the side door for a waif who demanded to see him. What would his fiancé Erna or Erna's father think?

"Don't you know anyone nearby? Someone you could stay with till morning?" asked Klara, as she nervously glanced through the window of the closed door.

"I only know Anton," demanded Vera. "Please tell him I am here."

"I can't do that. He isn't here." She lied, hoping Vera would leave.

Just then a familiar voice called, "Klara! Where are you? How long does it take to fetch a plate of strudel?"

The door opened. "What are you doing out here? To whom are you talking?"

Anton's face went white when he saw who was with Klara.

But, that was twenty years ago. Today was a day of celebrations. Vera's son Ivan shined his attention on Katya like the sun and the girl opened up to him, unfolding like the petals of a flower. She was no longer the frightened girl from Selna. Katya was happy, confident and felt wonderfully alive. For the first time

Katya was aware of the power a woman could have over a man who was infatuated with her. She could see that Ivan was totally bewitched by her and she reveled in the feeling it gave her. Katya had liked being with the Gypsy, Zolton, but she enjoyed Ivan's company even more. She found herself liking and trusting Ivan. Until now the only man she had trusted was Milan, who was like a father to her. In the past she had feared men and often tried to make herself invisible. She had tried to make herself unnoticeable by not speaking, by always looking down and even hiding away in Old Julia's house, being friendly with only Milan and his family.

Today she smiled, held her head high and looked into everyone's face, as she greeted them, feeling warm and friendly and safe. Yes, she felt safe!

"What lovely things the bride and groom have received," said Katya, admiring all the gifts heaped on a long table made of boards across sawhorses and covered with cloth. The gifts were not wrapped, but were openly on display to be admired. There were large pillows, mattresses and coverlets filled with goose down. There were crochet and knit tablecloths, and scarves to drape above the windows and hand-carved wooden bowls of various size and shape. And to mix liquids, a tool carved so that five spokes protruded. It looked like miniature spokes of a wheel, missing the outer rim. The stick would be placed between both palms and rubbed between the hands, the motion making the stick whirl, mixing the liquid.

Nearby was a small corral set aside especially for wedding gifts. Bright ribbons were tied here and there, making streamers that fluttered in the wind. This corral was for living wedding gifts, such as a pig, or a goat or a calf or some chickens.

Hand in hand, Katya and Ivan found themselves a place to sit at a table.

"Vanjo, where is your brach? Aren't you going to play for us?" called Ivan to a short, thin man with shaggy brown hair over his ears. Vanjo's eyes were bright and sharp, like a bird's. He wore brown pants and a white shirt, not the usual peasant garb.

"I can't play," he said, "I have a boil on my chest and it hurts terribly. Even the weight of this shirt gives me pain." He grimaced as he spoke, feeling the burning beneath his shirt.

"Oh," said Ivan, disappointed, "you're the best brach player here." Then seeing Vanjo looking at Katya, Ivan said smiling, "This is Katya. She is a sort of cousin."

"Zdravo" said Vanjo, wincing with pain, "Hello."

Katya smiled and nodded her head in a greeting. She started to say something then stopped herself.

"What is it?" said Ivan. "You started to say something."

Katya hesitated. "I don't mean to embarrass you," she said to Vanjo, "but may I see your boil?"

Vanjo turned his bird's eyes warily to Ivan, who only shrugged his shoulders.

"I know a little about healing," said Katya. "Sometimes it is very simple to cure a boil."

"Let her see your boil," urged Ivan.

Reluctantly and gingerly, Vanjo unbuttoned his shirt to expose an angry red protrusion above his left nipple. The inflammation made the left side of his chest decidedly larger than the right.

Katya put both hands to her mouth, as it was her thinking gesture, and leaned forward to inspect the furious eruption.

"Please, don't touch it," begged Vanjo.

"Come to the house with me," ordered Katya. "I know what to do."

Thinking she was going to lance the boil, Vanjo protested, "Oh, no, you're not going to cut me."

"Of course not," said Katya. "I'll make a poultice. Come now." She spoke softly, but with authority.

Vanjo rose from his seat reluctantly, giving Ivan a wary look. The two men followed Katya to the house. Ivan was smiling. He was delighted to learn something new about Katya, while Vanjo walked glumly, sure that he was in for more pain.

Vera was still on the porch watching the trio as they approached the house.

"Good-morning, children," she called out to them.

"Good morning, Mamitza," Ivan said, kissing his mother on the cheek.

Seeing Vanjo's open shirt and the red boil Vera said, "My God, Vanjo that must hurt."

"Katya is going to fix it," Ivan proudly announced.

"Is this true?" asked Vera. "You know what to do?"

"Yes, Mama," said Ivan before Katya could answer. "She knows what to do."

Now a small group of curious onlookers had gathered and sympathetic murmurs were registered when the boil was spotted.

"May I go in the house and get what I need?" asked Katya.

"Of course," Vera said. "Anything, anything you want."

"Wait here," said Katya, as she disappeared into the house.

Curious, Vera followed her into the kitchen and watched as Katya took a bar of homemade lye soap from the table. With a small knife Katya scraped the bar until she had several soap curls that she dropped into a nearby bowl. To the soap she added sugar and a little water, while Vera watched with much interest. Katya stirred the mixture adding water and sugar until it was the proper consistency. The sleeve of her blouse worked up as she mixed displaying the Gypsy bracelet.

Vera stared at the gold bracelet with its colored stones and unusual designs. Noticing Vera looking at the bracelet, Katya said, "It was a gift. It is supposed to protect me."

Vera moved closer, taking Katya's arm and inspected the bracelet.

"It looks like a Gypsy bracelet," Vera said.

Ignoring Vera's remark, Katya said, "I'll need a piece of soft cloth, something to cover the boil with."

Vera reached into a side cabinet and took out a soft piece of flannel. "Will this do?"

"It is perfect," said Katya, heading for the door.

Milan and Marko had joined the small group of onlookers waiting to see what Katya was going to do to the very nervous Vanjo.

"You will have to remove your shirt," said Katya.

With silent fascination the curious onlookers watched as she gently smeared the thick brown paste over the boil. She used every bit careful to mound it over the heart of the boil. Throughout Katya's ministrations, Vanjo was tense with the fear that she would touch the boil in some spot that would send a stab of pain into his chest, but it never happened. She was very gentle as she wrapped the flannel around his chest and back tying it into place when she was finished.

"If I am still here tomorrow," said Katya, "I'll unwrap it and see if it needs another poultice."

"Of course you'll be here," said Ivan. "Isn't that so, Cousin Milan?"

Milan and Marko stood watching as Vanjo buttoned his shirt, the curious onlookers drifting away for it seemed the show was over. A worried look registered on Milan's face. All this time he had not broached the subject of his visit. "I don't know." There was hesitation in his voice. "I must have a serious talk with your father."

Ivan looked to Katya who only shrugged her shoulders, for she had no idea what Milan's plans were or where he planned to take her.

A few stragglers overheard Milan and felt this "serious talk" might be interesting, so they clustered near.

Sensing Milan's discomfort among the eaves dropping neighbors, Marko said, "Come, Milan, let's walk."

"I would like to come along, Ta," said Ivan.

Marko gave his visiting cousin a look, as if asking if it would be all right.

"Of course," Milan nodded to Ivan, whose face broke out into a huge smile. Ivan couldn't wait to hear more about Katya, and he wanted to be available if it was necessary to convince Milan to stay a little longer.

Ivan gave his mother a big smile, nodded good-bye to Katya and walked beside his father and Milan away from the disappointed little gathering of curious neighbors. No new gossip. They were disappointed. None of them felt any embarrassment for wanting to know something that was none of their business.

The three men walked a while in silence. Both Milan and Marko wore the richly embroidered white pantaloons and festive shirts, while Ivan wore black riding pants, hand-me-downs from his godfather Anton, along with a shirt matching his father's.

The trio walked until they were past the wagons and clusters of people who might be within earshot. Finally Milan said, "Let's sit here."

They were under a large shade tree with Milan positioning himself so that his back leaned against the trunk of the tree, while Marko and Ivan sat cross-legged facing him.

"I don't know where to start," Milan frowned, his eyes dark. He scratched nervously at his beard fearing that once he told them all about Katya, Marko might think of her as 'bad luck' and not want her around. And yet, he loved his cousin and had to tell him the truth, no matter the consequences.

So Milan began to tell Marko and Ivan about Katya. He started with what he believed to be the true story of her birth, the death of her mother and the unborn baby, and the death of her father all in the same night. He told about the marriage Milan arranged for little orphan Anka, who was only a little over ten years old, to Elia Sokach. He explained that he had hoped that Anka and the baby Katya would be cared for by Elia. Then he told about Elia's cruelty over the years and how he would have attacked Katya if Old Julia hadn't taken the girl in to live with her. Milan told them about Old Julia teaching Katya all she knew about healing. At last he came to the part about the Turk buying Katya and her escape. Milan left out the encounter with the Gypsies, as he himself was still upset over it.

Milan paused, waiting for a reaction. He was afraid to go on, afraid to ask if Katya could stay with them. Now that he had seen the fine house, far finer than his own, and how his cousin lived, he was embarrassed to ask them to protect Katya.

Marko looked thoughtful as he gazed past Milan looking at nothing in particular. Young Ivan was visibly enthralled with the story. He couldn't get over what he had heard. Katya was like a heroine from an English novel. She was nothing like the girls he knew who only fed chickens, washed clothes or milked cows, and giggled whenever he rode by. Ivan wanted to shout out, *'We'll take care of her.'* But it wasn't for him to say. He looked at his father, who was lost in thought.

Marko was thinking of the night he had brought Vera to his little house. He never asked what had brought her to Klara's kitchen that night so long ago. At that moment he wondered if Destiny had brought Katya to Ivan, the way it had brought his beloved Vera to him.

"Ta," Ivan broke into his father's thoughts. "What, do you think?"

"About what?" Marko's mind was still in the past.

Meanwhile, up the hill at the Vladislav house, Anton's sister, Sofie was unhappy at the prospect of going to the wedding celebration alone. She had been ill the day before, but her affection for Marko and Vera would not keep her away. Marko had been a childhood friend and later Vera, too, had become a friend.

Sofie was Anton's younger sister and at thirty-three years of age looked older. She had Anton's coloring, fair-skinned with brown hair that Sofie wore in a thick braid coiled around her face. Her blue eyes were under finely arched brown brows and her pale lips were of a generous proportion. Her small, thin frame suggested frailty.

Because of her kindness and her genuine regard for people, all who knew Sofie loved her, the only exception being her sister-in-law, Ernesta. Sofie had long ago given up hope for a friendship with Erna. After a time the two women had settled into a cool, but polite relationship, since it was the only way they could sanely exist under the same roof. Sofie loved her brother very much and it pained her to see him unhappy. So she tried to make their existence in the strained household at least congenial.

To Sofie it was a mental strain living in a house that was in reality part hers, while by protocol her sister-in-law was mistress of the house. The estate belonged to Sofie and Anton equally until she married, then it would belong to Anton alone. Since her fiancé had died, Sofie never thought of marriage again, much to her sister-in-law Ernesta's disappointment. Ernesta's open dislike for Sofie depressed and depleted Sofie of her strength.

Sofie had hoped to go to the wedding celebration with Anton or her nephew Stefan. It was well into the morning and the young Stefan, Anton and Ernesta's only child had not returned from Zagreb.

This morning, the second day of the wedding celebration, Sofie and her sister-in-law, Ernesta, were in the simply furnished dining room at the table. Sofie was sipping her morning coffee and Ernesta toyed with some bread and jam. Both women wore white, long sleeved blouses gathered at the neck with colorful embroidery. Their long skirts were trimmed along the bottom with brightly stitched flowers. Instead of the heavy flaxen material worn by the peasants, theirs was of fine lightweight material. Ernesta's sleeves and skirt hem were decorated with beautiful hand crochet lace. These full skirts worn over the gathered blouses tended to add bulk to the frame. With Stefan's birth, Ernesta gained much weight and had lost what attractiveness she had possessed in her youth.

There was no conversation between the women. Only a cool politeness prevailed.

Ernesta was worried because of Stefan's absence, fearing some danger had befallen him. Along with the worry for her son, there was a brewing anger toward her husband. Anton had stayed out all night. She was sure he had flirted with the girls and became so drunk he couldn't make it home.

The dining room was not a large room, but the table could seat a dozen people comfortably. Anton and Ernesta seldom entertained. The only guest they ever had was Father Lahdra. When the priest came to visit, Ernesta and Anton were able to relax and the usual tension receded. Those evenings were actually enjoyable and even Sofie could have a good time. With the priest there, Ernesta could be most civil.

Both women heard the kitchen door open and they heard Anton's voice, "Good morning, Klara."

Sofie felt herself stiffen. Ernesta hated that Anton preferred to enter the house through the kitchen. She especially hated the easy manner Sofie and Anton had with Klara, who Ernesta felt *was just a servant.*

No amount of explaining could make Ernesta understand what the kitchen and Klara meant to both Sofie and Anton. As children, Anton and his little sister spent most of their time under the care of Barica, Klara's mother who was the cook back then. Sofie hardly remembered her own mother for she was very little when Amanda Vladislav died. The influenza had taken so many victims that winter so long ago. Her death had made their father a grieving widower who soothed his broken heart with travel, leaving the household help to care for the motherless brother and sister.

So the kitchen, which was Barica's domain, became for Anton and Sofie a place of love and comfort. Marko and Klara were cousins. Anton, Sofie, Klara and Marko did what children do. They played together and grew to adulthood loving one another.

Klara and Marko never crossed over the invisible line that separated them from Anton and Sofie. Generations of servitude bred into them the cognizance of their rank and Marko never ventured beyond it, though Klara on occasion dared to push it to the limit.

For Anton, coming through the kitchen would rekindle some warm feeling deep inside from childhood, and no amount of nagging from Ernesta could make him use the family entrance at the front of the house.

Seeing his wife and sister at the table caused Anton to momentarily pause at the door leading from the kitchen to the dining room.

"How are you, Ladies?" he said as he prepared himself for a sample of Ernesta's anger.

"Where have you been all night?" Ernesta's fleshy cheeks were flushed. "Don't you think Klara and the others know you were out all night?"

Anton looked pale and exhausted. "I was with Lahdra." His voice was hoarse.

Ernesta's black eyes narrowed, "I'm to believe you and a priest caroused all night together?"

Anton could see this conversation could easily escalate into a quarrel. "Leave me alone. I'm going to freshen up." He started across the room, but Ernesta leapt from her chair and blocked his way. "No!" Her voice shook with fury and her dark eyes sent out sparks. "We have to talk about the insane wedding gift you gave that Balaban boy."

Anton pushed past his wife, giving his sister Sofie a wan smile and a look that said, 'I don't need this.'

Ernesta was grabbing at his sleeve. "Tell me," she demanded, "how can you give your son's land away to that peasant?"

Anton's anger rose and he pulled Ernesta's hand from his sleeve squeezing it, wanting to hurt her. "It is my land, mine and Sofie's."

Ernesta pulled her hand from his grip, the pain reflecting in her face. "This land is meant for Stefan," she cried, her face red with anger. "How can you scatter it this way?"

Sofie wanted to say something. Anything to come to Anton's defense, but she dared not.

"We have much land. Four acres means very little to us, but it is the world to that young couple," said Anton, his voice weary.

"It was Stefan's land you gave away," Ernesta insisted.

As if beaten, Anton said with much effort, "Stefan doesn't care for this land or the house." His voice almost broke when he said, "He only cares what it is worth."

Ernesta opened her mouth to speak. Her eyes betrayed her. She knew what Anton meant. Still defending her son, she said, "That's not true. He loves this land as much as you do."

Anton's eyebrows rose. "Really, then why doesn't he know the names of all the people who live here and work for us? Why doesn't he listen to me when I try to explain the expenses and how we operate on a daily basis?"

"He's young." There was a faint pleading in Ernesta's voice. "He will be responsible when the time comes."

Sofie, trying to be invisible in her chair at the table, watched her brother and Ernesta in yet another heated argument over Stefan. She held her trembling hands tightly in her lap and studied the pattern of the crochet tablecloth. Ernesta could crochet beautifully. It seemed to be her only talent. Over the years she had made many crochet tablecloths, doilies, bedspreads, curtains and lace. One seldom saw her without one of her many hooks used to produce this finery. Right now Sofie felt like a slender piece of thread and wondered if Ernesta was going to 'hook' her into this quarrel as she had done so often in the past.

Three feet away from Sofie, Anton and Ernesta were face to face.

"He's young," repeated Ernesta. "You are too hard on him." Her tone grew bolder. "You are always criticizing him. You find fault with his studies and just about everything else about him."

Anton stared at his wife for what seemed a long time. He thought about his handsome, black haired son with heavy-hearted disappointment. Stefan had no interest in becoming a scholar. He had less interest in being a landowner and at twenty years of age showed no inclination toward any worthwhile adult activity. He was openly bored with his parents when he was home and couldn't wait to leave. When gone, he stayed away for days at a time. Yes, Anton criticized Stefan often and couldn't stop himself.

Sofie braced herself for Ernesta's burst of fury when she heard her brother say, "Ivan Balaban could take over this land and all its workers tomorrow."

Oh, God! Why did he have to mention, Ivan?

Ernesta pursed her lips and made slits of her eyes. The skin on her face seemed to tighten, her arms were tight at her side, her hands balled fists. She said in a low, controlled voice slightly shaking with emotion. "I *hate* the Balabans. I hate their perfect sons. I hate Marko because you think he should be your brother, when all he is...is the blacksmith. And," she nearly spat the words, "I hate that perfect little Balaban wife."

With her eyes blazing fire Ernesta straightened her shoulders and raised her chin. She slowly backed to the doorway leading to the front part of the house. "Listen to me, Anton Vladislav. This house and land will be my son's. You will not give anymore of it away. I will do anything to see Stefan gets what is his rightful due. No one will stand in my way." Her stare shifted to Sofie whose face was drained of color. "If I must, I will even kill for my son!" Sofie and Anton were both shocked speechless. Familiar as they were with Ernesta's angry outbursts, they had never seen her so venomous. It unsettled them both.

Slowly Sofie rose from the table, her face pale. She wanted to defend her brother, to remind Ernesta that half the house and land belonged to her.

"You needn't worry." Sofie's voice was soft and low. "I have no children. Whatever is mine will go to Stefan. No one will cheat Stefan of his proper inheritance."

Ernesta glared at her sister-in-law. In a cold, controlled voice she said, "I cannot stand the sight of you any longer." Then, Ernesta turned to Anton, "That includes you." Ernesta, stood framed in the doorway that led to the living quarters, said, "You will both understand that from this moment on, I only live for my son. I will stop anyone...*anyone*...who stands in the way of his inheritance. *Do you understand me?*"

Book II, Chapter 10

Just as Anton had loved Zagreb in his youth, so did his son, Stefan. 'Like father like son' didn't apply when it came to their fondness of the city. What each found appealing in Zagreb was as different as night is to day.

While Anton knew the historical points of interest, the stories of the great men who had lived there, the great architecture and the history of the invaders of Zagreb's past, Stefan knew a different Zagreb.

Anton's handsome son had short black curls, bright blue eyes, which had a mischievous glint to them. His nose was nicely proportioned above a nice mouth and a firm strong jaw. His smooth clear complexion was the envy of men and women alike, for scars and pockmarks were common at that time.

Many not so young or attractive men wanted his company and friendship, and were willing to pay for it. Paying for drinks, meals and carriages was a sure investment in meeting and acquiring beautiful women, for Stefan drew women like flowers attract butterflies. It was known in certain circles that older wealthy women were willing to pay for Stefan's company. Sometimes Stefan went out with these older women on a dare, but usually he did it for the money. He had decided long ago that it was tedious trying to live on his allowance or to face the interrogations of his father when funds were short.

There was a time Stefan could get extra money from his Aunt Sofie, but as he grew older, she became less generous so that now he never approached his aunt for help.

In times of financial desperation, Stefan would go home and work on his mother, whose heart he could break just by seeming unhappy. There had been only some rare times when she was reluctant to give him money, questioning why he needed so much. But more than once the clever Stefan had been able to convince his mother that his aunt and father were plotting to cut him out of his inheritance. That easily made Ernesta an ally with all the protective instincts of a tigress.

Tonight Stefan sat at an outdoor cafe, sipping thick Turkish coffee as he watched the continuous parade of Zagrebites passing by on their way to appointments or just for a pleasant evening's stroll. The evening breeze felt fresh and the air was scented with the fragrance of night blooming jasmine. Stefan looked quite handsome in his blue suit hand-tailored in Venice. His matching blue silk cravat was held in place by a gold stickpin, a gift from a grateful married woman, whose name he had long forgotten. He looked pleasantly bored as he leaned back casually in his chair.

Stefan's heavily fringed eyes studied each passer-by in the hopes of seeing someone he knew, someone who wanted a companion and had some money to spend. Usually by early evening, he was at Magda's, a popular gambling house with rooms upstairs where beautiful women of every color entertained anyone with money.

Tonight Stefan was short of funds. Sometimes when he went to Magda's, he would meet up with a willing gambling partner who would stake Stefan for the night. He couldn't go to Magda's alone tonight. Not tonight. Not without some money in his pockets. He was in debt to the house for a large sum and had only enough money to pay for his coffee. A brief look of annoyance flickered across his handsome face. He hated always searching out clever ways of finding money. After all it was ridiculous. His family had wealth. Why should he do without when his father was always giving something of value to the Balabans? God! How it annoyed him that his father was so devoted to Marko, his childhood friend, a blacksmith!

Stefan did not want to go home. He only did that as a last resort. Surely Aunt Sofie would be waiting for him to escort her to the Balaban wedding. He didn't want to go there! All of Stefan's life, it seemed his father praised the Balaban boys as if they were something better than the peasants there were. It was Ivan, the oldest who especially irritated Stefan. The lout learned to read and became insufferable with wanting to borrow books, and worse, to discuss them at length with Stefan's father.

It was at one of these times, when Stefan was home, that Anton had called out to him, "Come here my son. Ivan has completed Sir Richard Burton's, *Vikram and the Vampire*. It is his first adventure in reading English."

Stefan had descended the stairs seeing his father's excitement as he sat next to Ivan at the dining table. Books were scattered and the wine glasses filled. Seeing his son, Anton called, "Come, come here, Stefan. Let's hear what Ivan thought of the book." Bile rose in Stefan's throat. He hated Ivan. Never had his father's face shone with that same excitement when he looked at Stefan. Stefan felt that he saw only annoyance and disappointment reflected in his father's eyes. Now his father's eyes glistened with eager anticipation for Ivan.

"Sorry, Tata," he tried to sound genuinely disappointed, "I promised to go riding with some friends."

Anton wouldn't be dissuaded. "Please sit for a moment I want you to join us."

Reluctantly Stefan sat opposite his father. Ivan sat very near the Count, looking up briefly to smile a greeting at Stefan, his attention returning to the books.

"Was the English hard for you to understand?" Anton asked Ivan.

"I had to read slowly and used my dictionary often, but I believe I understood most of it," said Ivan.

Bored Stefan poured himself a glass of wine, leaned back in his chair and sipped the sweet liquid.

His eyes fell on a book he recognized. It was a book his father bought in Venice and had given to Stefan as a gift. It was Kipling's *The City of Dreadful Night and Other Sketches.* Stefan had never read the book and quite frankly didn't plan to. To read, one had to sit alone. Stefan didn't like being alone - he liked excitement. He liked the smell and warmth of women and the challenge of gambling and the laughter of entertaining companions. No, he didn't like to read. But, that didn't keep him from being annoyed and hurt now that he saw the gift from his father placed on the table before Ivan.

"What is this?" Stefan picked up the hand-sewn book.

"I'm giving it to Ivan to read," said his father.

Anton waived his hand at his son. "Oh, you aren't interested in the book. Ivan will enjoy it." It was as if Stefan had been dismissed.

Stefan wanted to say something. He felt his jaw clench. It didn't matter that he wasn't going to read it. He might someday, who knows? The point was that it belonged to him and he didn't want Ivan to have it. Ivan gazed at Stefan with golden hazel eyes as if he could read Stefan's mind. Stefan stared back for a moment not hiding his feelings. Then Stefan quickly rose, almost tipping his chair over.

"I must go. I'll be late." He said, escaping the keen comradeship between Anton and the peasant Ivan.

Now, seated at the cafe in Zagreb, Stefan shook his head as if to be rid of that sore memory. He motioned for the waiter to bring more coffee and resumed his scanning of the promenades.

Damn! He thought. Everyone I know is already with friends or at Magda's. He pulled a pocket watch from his vest and checked the time. Nine o'clock, it isn't that late!

Stefan had to keep himself from leaping up when he saw the lanky figure of Blaz Sukich. At the same moment Blaz saw Stefan and waved, threading the crowded tables to reach Stefan.

Blaz Sukich had pale, almost colorless blue eyes shaded by thick brown eyebrows. His brown hair was thinning slightly at the temples. The finely trimmed mustache and goatee on his thin face gave him the air of a scholar. Always neatly dressed, Blaz wore a tan suit with a yellow cravat. Only his diamond stickpin rivaled his smile in brilliance. He seemed so happy to find Stefan.

"Stefan!" he said warmly when he reached the table. He extended his hand for a handshake and said, "What a pleasant surprise. I was getting lonely."

Stefan took his hand and said with equal warmth, "Hard to believe you are ever lonely. Sit with me awhile. Perhaps we can think of something to do together."

When he sat at the tiny cafe table, Blaz's eyes didn't match his wide smile. He said, "Of course, it's no fun to be alone in Zagreb on such a lovely night." He looked at Stefan's demitasse cup and said, "I don't want coffee. Let's go where I can buy you a real drink."

This was what Stefan had hoped for, someone with money willing to finance the evening. It was perfect! "Where do you want to go?" he asked.

"Oh..." Blaz spread his hands and gave an indifferent shrug. "Magda's is always interesting."

Stefan paused. He didn't want to go to Magda's until he had some money to cover his debt. "There must be some new place with new faces," Stefan's voice trailed off.

Blaz ran his knuckles under his chin scratching his goatee. "I hear Magda has a new girl, very young, maybe thirteen or fourteen years old, a wild Gypsy girl with eyes as black as indigo." Before Stefan could refuse, Blaz slapped him on the shoulder and said, "Come! Let me pay for the whole evening…drinks, girls and food, all on me!" Then he said almost as an afterthought, "I'll even stake you at the tables if you wish."

This was what Stefan had been hoping for, a stake at the gambling tables. Surely his luck had changed, and he could win back what he needed to pay Magda and be in her good graces again.

Stefan didn't answer immediately. He didn't want to seem too eager, "If that's what you want." He tried to sound indifferent, "I suppose Magda's is as good as anywhere."

"Splendid decision," said Blaz, already on his feet, tossing wrinkled bills on the table to pay for Stefan's coffee. "Let's go, I'm anxious to see that beautiful Gypsy."

Blaz didn't hail a carriage. Instead they walked through the streets, their fine leather shoes echoing on the cobblestones with each step. Stefan had to walk briskly to keep up the pace set by Blaz.

"I think you should save your energy for the Gypsy," said Stefan, hurrying to keep up. "You won't have the strength to do anything."

Blaz laughed nervously and slowed his walk, trying not to appear so anxious.

At the open door of what looked to be a private home with a discreet stone edifice and windows heavily curtained for privacy, stood Magda greeting the arriving guests. Around the perimeter of the property was a large iron fence with an impressive iron gate. A guard sat in the shadows at the gate entrance only permitting those he recognized to enter.

It was hard to believe that Magda had ever been a great beauty, though legend had it so. No one knew her age. She had a protruding belly and enormous breasts, which she tried to hide under exotic caftans. Her pale brown hair showed some gray, along with a poor attempt at coloring it. She wore her hair piled on top of her head in loose curls. Her face was long, with eyes too small and mouth too thin. Her nose was bulbous and it was the only feature in proportion to her long face. She outlined her eyes with khol, which made them seem even smaller. Her cheeks were rouged and her lips were red. Even in the dim light, she was not an attractive sight.

Despite her size, doubtful age and looks, Magda was enormously popular and was liked by all her customers. She always wore a smile and exuded genuine warmth. She knew all her patrons by name and was willing to sit and be a good listener for great lengths of time, sympathetically listening to their problems like a loving aunt.

As Stefan and Blaz entered the door into a dimly lit vestibule, Stefan expected the usual hug and slap on the back from Magda. Tonight an uneasy feeling surrounded him. Magda's smile was different. It was there, but it was a nervous smile. The corners of her mouth seemed to twitch. Her eyes kept averting his. She stood so that she blocked the entrance to the huge gambling room just beyond the vestibule.

"How are you, Magda?" said Stefan, trying to ease the tension he felt. "You look lovely as always."

She acknowledged his compliment with another nervous, twitching smile. Her voice didn't sound natural when she said, "Let's have a private drink before you go upstairs." She guided them to a door at the left, which for all his visits, Stefan thought to be a storage closet. Instead it opened into a large room. Blaz entered first. Magda motioned for Stefan to follow Blaz, closing the door behind her. Blaz nervously glanced about, looked at Stefan, and then quickly looked away.

The room seemed to be a storage room. The only functional furniture was a long, heavily carved wooden table with a single chair behind it. It appeared to serve as a desk. Paintings of every size were carefully stacked against the wall behind rolls of oriental rugs. Against one wall was a large floor to ceiling bookcase, the width of the wall. It was loaded with porcelain vases and figurines. Marble statuary was placed carefully on the floor out of harm's way.

Magda looked at Blaz, who was very nervous, perspiration glistening at his temples. "I think you should leave now, Blaz. I want to talk with Stefan."

Blaz looked at Stefan, apologetically. His mouth was dry. He shook his head and said, "I'm so sorry, Stefan. I had no other choice."

Stefan stared at Blaz. "What in the world is going on? What are you talking about?" he asked.

"I'm sorry, Stefan," Blaz said again, his eyes searching Stefan's face for some sign of understanding. "I...I owed them more than I could pay. This was the only way I could get an extension of time to clear my debt."

"What are you saying?" demanded Stefan. He still didn't understand why they were in this room and not upstairs with the new Gypsy girl.

Blaz's voice caught as he said, "It was the only way they would give me more time. I couldn't find the money to pay what I owed. So, he said, if...if I brought you to him, he would give me another week."

"What him? What are you talking about?" Stefan turned to Magda, "You've trusted me before. Haven't I always paid you what I owed? What is going on?" Stefan's voice was rising now. He felt anger and confusion.

"You'd better go." Magda said again to Blaz, who quickly left without a backward glance.

Fear was creeping up Stefan's spine. Something was terribly wrong.

"I thought we were friends, Magda. Why are you treating me this way?" He tried to steady his voice, but failed.

Magda looked sincerely pained. "I know, Stefan," she said, biting her lower lip, smudging lipstick on her teeth. "I didn't want to do this."

His eyes were wide. "Do what?"

Magda reached her hand to touch Stefan's arm. He looked down at the brown spots on her hand, as if he had never seen those hands before.

Her voice was low and friendly as she tried to explain, "I have money problems too. The girls get sick, there are doctor bills. Just keeping food on the table for all of them costs a fortune.

Then, we had some big winners here and I had to pay out." She looked at him for some understanding. Seeing none, she went on, "I had to take in a partner. I couldn't afford to run the place alone anymore."

Just then a door opened. Not the one Stefan had entered, but another private side door.

Magda's new business partner was heavy-set. He was bald, with a round face and thick neck. He wore black pants, a fine white shirt with a vest woven with gold threads. On his head was a black fez and at his waist hung a money pouch.

Book II, Chapter 11

Her husband was still away. Eva Kosich, back in Selna, had no way of knowing if Milan and Katya were all right. Had they made it to his cousin Marko's house? Would Marko take in Katya? All these thoughts ran through her mind as Eva sat at her table. Rain splattered against the windows. It was early evening, but getting dark suggesting a heavy storm. She worried that Milan was not home yet. Eva's hand trembled slightly, as she brought the cup of hot tea to her mouth. In their sixteen years of marriage, this was the first time she and Milan were apart. He had now been gone five days and his absence worried her.

She had a gentle sweetness about her, always pleasant and kind. It was reflected in her eyes and her smile. A quiet woman, she was hard working and dependable.

Eva removed her ever-present babushka and scratched her scalp. Without looking into a mirror she loosened her hair, used her fingers as a comb then rewound her hair at the back of her head. She again positioned the scarf on her head, far over her forehead securely knotting it at the nape of her neck.

The tears were there, just behind her eyelids, ready to trickle down if she lost control. She couldn't lose control. The children were worried, also. Tata had never been away before.

Young Milan was the oldest and favored his father with the same tall build and dark hair. He was sixteen and doing as much work as his father. At the moment he was in the barn tending the cow. It wouldn't be long before he found himself a bride. She and Milan had hoped Katya and young Milan would marry. They were disappointed when Katya said she wasn't ready to marry.

Marica and Evica, now eleven and twelve, were pretty little girls. They both looked like their mother with the same pouting lips, the heavy lidded brown eyes and round rosy cheeks. They wore long braids. Another year or so and they would be married, with babushkas on their heads, the sign of a married woman.

There had been two more babies for Eva after Evica, but they each died soon after birth.

Eva had another child. One she put to her breast as if it were her own...Katya, poor Katya. The poor surviving twin, or so everyone thought, left to be raised by another child. Eva thought of Anka. What a sad, tortured little girl Anka had been, with the death of her mother and father on the same day and then a newborn baby to care for.

There was her terrible marriage to Elia Sokach! Now a tear trailed down Eva's cheek. It was she who suggested Milan bring Elia to the village to arrange the marriage to ten-year-old Anka. It was a decision she would regret until she was dead and buried.
"God forgive me." It was a prayer she had said a million times and would say a million times more.

She shook her head sadly at the memory of Elia's cruelty and the many times she hid the child bride Anka, and baby Katya, from Elia's drunken rages. Then, there were the times she and Old Julia would care for the beaten and battered Anka. Finally Old Julia took Katya into her own home to protect her from Elia. But, no one could take Anka away. She was married to Elia before the Altar and the church blessed the union.

Anka's whole life had been one of sadness. It was as if Anka had been a shadow. There was nothing memorable about her. She seldom spoke with her neighbors, out of fear or shame, or both. Her clothes had become threadbare and even ragged, keeping her from going to market, which was a social event, a place to meet one's friends. After Elia knocked out her front teeth, she seldom let anyone see her, except for Old Julia. A shadow...that's what Anka had been. Just a shadowy figure moving through her daily tasks for the years she was with Elia. Eva couldn't remember how many times Anka had been pregnant in her ten years with Elia. Each time, the frail girl miscarried. The beatings made carrying to term impossible for the thin woman-child.

Anka died in childbirth at twenty. Her wrinkled, sunken face looked fifty when they prepared her body for the funeral. A blessing thought Eva. Death had been her only way out of life's pain and misery.

Anka's only joy had been Katya. "A gift from my mother," she used to say proudly, back when she still mingled with her neighbors. Her pride in Katya's beauty and the girl's quick learning had no measure. Anything Old Julia showed Katya, the girl remembered.

When Old Julia took Katya to live in the house across the road, it broke Anka's heart. She knew it was best for Katya's safety, for Elia was a lecher around the girl.

Anka, The Shadow, had even thought of killing her mean husband. It used to consume a good part of her lonely existence, but she lacked the courage. After all those beatings, she was afraid.

Eva's thoughts returned to the present. She looked about the simply furnished room. Milan and young Milan had built the sturdy table and benches. Three beds were positioned against the walls. One bed was for the girls to share, one for Young Milan and one for the parents. A nice stool was next to the clay stove and several more were near the fireplace.

Many wooden bowls were on a shelf above the stove, all carved by her husband or son. She had many wooden spoons and forks. At the far end of the room Marica and Evica were seated at the loom, working on a new pattern. Her daughters had learned to weave so there was no shortage of cloth. She was so fortunate to have so much, so much more than some of her neighbors.

"Mama, look. Someone is coming," said the younger daughter, Evica looking out the window, into the now heavy rainfall, pointing to a figure walking towards the house.

"Is it your father?" Eva jumped to her feet hurrying to the door.

"No, Mama...it is Elia," said Marica, joining her sister at the window. "And he looks terrible."

Elia came through the gate made of tied tree limbs heading straight for Eva's door. She gasped when she saw him. His cheek was swollen, infected from the knife wound the Turk had inflicted. He had a dirty cloth tied around his head, looking as if he had a toothache.

Eva stepped in front of the door hoping to block his way. He was wet, filthy and smelled awful.

"What do you want, Elia?" she demanded. "Milan is not at home."

"Of course, he's not home! He's run away with that red-haired whore. You'll never see him again." The words were slurred because of his swollen cheek.

Eva ignored his remarks and asked, "What is wrong with you? Do you have a toothache?"

"I was attacked by thieves…on the road." He lied. "They cut my face. There must have been five of them."

Evica and Marica stood huddled together their mouths open in horror, at the sight of the pointy-faced man, made grotesque with the angry swelling on his cheek. The cloth tied about his face, only emphasized the wound.

"What do you want here?" demanded Eva, finding it hard to look at his disproportioned face.

Elia dropped his eyes and tried to sound humble, "I'm hungry. I'm sick with fever and can't cook for myself."

Eva couldn't believe what she was hearing. "And you want me to feed you?"

"Please, Kuma," he addressed her as a close friend, "I need help and you are a good woman."

Eva glanced at her visibly frightened daughters. They were standing at the far side of the room, staring at the wet figure of Elia in the doorway.

"Please, Kuma," he said again, "just a little warm soup."

As much as she disliked Elia, she couldn't ignore his pitiful condition. It wasn't in her nature to ignore someone in need. *I'll regret this.* She thought.

"Come in Elia. I'll give you some soup. But, that's all. Then you must go!"

"God bless you," said Elia, walking slowly to the table where he seated himself on the bench. "God bless you. You are a good woman."

From their side of the room, the girls could smell his foul odor.

Eva busied herself warming the soup in an iron pot. Wanting to hurry and get him out of the house, she said to Marica, "Get a bowl and some bread and a spoon. Put it in front of him."

Marica gave her mother a look that asked, *Why me?* Getting a stern look from her mother, the girl brought the utensils and bread to the table. She avoided looking at Elia dropping the things as near to him as she dared.

It was at that instant the crazed Elia grabbed Marica's wrist and twisted it. She gave out a scream. "Where is she?" Elia snarled. "Tell me where your father took her. I know he took Katya."

Later, when Eva would tell Milan what had happened, she wouldn't remember flying across the room from the stove and hitting Elia in the head with an iron kettle. She couldn't believe herself capable of it.

Marica, Evica and Eva had stood staring in stunned silence. Elia, not moving, lay on their earthen floor.

"Mama!" Young Milan's voice had startled Eva back to reality. Her young son stood in the doorway, milk bucket in his hand.

"Sveta Maria, Holy Mary! What have I done?" Eva's hands began to tremble. Her whole body was shaking.

Young Milan quickly closed the window and pulled the curtains closed for privacy. He was about to close the door, when he was startled by a shadowy figure in the doorway.

It was Stevo, Stevo, the burner of the mattress when Mila died. Stevo, who had loved Mila, Anka's Mother and regretted never asking for her hand; Stevo, who had discovered Mato's dead body in Father Lahdra's wagon.

They all stared at Stevo in silence. *Now, what? Now everyone will know Eva killed Elia. She would go to prison.*

Stevo stepped into the room and closed the door behind him. He pressed his finger to his lips, indicating they be quiet. He saw the fear in their faces. "Don't worry," he assured them, his voice low. "No one is going to know what happened here."

Stevo's white hair under a small cap was wet as was his handlebar mustache. His homespun pants and shirt were rain soaked.

"Girls, come, sit down," his voice was low. He motioned with his hands towards the table. "Milan, get a blanket."

Eva and her daughters obeyed the old man, sitting on the bench farthest from where Elia fell, blood seeping from his head wound.

The frightened girls sobbed softly, clutching their mother, seated one on each side of her.

Stevo knelt, looking closely at Elia's face.

"Give me a mirror," he demanded. With both frightened girls clinging to their mother, the three figures rose and moved as one entity across the room to a table where a comb and mirror lay. Eva untangled herself from the girls and brought the mirror to Stevo, who placed it over Elia's face.

"He's dead," Stevo said, seeing no fog on the mirror. Young Milan was at his side with the blanket. Without speaking, the two men wrapped the body in it. When they were finished they stood a moment just looking at one another. Young Milan didn't know what to expect or what to say. Stevo took charge.

"Milan get some wine or krushkovac or whatever you have. We're all going to have a drink...even the girls." No one challenged this order. When wine was poured they drank in silence, the glasses for the girls, filled only a third full.

When the old man felt Eva and the girls had calmed a bit, he said, "No one must know of this. I am sure I am the only one who saw Elia come here. I followed him in the rain and saw no one along the way. We will sit here quietly, calmly. Soon there will be full darkness."

Young Milan said, "We can take him into the woods and bury him there."

"I have an even simpler plan." Stevo said. "I already have a large hole, where I removed a dead tree stump. The hole is waiting for me to plant a young apple tree I moved from the field. We'll make the hole a little bigger if we have to. We can do it in the dark. The hole is at the back of my house far from the road. I don't think anyone will see us."

The rain beat harder on the roof and against the windows.

"In this hard rain, no one will go out. No one will see us," said Stevo.

Eva was regaining her composure. "Stevo, we will never forget this. When Milan comes home and hears how you helped us, he will do anything to repay you."

Stevo raised his hand, his skin like parchment, "There is nothing to pay. We will forget this night." Then he added, "Who will ask about Elia? No one! People will think he left for a better place. Really...no one will care."

And that was how it turned out. No one was concerned about his disappearance. Mildly curious perhaps, but no one missed him.

Elia was fine fertilizer for the young apple tree. In a short time it grew large and bore much fruit. Each year while he was alive, Stevo would go from door to door, sharing the fine fruit with his neighbors, until he died at the age of ninety.

Book II, Chapter 12

The morning following the Balaban wedding, after he said the daily mass, Father Lahdra knelt and prayed fervently for his friend Anton. Anton's strange behavior and his quick departure worried Lahdra. It was as if the priest carried his friend's pain. He felt leaden. His limbs were heavy, his heart and mind were burdened. He prayed for guidance, and he prayed that Anton would find inner peace for whatever it was that plagued him.

Father Lahdra stared up at the life-sized wooden crucifix as if it might speak to him. Lahdra loved this little church. It was one hundred years old and made of field rocks placed one atop the other. It stood high on a hill overlooking the green countryside with a golden steeple cross that shone in the sunlight like a comforting beacon visible for many miles. The interior of the church had beautiful statues and candle stands, which had been lovingly made by artisans for the 'Glory of God.' The fourteen Stations of the Cross, seven lining each side of the church, were hand carved and then beautifully painted. The ornate altar and side chair were said to have been carved in the Black Forest of Germany. At some time these were brought to Saint Joseph's by a Vladislav ancestor.

Finished with his duties, Lahdra dressed in his black priest's garb, genuflected before the altar, made the sign of the cross and headed for the house that was both rectory and his home. He was thinking about his journals where he recorded his daily thoughts. How was it he could not remember Katya or her family? She didn't resemble anyone from the village, as he recalled. Milan, on the other hand, he remembered well. He could even picture Milan's young bride Eva and their marriage. But, Katya was a mystery.

In the study, Lahdra went directly to his desk. From a deep, lower side drawer, he lifted out several leather-covered journals. He kept searching until he found the older ones with paper covers, from the days when leather bindings were a luxury. He put aside several of the journals after briefly glancing through them. Satisfied with his selection, Father Lahdra leaned back comfortably in his chair and opened the old book. The first sentence he read was:

'I am so unhappy here! The bishop ignores my many letters. I beg him to send me away from here. The people here in Selna are uneducated and superstitious. I have no one to share good company with'.

Father Lahdra was embarrassed by this entry. He felt ashamed that as a young priest he had so little patience with the peasants.

Thankfully he had matured since then. Quickly he turned the pages, leaving the cheerless reminder of his first parish behind. His eyes fell on the date, October 5, 1892. He smiled recalling that it was about that time he had his first meeting with Anton, the meeting which changed his life. Anton never admitted that he had a hand in Father Lahdra's being transferred to the Karlovac area, but Lhadra was certain Anton was the reason for the privileged transfer.

Father Lahdra looked at the page with his uneven handwriting. *How much my handwriting has changed*, he thought, looking at the meandering scrawl, at times illegible. He could almost feel the old unhappiness seeping back into him. He reminded himself that he was looking for information about Katya, to satisfy his curiosity about the girl, not to review his early years as an unhappy pastor. Once again he read:

October 5, 1892.

Yesterday, I was summoned to the convent located in the countryside near Novo Mesto, by Mother Superior. Greatly annoyed, I set out on my journey. It was a good three hours by horseback. There are many parishes much closer. Surely she could have called another priest who was located nearer. I didn't have a carriage and wasn't looking forward to riding a horse, but on the other hand, I was pleased for the excuse to get away from Selna. I am tired of reading letters from relatives who are in America and tired of the constant poverty around me.

It was late afternoon when I found the convent surrounded by a wall of stone resembling a fortress. In the wall was a large wooden door above which dangled a chain. Seeing no knocker, I pulled on the chain and heard a bell ring in the distance. I pulled on the chain several times thinking the bell wasn't loud enough to be heard. After a few moments, there was movement on the other side of the door and the sound of the latch being pulled. A tiny figure all in white homespun linen looked me over quickly and stepped away from the open door to let me enter.

I saw a large vegetable garden where neatly spaced rows of assorted vegetables grew. To the west was a small chapel with a bell and cross on the wooden roof. There before me was a rectangular building which I guessed to be the convent. Beyond the convent I saw a barn and stables, where a fine carriage stood. Nuns are poor, so the sight of such a splendid carriage aroused my curiosity.

"I'm Father Lahdra," I said to the nun who opened the door for me. "I was summoned."

The nun kept her head down, never once looking at me or speaking to me. She took the reins out of my hand and gestured toward the building I thought to be the convent. "I'm to go there?" I asked. Turning her face from me, her features hidden by the coarsely woven veil, the nun again motioned toward the building.

The structure was long and narrow with many windows, suggesting many individual rooms. The heavy wooden door with large metalwork hinges opened before I could knock. Standing in the open doorway was another nun also veiled and dressed all in off-white coarse cloth. The veil came low on her forehead, framing the most expressive dark eyes beneath finely arched brown eyebrows, suggesting she had dark hair. Her skin was pale and unlined and her mouth formed a mischievous smile.

When I heard the words, "It took you long enough to get here." I was speechless, for only then I recognized my cousin Manda. How was it I didn't know she had taken the veil?

"Is it you, Manda?" I asked. "Is it really you?"

"Come this way, Father," her voice had a no nonsense tone to it. She turned her back to me and walked briskly down a deserted narrow corridor lined with many doors on each side. I felt like a child again, and Manda was teasing just as she had when we played together as children.

I reached for her elbow to stop her, but at my touch she playfully pulled away and said in mock seriousness, "Surely you

must know we are not to have any physical contact with men."
Then she abruptly stopped before a door, identical to all the others,
and with a motion of her head indicated I should enter.

Manda was my favorite cousin and I had to stifle a smile as I
entered the cell. There I saw an older, obviously ill nun in a bed,
her colorless face framed by a white bonnet completely covering
her nearly hairless skull. The bonnet was tied under her bony chin.
She was attended by a white robed figure praying alongside the
bed. Seeing us, the praying nun rose without speaking and moved
to a corner of the small room. The only sound was the rustling of
her heavy skirts.

"Mother," Manda gently touched Mother Superior's hand.
"Father Lahdra has come to pray with you." Gone was the
playfulness. My cousin's face now reflected the solemnity of the
moment.

The old nun's pale watery eyes shifted from Manda to me. I
believe she understood I was a priest, though I could tell she was
very near death. In one hand I carried a small leather bag holding
my stole, prayer book, oils, and the communion host. With my
free hand I touched the old nun's hand and said, "Hello, Mother,
I've come to pray with you."

The room was very simple, indeed a cell. There was only the
tiny bed with a crucifix above it, a table on which lay some
religious books, and a statue of the Virgin Mary with a flickering
candle set before it. Hanging on wall hooks were the dying nun's
garments. One crude wooden chair stood alongside the bed. There
was a small bedside table I could use for the last rites.

"We must hurry, Father," whispered Manda. "We may not
have much time."

I placed my bag on the table, making the necessary
preparations, and kissing the stole I draped it about my neck.

"*Pax huie domui,*" I said, "Peace to this house." Manda and
the attending nun both knelt near the bed responding, "*Et omnibus
habitantibus in ea*...and to all who dwell herein." I placed the
Blessed Sacrament on the table and genuflected, placed the oil
next to the burse and replaced my white stole with a violet one.
Making the sign of the cross I sprinkled the dying nun with holy
water. The two kneeling nuns, said in Latin, "Sprinkle me, O lord,

with hyssop, and I shall be purified. Wash me, and I shall be whiter than snow."

I feared there was not time for the complete rite, so I hurried on to the absolution, then to the anointing, making the sign of the cross on eyes, mouth and all other parts of her body.

When at last I was finished and began putting away my things, Manda knelt beside the bed and said to Mother Superior, "I must leave you Mother, though I don't want to. The young Vladislav girl is here and very ill. I'm sure she would like to see Father Lahdra."

Mother Superior's eyes again looked as if they understood. I followed Manda out of the modest room.

We walked in silence down the long corridor, past many closed doors towards the back of the building. Beautiful paintings of the Blessed Virgin Mary, Saints and Angels hung in the corridor. Walking alongside Manda, I refrained from speaking to her, though I was eager to know how she came to be here and how it was she seemed to be in a position of authority.

As we neared one of the last doors, a figure emerged nearly colliding with us. It was a distraught young man, quite handsome. "Oh, forgive me Father, Sister," he said. "I have to go out and walk a bit." He seemed embarrassed to be leaving, quickly adding, "But, of course, now that you are here, I shall stay."

"Anton Vladislav," said Manda, "This is Father Lahdra. I took the liberty of asking him to pray with you and your sister."

A lie from the lips of my cousin, the nun.

The handsome man offered me his hand, "Thank you so much for coming, Father." He was very nervous as we shook hands. "My sister, Sofie, is very ill. I...I'm frightened for she has been caring for her fiancé who recently died. She may have come down with the same unknown malady."

Without speaking, Manda led us into the simply furnished room. Again a nun was in attendance, wiping the girl's pale face with a damp cloth.

The girl was young, slender and though her skin was colorless, she was pretty. Her brown hair was loose and disheveled, and her eyes were closed in sleep. Her breathing was even, and I somehow knew she was not dying, and would be well. I was so confident she would recover, that I only removed my stole and oils from my bag. Her sleep was so deep, that I decided to dispense with communion. I made the sign of the cross and began to pray, while the others in the room knelt and joined in. With the holy oil on my thumb, I made the sign of the cross on her sleeping eyes. *"Per istam sanctam unctionem* and his most loving mercy whatever sins you have committed by the use of your sight. Amen." I proceeded with the anointing until we said the Lord's Prayer and I finished with, "May the blessing of almighty God, the Father, and the Son, and the Holy Spirit, descend upon you and remain forever."

When Anton Vladislav, Manda and I were again in the corridor, Manda said, "I've taken the liberty of asking Father Lahdra to stay and dine with us. I thought you might enjoy his company."

"Why, yes, of course." The young man seemed genuinely pleased for he could not share a table with any of the nuns and dining with me might be better than being alone.

It would take too much time for me to write down all that we talked about. I must say it was a very pleasant evening and well worth the long trip to meet such a fine man and to share his company.

When he returned to his sister's bedside, I searched for my cousin. I walked along the corridor toward the front of the building, admiring the beautiful paintings, when I thought I heard something behind me. I turned and once again felt like a child, for Manda with that impish grin was walking behind me step-by-step. I meant to be stern, but seriousness gave way to giggles and Manda hit me hard on the arm to silence me. She said in a rather loud voice, so that she might be overheard, "Why, yes, Father, I shall be happy to show you to the chapel. Perhaps you will hear my confession."

We didn't speak or look at each other as we walked to the chapel, for fear of more giggling.

Once inside the confessional, I pulled back the screen and said, "When was your last confession?"

She nearly hissed at me. "Do you think I could make a confession to you?"

"Of course," I said, "after all, I am a priest."

"You are my little cousin," Manda whispered from the other side of the screen, "I must talk quickly and return to the convent, there is so much going on this evening."

"I don't understand," I said.

"This convent is sponsored by the Vladislav family. They are wealthy and very generous. Also they are kind, good people. They were returning from Trieste when Sofie Vladislav became too ill to travel. They needed to stop somewhere for help and we were near, so Anton Vladislav brought her here."

"I still don't understand what this has to do with me." My face was so close to the screen that I could feel Manda's warm breath as she whispered to me.

"They are powerful and influential." I recognized the exasperation in her voice. "It doesn't hurt to know such people...to be liked by such people."

There it was. She was again The General, for it was Manda who was the leader in our childhood playing. She was the best strategist in our games and the best negotiator when we were in trouble. Manda always did the explaining when we did something that earned the adult's disapproval. I was always in awe of her logical, if not so truthful, explanations. Now we were adults and she was still in charge, still planning little strategies.

"Manda," I kept my voice low, in case someone else was in the chapel, "we aren't children playing a game."

"Life is a game, Lahdra," her voice was low and soft. "If we win or lose depends on how we have played it. Lahdra...listen to me!" Her voice was urgent. "I know you can't be deceitful and that is what is so wonderful about you. But, don't let this opportunity go by without being your honest, good self. Anton Vladislav will recognize this in you and perhaps he can help get you a better position."

Before I could ask her how she knew I was unhappy in my parish, she explained, "Your mother has told my mother, and of course she told me you aren't happy in Selna."

We heard a sound, perhaps the door of the chapel opening and closing.

"I must go now! I hope I will see you before you leave in the morning."

I heard the confessional door open and she was gone. There was so much more I wanted to ask her. I would have thought her the most unlikely candidate for a nun and she didn't give me a chance to ask her when she got the calling.

After waiting a while, I decided no one was coming to make confession. I slid the screen cover, closing it and left the chapel. Darkness had fallen, but the lights from the convent guided me. I ate dinner with Anton Vladislav, but he seemed tired and distracted with worry for his sister.

After the meal, an older nun, short and heavy showed me to a tidy, simple cell of my own for the night. A flickering candle greeted me and was my companion as I said my evening prayers. I fell asleep on the tiny cot, fully clothed.

I returned to my little church and house in Selna about noon the next day. Waiting for me was a very excited Andrie, who with his wife help me with repairs, my garden and my meals.

"Father, I am so happy to see you!" Andrie said before I was out of my saddle. Andrie was usually a calm, easy-going man, and his agitated demeanor was disquieting to me.

"What is wrong?" I asked.

Andrie pointed to a plum tree with a man sprawled asleep beneath its branches.

"Who is that?" I asked.

"It is Mato Balich. He has lost his mind."

I alighted from my horse. "Surely, you're exaggerating," I stated.

Andrie shook his head. "No., Mato was at your door past midnight, yelling that ghosts were going to get him."

"He was probably drunk," I said disgustedly.

"I don't know," said Andrie, "He just kept wailing and going on about a baby and being punished by God and America money."

I really didn't want to deal with Mato. A glass of wine, some lunch and quiet time to think about the events of last night were my desire. I wanted to think about my cousin Manda and when I might see her again.

"Let's awaken him," I said to Andrie. "He should be sober by now."

Mato's body was already cold and stiffening when I touched his shoulder to shake him. I knew he was dead.

Andrie made the sign of the cross and fell to his knees in prayer. Before I could pray, a young boy came running, urgently calling my name. "Father Lahdra, Father Lahdra."

"What is it?" I was annoyed, for I wasn't pleased to find a dead man in my garden.

I recognized one of the boys from Selna. Quickly I rose and went to him, so that he would not see Mato's body. "What do you want?"

As I guided the boy out of the yard, he said, "Old Julia wants you to come quick! She says to hurry. She needs you."

Before he could finish his message to me I said, "Go to Andrie's house and his wife will give you something to eat and drink." I wanted him away from the yard, when we placed Mato into a wagon.

Later, when I came onto the only road leading into Selna, it seemed deserted. I looked into the yard and window of Old Julia's house and saw no one. I glanced about and saw a few figures coming down the hill at the far end of the village near the cemetery. I urged the horses onward with Mato's body well covered in the back of the rattling wagon, and preceded to the hill.

Seeing me, some villagers turned and headed back toward the cemetery. A tall, black-haired man, Milan's younger brother called out to me, "Thank God, you are here. Old Julia started the funeral, but she will be happy to see you."

"Started the funeral?" I said in disbelief. "What funeral?"

I was dumbfounded as I urged the horses along the clearing in the cemetery. The entire population of Selna was there. Men and women with tear-stained faces looked at me expectantly. I wasn't prepared for a funeral. My bag with holy water and prayer book were still tied on the saddle horn, left from my ride that morning,

I left the wagon with its lifeless cargo when I neared the open grave surrounded by the cluster of mourners. Old Julia said, "At last, you are here."

I saw the broken-hearted face of little Anka Balich in whose arms was a baby. My confusion as to whose funeral this was must have been evident, for Milan Kosich came to my side and whispered, "It is Mila Balich. She died during childbirth last night. One of the babies died unborn with her."

Back at his desk in Vladezemlo, Father Lahdra put down the journal. How had he forgotten that day? He believed Katya to be the baby that survived! Was it possible the beautiful young girl could be the daughter of Mato and Mila Balich? There was no family resemblance. The priest was disturbed by his discovery. The pieces didn't fit. He could not recall anyone from Selna or the surrounding villages even remotely resembling the beautiful red-haired, green-eyed beauty he had seen yesterday at the Balaban wedding festivities.

Book II, Chapter 13

Historians can't tell us how the tambura came to Croatia. Some say the Turks brought the stringed instrument to the Balkans 500 years ago. There is a story that in the year 591 A.D. Byzantine King Mauricius captured some Slavs who carried no weapons, just their musical instruments.

When Anton Vladislav was a young student at the University of Zagreb, he had the opportunity of hearing the singing group "Hrvatska Lira" or "Croatian Lire" perform, accompanied by a twelve-piece Tamburitza group under the direction of Slavko Shrepel.

Almost a hundred years later, the tambura would be played in rock 'n' roll bands and on the stages of Nashville in the United States.

But it was the peasant who made the Tambura the instrument of Croatia. It was the uneducated man who couldn't read or write, who learned songs by 'ear' and would play hours on end while he tended the livestock in the hills. These lonely herders accompanied themselves as they sang. In the evenings when the work was done, the sound of a tambura would summon the neighbors, who would gather to join in the singing or just to listen.

There were no songbooks, no special arrangements, just songs made up from life's experiences, accompanied by the heart-breaking plucking of the strings. This was the music of the lower classes...happy or sad. When the Croatians migrated to other lands they took the tambura with them, for it would remind them of home and their loved ones. It gave them comfort wherever they didn't know the language or had few friends.

Snatches of tambura music could be heard, as Sofie Vladislav and the housekeeper, Klara neared the Balaban farm.

The sounds of a kolo dance made both women smile, for it was an indication of a good time. The music along with fun-loving people would allay the uneasiness both women felt.

The quarrel that morning between Anton and Ernesta had left the air thick with malice. Young Stefan's absence added to the worry in the hearts of Sofie and her gray-haired friend and servant.

Though Stefan was spoiled and undependable, Sofie loved her nephew and was disappointed he hadn't kept his word to accompany her to the wedding party.

Klara urged the old mare while it grudgingly pulled the little cart. She was dressed in a white blouse brightly embroidered in festive colors, with flowers trailing up one sleeve across the bodice and down the other sleeve. The skirt was plain with only a wide band of hand-made lace at the hem. Both women would have been identically dressed in aprons of silk-embroidered flowers, but the housekeeper in a burst of artistic inspiration added leaves of various shades of green, making her's different.

Sofie had many fashionable continental clothes of silk and brocade, but she always felt happiest in the embroidered costumes of her region. The clean, crisp cloth with the embroidered designs warmed her heart. When she wore the costumes, it made her feel closer to the people who worked the land. Sofie loved the peasants and knew them all by name and their families. She would visit when a new baby was born or someone was ill, and always with a gift. Sofie was as comfortable in the cottages as she was in a grand house. It never mattered to Sofie what one had or didn't have. Teta Sofie was so loved that she was Godmother to an even dozen children. She was pleased with the display of affection she received and it made her even more generous.

Hearing the gay music, Sofie's blue eyes misted as she looked toward the Balaban's small farm. She remembered the night Ivan was born. He was her first Godchild. The next year she was there when Nikola was born, his little red fists shaking as if in anger. Today he was the bridegroom. How happy and proud Marko had been as each baby was born and how lovingly Marko had looked at his Vera.

"Klara," Sofie said, "do you realize after all these years we don't know where Vera came from? I mean...none of her people have ever come to visit and she never has mentioned a family." Turning towards Klara, Sofie asked, "Has Marko ever told you how he met Vera or anything about her family?"

Klara kept her eyes straight ahead. She remembered well the night young Vera came looking for Anton, as if it were yesterday, the night the family was entertaining Ernesta as a fiancé. "You know as much as I do," she lied.

Klara well remembered the night Vera appeared at her kitchen door, asking to see Anton, and how he left Vera at the steps, not happy to see her.

After her long trip mostly on foot, Vera had been tired, hungry, and had nowhere to go and knew no one. Klara felt sorry for Vera and was angry with Anton for his shameful treatment of the girl.

Feeling compassion for the girl, Klara had said, "Take this." She gave Vera a blanket and some bread. "Stay in the chapel until I come for you."

"And then what?" said Vera

"Just go and wait for me," said Klara. "I will come as soon as I can."

Marko came as soon as he got a message sent by his cousin Klara summoning him to the Vladislav house.

Together Marko and Klara entered the Chapel finding Vera lying on a bench wrapped in a blanket. Her face was stained with tears.

Gently, Klara touched Vera's shoulder. "Vera. This is my cousin, Marko. He is a good man and will take you to his house. You can stay there."

Vera rose to a sitting position, a wary look in her eyes.

Marko thought this stranger was lovely. He looked at the tears on her cheeks, and those golden brown eyes and wanted to protect her. "You can stay in the house," he said. "I will sleep in the barn. The barn is fine with me. I slept there while the house was being built."

Vera looked into Marko's smiling face. His hair was a bit long. He needed a shave. His body was compactly built. Because he was a blacksmith he had arms like logs. Vera sensed gentleness within him. His eyes were what Vera liked the best. They were warm and honest eyes. She trusted those eyes and never had reason to regret it.

The tiny cart rattled on the deeply rutted road. As Klara and Sofie neared the farmyard, the sounds of laughter and the music becoming louder and the smell of roasting meat was strong in the air. Sofie said, "I'm so glad Marko found someone like Vera. She is wonderful. It really doesn't matter where she came from." Then her voice caught. "Oh, Klara," she fought back tears, "I wish Vincent had lived. I wish I had a child getting married today."

The tears came, first in trickles down her cheeks, then in unleashed torrents. Her painful sobbing was so intense that Klara pulled the old mare to a stop and wrapped her arms around her friend. "I know Sofie, I know. I, too, would have liked a husband and children."

"Klara, I'm so sorry," Sofie was gaining control of her emotions, "how selfish of me. Of course you know what I feel. We are both alone. I'm sorry," she said again. "It was a moment of self-pity, an emotion best expressed in private." She wiped her eyes with a handkerchief pulled from her sleeve and patting Klara's arm said, "No more sad talk. We are here for a good time."

The two women continued the ride in silence. Klara the cook thought of Anton back when they were young and how she secretly loved him. No one knew. No one even suspected that her devotion to the family was based on one childhood kiss. Remembering that kiss from so long ago made Klara's stomach stir. Anton had come from a night out, more than a little tipsy. He came through the kitchen door as always, and seeing Klara, a pretty girl back then with long brown braids cascading down her slender back, he took her hand. Saying nothing, he had pulled her to him and hotly, passionately kissed her. When Klara had wrapped her arms around his neck, returning the kiss with equal passion, Anton stiffened. It was as if he sobered at once and realized what he was doing. "I'm sorry, Klara." He had said as he gently pulled her arms down from his shoulders. "I am so sorry." Then he turned and went into the dining room and Klara heard each step as he climbed the stairs to his room on the second floor.

The kiss was never to be repeated, though Klara waited for it. Actually she was still waiting, a long lost hope. It was never going to happen. She knew that. It was never mentioned. It was as if it had never occurred. Oh, but Klara knew it had. She could still feel that kiss and she could still remember the feel of his breath on her face and his arms around her waist.

"We are almost there." Sofie's voice brought Klara back to the moment pushing the servant's sweet memory aside. "I promise not to cry anymore," said Sofie. "I'm just getting older and wish things had turned out differently."

Klara flicked the reins and called to the mare, "Aide, Runa." The old horse wanted to stop to eat grass. Klara with eyes straight ahead said, "We can't fight our destinies. If we could, I would be married to a rich man living in a fine house with servants of my own."

Sofie gave Klara a long look, as if she were seeing her friend for the first time.

"I had no idea you felt that way." Sofie was truly surprised and a little hurt. She never thought of Klara as having any dreams or aspirations. Their eyes met for a moment, Klara looked back to the road.

"You are taking my remark personally," said Klara. "Don't. I love you all. Oh, well, not Ernesta, and I am not too crazy about Stefan. But, I would be lying if I didn't admit I would love to have someone do cooking and cleaning for me." Her voice had an edge to it as she said, "I'd like to sit and crochet, resting my feet on a velvet footstool."

"I never realized you felt that way," Sophie said again. This time apologetically. "I just never thought about it. You've been in the kitchen since we were children. I'm ashamed to say that I've never thought of you as being anywhere else."

"I'm old and I'm tired." Klara was sorry she had exposed so much of herself.

What did it matter, nothing was going to change. Her grandmother had been owned by the Vladislav family, later her mother and father had been serfs. Klara probably could have left, if she really wanted to, but she chose to stay. She wanted to stay with the only family she knew and loved. "I'm ready for bed earlier each evening and my legs get tired and ache. Sometimes I want to just sit and put them up."

"What does it matter?" she said, trying to sound casual. "My destiny was to stay and work for your family, just as my family before me." Quietly she said, "Our destinies are not so different." She looked at Sofie. "You are still in the house, serving Anton and Ernesta in your own way. You would be happier in your own home, but Destiny had other plans for you. That's all life is...just waiting around to see what Destiny has mapped out for us."

Sofie said nothing to her servant-friend-confidant. They rode in silence the rest of the way, listening to the music. Sofie had a strange feeling. She couldn't identify it. She just knew nothing was going to be the same anymore. It had started that morning with the argument between Anton and Ernesta. Then this conversation with Klara left Sofie feeling uneasy. Oh, how she wished Vincent hadn't died. If he had lived, they would be married, hopefully with children, living in a lovely house somewhere in Trieste.

"Kuma Sofie! Teta Klara!" Ivan was running toward the cart when he saw them. His face was as bright and happy as a child's on Christmas morning. He adored these two women and they couldn't help but return his affection.

When the cart stopped, Ivan leapt onto the side of it and kissed first Sofie and then Klara. "Where have you been?" he demanded. "I was afraid you weren't coming. Are you all right? You aren't sick or anything." The words tumbled out of Ivan's mouth in his excitement at seeing the women.

Sofie gave Ivan a hug and had to laugh at his display of affection. "We're fine," said Sofie. "I felt a little tired yesterday, but I was determined to come today."

Lifting Sofie down from the cart, Ivan said, "I hope you aren't too tired to dance with me." Klara had started to climb down on her own, but Ivan took her hand and helped her also. "What about you, Teta Klara? Will you promise me a dance?"

"A slow one," she said smiling.

Ivan's happy mood was infectious as he stepped in between the two women and took each by the arm. He looked at their feet, did a quick skip and the three headed toward the music, stepping in unison as if they were in a chorus line.

Vera Balaban was seated at one of the tables shaded by a large pear tree, where the leaves were casting playful shadows across her pretty face. She smiled as she saw her oldest son with the gray-haired Klara and the tiny Sofie, skipping and laughing like children. Vera rose to greet her old friends.

"Come," she called, motioning for them to join her. "Sit here in the shade."

"Bring something to drink," she said to Ivan. The three women exchanged hugs and kisses before they sat at the table.

"Tell me," said Klara, "How is it Ivan is acting as happy as a bridegroom, when it is his brother who got married."

"I think he is in love," said Vera in a conspiratorial tone. "Marko's cousin Milan from Selna brought the girl here. It's a strange story. The girl's mother died the night Katya was born. Marko's cousin and his wife helped the older sister, herself just a little girl raise Katya. Then the sister died and she was taken care of by the village herbalist. It is all very sad. "There..." Vera pointed towards the table on which stood two barrels of wine. "See the girl he is speaking to, the one with the red hair?"

Aunt Sofie was distracted by an argument at a nearby table. Two old grandmothers, Babas, dressed all in black with black babushkas on their head were arguing over who would get the roasted lamb's head, its baked eyes a delicacy.

"I hurried to be here first," the one with missing front teeth said. Her face was like parchment.

"You should hurry as fast when your pigs get into my garden," the other old Baba retorted, wagging a bony finger at her adversary.

"I was here first. It is mine," the first Baba exclaimed.

A shirtless man in a greasy apron, smelling of smoke and garlic brought the lamb head to the table wrapped in paper. Both women grabbed for the wrapped head, but the man swung the prize upward out of their reach.

"Sit down and be quiet," he ordered them. "Must you two fight over everything?'

"Don't touch it!" he demanded as he placed the wrapped head on the table removing the top layer of paper. Before either woman could reach for it, he pulled out a sharp cleaver tucked in the back of his apron and with a swift swing of the cleaver, whacked the head cleanly between the eyes, leaving almost equal portions on the paper.

"There! Now, I haven't played favorites with my grandmothers. You each have the lamb's head." He walked away rolling his eyes to the sky, as the guests nearby all laughed at what was evidence of an on going rivalry between the two women.

Sofie, too, laughed good-naturedly over the lamb head spectacle, she then turned and looked toward the table where Ivan had gone to get the drinks.

The wild, red hair was the first thing Sofie noticed. *Vincent. His hair had been that same coppery color!*

Book II, Chapter 14

Sofie, restless in her bed thinking of the wedding couldn't sleep. It was as if the past had washed over her. *That red hair*! Katya's red hair was the trigger that resurrected Sofie's sad memories from long ago. Memories of her love for Vincent, his battle with the unknown illness that took his life, thus altering Sofie's life.

On her bedside table was a glass oil lamp with a barely visible glow. Sofie adjusted the small knob, raising the wick bringing more brightness to that part of the room. She picked up a small square picture from her bedside table. It was a portrait of Vincent, hand-painted on ivory, the wooden frame embedded with mother of pearl. The slender face depicted in the miniature portrait had fine delicate features with pale green eyes that seemed to stare at Sofie. For fifteen years the little portrait was on this same table, at her bedside, but it never troubled her the way it did this night. Sofie studied the painting as if looking at it for the first time. She looked at the red hair combed back close to his head. The artist hadn't captured the true fiery color, the color she had seen today on the head of the girl from Selna.

She barely remembered the events of the afternoon at the party, for most of the time her mind had been elsewhere. She couldn't remember the ride home from the wedding party or what she and Klara talked about, if they talked at all. Surely they talked. But, Sofie had only wanted to be alone...alone with her thoughts and memories of Vincent.

Had she said good-bye to Marko and Vera? My goodness! She didn't remember.

Carefully Sofie put the miniature painting of Vincent on the side table and walked to her window. That part of the room was in shadows, with most of the light from the oil lamp flickering on the tablecloth covered thick with red and black embroidery.

Staring out at the clear sky and the waning moon, Sofie tried to remember the events of the day. Surely she had spoken to all her neighbors and their children. She always did that wherever she went. Why couldn't she remember the bride and groom?

But, she did remember Katya...that hair...the eyes glowing green when the sun hit them. Sofie barely remembered what was said when Ivan proudly made introductions, for at the time Sofie could only think about how the girl could pass for Vincent's sister.

In her mind she could see the man she had loved, the man she had meant to marry despite objections by her father. She remembered Vincent looking so thin and frail, sunken like a heavy statue in a mattress of goose down. The once beautiful face had become gray, the greenish-brown eyes milky. His beautiful red hair limp on the pillow had come out in clumps. For two months Sofie was at his bedside, in that lovely room full of books, paintings and furniture designed with inlaid pieces of colored woods and knobs of ivory. The different woods on the furniture formed geometric patterns all of which Sofie found intriguing and more appealing than the floral French patterns. Sofie would have been very happy in Trieste with Vincent and his mother, if he had lived. She loved Vincent so much that she ignored the letters from her brother demanding her return home. Anton felt it unseemly that an unmarried girl should spend so much time at the home of a man, not her husband, even if chaperoned by his mother.

Day after day Sofie had watched her wonderful Vincent grow thinner and more pale, his breathing a struggle. Doctors from Venice and Zagreb had been to see him at the Kurecka home in Trieste, but each left shaking his head, offering no encouragement. The doctors would examine Vincent and ask the same questions. "When did he become ill? Had he been traveling? Could he have brought an illness back with him? What had he eaten? Could he have been poisoned?"

The first doctor to see Vincent Kurecka was the local physician from Trieste. The small man was wearing wire spectacles, which slipped on his nose as he bent his thin torso over Vincent examining carefully the oddly bruised body, lifting the limbs, putting pressure on the groin, and listening to the heart. When he was finished, he pronounced that Vincent should be bled to purify the system. From his scuffed and badly worn tapestry cloth medical bag, he pulled out a jar of leeches.

Vincent's mother Lucia was a handsome woman, short, plump, with brown hair graying at the temples. "Do what you must," she said, holding Sofia's moist hand for comfort, as they nervously waited for the gruesome procedure to begin. The worry lines on her forehead had become permanently etched.

Dr. Josep Bergone removed the leeches with a wooden stick fished out of his bag. He looked at the first ugly two-inch brown flat worm. "Pull the sheet away," the Doctor ordered. Both Lucia and Sofie obeyed. Vincent's naked body was patched with bruises. Quickly his mother placed a towel over his groin area so as not to embarrass the young Sofie. She needn't have bothered. Sofie and Vincent were not strangers to each other's bodies.

The Doctor placed a leech first on Vincent's chest. Then, he placed another, carefully on each arm and then each leg, being sure they covered a bruise. It was both disgusting and fascinating to watch the ugly flat worm-like creatures start to grow into longer, firmer forms. Leeching was a common practice, believed to be a health-giving procedure. It didn't take very long for the leeches to gorge themselves, just a matter of minutes. Sofie nearly gagged when Dr. Bergone, using a small metal spatula wedged under the blood-filled leech, prying it off, leaving a red spot where the leech's sucker had been attached. One by one he removed the disgusting parasites, returning them to the glass bottle. He then carefully placed the bottle in his medical bag.

Dr. Bergone was never called back after the phlebotomy, for Vincent became worse and Signora Kurecka had lost what little faith she had in leeches.

The doctor from Zagreb, a heavy man with a large mustache and thick sideburns, recommended Vincent should be placed in a health sanitarium on the Coast. He was sure the warm sun and fresh air along with a diet of rich broths would make Vincent well again.

It is ridiculous, thought Signora Kurecka, their house overlooked the Adriatic and there was plenty of sun on the terrace. Her cook had already been making rich broths which Sofie spoon-fed Vincent.

The last doctor, a serious physician from Venice stayed two days. He was younger than the other two doctors had been, but his care was one of a dedicated healer. His young face showed mature concern as he studied his patient. His final diagnosis was that Vincent was gravely ill and should be in a hospital, receiving full medical attention round the clock. "Possibly surgery could improve his condition," the young Doctor had said.

"What kind of surgery?" Vincent's mother asked. The doctor started to speak then just shrugged his shoulders for he wasn't sure.

Roentgen, the German physicist had discovered X-rays in 1895, but the procedure had not been developed enough to help patients as it does today.

Lucia Kurecka knew her son would not get better. Three doctors were baffled, though the only one who seemed to admit to the gravity of Vincent's condition was young Doctor Parelli from Venice. No one knew that Vincent had leukemia and that the leeches taking his already poor blood, only made him weaker. He was dreadfully thin, unable to eat, and his belly was swollen. At times his breathing was no more than gasps which became painful coughs.

Vincent's mother Lucia, alone in her room, dropped a pillow on the floor before the statue of the Madonna. With rosary in hand, she knelt on the pillow, which protected her knees from the stone floor, and completed the beads three times. She prayed for guidance, wanting to do what was best for her only child. Her belief in the Virgin Mary was strong, as was her Catholic faith. Lucia was Italian. Her family could be traced to the time when Trieste was a Roman colony. Her family had been in the business of importing for many years, their ships traveled the Adriatic, carrying cargo to buy and sell. Before she was twelve years old, Lucia had been up and down the Adriatic and on the Mediterranean as far as The Strait of Gibraltar. Her older brother died as a baby, and no more children came after Lucia. She became her father's heir and the love of his life. He poured into her all he could teach her. Against her mother's protestations, he took Lucia on the ships whenever possible to expand her knowledge of the business world.

"She's only a child," her mother had cried. "Don't take her from me. I am lonely without her."

"Then come with us," her father would say.

"You are cruel. You know how ill I am on the sea." Lucia's mother would wring her hands, tears in her dark, Italian eyes.

"You have no right to take my daughter from me."

"I must teach her all I can," her father would argue. "Do you think I am going to give this business to your nephew? Lucia will inherit it all and she will be wise enough to control what goes on. I don't want her cheated or robbed." Glaring at his wife, he would add, "Can you understand that?"

Her reply was always the same, "It is unseemly for a woman to work in the world with men. You are making a joke of her."

Aleksander Kurecka, Vincent's father came to work for the Renaldi Trading Company as head accountant when Lucia was seventeen. He said he was from Austria and presented a letter of introduction from his professor. At twenty-one he had fine features, hazel eyes, a long thin face and reddish-blond hair. He had the bookish look of an accountant. He was polite, had lovely manners, and always dressed in a suit. It became apparent that he only owned two suits, but he was always neatly attired, with clean shirt, handkerchief and gloves.

Vincenti Renaldi watched his accountant closely. The young man was meticulous in his bookkeeping. Soon he knew everyone at the Trading Company by name and their position, all the way down to the dockworkers. He was polite to them all. Aleksander was very careful never to behave in a manner that would place him above another employee. Of course he was almost as important as Vincenti Renaldi as far as the day-to-day activities went, though his salary didn't reflect his valuable position.

For six months Vincenti watched Aleksander Kurecka closely, even going so far as to test his honesty by leaving money lying about or deliberately entering the wrong amounts of shipped items on day sheets. Aleksander always caught the errors and corrected them. It would have been a simple thing for him to divert the money to his own pocket. But, he never did. Each time Vincenti Renaldi would record fifteen barrels instead of let's say eighteen, Aleksander would catch the error and faithfully report it.

Almost daily, Lucia went to the Trading Company causing much grief to her mother who wanted to see her daughter married. Frail, small Anna Renaldi was sure no one of any social standing would want a young woman who associated daily with dockworkers. When Anna wasn't swearing at her husband, she was praying to the Madonna to provide a fine husband for Lucia.

While his wife prayed, Vincenti watched closely as the young Aleksander taught Lucia accounting. He was impressed when the young man showed her the many ways she could be cheated. Aleksander never over-stepped himself with the beautiful Lucia, even when she leaned closely over the account books, deliberately letting her hair brush against his face. Lucia found the shy accountant attractive, but she too knew her place. However, she couldn't help touching him when the occasion presented itself.

With unemotional detachment, Vincenti Renaldi watched his daughter and Aleksander daily. For three months he watched. He watched to see if the young man would respond to Lucia's subtle encouragement. Vincenti thought he detected an emotional interest between Lucia and his bookkeeper though he did nothing to encourage them. He only watched.

Trieste was part of the Austrian Empire populated with both Slovenians and Italians. The Italians supported a small opera house, where once a month traveling opera companies would come to perform. The Renaldi family had a box and went without fail each time a performance was given. On one particular night *The Barber of Seville* was offered. Vincenti Renaldi had never noticed Aleksander Kurecka in the audience before. Tonight he couldn't help but notice the young man, since Lucia's eyes were on Aleks seated below on the main floor. She kept looking at the reddish coppery head, which several times during the evening turned upward towards the Renaldi box.

"Who is that young man, the one that keeps looking this way?" asked Lucia's mother, using her lace fan as a pointer.

"It is my accountant," answered Vincenti, calmly.

"Don't look at him, Lucia," demanded Signora Renaldi, annoyed. "You don't want to encourage him."

Some days later Lucia's father and Aleksander were alone in the office of the trading company.

"Tell me about your family," said Vincenti.

"I have no family." Aleksander answered, a little surprised at the personal question. Until now every conversation had to do only with business. "I was raised by my professor and his wife. They knew my parents and took me in when my mother and father died of the fever."

"You have no relatives, no one?"

"No, I am alone."

Vincenti Renaldi did not say the rosary for guidance, as his wife did. Instead, he left his office and went for long walks along the beautiful coastline of the Adriatic and stared at the sea. He did his best thinking looking at the sea. It calmed him, soothed him...he loved her...the sea. He could think clearly when mesmerized by the waves. It was people that befuddled his thinking, people with useless opinions. But the sea, it was his friend. It had made him a rich man and traveling on her had taught him much about places and people. Especially about people...people of different countries and tongues. One needed some inner sense or instinct about people when one didn't understand their language. You had to look into their eyes, read their faces and mannerisms. It could tell you much about their character.

Signore Renaldi had to be sure about Aleksander Kurecka. Who ever married Lucia would have control over the business. What if she married the wrong man and he was cruel to her, possibly take everything away from her leaving her destitute?

Renaldi knew his wife's nephew, Carlo, was waiting to take over. It had even been hinted that Lucia and Carlo should marry. Hint was a mild word considering the crusade his wife Anna launched when Lucia became sixteen. Carlo and his family came regularly for meals and visits, trying to encourage a romance. Romance wasn't necessary, since Lucia would marry whomever her father chose. Vincenti wanted to give his daughter love, not just a husband. He wanted her to have the magic of romance that his own arranged marriage never possessed. Was it possible, he wondered, to have a perfect marriage?

Vincenti sat on the stones lining the beach and stared at the clear blue water, each wave splashing into white caps as it rolled onto the beach. "Tell me, my friend," he said to the sea, "what should I do?"

Lucia Renaldi and Aleksander Kurecka were married in a Catholic ceremony, accompanied by the unhappy sobs of Signora Renaldi and her sister, Carlo's mother. Now, Carlo would have to look elsewhere for his fortune.

Vincenti Renaldi, dressed in a new black suit with a white silk shirt and maroon cravat, was a happy man. He knew in his soul he had made the right choice for his dearest Lucia and the Renaldi Trading Company. He watched the priest bless the rings and hoped for many grandsons. *Who knows what the future holds*? He thought. Perhaps God plans for the Renaldi's to have ships going to ports all around the world. Yes, many grandsons, that was what he wanted, and they would be smart. With Lucia and Aleksander for parents, they were sure to be brilliant children.

But twenty years later, the only child of Aleks and Lucia lay gravely ill. Constantly at his side were his mother and the woman he hoped to marry. Nursing Vincent day and night with little sleep seemed to wear on Sofie. She was losing weight and had no appetite. There were times when she felt weak and faint, which frightened Vincent's mother. Sofie noticed that her periods were very light, almost nothing at all. She only had a few dots of blood on her muslin 'monthly' cloths. These had to be signs of her exhaustion. Her body was no doubt telling her she was pushing it to the limits with her round the clock care of her beloved Vincent.

"Sofie," Lucia said one day, "as much as I want you here, perhaps your brother is right. You look ill. Perhaps it would be better for you to go home."

Sofie was near tears. "Please let me stay. I can't leave Vincent. I won't leave him," she was adamant. "You know we want to marry. I don't care what my family wants. I want to stay with Vincent for the rest of my life."

The older woman put her arms around the grieving young girl. She felt her thin frame and was worried for her.

"Sofie," her voice was low and soft, "I have a letter from your brother. He will be here tomorrow and he means to take you home. I can do nothing to stop him. After all, he is speaking for your father, and you are but a young girl."

"Oh, no!" Sofie turned her face into the woman's shoulder and cried. They both knew she had to go with her brother. She was a young girl with no rights of her own. If she refused to return home, then legal steps would be taken to remove her from the Kurecka home. The home Sofie had come to love.

"I wish Vincent and I had gone ahead and married, instead of waiting for my Father's blessing," said Sofie. "If I were married, then my Father would no longer have any rights. Those would be my husband's."

Vincent's mother looked at the sobbing girl seated on a chaise. She had grown to love this girl, to think of her as a daughter. Sofie had become a strong and comforting companion to the older woman during this terrible time of stress. In a moment of selfishness, the old lady had a thought.

"What if you *were* married? Then, your brother could not take you away from us." She looked long at Sofie, watching for the girl's reaction.

Sofie raised her head. With the back of her hand, she wiped away the tears from her cheeks. "How can that be? My brother will be here tomorrow. It takes time to plan a wedding and to post the bans in the church."

Lucia sat beside Sofie, taking the girl's hand in hers.

"I know I can bypass the bans. I have friends in the Church. Unspoken favors are owed and should gladly be repaid. Let me send a servant to the Cathedral. We will do this tonight. Your brother will have to return without you."

Sofie's pale face brightened and her eyes shone. The women hugged happily, for they had found a solution.

Book II, Chapter 15

Anton sat in the impressive foyer of Signora Kurecka's home, its shiny marble floor spread out before him.

The décor was so different from his father's house, so elegant. Colorful Turkish rugs with intricate designs lay on the floor and large Flemish tapestries adorned the walls alongside large paintings. Curtains made of thick woolen weave hung beside the doorways ready to be pulled across the openings to bar any invading cold drafts. Marble statues befitting a museum seemed at home in this house, as did the many Asian vases and urns that Anton studied with awe.

His father was sure that a marriage between Sofie and "THAT" Italian was unsuitable, but Anton wasn't so sure, now that he could see how well the Kureckas lived.

Trieste the city, part of the Austrian empire, was mainly populated with Italians, with only about a thirty-five percent Slovenian population. The rural areas outside the city were more than ninety-five percent Slovene. For that very reason many of the people spoke both Italian and Slovene.

A teary-eyed servant girl had met Anton at the gate. The slight, dark haired girl held a corner of her white apron up to her face, in place of a handkerchief. She showed Anton to the foyer where he now waited for his sister. He had not been there long, but was becoming annoyed at being kept waiting. After all, Sofie knew he was coming and he had expected her to be packed and ready.

The house seemed unusually quiet, except for some muffled sounds from the second floor. Anton's eyes followed the wide marble stairs leading to the second level, which surrounded the foyer as a balcony might surround a theatre.

He was running out of patience. Making him wait was plainly rude. He at least expected the hostess to greet him, but she was nowhere to be seen. In fact, now he saw no one, not even the servant girl.

Anton reached into his jacket pocket for a cigarette then stopped. It wasn't proper to smoke in a home where one was a guest unless invited to do so. He was becoming nervous. He wanted to do something with his hands. His eyes kept searching the landing above him. Somewhere above him a door opened and he heard what he thought was crying, then the door closed and it was quiet once more. He counted the stairs leading up and there were twenty-four. He studied the Nubian newel posts on each side of the staircase. Each held a gleaming brass plate with a large candle on it. Each candle was covered with a glass chimney to protect the flame from drafts.

Anton stood up, brushed his brown pants of some imaginary lint and finding a large mirror, looked at his reflection as he straightened his matching brown jacket, with dark brown trim at the collar and sleeves.

He thought he looked nice enough to represent Sofie's family.

Now this was enough! Annoyed, he wasn't going to take this rudeness any longer. Anton looked about the main floor where he waited and seeing no one, mounted the stairs. At the top of the stairs he heard sounds and walked to the door from where he thought the sounds came.

Gently he knocked...there was silence. Not a sound. He knocked with a bit more force.

Slowly the door opened. A woman who Anton took to be Signora Kurecka, her face with red eyes swollen from crying, moved out of the way to let Anton enter without saying a word.

The drapes were drawn making a candle necessary in the gloom. The strong odor of urine and illness permeated the air. Anton wished he could hold his breath, not breathe in this foul odor

Anton's eyes followed the Signora's to the bed, where he saw a man lying in a large, fancy wooden bed, with Sofie prostrate across the man lying on the bed.

"Sophie! What are you doing?" Anton was at the bed in an instant, trying to lift Sofie to her feet, but she fought him.

"Sofie...stop it!" Anton tried to still his sister's fists. She looked pale, her eyes red from crying.

Signora Kurecka's gentle hand on Anton's shoulder distracted him. He let go of Sofie and his sister immediately fell back on the bed, now sobbing uncontrollably.

"Please, Anton. May I call you Anton?" Her voice was soft and gentle. Her Croatian was very good, but spoken with a slight Italian accent. "Please be patient with Sofie. You see, Vincent..." the words caught in her throat, "You see..." she began again, "Vincent died last night."

Anton stared at his crying sister. His emotions were mixed. Now he could take his sister home and not have to worry about her hopes of marrying this stranger. The news made Anton momentarily speechless. After a few moments he said to Signora Kurecka, "I am so sorry. We had no idea Vincent was so ill." He searched for more words, "We just didn't know." The Signora nodded her thanks.

Anton moved to the bedside near his sobbing sister. He was shocked at the sight of the dead Vincent. In no way could he see that Vincent had once been a handsome man. Anton looked down at a gray sunken face, almost the face of a skeleton. Hair that was once red was now a pale, yellow-orange and thin. So much hair had fallen out during his illness.

Anton's eyes moved to his sister. She was so thin! Her small hands clutching the bedspread were bony and the skin appeared transparent.

My God! She has caught his illness. Oh, God, no!

He had to get her home, home where she would be cared for, away from this house of death. This couldn't be happening! Not to Sofie. Not his little sister.

"Sofie..." he said gently, "let me take you home."

"No." Her reply was muffled, her face buried in the covers, her arms around Vincent.

Anton felt a shiver. It was unpleasant, even gruesome to see his little sister hugging this corpse.

"I won't leave him," she sobbed, "I can't leave him."

Anton looked to Signora Kurecka for some assistance, but she was full of grief looking at her dead son and the sobbing Sofie.

Anton touched the mourning woman's arm. "Please," he said, "help me get her home. She looks ill and needs care."

The old woman wore a black high-collared dress. The only color she had worn since the day her beloved husband died ten years earlier. At her throat was a large carved cameo of red coral. The cameo was the only bright color she allowed herself to wear, because it had been the gift that her husband had given to her as a wedding present.

Lucia Kurecka smoothed her dress in a nervous movement. She cleared her throat. "I...we," she motioned to Sofie, "we would like to remain together."

"What do you mean *together*?" Anton's eyes narrowed.

"Well...you see..." she stammered, "Sofie was about to marry Vincent last night. But...but, he died before the priest arrived."

For a moment Anton couldn't grasp what he had heard. *Sofie wanted to marry this horrible looking corpse. Surely he couldn't have looked any better when he was still breathing.*

"I don't understand," said Anton. "I know that my father gave no permission for a marriage."

Signora Kurecka looked away. "I know," she said softly. "But, once Sofie and Vincent were married," she turned to him nervously, "Sofie would be able to stay with us. You couldn't take her away."

Anton could feel his face redden. Anger was building within him. Sofie had stopped sobbing and turned her tear-stained face expectantly toward Anton. Her thin face was pale, large dark circles surrounded her red eyes.

Anton was angry that his father had allowed her to come to this house so often on extended stays. For the past year she made monthly visits, staying longer each time. Now there was the possibility that she was also dying of whatever unknown ailment Vincent had.

"I am taking Sofie home!" Anton surprised himself with the firm tone of his voice. "My father sent me to bring her home. He did not expect me to bring her home ill."

"No!" cried out Sofie, as she raised herself from the bed and for the first time, Anton saw how the dress hung loosely on the girl's body. Sofie wrapped her arms around Lucia Kurecka and sobbed into the woman's shoulder, "I don't want to leave you."

"I know, I know," soothed the woman holding on to Sofie. "I want you to stay."

Angry at the sight of Sofie clinging to this woman who was a stranger to their family, Anton took hold of Sofie's arm and pulled her away from the Signora.

"You belong home with your family."

"I want Signora to be my family." Sofie held her arms close to her body, bent at the elbows hands held upward, palms open, distancing herself from Anton.

"You don't know what you are saying," Anton tried not to let the anger show in his voice. "This is not your family. Your father and friends are waiting for your return."

Signora Kurecka moved to Sofie. She put her arm around the girl, saying, "Perhaps she could stay a while longer. We could comfort one another."

Sofie again buried her face in the woman's shoulder, finding safety from her brother.

Anton did not like the influence this woman had over his sister. This was out of control. This woman was not a relative, not even a family friend. She had no right to influence Sofie's thinking, as she appeared to be doing.

Controlling his emotions, Anton said, "You will please gather Sofie's things. We are leaving shortly."

Holding Sofie with one arm, Signora Kurecka reached out to Anton with the other, "But surely you will stay for the funeral."

Anton turned his back to the women heading for the door, "Absolutely not! We are leaving within the hour."

As he left the room, he heard Sofie's loud sobs again and some faint words that she was "not leaving."

The carriage that Anton had driven to Trieste was suitable for a nice leisurely ride, but not suitable for the transport of an ill woman. Anton drove the horse, while Sofie half-sat, half-lay on the wooden carriage seat. It was padded and covered with leather, but still it was not comfortable for the sick Sofie.

The departure was not pleasant. The sobs of Signora Kurecka, the bursts of anger from Sofie and finally, the threats from Anton to call the authorities, made the women give in.

Sofie and Anton did leave within the hour. Her clothes were gathered into a carpetbag. A basket of cheese, salami and some water and wine were provided by Signora Kurecka, though neither Anton nor Sofie would feel like eating.

The teary good-byes between Sofie and Signora Kurecka both angered and sickened Anton. He greatly resented the affection Sofie had for the woman. It angered him that Sofie was willing to stay with Signora Kurecka and seemingly forget her own family.

After about an hour's carriage ride, Sofie's sobs subsided. Her eyes were swollen from crying and she sniffled a great deal.

Anton looked back at his sister, who was uncomfortably trying to lie on the narrow carriage seat. Seeing her so sad, so sick and uncomfortable, he said, "Sofie...I am so sorry. I wish we could have known Vincent."

Silence...

"I'm frightened for you. You look so ill. You need care." He *was* afraid. Anton had never seen her look so ill, not even when some illness had gone through the whole village, giving almost everyone a fever, making them weak and bed-ridden. Back in the village during the influenza, she had looked awful, but she had pulled through. Even with the influenza Sophie had never looked as bad as she did now, pale, sweating, and gasping for breath.

She still didn't reply. He wanted to make some conversation with her, something to re-establish the brother-sister bond they had always shared. He wasn't sure what to say that would once again connect them.

He tried again, "Sofie?"

More silence.

"Sofie, someday you will meet someone you will love as much as you think you loved Vincent. You will marry and have a family. It just takes time to get over something like this."

After a long pause, Sofie said weakly, "I hate you."

Book II, Chapter 16

Sick in the back of the carriage Sofie vowed that she would never forgive Anton for taking her away from Vincent's home. It was where she wanted to be. She needed to be near Vincent's mother. She wanted to be in his room near the books he loved and the ship models he collected. Sofie wanted to be with Lucia Kurecka so that the woman could tell her all the things she didn't know about Vincent. She wanted to know the things he did as a child. Sofie didn't know Vincent's favorite color. Why didn't she know that? There was so much she didn't know and it pained her. She wanted his home to be her home.

Sofie had no idea how exhausted her body had become. She only knew that she couldn't sit upright in the carriage. Those last weeks of caring for Vincent, with nearly sleepless nights watching over him, wore her out. She would gladly do it still, if only he were alive! The sorrow…the bone deep sorrow had sapped her of her last ounce of strength. She was so hot…and tired. Anton said she was sick. Was she sick? Is that why she felt so weak? What did it matter? She didn't care if she was sick. Would she be with Vincent if she died? Could she have the same illness that Vincent had? Could she really die?

Anton, sitting in the driver's seat of the small carriage, was grateful for the bit of fringed cover overhead, for it protected Sofie from the warm sun. Any other time the warmth would be welcome, but Sofie was perspiring and her face was red. Anton wanted to whip the horse to a gallop, but was afraid the jostling would hurt Sofie as she half lay on the narrow seat. With every bump Anton heard Sofie's soft moan.

His anger had melted into worry with each kilometer. Doubt plagued him. Should they have stayed in Trieste and called a doctor for his sister? Could they be sure that she had the same illness as Vincent had? Or was it something worse? What will his father say when he brings Sofie home so ill?

Anton turned his head for another look at Sofie. She had slid to the floor of the carriage in a seated position, her head resting on the seat, her face glistening with perspiration.

Why did he bring this little carriage? If he had only known, he would have brought a wagon. In a wagon Sofie could properly lie down.

Anton reined the horse.

"Would you like some water...or some wine?" Anton dug through the basket supplied by the caring Lucia.

"I don't suppose you feel like eating something."

Sofie didn't answer. Her eyes were closed and her breathing was labored.

Anton poured water on his handkerchief and wiped Sofie's reddened face with it. "Does that feel better? Would you try and drink some water?"

"Oh, Vincent..." Sofie softly moaned. "I want to be with you."

A chill ran through Anton. *My God! She wants to die. My darling sister Sofie wants to join Vincent.*

"Please, Sofie...don't die. You aren't going to die." He tried to sound confident, but he was afraid for her. This couldn't be happening to his darling Sofie. They had been so close all their lives. Their mother died when they were very little and their father in his grief left them in the care of servants. Sofie and Anton had shared so much growing up. It seemed to him that they had spent almost every minute of every day together, along with Marko and Klara. It couldn't end now.

They were meant to have weddings, to produce children, and, to be Godparents to one another's children.

Anton stared at Sofie unsure what to do. She was so pale, so warm. He wet the handkerchief once more and then laid it over her head, cooling her reddened her face.

"Sofie..."

She didn't answer.

He raised his sister's small hand to his lips and gently kissed it. Anton had to get her home...home where she would get good care.

Anton moved back to the front seat of the carriage. He sat in the driver's seat slightly sideways, looking back often, for any change in Sofie's condition. He urged the horse to trot a little faster, less concerned with the bouncing now and more with getting Sofie home.

Sofie's moans terrified Anton. He prayed to God for help. He promised anything…everything…just let Sofie live. He would never quarrel with her again. Never! Whatever she wanted he would let her have. Anton begged God to watch over Sofie. *Make her well and I will find her a wonderful husband.* A husband that would make her forget, forget she ever loved Vincent. She would have babies and be happy.

Then he saw it! There in the distance was a huge cross. It was a sign from God. It had to be! He heard Sofie moan again calling out Vincent's name. Anton knew what he must do.

The convent! The nuns would nurse her. They could call a doctor.

Please God! Let there be someone here who will know what to do to save my Sofie.

Anton carried Sofie in his arms as he followed the young nun, almost running past other nuns with astonished looks on their faces.

"Come this way," the nun said her voice urgent. "There is a room at the end of the corridor."

The nun was young, pretty and not at all bashful or shy as most of the nuns in the convent were. She did not hide her face from strangers. Sister Manda seemed to be in charge, which was unusual for one so young.

"There…put her on the bed," she motioned to the small bed in a room bare of any decorations, other than a cross on the wall. There was a chair beside the bed, and a small table covered with a white linen cloth.

"Sister," the nun called to a passing nun who stopped at the open door to look in, "Please undress Miss Vladislav and have someone get some towels to bathe her."

The nun at the door motioned to another passing nun and the two hurried into the room and began to undo the moaning Sofie's dress.

Sister Manda touched Anton's arm lightly, "Let's go out for a breath of air. You can tell me when your sister first became ill."

Anton nervously glanced back at Sofie, not wanting to leave her, but allowed himself to be led out of the room by the Sister.

One of the nuns was removing Sofie's shoes, while the other was undoing the hooks on her dress.

When they were outside, Sister Manda said, "Please...we can sit in the garden and you can tell me what I need to know."

When Anton was seated in the shade under a large apple tree on a crudely made bench, another nun appeared with a pitcher of ice-cold well water and a tall glass. She filled his glass without looking at Anton or speaking. When she finished she looked to Manda for instructions...as if she knew there would be one coming.

"Send for the priest from Selna." Sister Manda saw the questioning look on the other nun's face, for Selna was three hours away and there were priests in closer villages able to come sooner to the convent. "The priest from Selna," she repeated her voice low, but firm.

"Yes, Sister," the nun obediently left, leaving the pitcher of water on the table. All the nuns seemed like shadows in white, never really looking at anyone, sort of drifting about attending to their duties. All were so similar...except for Sister Manda. She was so direct, so in command. No shadowy ghost, this Sister.

"Tell me..." she said again to Anton. "What are her symptoms?"

Seated in the cool garden at the back of the convent, Anton told Sister Manda how Sofie had gone to Trieste several times over the past few months and how she cared for Vincent during his illness. He was sure she had succumbed to the same unknown disease Vincent had and now Anton feared Sofie would also die.

Seeing that Anton was pale with fatigue and worry, Manda asked, "Would you like to lie down and rest? We have more rooms."

"I couldn't rest. Not until I know my sister is going to be well."

"Then stay here where it is cool. I shall return as soon as I can to tell you how your sister is doing."

Anton started to rise, "I want to be with her."

"Please," protested Manda "we are good nurses. We will take very good care of her. You stay here and rest, you look exhausted. We will come with news if there is any change.

Anton was tired, more tired than he realized. He crossed his arms on the table and rested his head on his arms. *Only for a moment*, he thought. *I will close my eyes just for a moment.*

One of the nuns came out of the room where Sofie was resting.

"Sister," she said to Manda, "come, take a look at Miss Vladislav."

As Manda approached the bed, the other nun raised the bed sheet to show the thin body of Sofie, with only the slightest protruding belly of a pregnant woman.

Manda was speechless for just a moment.

"We can't let Anton Vladislav know of this! He thinks his sister is ill and may die. Oh dear," Manda sat on the chair next to the bed.

"Close the door." Her voice was a hushed whisper.

She had to think. The Vladislavs were the sole support of the convent. Would they be so generous if they thought all the nuns knew Sofie was pregnant? And not married?

The taller nun, the one with the acne scarred face, asked, "Shall I send for the doctor?"

"No…no…" Manda was thinking out loud. "No. I don't want anyone to know about this, just the three of us." The other nun was short and plump, with a pink-cheeked face. She spoke for the first time. "Don't you think many people are going to know about this? How does one keep this a secret?"

"I don't know," Manda sounded weary. "Let me think…"

Sofie moaned and cried out in pain.

"Mother of God," cried the tall nun. "Look at her!"

The bed was wet and Sofie was writhing in pain.

"What is happening?" Manda was alarmed. "She can't be having the baby…she is too small. It is too soon. She can't be to term."

When Sofie cried out again, Manda put her hand over the woman's mouth to stifle the cry. "I don't want Vladislav to hear her." To the short nun she said, "Go out to the back door and see that Anton Vladislav does not come into convent"

"What am I to do if he wants to come in?" The little nun asked sharply.

"Just don't let him come this far. Distract him."

Sofie was delirious and appeared to fade in and out of consciousness.

With her hand still covering Sofie's mouth, trying not to smother her, Manda said to the taller nun, "With all your weight, push on her belly."

"Are you mad?" The nun was shocked. "I will kill her or the baby or both."

"Do it!" demanded Manda. "How long would this convent survive without the generosity of the Vladislavs? Push on her stomach…now!"

The tall nun, whose name was Sister Fillipa, said, "May this be on your conscience, Manda. I think you are out of your mind."

Some time later, while Anton was in the Chapel praying for his sister to recover, Sister Manda buried something wrapped in a piece of coarse homespun cloth at the far end of the garden, near the wall.

Book II, Chapter 17

Anton and Ernesta each had separate sleeping areas within one large room, connected by an arched opening in the wall. A drape hung there for privacy, yet it could have been a locked iron gate instead of soft velvet, for it had been years since there had been any late night traveling through the archway.

Ernesta's side of the room was decorated in a very feminine manner. Her high bed was covered with a heavy crochet spread, and the trim on her sheets and pillowcases also had crochet lace edgings. There was a step stool to help her climb onto her high bed. It was embroidered with colorful flowers and green leaves.

Now standing at her window she held the crochet lace curtain aside, as she watched the road hoping to see her son Stephan arriving home.

On one side of the arched entry to Anton's side of the room stood a dark walnut wardrobe cabinet, heavily carved with lion's paw feet. It held Ernesta's dresses and hats. A secret drawer, which was disguised as a carved panel at the bottom of the chiffonier cabinet, could be pulled out to store valuables.

Instead of a dresser, a small cabinet with two long swinging doors was on the other side of the arched entry. When opened it displayed a row of shelves filled with some of Ernesta's personal items, such as books, writing papers, pictures and mementos. On the cabinet was a crochet runner, more of Ernesta's handwork, on which were displayed some of her favorite things: a depiction of her beloved Stefan as a little boy and a more recent one, showing what a handsome young man he had grown to be. There was a picture of Ernesta as a pretty young girl. This same picture once stood on Anton's bedside table.

Some years earlier, an angry Ernesta had taken the photo from Anton's table, at the time feeling it was hypocrisy to have the picture next to his sleeping head. She no longer remembered why she had been angry enough to take the picture. But she did remember that Anton never mentioned it was gone. In reality, at one point when he was pouring himself some water from a decanter, he had felt something was different about the tabletop, but he couldn't remember what it could be.

Looking into Anton's room one could see all the hand work Ernesta had lovingly made for him. The bed had pillowslips and sheets with tiny trims of her crochet lace. The footstool before his reading chair had a maroon needlepoint cover with the initial V in gold threads. She had been careful to match the maroon color of the drape showing on his side of the archway. On the round bedside table was a lace cloth she had made. Always placed on it were his glass and water decanter, as well as his prayer book and whatever current novel he might be reading. In the prayer book was a crochet bookmark she had made with a cross in its design. Ernesta had stiffened the lace with sugar water. All these things were done long ago when she was young and still in love with Anton.

Ernesta heard the approach of the carriage. She recognized the carriage immediately as Father Lahdra's. Ernesta was always happy to have Lahdra's company.

Downstairs, unknown to Ernesta, Anton was already seated at the table in the room that served as the dining area, with Sofie, and Klara. When Klara heard Ernesta coming down the stairs, she quickly rose with her coffee cup and disappeared into the kitchen. Ernesta did not like it that Klara at times behaved like a member of the family and not the servant that she was.

Taking a seat opposite Anton, Ernesta said, "Perhaps you can confess to Father Lahdra why you give away your son's inheritance. He is in the courtyard now."

Pleased with an excuse to avoid Ernesta's sarcasm, Anton dropped his napkin and went to the door. He opened it just as the priest was about to knock. Seeing the surprised look on Lahdra's face, Anton said, "Erna saw you from her window and told us you were here. How nice to see you so soon. Come in, come in." Then he called to Klara, "Coffee and bread for Father Lahdra."

As the men were seating themselves, Klara came in with a tray of steaming coffee and warm milk. Also on the tray was a plate of warm aromatic bread from the oven. Dishes of butter and apricot jam were already on the table.

"The bread smells wonderful," said Lahdra to a beaming Klara.

"Good morning, Sofie." He said as he sat down, then he nodded to the mistress of the house, "You are looking well today, Ernesta."

She smiled at the priest, genuinely happy for his company. She could put aside her foul mood for the time being. "Thank you. Have your coffee and bread."

Lahdra sat opposite Sofie watching Anton cut off a large slice of steaming bread. Anton placed the bread on the plate and handed it to Lahdra.

"I thought we would have some cake for breakfast, but Klara's bread is always delicious," said Anton.

"It is as good as cake to me," said Lahdra, spreading butter on the slice.

"And you, Erna?" smiled Anton. "May I slice some bread for you? No?" He frowned teasing her. "You should have some. It is best when it is still warm."

Ernesta ignored Anton. To the priest she said, "Father, how is it you are out and about so early?" She quickly added, "We are delighted to have you. I didn't mean it to sound as if you are not welcome."

Lahdra smiled. "I know, Erna. Your hospitality is most generous." He bit into the bread, enjoying it immensely. "I came to tell Anton and Sofie that I discovered who the new girl at the wedding party is."

"We know who she is," said Anton. "She is the godchild of Marko's cousin, Milan."

"Yes, she is that," said Lahdra, "but there is much more to her story."

"Whom are you talking about?" asked Ernesta. "What new girl?"

Sofie reached for a small piece of bread and said, "The girl that Ivan is in love with, the one with the red hair."

"We don't know that he is in love," said Anton.

"Oh, yes, he is," said Sofie. "A blind person could see that."

"I don't understand all this interest in some girl," said Ernesta. "Who cares if Ivan Balaban is interested in her? Bring me a fresh cup," she called to Klara. "This one is not clean."

Klara placed a fresh cup before Ernesta, with a bit more noise than necessary when she set it down and took away the perfectly fine cup Ernesta wanted replaced. This was one of Ernesta's power games she played with Klara, who long ago learned to ignore them.

"The girl's story is fascinating," said Lahdra, taking a sip of his coffee. "She was born on the same night we met. Remember? The night Sofie was ill at the convent?"

"How is it you know that?" asked Anton.

"I couldn't remember anyone from the time I was in Selna who resembled this beautiful girl. So, I got out my old journals and found that she had been born that same night. The night we met. And..." he went on before he could be interrupted. "Her twin died with the mother after Katya was born."

"Oh, my," said Sofie, her eyes wide. Even Ernesta seemed interested.

"There is more," said Lahdra, making sure he had all of their attention. "Not only did the mother die during the birth, but I found the father dead under a tree in my yard, when I returned from the convent."

There were gasps of surprise from all three at the table, and a murmur of surprise from Klara, who was listening at the door.

Anton was the first to speak. "Then, she was left an orphan?"

"Not really," said Father Lahdra. "She had a 10 year old sister. Or maybe she was older...I don't really remember."

"Another child," said Sofie softly. "How could a child take care of a baby?"

Lahdra pushed the plate out of his way, resting his arms on the table.

Sofie, Anton and Ernesta all leaned forward with interest as he went on with his story.

"There was an old woman in the village, a healer, and some said a witch, who summoned Milan...you remember...Katya's Godfather. His wife had just had a baby and became the wet nurse for baby Katya.

The sister, Anka, lived alone in the home with her baby sister. Directly across the road was the house of the healer, Old Julia. She kept a close eye on Anka and the baby. Then of course, Milan's wife Eva saw the baby several times a day to feed it and helped however she could.

As I recall," he paused, "about the time I left to come here, Milan had found a husband for Anka."

"What a blessing," said Sofie, "someone to take care of them."

"Not really," said Father Lahdra. "It turned out that Elia Sokach was a terrible man. He regularly beat the young bride, Anka, who appeared to me to be a pale, little thing."

"Didn't anyone stop him?" Ernesta was outraged. "Surely the men in the village put a stop to it."

"Not really," said Lahdra. "You see in the village the husband is the master of the house. Anka had no brothers or uncles to defend her. Though as I recall, the godfather Milan did threaten Elia."

"And the beatings stopped?" asked Sofie.

"I don't know what happened after I left to come here to Saint Joseph's. I lost touch with the people in Selna. It was a sad place." He paused and looked into the distance, as if remembering something. "I was very sad there…it was a poor village with poor people."

His gaze returned to Anton. "You will never know how grateful I have been all these years that you used your influence to have me transferred here, to St. Joseph's, even though you will not admit it."

Later that day, alone in the garden, Sofie remembered the morning she awoke in the convent, those many years ago. She vaguely remembered being carried down a hallway with many religious paintings. She also remembered the strange dream she had of a nun pushing on her stomach. It was a dream she had often throughout the years. And she recalled that her monthly period had returned after months of only a bit of spotting. She thought she had a light period because of the stress of caring for Vincent.

The story Lahdra told them played over and over in her mind. What a wretched life this lovely girl must have had! Sofie walked through the garden behind the house and sat for a while in the old Vladislav chapel staring for some time at the carved wood statue of the Blessed Virgin.

She made up her mind what she would do! Sofie would not discuss her decision with anyone. Not Anton, Ernesta or Klara.

Tomorrow morning she would go to the Balaban farm.

Ernesta paced back and forth waiting for Anton to appear from wherever he had gone to when Father Lahdra had left.

Sounds from the yard sent Ernesta to the door ready to give Anton a piece of her mind. But when she opened the door, it was her son Stefan, who sheepishly grinned at her.

"Mamitza," he said, "how nice that yours is the first face I see."

"My darling boy," she said as she embraced him. "This is a surprise. I was expecting your father."

"I hope you aren't too disappointed," teased Stefan, his arm around his mother's shoulder.

"Of course not," she said. "You are my very most favorite person in the whole world."

"Good," said Stefan. "Then you won't mind if I'm home for awhile."

"Oh?" Ernesta gave her son a long look. His stays at home were brief, usually only long enough to change clothes and get some money from his mother.

"Yes," he lied, "I missed the family and wanted to spend some time with all of you." He gave his mother what he hoped was a sincere-looking smile. "Besides, I had promised Teta Sofie I would go to the wedding with her. I missed it, didn't I?"

Ernesta watched her son remove his dusty boots and a cold chill passed over her. Her intuition warned her something was very wrong. Stefan's manner was unnaturally light-hearted. Ernesta knew her only child very well and her instincts told her he was in trouble. She wanted to ask him what was wrong, but stopped herself. If there were troubles, she would know soon enough. And if it was nothing serious, well then, time would take care of the problem.

"Are you hungry?" She asked.

"Yes, I'm starved," Stefan said. "I didn't take the time to stop and eat on the way home."

"Well then," said Ernesta, "go to your room and wash up, while I tell Klara you are here and hungry."

In his room, Stefan saw his pale reflection in the mirror over the washstand and wondered if his mother had noticed anything unusual. He had spent the last night and all the morning thinking about the debt he owed at Magda's. Stefan was frightened...really frightened. Magda's new partner was cold and threatening. He had already decided not to mention the gambling debt to his father who would not be sympathetic at all. His Teta Sofie would tell his father, so better not to confide in her. That left his mother. He would take his time...not rush into the matter. He had a week...that was what Magda's grim partner had said, 'Only one week, then the debt doubles and I come looking for you.' Stefan felt chilled, though there was perspiration on his forehead. He had to stay calm, he told himself. He noticed that his hand trembled as he reached for a towel. He had time to come up with the money. *Just be calm.* He told himself again.

Book II, Chapter 18

Sofie's original plan had been to have Katya come to the Vladislav home as household help for Klara. Now the girl was upstairs in an attic room, not as kitchen help, but as a companion to Sofie. No family discussion took place concerning Sofie's decision. She just did it. Katya had completely invaded Sofie's thoughts. Sofie had to have Katya near. The girl so reminded her of Vincent that Sofie couldn't bear to be separated from her. Sofie hoped Katya could be a friend. Maybe that was too much to wish for, but she needed someone in her life. Klara the cook was a friend from childhood, but their positions separated them. Klara couldn't walk away from her duties to spend a day with Sofie. Her sister-in-law, Ernesta, was never a confidant and now she might even be an enemy...who knew? Handsome, spoiled Stefan was only in love with himself. He didn't have time for his parents, much less an old-maid aunt...especially since she had stopped giving him money. Her brother Anton loved her. She knew that. But, they didn't seem to spend much time together. He was always off somewhere...and he had Father Lahdra as a good friend. That was what Sofie wanted, a good friend such as Anton had in Father Ladra.

Young Ivan Balaban was very disappointed when Katya agreed to Sofie's offer of living at the Vladislav house. He would gladly have built a small house on his father's property, just to keep Katya near. He was ready to propose marriage, but three days didn't seem a respectable enough time before asking. Furthermore, he had no idea how Katya felt about him. Ivan was devastated when Katya left with Sofie. He wanted to hold her, to kiss her, to make her promise never to forget him. But, he didn't do any of those things. He bravely bid her good-bye with a promise to come visiting often.

In the immaculately clean attic room, once the bedroom of the governess briefly engaged after Sofie and Anton's mother died, Katya absent-mindedly untied her bundle, her eyes surveying the room. The walls and floor were wooden planks of a walnut color...no dirt floor or clay walls here. The headboard of the bed

was decorated with hand carved flowers. A three-drawer
washstand with a mirror above it awaited her meager possessions.
A straight-backed chair also with flowers carved on its slats was
next to the bed. A bi-fold screen covered with blue cloth stood in a
corner. The most intriguing piece of furniture, something Katya
had never seen before, was the wardrobe. A large mirror on the
door showed her reflection. It was the largest mirror she had ever
seen...it was the full size of the door. Curiosity got the better of her
and she pulled on the brass handle swinging the door open to
reveal a symphony of colorful fabrics. Dresses made of fabrics
Katya didn't know existed hung neatly in a row. She reached out
and touched the silks and taffetas. They felt wonderful to her
touch, nothing like the coarse homespun she was wearing. *What
must it feel like to have this fabric next to one's body*, she
wondered? Beneath the open door, Katya saw a drawer. Kneeling,
she pulled it open to reveal several pairs of shoes, neatly standing
in a row.

Slowly, almost reluctantly Katya closed the drawer, then the
wardrobe door. When the door closed, the mirror caught the
reflection of the silent figure of Sofie standing in the doorway.

"I never wore those dresses," Sofie said softly. "They were
part of my trousseau."

Seeing that Katya didn't understand the word 'trousseau,'
Sofie said, "I wanted to be married and these were the clothes I
planned to take with me." Sofie walked to the wardrobe and pulled
open the door. "I never wore these. After Vincent died, I didn't
want to see them...to be reminded."

"Then, I'm sorry it was I who opened that door," said Katya.
"I was just curious."

"No, not at all," said Sofie. "It's a shame these have been
unused for so long."

Impulsively, Sofie said, "Would you like to see what else I
had?"

"Of course!" said Katya, flushed with the excitement of
seeing new things, things she had never even dreamed of.

Sofie walked to an inside wall of the small room and pulled
on an almost concealed wooden knob. In the wall was a door
opening onto the unfinished attic.

"Come, follow me," said Sofie, offering her hand and leading Katya into the dim interior of the attic. "It is too dark to see in here, but I'll hand you the trunks and we can look at them in your room."

For the next few minutes, Sofie and Katya dragged heavy trunks into the middle of the small attic bedroom. Some were made of leather others of wicker. There were several cloth covered round travel cases. Finally, both women, warm from the work, sat on the floor before one of the trunks. Sofie undid the leather straps feeling flushed and excited. She had not seen these things since they were put away fifteen years ago. Until this moment she could never bring herself to look at them. Now she was eager to open them and share her past happiness with Katya...the time before Vincent's illness.

The first trunk held fine linen tablecloths and napkins, each delicately embroidered with the initial K, for Kurecka. These were not brightly embroidered in the ethnic manner of the peasants, but delicately with the thread matching the cream color of the cloth.

"Oh, Teta Sofie," said Katya, her finger caressing the fine embroidery. "These are very beautiful."

"See," Sofie pointed to the "K" on the napkins. "These have your monogram on them."

Again Katya's expression was blank, for she didn't know what a monogram was.

Quickly Sofie said, "It is the first letter of your name."

Katya picked up the napkin, once more running her fingers over the letter K saying, "I've never seen this before. I don't know how to write."

"We'll change that," said Sofie. "Starting tonight...right after dinner, your education will begin." Then, she continued pulling things out of the trunk.

Katya's brain was in a whirl as she watched Aunt Sofie open each trunk and explain where the pieces were made and their use. She saw things she never knew existed, such as silver tongs to carry sugar cubes. What is a cube, Katya wondered? There was a beautiful glass "Bride's Basket" hand-blown in Venice. It had no other use than to sit on a table for fruit or candy...a thing of beauty. Then, there were the small ivory carved rings for the napkins. Katya couldn't imagine what one did with the napkins or the rings.

Sofie was thoroughly enjoying herself. She un-wrapped each object with renewed pleasure. The excitement in Katya's eyes was a joy Sofie could not have imagined. Sharing her stories about the items and their uses was a delightful experience for Sofie.

When Sofie un-wrapped the cloth protecting a silver hand-mirror, ornately embellished on the back, Katya picked it up and studied it. "Look," she said, showing Sofie the 'K' engraved in the middle of the back, "my monogram." Then, she placed the mirror on the bed and examined the matching comb and brush.

The heaviest trunk was left for last. "Oh, I remember these," said Sofie, pleased with her find. "Isn't it strange how you can put something out of your mind? I haven't thought about these since I put them away." Sofie stopped talking when she saw Katya on her knees holding a plate, silently staring at the pattern. Katya ran her fingers across the hand-painted images of a young man and girl in peasant dress. There was a girl on one side of the gate and the boy on the other, a bouquet of flowers in his hands, offering them to her. They were obviously lovers.

"Do you like those?" asked Sofie. "Each one is different. See, here is one showing an angry father chasing a boy away from his daughter."

Katya picked up a cup depicting a wedding scene and it could have been painted at the Balaban wedding, for Katya saw musicians, dancers and a bride and groom, all in miniature on the side of the cup. Katya kept un-wrapping the dishes, bowls, and pitchers, studying each scene for some time. There were even drinking glasses and beer mugs, all with everyday village scenes painted on them. Sofie said nothing. She watched with pleasure, the enraptured look on Katya's face.

After examining each piece and putting them once again in the trunk, Katya said, "Everything is beautiful."

While Katya and Sofie pulled and tugged the trunks back into the storage space of the attic, Sofie remembered where the dishes had come from. She had secretly ordered them, not letting her family know she was building a trousseau. The pictures on each serving piece, beautifully painted by a local artist, were meant to remind Sofie of her home when she moved away after her marriage.

"I have a thought," said Sofie, as they sat resting on the bed after everything was put away. "You don't have very many clothes. Perhaps something in the wardrobe could be altered for you. I would be so happy if you could use them."

Katya wanted desperately to try on the dresses, for they reminded her of the beautiful woman in the yellow dress wearing the black and yellow hat, she had seen while riding through Zagreb, the grand woman descending the carriage at the hotel. That ride with Milan was only a few days earlier, yet it seemed so long ago. Katya was almost tongue-tied with excitement, but she managed to say, "Oh, Teta Sofie! I've never worn such clothes."

"Let's see how they look," said Sofie, as she pulled open the mirrored door of the wooden cabinet removing two dresses. "You can go behind the screen and undress. I'll hand you a dress and you come out when you need to be buttoned up."

Katya's face shone with excitement as she hurried behind the screen. She undressed not knowing what to do with her skirts, so she draped them over the top of the screen and stepped into a pale yellow dress. Katya pulled the bodice up and slipped her arms into the sleeves. She stepped from behind the screen to the waiting Sofie, who started fastening the dress at the back. When Sofie fastened the last metal hook and eye, she said, "Now step out, away from me. I want to see what alterations we need to make."

Katya, flushed with excitement did as she was told. The skirt rustling as she stepped away from Teta Sofie.

After a long silence, Katya said, "Well, what's wrong? Why aren't you saying something?"

"I...I'm amazed," said Sofie, softly. "I can't believe how well the dress fits you. The shoulders are perfect, the waist hits at the right spot, the sleeve length is correct and the hemline doesn't need to be altered even a centimeter."

Sofie wanted to say something about the elaborate bracelet at Katya's wrist, it didn't seem to go with her new look, but she said nothing.

Katya turned from Sofie and faced the mirror and gazed at the stranger before her. Out of the peasant clothes and into this metropolitan fashion, she was someone else. For the first time in her life, her wild red hair seemed wrong.

Seeing the frown on Katya's face, Sofie asked, "What's wrong."

"My hair," Katya moved closer to the mirror for a better look.

"Come sit in the chair," said Sofie, and Katya obeyed. Sofie took what she deliberately didn't repack, the silver brush from the bed, leaving its companion mirror and comb still on the coverlet. With Katya seated before the mirror and Sofie behind her, the older woman began to gently brush the lush red tresses. Katya said nothing, enjoying this new sensation...this feeling of being cared for.

Sofie willed the tears that gathered in her eyes not to roll down her cheeks. Was this what a mother felt when she did her daughter's hair? What an exquisite feeling this was — to make someone happy, to share memories, to comb a daughter's hair. She felt like the mother she never was. Sofie liked this feeling and she wanted more. She decided she would be a teacher to Katya and a mother and a friend and whatever else the girl needed. That was it! Sofie enjoyed being needed!

Sofie pulled Katya's hair smoothly back to the nape of her neck and coiled a braid low at the back of her head. Katya stared with fascination at the metamorphosis. Instead of the wild-haired peasant girl, a sophisticated beauty looked back at her.

"Do you like what you see?" asked Sofie, softly, impressed with the transformation.

"Oh, Yes!" whispered Katya awed by her reflection. "I want to be that person forever."

"Then I will teach you all you need to know. You are already a very polite girl, but the girl you see in the mirror needs to know more and to be more than that." Talking to the Katya's reflection in the mirror Teta Sofie asked, "Are you willing to be a student, as if you were in school."

"Of course, I will do whatever you say...whatever it takes to remain this way."

Arriving from his duties as a landowner, Anton was verbally assaulted by Erna as he came into the house. In a huff Erna told Anton no stranger was coming into the house and that was that!

She said a lot of other things, all of which Anton dismissed, as he usually did when Ernesta became dictatorial.

He had gone upstairs to see for himself what all the commotion was about. Unnoticed at the open door of the attic room, Anton watched not only the transformation of Katya, but the rebirth of his sister. A part of Sofie had died when she came back from Trieste after Vincent's death. A part of her had been gone all these years and Anton was near tears as he watched his beloved Sofie return to the sister he had lost so long ago.

Anton thought his Sofie looked years younger and that her laugh had a new lilt to it, or was it the old laugh of long ago, returned.

Very quietly he turned away from the open door and the happy chatter within knowing full well he had an inevitable battle awaiting him downstairs with Erna.

Book II, Chapter 19

Stefan could almost feel the tenseness in the air, as he descended the stairs to have breakfast. His parents and Aunt Sofie, in a somber mood, were at the table having breakfast. The three brightened when they saw him. He was the diversion they all needed, the one neutral bond they shared.

Stefan dutifully kissed his mother on the forehead, then his aunt and lastly his father, who joyfully slapped his son on the back in the form of a greeting.

"It is good to have you home, my son," said Anton. "You have been missed. Sit here...next to me and tell me what is new in Zagreb."

Before Stefan could speak, Katya entered the room carrying a platter of prune filled Kolachky pastries sprinkled with powdered sugar. Seeing this beautiful, young stranger dressed in a continental full–skirted tan dress with pearl buttons down the front trimmed with lace collar and cuffs, Stefan rose politely. Her hair was smooth against her head, coiled in a soft bun at the back, making her green eyes more prominent.

Erna frowned when she saw the pleased look on Stefan's face. "Put the plate down," she ordered, "and get more coffee." To Stefan, who was still standing, napkin in hand, she said, "Your aunt brings a girl in the house to be a servant and then tries to make a lady of her."

Slowly Stefan sat down, watching one of the most beautiful girls he had ever seen retreat to the kitchen. The girl looked confused and embarrassed.

Earlier, when Katya came down for breakfast, she was happy with the way she was dressed and how she looked. She wanted so much to please the Vladislavs, especially Sofie. Katya was grateful for the chance to live in this fine house and to be educated by Sofie.

She had come down to see Anton, Sofie, and Ernesta already seated at the table. Sofie had smiled warmly and motioned for Katya to sit next to her. Before Katya could be seated, Ernesta said, "I believe you are bit over-dressed to be working in the kitchen."

It was as if Katya had been slapped in the face.

"Erna! Please don't be that way," said Sofie.

"Erna," said Anton, "I thought this was settled last night."

Katya with cheeks flaming headed for the kitchen, tears stinging her eyes.

Klara heard it all and could only pat Katya sympathetically on the shoulder.

"We have all felt Erna's sharp tongue," said Klara, "even Anton, and especially Sofie."

Ernesta's treatment of Katya only added to the tense mood

Katya poured Ernesta's coffee first. All at the table noticed her trembling hand spilling some of the coffee onto the cloth.

"For Heaven's sake," said Ernesta. "You can't even pour coffee."

"Mamitza!" said Stefan, seeing Katya's hurt look. "Don't be this way. Not on my first morning home."

Katya stood not moving, coffee pot in hand. Stefan rose, took the pot from her hand. He felt her body shaking as he took her hand leading her to the chair next to Sofie. He then proceeded to pour the coffee, himself.

"What are you doing?" demanded Ernesta. "We have servants to do that!"

Sofie took Katya's still trembling hand into her own. It was a cold hand.

Sofie said, "Erna...I have let you be the mistress of this house because you are the wife of my brother." Sofie raised her hand to still Erna, who was ready to interrupt.

"You understood that I wanted Katya as my companion. Yes, I know, at first I thought she could help Klara, but I have changed my mind. Katya is not a servant. She is my companion and I hope will be my friend." Looking coolly at Erna, she added, "We all know you aren't my friend."

Anton remembered Sofie's happy laughter he had heard at the attic room door the evening before. The sort of laughter he missed hearing all these long years since Vincent's death.

Anton spoke directly to Katya, who was still trembling, her eyes brimming with tears.

"Katya, please look at me."

When she raised her face, a tear rolled down her check and Sofie was heartsick when she saw it.

"I welcome you to our home as my sister's companion. From now on, you will not be asked to do household tasks."

Ernesta's face had gone from red to nearly blue with anger.

Not looking at his wife, Anton raised an open hand at her, his way of showing her she was not to say a word.

Still standing with the coffee pot in his hand, Stefan's eyes moved from his mother to his father and then rested on the lovely Katya. He could almost feel her hurt. He wanted to protect her.

Taking a clean cup and saucer from the center of the table, Stefan poured Katya some coffee. He reached over for the pitcher of warmed milk and placed it before her.

Raising the coffee pot as in a toast he said, "And I welcome you to this house as Teta Sofie's companion."

Ernesta rattled the table as she rose, flinging down her napkin. Without a backward glance, she stormed out of the house.

Klara, listening at the kitchen door, hearing it all and seeing Ernesta's departure, made the sign of the cross saying, "God help us all."

After breakfast, Stefan knew he had made a mistake by taking Sofie's side against his only ally, his mother. He had been struck by Katya's beauty and wanted to be the gallant knight. By protecting the damsel in distress, he had alienated his last definite source of financing.

This wasn't the same as being a bad little boy and cajoling his mother into forgiving him for sassing or breaking something or telling a lie. This time he had crossed over to the enemy. He was a deserter. Deserters got shot. This deserter was in BIG trouble if he didn't come up with money to pay his gambling debt. Stefan felt queasy just thinking about the Turk at Magda's. He remembered those cold threatening eyes and he shuddered.

It was too soon to try and make up with his mother. As a matter of fact, he didn't have a clue how he was going to do so. He decided to give her time to cool down, hoping she would do so and not get angrier.

He thought he might spend the day with his father. Now was as good a time as any to please his father by showing interest in the land and how it was managed. Actually, Stefan found all the day-to-day management of the land a bore. He really didn't care how many pigs they had, or how many calves were born. He did like seeing the foals though, but only because he liked horses and riding.

Ernesta, feeling both hurt and angry, walked along the rock piled wall around their house. She didn't want to go back and see any of the family. She looked out at the valley below seeing the cluster of small modest wooden dwellings. Here and there on a chimney was a large stork's nest. In the distance she saw a stork as it descended and settled onto a nest. In these parts it was considered good-luck to have a stork nest on one's chimney. Ernesta glanced at her chimney. They had never had a stork's nest. To her, it was another example of all the bad luck she felt had befallen her marriage.

Ernesta assumed her marriage to Anton would mirror the marriage of her parents. Her mother and father had loved one another very much and enjoyed each other's company tremendously, sharing all their interests. If one of them enjoyed a book, the other had to read it and then they would discuss it. If one wanted to go to the country, the other was ready and willing. It was the same with social events...they did everything together.

"We're like milk and sugar," Ernesta's father used to say. "We go everywhere together." Then her mother would laugh and reach out to touch his hand.

Ernesta couldn't remember the last time she had touched Anton's hand in an affectionate manner.

Then there was the running of the house.

Sofie and Ernesta always helped with the cleaning, a task which Ernesta greatly resented. She never understood why there weren't more servants to do the menial tasks. When she was first married, Ernesta didn't challenge this procedure, for as a new bride she wanted to please her husband. As the years passed when she suggested more help, Anton would only say, "What else do you have to do, beside your needlework and caring for the house?"

She was in a marriage with a man who did not love her. She lived in a house, which after twenty years was still not completely hers. The friends from her youth had disappeared over the years and she blamed Anton's indifference to them as the cause. In her unhappiness, she was sure that Sofie and Klara conspired against her. She only had Stefan...beautiful Stefan. And today, that foolish boy had betrayed her. In time she would fix that too. She could stand every slight, every insult from Anton knowing that someday the Vladislav lands and title would go to Stefan. Stefan was hers. Anton could try all he wanted to win the boy's affection. Stefan was and always would be *hers.*

And now this Katya...a girl who was supposed to be a servant becomes a houseguest. A companion to Sofie! *What about a companion for me?* she thought, feeling very lonely and abandoned, but...not for long. She needed to think. Somehow she had to get rid of Sofie and that Katya. She didn't like the way her foolish son looked at the girl. He didn't know she was just an uneducated peasant. She was certainly not a girl for him to waste his time on!

Katya was gone from the Balaban house for only one day and Ivan missed her terribly. He loved seeing her in the kitchen with his mother. He loved seeing her walk across the barnyard with a pail of milk in hand, her bright coppery curls wild in the wind. How he loved those wild curls. In the sunlight her eyes were as green as emeralds. She was his light-skinned Gypsy. He liked to think of her as a Gypsy. How he loved that she was so different from the usual village girls. None dared have their hair loose as she did. It was braids only. Then, when married, a colored scarf. And last when widowed, the black babushka.

He had to see her. It wasn't unusual for him to visit his Godfather, so he was sure no one would mind if he dropped in to see Katya. After all, he thought, he could help with her reading lessons.

It was after lunchtime and he felt it was an appropriate time to visit. Behind the Vladislav chapel was a huge walnut tree offering much shade. That was where he saw her. He almost didn't recognize her. Her hair was pulled smoothly back into a bun. Gone were her full skirts and embroidered blouse. Now she wore a tan dress with pearl buttons. She looked so tiny...and so different.

When she saw him, she said, "Hello, Ivan." Just like that. "Hello, Ivan." He expected her to be surprised, pleased, happy, excited. But she showed none of that just, "Hello, Ivan."

He was hurt. In the morning at his father's home, she was so happy, so cheerful, smiling...HAPPY to see him. She not only looked different, but she was different.

Ivan sat on the bench next to her. "Are you alright?" he asked. "Is anything wrong? You don't seem like yourself."

"Just *who am I*?" She demanded angrily. "I don't belong anywhere. I didn't belong in Selna, where I was born. Everyone told me I was different! I don't belong here because I am not good enough." She stared at him as if he could give her an answer.

After a bit of silence, he said softly, "You belong with me on my Father's land. I can build you a house and you can be barefoot with your hair wild."

Katya stared at him as if he were out of his mind. "You want me to be a peasant again? How can you ask me to be that?"

"Because that is what you are." His heart was heavy. His Katya *was gone*. He could feel it. His wild Gypsy girl was gone and he didn't know who this sophisticated-looking girl was. "You don't belong here. Ernesta Vladislav will make your life miserable. We all know what she is like."

"Oh, no," said Katya, "she will be no trouble. The family is against her. Even her son Stefan welcomed me into the family," Kayta said proudly.

At that Ivan's eyes darkened. "Stefan is back? When did he arrive?"

"I don't know...maybe yesterday. He was wonderful. He led me to a chair and served me coffee. As if I am important! He made his mother so angry she couldn't speak. She stormed out of the house." At that Katya smiled remembering that Stefan had been her champion.

Ivan felt sick. This wasn't the visit he had planned or the reception he had expected.

"Look," said Katya, "there is Stefan, now. He just came out of the house."

When Ivan saw the happy look on Katya's face, the look he had expected for himself, he arose from his place next to her. He mounted his waiting horse and without a word, rode away.

At supper that evening, Katya could not bring herself to sit at the table with the family. She was still uncomfortable near Ernesta. Sofie gave up trying to convince her to join them. Instead Katya ate in the kitchen with Klara, though she did not help with the serving.

Ernesta was surprisingly calm. Not openly warm or forgiving, for she was not ready to forgive. During the quiet meal, with a somewhat strained atmosphere, Ernesta said to Sofie, "Wouldn't you like to take your companion to Trieste to meet your friend, Signora Kurecka? I think Katya would love seeing the coast."

Book II, Chapter 20

Katya was so excited during the carriage ride to Trieste that Sofie almost forgot the uneasiness she felt with Ernesta's suggestion that they make the trip. In fact, she was so uneasy about it that she instructed their driver, Yura, one of the stable hands, to come back in a week. Any other time, she would have stayed a month, but not this time. Something was amiss. Ernesta was being almost...sweet.

Signora Kurecka garbed as usual in black, always wearing the beautiful carved coral cameo at her throat, stood in the courtyard waiting for Sophie. Lucia was now a bit heavier, a bit older with more gray at her temples, but still a handsome woman with bright eyes.

Those eyes widened when she saw Katya step from the carriage. For a moment, just a brief moment, she thought she might faint, but didn't.

Seeing the look on Lucia's face, Sofie said, "I'm sorry. I think I should have warned you." She hugged the older woman and kissed her on both cheeks. "I had the same reaction the first time I saw her."

Turning to Katya, Sofie said, "Katya this is my dearest friend in the whole world, Signora Kurecka." Katya extended her hand to Signora Kurecka. "I am so happy to meet you," said Katya.

Lucia took Katya's hand and held it, staring into the girl's face and looking into those green eyes. She asked, "Where are you from?"

"I was born in a small village near Zagreb, called Selna."

Still holding her hand Lucia asked, "And your people, who are they?"

Embarrassed by the interest and that the Signora was still holding her hand, Katya stammered, "I have no people. My family is dead...I mean they all died."

Servants appeared gathering the carpetbags carrying them into the house, and Yura, promising to return in a week was already on his way back to Vladezemla. Anton's land was called Vladezemla, which meant Vlad's land.

Lucia held Katya's hand as she led her into the house. "Tell me Katya, how old are you."

"I will soon be 16."

"My Vincent...that is my son, Vincent, died almost 16 years ago." She reached out and touched Katya's smoothed hair. "It is remarkable. Isn't it, Sofie? She has the same color hair that Vincent had."

The Signora's house was breathtaking to Katya. It was something she, of course, had never seen and couldn't possibly have imagined. It was a white stone house over-looking the Adriatic Sea.

Katya had never seen large woven tapestries such as were on the walls of the house. She knew the woven work of the peasant women, which were nothing like these woven of gold and silver threads. Naked statues on marble pedestals seemed to be everywhere. Marble urns large enough to hold a child stood at the doorways like sentries. The sweet sea air moved the filmy white curtains at the large doorway leading to a terrace. There potted plants surrounded a naked breasted mermaid made of stone, the clear water shooting up around her.

Upstairs, the room chosen for Katya had a small balcony. Katya loved that balcony. She was above everything and could see far out into the city and out onto the Jadran...the Adriatic. She loved the smell of the sea. There was no smell of grass or manure, only the smell of flowers and the sea. She loved the sea. She had never seen it before, never knew it could be so large. Never knew it existed. *But she loved it.*

"How long are you staying?" asked Lucia, pouring Sofie a blended juice drink of different melons from a brightly painted pitcher. They were seated on the enclosed terrace in the shade among fragrant blooming roses.

"A week."

"Only a week? Why? You always stay longer."

Sofie sipped her drink. "There is something afoot back home. I think my brother may need me."

"Trouble with your sister-in-law?"

"I can't be sure. I just have this feeling that Katya and I were sent away for a reason."

"Speaking of Katya," said the older woman, "tell me about her. I find that I cannot stop staring at her."

"Oh, I know," said Sofie. "It is as if I can't get enough of looking at her."

Lucia nodded, "Yes...yes."

Sofie told her all that she knew about Katya. How she first met Katya at the Balaban wedding, and then all that Father Lahdra knew of Katya's family and the strange way her mother, twin and father died within hours of each other.

"Has she been educated, at all?" asked the Signora.

"No, but she learns very quickly and is eager to learn anything and everything."

"There is a natural elegance about her," said the Signora.

"The transformation came about when I showed her the dresses from my trousseau, which by the way fit her perfectly with no alterations."

"Really?"

"She prefers the continental styles to those of the village. However, I personally find the peasant clothes so much more comfortable when I am home. Katya even moves differently when she wears the continental clothing."

Just then, Katya appeared from within the house, somewhat shyly. "I hope you don't mind, but I have been going through your house looking at things." Quickly she added, "I didn't touch anything...really...I just looked."

"Come sit down, my dear. Let me pour you a drink," said the Signora.

Katya took the glass and sipped it. She had never tasted anything like it before.

Sofie and the Signora laughed, seeing the look of wonderment on Katya's face.

"It is juice from melons. Our ships bring them to us from Africa," said the Signora.

Melons? Africa? What were these things, thought Katya?

Seeing Katya's Gypsy bracelet slip down to her wrist from its hiding place under her long sleeve, Lucia asked, "May I see your bracelet?"

Hesitantly, Katya reached her hand out so that the bracelet could be seen.

"This is remarkable work," said Lucia, as if speaking to herself. "These are some sorts of ancient designs. And...I do believe the stones could be real." Looking up she asked, "How did you come by such a treasure?"

Katya felt embarrassed at the attention to her bracelet. "It was given to me be a Gypsy Queen," she said.

Still holding Katya's hand, Lucia Kurecka looked at Sofie. "This is remarkable. I think this is very valuable. What did you have to trade for this, may I ask?"

"I didn't trade anything." said Katya, her arm still extended. "Valina, the Gypsy Queen read my fortune...first in my hand and then in a crystal ball."

Sofie had not heard this story before and now both women looked at Katya intently. Katya went on, "You see, according to Valina, I am in some sort of danger. She made me promise to never take off the bracelet...that it would save me from harm."

"Well," said the Signora, "that is some lucky charm. I am sure it is quite old, perhaps from India or Assyria."

"What sort of danger?" asked Sofie.

"I don't know," said Katya. "She said I was *'put where I didn't belong, but that I would find my rightful place.'*"

"Do you know what that means?" asked Sofie.

"No...and I don't know where I belong," said Katya.

Later that day, Sofie and the Signora couldn't stop laughing good-naturedly at Katya as they walked along the short distance to the Renaldi warehouse located on the wharf. Watching Katya was like watching a three year old discover new things and ask endless questions. It was a delight for the women to see Katya's reactions to the baskets of sea creatures for sale.

The tangle of eels slithering in the woven grass baskets, the crabs, lobsters and clams brought squeals of wonderment and delight. Pointing to the eels wriggling against one another Katya asked, "What do you do with these?"

"Eat them," replied Sofie and Lucia in unison.

"Ooooh!" said Katya, wrinkling her noise.

But it was the hanging swordfish that made Katya's eyes grow large. She could have been an alien from another planet for these were things she had never seen, never knew about.

The ships! Those gorgeous cargo ships with their billowing sails were beautiful to Katya's eyes. Something else she had never seen, never knew existed.

"Oh, Teta Sofie," Katya nearly swooned. "Look at those ships. Aren't they beautiful? Where do they go? Can we go on one?"

Laughing at the girl's enthusiasm Sofie said, "No dear, not this time. Actually," she added, "I have never been on the cargo ships."

"Whose are they…the ships, I mean?" said Katya.

"That one is mine," Lucia pointed with her closed sun umbrella. "It is the Vincenti, named after my son." It has sailed the Adriatic and the Mediterranean, stopping at ports to buy and sell things for me."

The Vincenti was a four masted schooner. Its sails could be raised by gasoline hoisting engines, reducing the need for sailors. The gas hoists were an economic move on the Signora's part, reducing expenses. It was a good ship for coastal trading.

"Can the ship go to America?" asked Katya. "I have heard that people want to go to America."

"Yes, she is capable of ocean travel to America," said the Signora.

"But, I don't have my ships venture that far. I have plenty of trade on this side of the hemisphere."

Hmm, hemisphere…Another word Katya didn't know. But she didn't interrupt the two friends to ask what it meant.

On the wharf in front of a two story, unimpressive warehouse were crates made of woven grasses or wicker. In faded paint one could read RENALDI SHIPPING AND IMPORTING. The main floor held the storage and sorting area, while the offices were upstairs. Stacks of porcelain vases, beaten metal bowls and trays, brassware, exotic fabrics and woodcarvings were everywhere, being sorted for selling or shipping.

Once inside, the three women ascended the wooden steps to the offices, all the while, Katya's eyes scanned everything. Lucia now had what had been her father's office, then later her husband

Aleksy's office. It still looked like a man's office. Lucia did nothing to change the décor, nothing to make it hers. In her heart she felt her father had built the business and Aleksy made it grow so it belonged to them. She was now the caretaker of the import business. With her only child gone, the business was hers to oversee.

Her office had a wooden file cabinet and a large wooden desk made so that two people could use the desk at the same time. It was wide enough that chairs could be placed opposite each other with the bookkeepers working facing one another. Today at one side of the desk sat a short, balding man with a black mustache. The creases around his eyes crinkled when he saw his cousin and her guests appear. Carlo, the cousin who wanted to marry Lucia when she was a young girl, rose to greet the women.

He nodded to his cousin, took Sofie's hand and brought it close to his mouth, but not touching them with his lips. "Signorina Sofie, such a pleasure to see you. We do not see enough of you."

"Hello, Carlo. It is always nice to see you, too," said Sofie. "Please meet my traveling companion, Katya."

Carlo paused, staring at Katya's face and hair, before taking her hand. It was apparent, that he also thought he saw a resemblance to Vincent.

"How nice to meet you." he said, with a bow, looking from his cousin to Sofie, waiting for an explanation at the resemblance, which didn't come.

Sofie looked through the glass to the adjoining office and said, "I see you have Carlo the Son working here. A younger version of the father looked up briefly, smiled and waived. He would have come to greet them, but was stopped by a worker asking a question.

"Of course," said Carlo the Father, forcing his eyes from Katya's face. "We need to keep the business in the family."

Carlo did not see the displeased look on the Lucia's face when she heard the remark, 'keep it in the family.'

Later that evening, after a supper of fresh tomatoes, a salad of marinated green peppers and fresh fish cooked on an outdoor clay stove, Sofie, Katya and the Signora sipped strong Turkish coffee served in tiny cups held in silver holders.

Katya was content to sit and listen to the two old friends, as they reminisced and shared confidences. It was nice to share in the warm, genuine friendship of these women so that Katya didn't feel she needed to contribute to the conversation, unless invited to.

"I am greatly troubled, Sofie," said the Signora with a sigh.

"Why, what is wrong?"

"That remark Carlo made, about keeping the business in the family."

"So?" said Sofie.

"My father would turn over in his grave if the business ended up in my aunt's side of the family. You see my father, with no help from any of the family, built the Renaldi Import business. When it became a success, my Mother and my Aunt wanted me to marry Carlo, so that the business would some day become his."

"I can understand that," said Sofie.

"However, I didn't love Carlo...and...I knew how much it had galled my father that no one would help him when he was starting out. But, when the business became a success, they all wanted to be a part of it."

She brushed some spilled sugar from the tablecloth. "Aleksy was a wonderful businessman, and Vincent would have been also, if...if," her voice trailed off.

Sofie reached across the table and patted the woman's hand to comfort her. "I know," she said. "I know."

"It will probably end up in the hands of Carlo the Son. Then, it will be the end of the Renaldi Shipping and Trading Company."

"Why do you say that?" said Sofie. "Surely that wouldn't happen."

"Yes, it will happen, if Carlo the Son gets control. He comes to work only because he must and because he thinks I will be impressed and since I have no heir, that I will leave it all to him." She threw her hands up in despair. "He is not a business man. He doesn't love what he is doing. When a new shipment comes in, he is bored. No excitement, no plans for expansion."

To Sofie she pleaded, "Come live with me. Let me teach you what I know. We can run the business together." She paused. "I am tired, Sofie. I am tired of doing it alone... trying to keep control alone. And...it makes me even more tired when I think that it could be for nothing. That someday Young Carlo will be a playboy on the efforts of my father and my husband.

Katya felt uneasy when she heard Lucia's plea for Sofie to live in Trieste. What did that mean? Would she leave Katya behind, if she did move to Trieste? What would become of her then, alone back at Vladezemla?

"Oh, my dear, Lucia, I wish I could have stayed when Vincent died. We could have been a family, you and I," said Sofie.

"We still can," said the Signora, wiping a tear from her eye. In my heart you have always been Vincent's wife."

The two women hugged one another and softly sobbed for the loss of Vincent and what might have been.

Katya felt she should not be watching something so personal taking place, so she quietly slipped away, went into the house, and climbed the marble stairs to her room. From the balcony she looked at the night sky and the glow of lights in the city. She loved it here. It was so beautiful, so peaceful. Then there was the sound of the sea. It soothed her. She could listen to it forever, she thought.

Below in the garden, a maid, very young, with straw colored hair and a gap toothed smile, dressed in a black skirt, black stockings, white blouse and a white bib apron, set a decanter of wine on the table. She also placed two crystal glasses before Lucia.

"That's all, Mia," said the Signora, "You can go home if you are finished."

"Gratzie," said the girl with a small curtsey.

"I meant what I said," continued the Signora. "I wish you would come live with me."

"I don't know," said Sofie thoughtfully, "I think it is too late. I am too old to change my life. Then there is my family…"

"I know you love your brother," said the Signora. "But he has a wife and a son. It is as if you are a guest in the house, even though it is partly yours. Isn't that so?"

"Oh, Lucia…I am too old…it is too late for me."

"It is never too late for a change, especially a change for the better." Lucia poured the wine for them both. "I have decided that I am leaving the house and everything in it, to you."

Sofie was speechless. She stammered, "But…I mean…why?"

"I told you…to me you are my daughter-in-law. You would have been married to Vincent, if the Priest hadn't dawdled when he was called." She waived her hand in the air dismissively. "He probably stopped to have an espresso or a wine and by the time he got here, it was the last rites he performed, instead of a marriage. What does it matter?" She slapped the table for emphasis. "In my heart you are Vincent's wife."

She looked out past Sofie, past the latticed terrace wall, out to the sea. "When you left here, I had hoped you were pregnant." The Signora saw the look of surprise on Sofie's face. "Oh come, Dear. You two were in love. It was natural that you would make love. I hoped that you might find yourself pregnant. I fantasized that your family would be disgraced and turn you out. Then, you would have come to me," she laughed ruefully, "then we would raise the child together and my little dynasty would continue. But…" She spread her hands out and shrugged her shoulders, "That's destiny."

Book II, Chapter 21

A contented Anton Vladislav was visiting with Father Ladra. The men sat outdoors in back of the priest's home, drinking coffee and sharing strudel. Anton was in his usual riding attire, today in his favorite maroon trousers and coat. The priest was dressed casually in a loose white peasant shirt with tiny embroidery around the neckline and sleeves, over loose brown pants. The sun was warm and comforting and the gentle breeze was fragrant with the scents from a nearby herb garden.

"Sofie and Katya went to Trieste for a week," said Anton. "They should be returning today."

"I cannot believe how happy Sofie was before they left for Trieste," he continued. "She is a different person since Katya has come to live with us." He sipped his coffee, sweet with sugar and milk.

"And, Ernesta," Lahdra asked, looking at his friend, his eyebrows raised in doubt. "You haven't said much about Ernesta."

Anton leaned back in his chair, made a face as if searching for the right words. "You know how Erna is about servants. I think she resents the girl being treated as a member of the family by Sofie. I'm afraid I'm just as guilty. I enjoy the girl's company."

After a moment's pause he said, "I can tell you Erna is not happy about the girl being in the house. I'm not sure if she dislikes Katya or is annoyed that Sofie didn't consult her before bringing the girl in."

Lahdra nodded his head in agreement.

"Did I tell you Stefan has been home? Yes, of course I told you. He is changed, too," said Anton.

"No, I didn't know," said Lahdra. "How has he changed?"

"Oh, well!" Anton smiled broadly. "Stefan has shown an interest in the workings of our holdings. Yes, I know it's hard to believe. He even asked me how many pigs we have. Can you believe that?" Anton shook his head in wonder, as if he couldn't believe it himself. "Then Stefan wanted to know how we pay each family for their work. He has never cared about money before or the working of the land. I must tell you, Lahdra, this new interest of his has shown me he has grown up. It is such a relief to see this new mature attitude of his. I must admit that for a very long time now, I've wondered who would take over should something happen to me." Anton took another bite of strudel.

Lahdra said, "I'm pleased things are going well for you. You've been in my prayers ever since the Balaban wedding." Then, he asked, "What is new with Ivan? He seemed very fond of Katya." He added, "Almost everyone likes the girl."

"That's another story," said Anton. "You know Ivan and Stefan have always had a rather strained relationship. Ivan came to visit Katya one day and it was a somewhat uncomfortable time."

"What do you mean?"

"Well, first of all, Ivan seemed upset by the new clothes Katya was wearing. She has taken to wearing the cosmopolitan dress of the city, rather than her peasant skirts. The clothes suit her and she looks wonderfully sophisticated in them. Her hair is pulled back in a very becoming manner, not long and loose. You could pass her by and not recognize her."

"Perhaps Ivan feels threatened by the changes," said the priest. "He may think she prefers a different kind of life...a life he can't give her."

"Do you think it's that serious?" Anton asked. "You're talking long term. I hadn't thought that far. But, you might be right. Ivan looked very sad when he left and he hasn't been back since."

Both men sat in silence. After a while, Anton said, "I have this strong need to know more about the Katya, for myself and for Sofie." Anton looked down at his boot and brushed off some dried mud. "That bracelet she wears is a mystery. Do you remember it?"

"No," said the priest. "What bracelet? What is the mystery?"

"Well," said Anton leaning forward, "it looks to be a very valuable bracelet. When anyone comments on it, she just pulls her sleeve over it and says nothing. "Someone said it was an amulet for protection."

"Sounds like witch talk to me, or Gypsy nonsense," said Lahdra, frowning. He had enough of village superstitions to fill a book. "Isn't she an herbalist? A healer of sorts, I heard?"

"She does know her poultices and teas." admitted Anton. "One of the men working in the barn, Yura, you know him." The priest nodded that he did know Yura, so Anton went on with his story. "Well, he scraped his leg badly on a nail. He did the usual, you know, cleaned it with his own urine, but it started to hurt and swell. When Katya heard of it, she went into the woods, came back with a basket full of twigs and leaves. Boiled the nasty smelling stuff, all the while disturbing Klara in the kitchen, then wrapped it over the wound. Two days later he was walking as if nothing had happened." Anton realized he was proud of Katya's accomplishment, "Klara was so impressed she let Katya make a poultice for that knee of hers, the one that aches from time to time."

The priest nodded. He found this fascinating.

"I so enjoy watching Sofie when she is with Katya," said Anton. "Sofie shines with happiness. She's a girl again, Lahdra." He leaned forward, his elbows resting on the table, "I find it fascinating comparing the two." He went on to explain, "For instance, their hands. They have the same small hands and delicate fingers. All of Sofie's clothes from her trousseau fit Katya with no alterations. Isn't that interesting?"

Later on his way home, Anton passed the Balaban farm and concerned about Ivan, he decided to stop for a visit.

Not far from the house shared by Vera and Marko, another structure was being built for Nikola and Luba, the newlyweds. Amid the pounding could be heard some swearing followed by good-natured laughter. With several men helping, the house would be completed in a few days. The workers were paid in food and drink along with the understanding that should any of them need help, it would be given.

The newlywed, Nikola, was straddling a beam on the roof when he spotted Anton. "Kum," he called, "did you bring a hammer?" This was followed by more laughter for everyone knew it was a joke, though Anton was known to pitch in from time to time.

"Why aren't you taking care of your beautiful bride?" called Anton to Nikola. "Wouldn't her company be more pleasant than an afternoon with these ruffians?"

More raucous laughter was followed by several comments on the duties of a new husband.

Spotting Ivan coming out of the barn, beyond the new structure, Anton gave the men a wave good-bye and called out to them to, "Hit the nails and not their thumbs."

The look on Ivan's face displeased Anton. Always in the past Ivan's face would light up when he saw his godfather. It always meant a new book or lively conversation, something Ivan looked forward to and enjoyed. But today the young man's face wore a frown. He greeted Anton politely, without a smile. Ivan put out his hand, "Zdravo, Kum. How are you?"

"I am fine, but you don't look so fine to me. Are you all right?"

Ivan answered the question with a shrug of his shoulders. He looked at Anton's face then nervously looked away. For a moment the two men stood in an uncomfortable silence. Anton said, "You seemed very upset when you left my house. Did you know that Sofie and Katya are returning today from Trieste?"

At the mention of her name, Ivan's head snapped towards Anton. He stared into the older man's eyes, shook his head slowly, as if to say, *what is the use*? Then, he looked away again. Ivan didn't want to say what was on his mind for fear of insulting his godfather. He felt it would offend Anton if Ivan told him how much he hated the change in Katya. He wanted the wild haired peasant girl, not the 'proper lady' Sofie was trying to make of her.

Feeling ill at ease, Anton said, "Ivan, my boy, I have known you since you were born. I would like to think you could say anything to me. I will respect your feelings and try to help if I can."

Ivan leaned against the side of the barn. He looked at his godfather nervously, and then his gaze fixed on something in the distance, not really seeing anything. It was evident he was struggling with himself trying to decide if he should speak what was on his mind. At last he said, "I don't know who she is anymore." There was pain in his voice. "She doesn't care if I come to visit or not. All Katya cares about is learning to read, learning to be a lady and dressing like a city woman. She has no time for me!"

Ivan's pain cut through Anton like a knife. He wanted desperately to help the young man, to take away the anguish he could see on the handsome face.

"Are you in love with Katya?"

Ivan kicked the ground with his toe. "I must be or I wouldn't be so miserable."

"Tell me, Ivan, have you told Katya how you feel?"

"How could I?" His voice bristled with anger. "Before I knew it, she was gone, up to your house with Teta Sofie. In one day later she was a different person. Then, she leaves for Trieste with Teta Sofie. That kind of a girl doesn't want a blacksmith's son for a companion."

Anton feared Ivan was right. In a brief time Katya's transformation was such that she seemed more suited to a drawing room than a peasant cottage. Anton felt sick. If Ivan had his birthright and lived in Anton's home instead of Marko's little cottage, Ivan would not feel inferior. There was nothing Anton could do...there was nothing he could think of to say.

At Vladezemlo in her room, Ernesta fluffed her pillows and draped them on the ledge of the open windows for airing. There had been a time when she would hold Anton's pillows to her face, breath in Anton's scent and been erotically affected by the smell. Now she mechanically plopped the pillows in the sunlight without a thought.

She never liked house cleaning, but it kept her occupied. For a time she fought it, but as time passed, she accepted that she was not living the life she had wished for. Ernesta dusted, made the bed and did some general tidying.

As she did her tasks she thought of Sofie and Katya's arrival sometime that day. This disappointed Ernesta, as she didn't miss them at all. In fact, she rather liked having the place almost to herself. Stefan was with his father most of the days, trying to learn all he could about managing the land, or so he told everyone. Ernesta found this change in him remarkable and somewhat doubtful. She wished it were true, but she knew her son too well to believe he suddenly lost interest in his 'life of pleasure' in Zagreb for the boredom of the country side.

Ernesta always very neat and precise was careful to put things back in their proper place. She noticed the secret drawer at the bottom of the cabinet, slightly open. This was unusual, for Ernesta always closed doors and drawers. Wondering when she had been so hurried that she would have left the secret drawer open, Ernesta started to push it closed. The slightly open door had the air of mystery or surprise, neither of which Ernesta liked. She never liked the unexpected. For her things had to be planned and details laid out. Ernesta knelt down and pulled the drawer out so she could look in it. This is where she kept her most private and valued possessions.

What she saw, or rather what she didn't see, made her heart pound. It felt as if it were knocking on her rib cage. The blue and gold box was nowhere in sight. Frantically she rummaged through the pictures and letters searching for the missing box for it held the amethyst and diamond earrings her mother had given Ernesta as a gift on her wedding to Anton. Her mother had always worn the earrings on the most festive occasions. The earrings were gold, each with a rose cut diamond from which hung an amethyst as large as Ernesta's thumbnail. Ernesta let out a sob. The earrings had been her most prized possessions.

These were the earrings her mother had worn to a ball in Vienna when her father was an officer in the Austrian Cavalry. Her mother told her that once Franz Joseph himself looked at her and smiled.

Oh, how Ernesta used to dream of wearing them to the opera or the theater or even to some foreign royal court. The only time had she worn them was on her wedding day. Marriage to Anton didn't bring the glittering social life she had expected and now the earrings were gone! It didn't matter that she had no occasion to wear them. They represented her dreams, her lost dreams.

"Oh Stefan..." she cried, grief overtaking her, "how could you do this to me?"

She knew he had come home for a reason. Stefan was in trouble and she knew it. He was being too polite, too attentive, too interested in everything and everyone. She had known something was wrong, so why hadn't she asked him about it? She knew why she hadn't asked. It was because she had hoped he had become a man and would find his own solutions to his problems. Well, it looked as if he found a solution...stealing her precious earrings.

She cried for a long time. It was broken hearted sobbing, the sobs of defeat. He was HER son. She had dreamed of the day when Stefan would inherit the land. Then Ernesta hoped to live the way she had wanted to. She would entertain officials and dignitaries and travel to foreign lands. Her house would be full of servants and she would never make a bed again.

Ashes...her dreams were ashes, blown away by the winds of disappointment. Like everyone else in this house, Stefan had betrayed her.

Klara seldom went up to the bedrooms. Her legs ached often, especially in cold or damp weather. Today each step was a cruel reminder that she was getting older. Klara hated getting older. It made her angry that she was no longer a young woman. There were days when all she did was dwell in self-pity, sorry that she had not married and had children. Sorry she never knew the love of a man or held a child to her breast. Sorry that she was foolish enough to think Anton and Sofie were family enough for her.

The first room she looked into was Stefan's which she found empty. Next, she saw that Anton's room was in order with the pillows airing at the window.

The sight in Ernesta's room was unsettling. Ernesta was seated in a rocker, the chair moving in rhythm like a metronome, a riding crop across her lap.

Moving closer to the chair Klara could see something was wrong with Ernesta. Rocking back and forth, Ernesta seemed in a trance, her eyes were open, but she saw nothing.

"Erna, Ernesta," said Klara, "are you alright?" When Ernesta didn't answer, Klara cautiously reached out and touched the woman's shoulder. Getting no response, Klara gently poked, not daring to shake. Without moving her head, Ernesta eerily shifted her eyes upward at Klara and stared at the servant for a moment, then slowly lowered her eyes again. Frightened by what she saw Klara slowly backed away. She preferred the sarcastic, rude Ernesta to this stone-like sphinx. At that moment Klara would have been happy to hear one of Ernesta's caustic remarks with which she could make her exit. Instead Klara backed out of the room, never taking her eyes from the frightening figure of Ernesta rocking to and fro. Klara hadn't seen Ernesta with a riding crop since her earlier days as a young bride, when she and Anton still enjoyed each other's company. *Was Ernesta thinking of riding?* Klara felt a cold shiver of doom run through her as she painfully descended the stairs for the refuge of her kitchen.

Book II, Chapter 22

Stefan would have preferred to ride in a carriage all the way to Zagreb, it would have been more comfortable and look a bit more elegant. Instead he urged his horse onward with his heels.

The seven days Stefan had to raise the money for his gambling debt went by rapidly. Stefan watched each sunrise and sunset with uneasiness for time seemed to condense, to diminish and disappear. Where had the morning gone? Was it already evening? Even the nights of tossing and turning, worrying about money, should have seemed endless, but no, the cock crowed too soon marking off another day.

Stefan never got around to asking his mother for the money with which to clear his debt. He just couldn't do it. He had siphoned so much money from all of his family for frivolities that now when he really needed bailing out, he found himself unable to ask for more. Worse, he feared the family might disown him. The thought had never occurred to him before, but recent events led him to believe that being the only son was no longer a position of power. There were the Balaban boys, Ivan and Nikola, who were great favorites of his father, receiving portions of land as wedding gifts and God only knows what else. And Sofie had a new companion whom she absolutely adored. Stefan could see the affection in his aunt's face whenever his aunt looked at the girl. Granted the girl was a beauty, but who was she, really? There was no denying that it unsettled him to realize he was no longer Sofie's pet.

Being certain he had somehow forfeited his place as family favorite, he was afraid to tell his mother how much money he needed. With remorse, he realized he had squandered his time at school and had done nothing to instill parental pride. His mother was his last ally, and he feared he might have lost her loyalty. He dreaded the thought of seeing any disappointment reflected in her eyes or possible rejection if he let her know how foolish and reckless he had been by his excessive gambling.

Stefan had really planned to steal Katya's unusual bracelet. He thought about it. But, when she and Sofie left for Trieste the opportunity was gone.

Stefan remembered playing in his mother's secret drawer as a little boy. She would show him her souvenirs along with the amethyst and diamond earrings that had belonged to his grandmother. His mother would never miss the earrings...it wasn't as if they were her favorites, he reasoned. He could never remember seeing her wear them. Wouldn't she have worn the earrings if they were important to her? So, Stefan took the blue and gold box certain his mother would never miss them and satisfied they were not important to her.

Today was the eighth day. Stefan had the earrings, and once he gave them to Magda, it would be over. What if Magda wasn't there and he had to see her partner? Stefan shuddered at the thought of Madga's large, dark and intimidating partner.

So lost in his thoughts was Stefan, that he hadn't noticed an approaching rider until they nearly passed one another.

Stefan saw the fez. Surely his eyes were playing tricks on him. But no! He recognized the solid figure looming before him as that of Magda's sinister business partner, wearing a menacing smile on those thick lips.

A long time later, as Stefan rode back through the gates of his father's estate, he was still very shaken by his encounter with the frightening Turk. Stefan was used to polite respect and deferential treatment, not the rude, threatening encounter he experienced at the hands of Magda's new partner.

Stefan had tried to hide his surprise upon seeing the Turk and smiled affably, greeting him in a friendly manner. "Hello, my friend," he had said, "I was on my way to Zagreb to pay my debt." Nervously he added, "How kind of you to save me the trouble of traveling all the way."

The Turk only smiled, not a friendly warm smile, but a cruel twisted grin that made Stefan uneasy.

Both men were still on horseback. The Turk made no move to dismount, nor did he return Stefan's greeting. Stefan's uneasiness grew and he found himself talking rapidly.

"I'm sure what I have here is more than enough to cover my debt." He offered the box to the Turk, who was slow in taking it. "It's very valuable, been in my family for a very long time." Still the Turk said nothing, only examined the earrings, holding them up to the light. "You see the diamonds are very clear and the amethyst color very deep." Stefan realized he was sounding like a street-seller, verbally enhancing his wares, so he forced himself to be silent.

After an uncomfortably long time, while Stefan could feel the perspiration on his forehead but dared not wipe it away for fear of drawing attention to his nervousness, the Turk deposited Ernesta's treasures in his pocket. To Stefan's relief the Turk turned his horse to head back towards Zagreb.

"These earrings," the Turk patted his pocket, "would have been enough to handle your debt had you brought them to me yesterday."

Stefan's mouth fell open. "But..." he started to protest.

The Turk interrupted, "Since it is the eighth day and I had to come looking for you, you still owe me the same amount...again." It pleased him to see the look of shock on Stefan's face. How he disliked these spoiled rich boys, who wasted time and squandered money. Young men like Stefan wouldn't make it one week on the streets, not the way Abuh had to fight and scrape from the time he was nine years old and alone. Oh, what pleasure he got from toying with the likes of Stefan! "So my young friend," there was that awful smile, more of a smirk, "I shall give you another seven days...or the debt doubles again."

Stefan was sick. He wanted to throw up, but didn't dare show his feelings. He couldn't speak, couldn't protest or bargain. He just didn't know how to deal with someone like this.

The Turk didn't bother to say good-bye, just urged his horse on. Stefan heard laughter as the man in the black fez slowly rode away towards Zagreb.

It was well past noon and the sun was hot when Stefan, home once more, gave his horse to a stable hand. Stefan never used the kitchen door to enter the house, the way Sofie and his Father did. But today, without thinking, he went through the kitchen door to find Klara at the table sipping tea. She didn't get up, only said, "Your father isn't home and Sofie is not back from Trieste yet." Her voice was low and sounded strange.

Stefan couldn't understand why he was getting this report on the whereabouts of the family. Klara continued, "Your mother is up in her room. There is something wrong. I don't know what, maybe a stroke of some kind."

"What are you saying?" Stefan didn't understand.

"Go see for yourself." said Klara, sadly.

Stefan flew past Klara who didn't rise to follow. The old servant didn't want to see Ernesta that way, with strange staring eyes that didn't seem to see, and the whip in her lap, something she hadn't touched in fifteen years or more. No, Klara didn't like what she had seen. *It is an omen.* She thought. *There are more bad things to come.*

"Boze Moj...My God," she said almost as a prayer.

Stefan mounted the stairs two, three at a time. He paused at the open door leading to his mother's room. "Please, God, let her be alright." Ernesta was the only person he could count on. Even if he hadn't told her about the debt, she was his closest ally in the family. She had to be alright. His handsome face was twisted with the strain and fear he felt. "Mamitza," he said it softly trying not to sound as fearful as he was. He could see his mother's profile move back and forth as she rocked in her chair, the riding crop still across her lap. "Mamitza?" He moved closer with more urgency in his voice. She never moved. Cautiously Stefan stood in front of her, not sure if she could hear him.

He was directly in front of his mother and she never looked up. Ernesta rocked and stared right through him at the window as if waiting for someone. Stefan felt a coldness grip his chest, as if his heart had turned to ice. He reached out and very gently touched her shoulder, as if she were made of glass. She didn't seem to see him or feel his touch. He knelt right in front of her and looked into her eyes and for the second time that day felt sick. It was as if his mother was gone. The eyes were vacant. In a very low, pleading voice Stefan said, "Oh, Mamitza! Please, please answer me. Look at me!" Stefan waited for a response and when none came he exclaimed, "Oh Christ, now what will happen to me?"

In his panic, he leapt to his feet glancing around the room assessing the value of things he might use to pay off the Turk. He picked up the double frame holding his grandparent's likenesses. He soon decided the frame was ornate brass and not the gold he had hoped for. Perhaps she had some gold coins or other money stashed in her room. He looked in the cabinet of the bedside table and only found a chamber pot. He didn't bother to go through the wardrobe again, for that was where he had found the earrings and he already knew what was in there. A small dressing table had three narrow drawers where he found gloves, babushkas, laces, but no coins.

Stefan ran his fingers through his thick, dark hair. He could feel his heart pounding in his head and even in his hands. He had to get out of the room. He needed to think and his brain didn't seem to be working.

That was when the first blow came. He didn't see Ernesta rise from her rocker. The riding crop, held high above her head, came swiftly smashing onto his back as he pondered what to do next, where to find some money. The blow startled him and sent him flying into the wall, where he tried to turn around, only to feel more stinging blows. Each strike of the crop seemed to come faster and harder than the one before. He covered his face with his arms and screamed, "What is the matter with you? What are you doing?"

Ernesta said nothing. She just kept whipping her only son, her beloved Stefan who had betrayed her.

Stefan managed to escape the raining blows, now accompanied by curses. He escaped running past a horrified Sofie who upon her arrival home had been sent upstairs by Klara. The sight of Ernesta beating Stefan left her speechless. Had Ernesta lost her mind? Was she insane?

Ernesta stood facing the doorway, her face dark with anger. She only stared at Sofie, who backed away slowly, feeling along the wall with her hand until she felt the stair rail. Sofie's body was trembling as she stumbled, almost falling down the stairs in the hopes of finding Anton.

Stefan was trembling also. He now stood outside the house, his body stinging from the whip lashing. His teeth chattered although he was standing in the warm afternoon sun. For a moment he turned in a circle, not sure where to go, where he could be alone to think. Too many emotions were whirling about within him. He needed to think. He was frightened...*really frightened.* He was afraid his mother had gone mad and he was frightened of Magda's sinister partner. What would the Turk do? Come to the house and confront Stefan's father? Beat up Stefan? Maybe kill him?

When Sofie and Katya had returned from Trieste, Katya did not go into the house. Instead she went to the chapel. She had to think. Think about the offer Signora Lucia had made to Sofie. What if Sofie went to Trieste and left her on her own? Would Sofie leave her?

Not knowing someone was in the chapel, Stefan went inside. He didn't kneel or sit down, for he was too nervous. He paced back and forth, muttering things like, "Dear God, what am I to do?" and then as a prayer, "Please do something with my mother." He shuddered again when he remembered the wild woman his mother had become.

Now what was he going to do? His mother had been his only hope. He should have talked to her before she went mad. *Madness...is it curable?* He wondered. *How long would it take?* Too long, he decided. He had no way out. Maybe he could go to England or America. That plan didn't appeal to him. What would he do in those countries? He wasn't skilled at any profession. All his life he had assumed he would take over his father's lands.

He was staring up at the crucifix of the tortured Jesus, wondering if the Turk had ever murdered anyone.

He had no choice, but to tell his father everything and take whatever anger his father would drop on him. After the horsewhipping his mother had given him, Anton surely couldn't do worse. What if Ernesta had told Anton that their son had stolen her earrings? Stefan would deny it. There was no way they would know he had taken them. With his mother in such a strange state, verging on insanity, his father might be a little more vulnerable, more forgiving. That was it! He would tell his father about the debt and hope for the best, and hope his father wouldn't resort to whipping him. Though for the money, he would take a beating. What if his father disowned him? Stefan pushed that thought out of his mind.

Lost in his thoughts, he still hadn't noticed that he was not alone in the chapel.

Stefan caught his breath when he saw Katya looking at him. This was too good to be true. No one was around. They were alone! The bracelet! Maybe he could slip the bracelet off her wrist without her knowing it. Then he wouldn't have to tell his father anything. It was too wonderful. His prayers, however poor they may have been, were being answered. He nearly laughed out loud.

"Hello, Katya, I'm sorry, I'm so sorry. I didn't mean to intrude in your prayers."

"That's alright," Katya said, smiling as she looked up at him. "I was really only sitting here and thinking."

"May I sit with you?" he asked, smiling charmingly.

"Of course," she said, moving to make room for him.

He looked at her wrist and saw the bracelet peeking out from under the sleeve of her blue cotton travel dress. "I see you are still wearing the mysterious bracelet," he said.

Katya glanced down at it. As always, she started to hide it, but Stefan stopped her. "May I see it? It is so unusual."

She raised her hand for him to better see it. She was so naive that he wanted to laugh. He looked at the circles and half moons and stars, all set with stones he was sure were real. Wanting to see how the clasp worked, he said, "Could you take it off, so that I can get a better look?"

"Oh, I never take it off." She was running her fingers over the bracelet. "It protects me." She dropped her arm to her side and pulled her dress sleeve down over the bracelet, back to its hiding place.

His chance to get the bracelet was gone. He would have to continue to be friendly with her until he got another chance to take it.

She was exceptionally pretty for a peasant. It wouldn't be too hard for him to be kind to her. Also, it would please his aunt and father if he spent some time with Katya, maybe helping with her studies.

"Come," he said, "let's go out in the sunlight, it's a bit damp in here."

It had taken Anton a long time to convince Ivan that he should come to welcome Sofie and Katya home from their trip to

Trieste. This time Ivan was to let her know of his feelings for her
and to see what her feelings for him might be.

When Anton reached his inner yard at Vladezemla, with Ivan
riding alongside him, he wished he had minded his own business.

An already unhappy Ivan saw Katya walking with Stefan.
She was dressed in a blue dress, her arm through Stefan's and she
was laughing. Seeing Katya looking so pleased and happy with
Stefan, Ivan turned his horse around and without a word to Anton
headed out the gate to the road and home.

Ivan swore to himself that he would never return.

Anton stared at the figure of Ivan on horseback riding away
and he was sickened. He wanted so much to do something for
Ivan, to make him happy, but he had failed miserably.

"Anton! Anton!" Sofie came running from the house,
stumbling and motioning to him. He jumped from his horse and
hurried towards his almost hysterical sister. Stefan and Katya
reached Sofie about the same time as Anton.

"My God, she has gone mad!" Sofie sobbed falling into her
brother's arms. "I'm terrified of her." Noticing Stefan, Sofie said,
"Tell your father. Tell him how she whipped you." Grabbing
Stefan's hand she held it in front of Anton's face, so he could see
the red welts. Katya's eyes grew wide at the bruised hands she
hadn't noticed in the chapel.

This couldn't be. Ernesta adored Stefan more than her own
life, or so Anton had always thought.

Katya stayed down in the kitchen with Klara, while Anton,
Sofie and Stefan went up to Ernesta's room. They found her sitting
in her rocker, whip across her lap.

Anton and Stefan approached Ernesta with caution while
Sofie stayed in the safety of the doorway. Stefan stood
apprehensively behind his father, just in case another barrage with
the whip came.

With a gentle voice no one had heard before, Anton said,
"Erna...Erna, tell me what's the matter." When she didn't
acknowledge his presence he took her hand.

"Be careful!" Sofie warned, "She may attack you the way she
did Stefan."

It was very sad to see someone who had been so willful and
strong, so vocal with her thoughts, sit there as if she were empty of

all thoughts and feelings. Anton knelt before her, still holding her hand. "Erna...did something happen to you? Please tell me." He spoke softly, soothingly. "Is there anything I can do for you? Tell me and I will do it."

The three waited for a response. All they heard was the chirping of birds and the whinny of horse through an open window. A fly buzzed by and landed on Ernesta's face. When she made no move to shoo it away, Anton did it for her.

Sofie cautiously moved a couple of steps into the room. "Tell your father how she beat you and swore at you," she urged. "Tell him."

Not sure what had brought on his mother's anger and not wanting to revive it, Stefan said, "Oh, it wasn't that bad."

"You don't have to be brave," said Sofie to Stefan. "Your father must know how bad it was. He has to know!"

"Son," said Anton, still kneeling on the floor before Ernesta and not looking up, "send for a doctor or go yourself. And Sofie, tell Klara I will take my meals here with Ernesta. I don't want to leave her."

When Stefan and his aunt were gone, Anton took both Ernesta's hands in his. "Erna, I am going into my room just for a moment. I want to take off my boots and this dusty jacket. I'll be right there, just in my room. When I come back, I'll bring a chair and a book and I'll read to you, if you wish." He looked into her eyes and thought he saw a flicker of recognition and it encouraged him. "I'll draw the drape open so you can hear me and know I am near. I'll only be a moment. Then I'll stay with you for as long as you need me."

Ernesta heard the drape separating their sleeping quarters being drawn aside. She heard his boots hit the floor and the sounds of him moving about his room. For years Ernesta had fought, yelled, threatened, used sarcasm, and any other weapon she could think of to get her way. Nothing had worked...until now. She found her silence to be very controlling. A tiny smile played on her lips. *Why hadn't she thought of this before?*

Book II, Chapter 23

It was a beautiful day, ripe with floral scented breezes mingled with the aroma of roasting meat. A warm sun shone from a cloudless blue sky, none of which Ivan noticed. He was in a dark mood as he rode over the fields, not really seeing where he was going, for he was so lost in his thoughts. He never should have told his mother he was thinking of going to America. It wasn't really a decision, just a thought. He wanted to hurt someone, as if it might release some of his own pain, so he said what he knew would wound Vera. Now he was sorry for lashing out at his sweet Mother.

If only he could rid his mind of Katya. Thoughts of her were never really gone for any length of time. The memory of her would weave in and out like tight fabric in his brain until he couldn't think of anything else. He knew that when he said he would go to America, it wasn't the answer. He saw Katya everywhere, even when she wasn't present. His mind had taken to playing tricks on him. Looking across a field he thought he saw her walking in the distance, her red hair gleaming in the sunlight. When he looked again, it would be only a dog, hunting in the fields or a large bird taking flight.

He was angry with everyone. He was angry with his brother for being so happy with his child-bride, Luba. He was angry with his mother and father for having the pained looks parents get when they can't make something right, but wish they could. Most of all he was angry with cousin Milan for bringing Katya into his life. He was angry with Stefan for being near Katya each day. He was angry with his godfather, Anton, for allowing Katya in his home. He was angry with Katya for leaving him and becoming someone he didn't know. And finally, he was angry with himself for not being able to erase her from his mind. She haunted his every waking moment and then invaded his dreams at night.

At that very moment while riding he thought he saw her in the forest, picking up twigs. He urged his horse closer. Instead of Katya, he found a young Gypsy girl alone gathering twigs for a fire. Her hair was black, not red. His mind was still playing tricks.

The girl recognized him, "So, it is the Scholar. How are you Ivan?"

"Is that you, Roha?" He recognized the pretty girl who was to marry the Gypsy Queen's grandson, Zoltan.

"Yes, Scholar, I am Roha." She gave him a warm flirty smile. "Come to the camp. It is near and everyone will be happy to see you." She watched as he dismounted and said, "Where is your book…in the saddle bag?"

"I don't have a book with me. I was only out for a ride."

"I have seen you every year since I was a little girl and you a little boy. This is the first time I see you without a book." She was barefooted, wearing a red skirt and blouse and in her ears, gold earrings glinted in the sunlight. "Does it mean you have learned all there is to know?"

"Of course not," he said. If he had not been so troubled he would have laughed, instead he walked without any more conversation. Roha looked up at him with her dark, Gypsy eyes and sensing he was troubled didn't say anything more on the way to the camp.

There were many wagons, more than when Katya had been to their temporary camp when escaping Selna. The Gypsies were gathering for their annual trip across Italy to France.

Each May the Gypsies made a pilgrimage to Saintes Maries de la Mer in the south of France to honor Sara the Black, a servant girl they consider their Patron Saint. The story told is that in the year 42 A.D., Sara was the Egyptian servant of the sisters of the Blessed Virgin Mary, who were Saint Mary Salome and Saint Mary Jacob. The three women had drifted from the Holy Land in a small boat with no oars or sails until they safely landed along the southern coast of France to the Ile de la Camargue. Candles are lit at the statue of Sara where a procession is attended by the more pious Gypsies, while others only come to enjoy the two-day feasting.

Now Roha's tribe waited for others to join them, as they continued their journey to France, only stopping when necessary to earn money or to rest.

"Ivan! Ivan!" An excited Zolton came running towards the handsome fair-skinned man. He wrapped his arms around Ivan's shoulders, giving his friend an embrace. "How wonderful it is to see you. Did you know we were here?"

"No, I was out riding when I saw Roha," said Ivan.

"Come, we must see my Grandmother," said Zolton. He led Ivan toward the wagons, while Roha walked behind with the kindling in her arms.

It was a large encampment with many caravans. Horses and goats grazed lazily together, while dogs were tied in the shade of the rolling homes.

A street performer the day before, now a prisoner in a cage, a monkey patiently waited to be fed. Several small fires were tended by sultry looking women, while dark men with sullen faces watched Ivan and Zolton arm in arm walk toward Valina's brightly painted home on wheels. The suspicious looks changed to smiles when the men recognized Ivan and waved to him. Ivan returned the waves as he and Zolton walked through the trampled grass. Almost naked children ran and played among the wagons, while men fashioned wooden bowels and troughs out of cut-up tree trunks, to be sold later in their travels. These people were experts at living in the open. The whole country was their home, with free grass for their horses and water from any stream to drink and fish to catch. Clever and cunning, dressed in rags, a Gypsy might have hidden gold sewn in his clothing. The gold wasn't always real. Sometimes it was an alloy with which to fool the buyer.

Now, the Gypsies were carefree, but in less than twenty-five years many Gypsies would be herded into concentration camps. Then...in less than fifty years, there would be parts of Europe where the wandering Gypsy would be forced to give up his free life to settle in one place. From the time Ivan was a small boy his father permitted the Gypsies to camp on his land. Ivan, caught up in his worries, had forgotten that it was time for their annual pilgrimage. Each year the Gypsies came to the large field near Marko and Vera's house, where they told fortunes, offered to make repairs, or sell and trade items they had gathered in their travels. Ivan had heard all the stories of Gypsies stealing babies and livestock, and of cheating people. But Ivan and his family never had such an experience. The Gypsies were grateful to have a place to stay without fear of being run off, beaten or jailed, so they never harmed the Balich's or anyone else in the vicinity. Occasionally a chicken might disappear or a gold ring might turn a buyer's finger green.

Ivan's father Marko was a superstitious man, as were most of the peasants, and he considered the Gypsies 'Good Luck' for him. It had been only two or three days after Vera had come to live in Marko's little one room home, that the Gypsies first came. That time Marko let them stay on his land more out of fear than kindness. He was afraid they would steal from him or harm him or worse, put a curse on him. Marko had heard that the old, ugly, Gypsy women were really witches able to cast powerful spells, such as turning women into cats. He had heard long ago of the village of cat people in Serbia and often wondered if the story was true.

The Queen of the Gypsies herself told his and Vera's fortune. She promised them 'A lifetime of love and contentment. Children will make you proud and friends shall always love and admire you.' It was the usual kind of fortune, but Valina who really had the 'gift' felt there was truth in what she told them. At that time, Valina had seen the unhappiness in young Vera's eyes and she suspected the girl was pregnant. Most of all, she saw the look of love in Marko's face and felt all would be well for these two. She also sensed they had just met and were only beginning to know one another.

So, when Vera turned to Marko for love and gave him a son, and Anton was generous in so many ways, Marko saw the Gypsy's prophecy as true. From that year on, the Gypsies were welcome to camp whenever they came through on their travels.

Now on this warm day, Valina was seated on the steps, which could be pulled up to disappear into the caravan. She watched as her grandson, the pretty Roha, and the sad-faced Ivan came towards her. Her talent for reading faces immediately assessed that Ivan was deeply troubled. At his age what could it be? If his parents were well, then it had to be of a romantic nature, after all he was young and healthy with normal passions. Fortune telling wasn't so hard. One just had to know human nature and the usual human disappointments. As the trio drew nearer, Valina became aware of Ivan's aura. The dark shadow out-lining Ivan's body meant he was in trouble. Someone meant him harm and the darkness indicated that the trouble was already manifesting. She felt a grandmotherly concern for Ivan. After all she knew him from the time he was a baby and watched him grow into a fine, young man.

"Come give me a hug," she said, descending the short steps to the grass below her red and yellow painted doorway. "Ivan, this is such a surprise. We were planning on coming to your home as soon as two more families join us."

"Grandmother," Ivan said, bowing his head in respect.

Ivan was genuinely happy to see the old woman. It was a wonder to him that she never seemed to grow older or that her looks never changed. To Ivan she looked the same year after year, her eyes bright, her hair black had only touches of gray, and her skin was smooth. This was unusual for most Gypsies looked older than their years, the result of living a hard life outdoors.

Ivan gave her a hug and a kiss on each cheek, stepping back waiting for her to look into his hand to predict the future, for she always did that when they met, but not this time. Instead Valina said, "Come, Ivan, let's walk."

Zolton and Roha stood in silent surprise, as Valina led Ivan away from her caravan, past the fire with the roasting hedge hogs and away from anyone who might hear them. They walked not speaking, side-by-side, through ankle high grass dotted with fragrant purple violets. When Valina was sure of their privacy, she sat on a fallen tree trunk. She motioned for Ivan to sit next to her.

"Now you must tell me how your parents are," she said this as she studied his face intently, to determine if what he was to say would be the truth or not.

"They are well," he said, wondering why they had to come away from the camp for this conversation.

"And, your Mother…anything troubling her?" Valina's eyes studied Ivan's face. He hesitated a moment before answering. Only a moment, but it told Valina there was something wrong.

Ivan was ready to say, 'No, not at all.' But, he knew Valina too well to keep the truth from her. She always seemed to know what was or what would be. He didn't dare risk their friendship with a lie.

He looked away from her to the tree line beyond where they sat. "I've upset my mother very much." His voice was low, ashamed. "I wanted to hurt her, so I told her I was going to America." He avoided looking at Valina, but could feel her black eyes on him, hot, like burning coals.

"Are you really going to America?"

"No, yes...no, I don't know!" He kicked at a pebble hoping she would take her eyes from his face, but the kick didn't distract her. After an uncomfortable silence, he turned to look into her round, dark face and into those black eyes that could see what wasn't there. "I have to go somewhere...anywhere. I must get away from here."

"What have you done that you must run away? You are not a criminal who must hide."

Now, she took his hand and turned it palm up. She drew it close to her face and studied the lines. His hand had always interested her. It showed so much that was not evident in his life. There was wealth, yet his family was not wealthy. Fame was there in his lines. That could come later, perhaps when he was older. From the time he was a little boy, conflict was evident in his hand. Valina traced the conflict line...deeper now with two menacing lines crossing it. Her finger moved to the love line...had it been broken before? She couldn't remember. The travel line was long and deep. Yes, he would break his mother's heart by going away.

As she closed his hand, Valina thought she saw death. Had she really seen it in his hand, or had it been a premonition?

Valina looked up from his hand and saw the red-haired girl...the girl Zolton found in the orchard only a short time ago. There! On the ground before her! She saw Katya lying with blood on her forehead and her fiery hair billowing around her head in the grass. Katya was wearing a brightly embroidered blouse and skirt. Her feet were bare.

In an instant the vision was gone.

In Zagreb, Mustafa, a Gypsy stood on the busy street on market day, watching his wife and daughter across the street, where they were selling bouquets of violets and hand-made twig baskets to the shoppers.

Mustafa and his wife, Gulja were very dark-skinned Gypsies, their features very Indian and not softened by the mixture of European blood. Their seven-year-old daughter, Fikria could have

stepped out of a page of the Arabian Nights, for she was as
beautiful as her parents were plain. Fikria always sold all her
flowers, because buyers would want to stop and admire her
mysteriously dark beauty as they paid for the tiny bunches of
violets held together with coarse string.

Mustafa wore brown trousers and a once white shirt, now
dirty with sweat and dust. His leather vest was old, trimmed with
coins from Persia. His shoes were leather sandals. Gulja and Fikria
were both barefooted and dressed in faded skirts and blouses. Both
mother and daughter wore purple shawls over their heads,
obviously new acquisitions for they were much cleaner than the
rest of their clothing.

From behind Mustafa a man asked, "What have you found on
your travels that I might want?"

Turning to face the speaker, Mustafa said, "How are you, my
friend?" He shook hands with the man who wore a black fez and
was dressed in black pants, a white clean shirt and a black vest, as
always from his waist hung a heavy pouch. Mustafa's eyes sought
the bag of coins.

"I have nothing of any value this time," said Mustafa,
disappointed that none of the coins in the pouch would be his
today.

"You wouldn't sell to someone else before offering to me
first, would you?" The Turk studied the Gypsy's face.

"No! You are most fair. I will have something for you when
we return from France." Mustafa tried to sound convincing, but he
never knew what he would come upon or what he could get.

The Turk wasn't looking at Mustafa as he spoke, but at the
pretty Fikria. "I am going to need some help in a day or so. I know
you camp near the Vladislav land, and I have some unfinished
business with his son." He looked away from the pretty daughter
to Mustafa, "I would like for you to come with me. I will pay you
for your time...and who knows what else might develop?"

Mustafa grinned at the prospect of making some money,
showing a gap between his uneven teeth. He liked the Turk.
Mustafa and the Turk understood each other. They were survivors.
There had been many dealings between the two men, no questions
asked, no explanations made, just a deal or a trade. It didn't matter

what, as long as each man felt he had profited from the transaction.

"Yes," said Mustafa, "I will go with you. Where shall we meet?"

"I will find you at the camp near the Vladislav home, watch for me. I think I should be there day after tomorrow." Then, he looked at Mustafa's pretty daughter again.

"Your daughter is very beautiful," he said.

Mustafa smiled proudly. "I have already been given offers to buy her as a bride, many offers." he added.

"I should like to make an offer," said the Turk.

Mustafa's smile faded, as he looked at his prize, his treasure, his beloved daughter. He knew the Turk didn't want Fikria as his bride.

Book II, Chapter 24

The last few days were tortuous for usually happy Vera Balaban. Ivan was in a melancholy mood and it made both his parents uneasy. No subtle questioning could draw from him the cause for the dark cloud that hung over the usually happy household. They all felt he was pining over Katya. Even the brotherly joking of Nikola couldn't brighten Ivan's brooding continence. Meals were eaten in an uncomfortable silence when Ivan was there. When he didn't join his parents for dinner, Marko and Vera, burdened with worry, had little appetite. Gone was the joking or the laughing and animated conversations. Ivan would disappear for hours on his horse, returning with the beast lathered. When he wasn't trying to break his neck on horseback, Ivan would go into the woods for hours at a time. Going into the woods wasn't that unusual for Ivan, but going without a book was.

Ivan's handsome face had become thinner with dark circles under his eyes giving him a haunted look. Vera wanted to blame his mood and his loss of appetite on illness, but in her heart she knew better. She knew it had something to do with the elusive Katya. Vera and Marko had not seen Katya or Aunt Sofie since the girl went to live in the large house. They heard that Sofie and Katya took a trip to Trieste.

Vera remembered how happy Ivan had been with Katya. The couple had danced together, laughed and gone for walks, and looked like a couple falling in love. Vera had been so pleased for she wanted her son to be in love...to know the joy of sharing and becoming one with another person. To have that one special person who was meant only for you and no one else. When she had such romantic thoughts it was Marko she was thinking of, not Anton. She had been able to exorcise the handsome Anton from her heart many years ago. The passion she once had for him was replaced by the solid, sweet love she had for Marko. Since that fateful night twenty-one years ago when Vera went to the Vladislav house on the night of Anton and Ernesta's engagement party, Vera never returned there. Marko never encouraged her. He just let it be.

That's why *this* journey was a momentous occasion. Vera, with a babushka covering her light brown hair, walked purposefully across the fields in the direction of Anton's property. She had waited until Marko went into the shed to do some blacksmithing before she headed out. For twenty years her plan had been to die an old woman without ever returning to the house where she had known such stinging humiliation. And she wouldn't be going there now, if Ivan had not said, "I'm going away. I want to get as far away from here as I can."

The words had been a knife in Vera's heart. She had always hoped Ivan would build a house nearby as Nikola had. Vera thought her life would be full with daughters-in-laws and grandchildren.

Vera stopped walking to catch her breath. It pained her to breathe for she wasn't used to walking so far. The shortcut she chose was uphill and strenuous. Vera bent over to ease the tightness she was feeling in her chest. She decided to sit on the grass for a moment. In her desire to hurry she had been running up the slope instead of walking.

From her vantage point she could see a group of women doing their laundry at a stream situated at the foot of the hill. She watched as a woman expertly wet a piece of clothing, rubbed it with a bar of lard soap and then beat the soapy article on the rocks. When the woman was satisfied she had beaten all the dirt out, she rinsed it in the stream. She took one end of whatever she had been washing, while a companion took the other, then twisting in opposite directions, the women would wring as much water as possible from it. Shirts and blouses were small enough to drape over a bush to dry, while tablecloths and sheets were spread out on the soft grass. Vera had no idea how long she had been sitting there watching the barefooted women, all with babushkas on their heads and skirts hiked up above their knees to keep the fabric dry. A woman approached the stream, gracefully balancing a full laundry basket on her head.

As Vera sat there, Ivan's words came back to her. She remembered how she had felt his hurt and anger as he said, "I want to go far away from here. I want to go to America."

America! Dear God, not America! Vera knew of too many men who left their families for America. Some kept in touch, others disappeared for whatever reasons.

It was easy to get lost in America. Vera felt sick. As a mother she had to do something for her child. He needed her help now as much as he had when he was a toddler reaching for something that could burn him or worse.

From the day her sons were born Vera had protected them and even now that they were adults, she couldn't stop.

Her love of family was so strong she would easily die for Marko, Ivan or Nikola if she must. She had been blessed since the night Marko came to the chapel, taking her, numb as she was with shame to his little home.

Vera got up from her resting place not bothering to shake out her skirts and resumed her ascent.

All the land stretching before her belonged to the Vladislavs. A wall made up of stacked fieldstones surrounded the house, barn and chapel. Vera didn't bother going to the main entrance where the gate was, instead she sat on the low wall and swung her legs over. Taking short cuts through someone else's property was an accepted practice in these parts.

The little chapel where Nikola and the shy Luba were married was nearest the wall. Vera felt a pang of remorse as she looked at the chapel, for she hadn't even come for her son's wedding. How odd, she thought, Nikola never questioned her absence, just as Marko never questioned her avoidance of the Vladislav property. *Maybe she should have gone to the wedding. After all, she was here now wasn't she?*

Beyond the chapel was the barn, also made of stone and weathered beams. Inside were kept the horses and the three carriages. One was a work wagon, another was the small carriage Sofie and Klara had taken to the Balaban's the day of the wedding. The last one was a large enclosed coach. It had been in the family for as long as anyone could remember. As children Anton and Sofie rode in it when they traveled to Reijka, spending their summers on the coast. This coach also carried Sofie to Trieste when she went to care for her beloved Vincent when he had been so very ill.

Vera saw the house. It stood opposite the barn, looking deceptively warm and cozy with bright flowers blooming cheerfully near the stone exterior. A large kitchen garden led Vera's eyes to the three steps leading to the kitchen door. She was seeing it for the first time, for it had been night when she had been here so long ago.

Shading the house was a huge tree perhaps two hundred years old, for its limbs were thick as the trunks of younger trees, with its own trunk so large two men with out-stretched arms could barely touch each other. Under its protective branches and in the cool of the tree's shade was a bench. That was where Vera saw Katya. If her red hair had been covered, Vera would not have recognized the young girl in the yellow dress, with trim collar and slender sleeves, holding a book over a billowing full skirt.

Vera felt sick. So many girls would gladly marry Ivan, but he had fallen in love with Katya. How could her Ivan compete with the affluent Stefan? Vera was angry with Katya, for it was Katya who broke her Ivan's heart...for taking on finer ways and trying to be something she was not...for trying to be a lady when she was not...for making her son want to go to America!

Vera looked away. She couldn't bear to look at Katya.

In the house, changes had been made. Klara with her arthritic knees was not able to climb the stairs, so Yura, the man in charge of the barn and of driving Sofie to Trieste, had a fourteen- year old daughter Mara, who was called in to help.

Klara was happy to have the girl's help. Now she had someone to send to the chicken coop for fresh eggs and to the barn for milk. Klara was especially happy that she didn't have to climb the stairs to Ernesta's room with meals during Erna's odd illness.

Answering the knock, Klara saw Vera's face and was sure some tragedy had occurred. "What is it? Who is hurt? Is it Marko? Ivan? Nikola?" Klara was visibly upset. What else would bring Vera here after all these years, but an emergency?

"I must speak with Anton," said, Vera.

"I have no idea where Anton is," said, Klara, her shaky voice betraying her nervousness. "Why do you want him?"

Vera covered her face, fighting off tears, "I don't know whom else to turn to. I must talk to him about Ivan."

"About, Ivan. I'm not sure that is wise. At least not here." Klara turned her head upward and rolled her eyes toward the ceiling, indicating the nearness of Ernesta.

"I know, I know, but I'm beside myself. I am paralyzed with worry. I can't do the simplest task. My mind is full of fear for Ivan. He can't go to America. Not this way, not so full of anger." Then she said, "Aren't you going to let me in?"

Once inside, Vera sat at the kitchen table. Klara reluctantly, poured her friend a cup of coffee left from breakfast, hoping no one knew Vera was in her kitchen. "Here, drink this. It may be a little strong, but it's still good." She watched as Vera took a sip. "Now then, what is this talk of America? When did this come into his head?"

"When Katya came to live here." Vera sounded defeated. "What can a mother do when her son is in love and the one he loves doesn't love him in return? Am I supposed to march all the eligible girls in front of him and say 'pick one?' Klara, I tell you, if Ivan leaves for America, I think I will lose my mind."

"I've seen the change in Katya, too," admitted Klara. "She is obsessed with learning. Almost the entire day is spent with lessons. After dinner, she goes to her room and reads."

"And Stefan," a touch of sarcasm was in Vera's voice. "Is he her teacher?"

Klara caught the implication. "I don't think there is any romance between them, if that is what you are suggesting. Stefan is helping Katya only because Sophie asked him to."

At that moment, Sophie coming down the stairs saw Mara, the new hired girl with her ear pressed against the kitchen door.

"What are you doing eavesdropping here?" demanded Sophie.

"I didn't want to intrude on the conversation," said the quick-thinking snoop. "Klara and Vera Balaban are in the kitchen."

When Sophie heard Vera was in the kitchen, her heart started to pound. Something must have happened to Marko or one of the boys. She pushed the little eavesdropper out of the way and went through the door.

"Vera, what has happened?" Sophie ran to her friend's side, concern in her eyes and voice. "Is someone ill? Has there been an accident? Why are you here?"

"I must speak to Anton," said Vera. "He will know what to do. He will help me."

Sophie gave Klara a questioning look and the white haired woman answered with, "Ivan wants to leave for America."

"But, why?" Sophie was bewildered.

Vera was now sobbing, unable to reply, so Klara said, "Because he is in love with Katya. Because you brought her to this house and have changed her from an ordinary peasant girl to one who is masquerading as a lady."

"Oh, my…" It was all Sophie could say as she sank onto the bench next to Klara.

Vera was the first to break the uneasy silence that settled among the three friends.

"Anton will know what to do," she said.

"But Vera," said Sophie, "Anton is only the godfather. I don't know how much influence he will have on Ivan."

For the briefest moment, when Sophie had said, 'He is only the godfather,' Klara and Vera's eyes met, for Klara knew the long-kept secret.

The outer kitchen door opened and a surprised Anton stood staring at the three women. Seeing Vera in his kitchen seated at the table with a coffee cup was an unbelievable sight. He quickly regained his composure and tried to sound casual.

"Vera, how nice to see you, what a wonderful surprise," his voice sounded strained, unnatural to his own ears and it displeased him.

Before he could take a step, Vera was up and across the room in front of him.

"We must talk. You have to help me." She grabbed his arm and pushed him back, out through the door and down the steps.

Her hand was at his back, shoving him farther from the door and away from anyone who might hear them. They finally stopped walking when they reached the stone wall near the chapel.

"Are you going to tell me what is going on? Something terrible must have happened. You haven't been here since…since…well, you know." Anton said.

"You must stop Ivan from going to America." Her voice was high-pitched as she fought off tears. "It is your fault that he is leaving."

"What are you talking about? What is my fault and why is he leaving?"

"Because he is in love with Katya and it looks as if you are grooming her for your other son!"

"That's not true. Stefan and Katya are only friends." Anton felt weak. He leaned against the wall to steady himself. "I know Ivan is hurt. I could see it, but I don't know what to do. America? Are you sure he wants to go to America?" Anton didn't want to lose Ivan. If Ivan went to America it could mean he might never see him again. For twenty years Anton had felt the loss of his first-born son, but having him near and in the care of Marko and Vera made it bearable. Visiting often in the roll of an influential godfather had given him some amount of satisfaction. But, America...he didn't want to lose Ivan to America.

"I don't know what I can do." he repeated. His concern for Erna had put Ivan out of his mind and now he felt guilty.

"You had better think of something." Vera's words came out in jabs like a sharp knife. "Ivan has been cheated out of his rightful place in the world and I have kept my mouth shut. He has been cheated out of his fortune and his title. I will not let him be cheated in love by your Stefan." Her cheeks were flushed with anger. "Everyone knows how Stefan has wasted his years at school while Ivan carries home the books you give him wrapped in cloth, so as not to soil them. He spends the nights reading by candlelight thrilled to be learning something new, while your Stefan plays with the women and the cards. Oh yes, we have heard the stories and are embarrassed for you."

Anton dropped his head. He didn't want to hear what Vera was saying. He wanted her to go away. Ever since the night Marko took Vera home and married her, asking no questions, Anton carried a guilt that never left him. Anton had tried to be generous, using his role as godfather to Ivan and his childhood friend Marko as the reasons for the many gifts.

Vera's words had stung him. She was right about Stefan, but Anton loved Stefan as much as he loved Ivan. He regretted that his second son wasn't a scholar and felt some shame that his neighbors knew of Stefan's escapades. For all the past displays of anger and disappointment Anton had felt for Stefan, he was now full of parental protection when he heard Vera's hurtful words. Anton pushed himself away from the wall and started to walk away from Vera towards the chapel.

"Where are you going?" She couldn't believe he was walking away from her.

"I have to pray."

"Pray that my son doesn't leave," she said venomously. "If I lose Ivan, I will curse you till I die and you will regret ever having known me."

Anton stopped walking and looked at Vera. He returned her look of anger with a blank stare. He needed peace and quiet to think and the chapel would provide this.

"Go home, Vera." His voice was full of sadness as he turned his back to her.

Vera watched Anton until he entered the chapel. With tears streaming down her face, she once again lifted herself over the stone wall and ran down the hill towards her home.

From behind a tall rosebush stepped a shaken Stefan. What he overheard made him physically ill. No wonder his father was so interested in Ivan! His mother had been right to think Anton might turn the land over to Ivan. Ivan was Anton's bastard son. Stefan's face was flushed, as he headed for his mother's room.

Anton had so much concern for Ernesta that the night before when he sat with her, he had spoon fed her dinner. Then when Klara and Sofie had her undressed and in bed, he read to her. When she fell asleep, he never left her side, sleeping in a rocker next to her bed.

Erna was touched by Anton's concern and his attention. She was so hurt by Stefan's betrayal and the theft of her earrings. She didn't want to speak to anyone, certainly not Sofie. She wished Sofie and Katya had stayed in Trieste longer. Most of all, she didn't want to see or speak to Stefan. The one person she loved the most in the whole world had betrayed her and the hurt had shut everything down within her.

With all his caring attention, Erna eventually got tired of even Anton being at her side. She wanted to be left alone and alone she was, so to speak. Her last ally, Stefan, had turned against her, or so she felt.

At one point last evening, while Anton talked on and on, making conversation, he said, "Tell me, Erna. What is the matter? Perhaps I can help."

It was then she turned her head and looked into his eyes.

He looked so pleased. "Erna! You understand! You heard me."

Still, she didn't want to talk, so she looked away.

Anton's concern for her had stirred old feelings within her. She thought perhaps there was a chance their lives could change for the better.

Those feelings of change were brief. There could be no change for the better.

Today, Erna watching from her window saw Vera and Anton in what looked like a heated conversation. *Never* in twenty years had that woman been to the house and now she was in the yard having a long conversation with Anton.

Stefan, badly shaken by the exchange he had overheard between his father and Vera Balaban, headed for his room when through the open doorway, he saw his mother standing at the window.

"Mamtiza!" He was surprised. "Are you feeling better?"

With her back to him, staring out the window, she answered coldly, "Not really."

"Thank God, you are well," his voice choked. "I don't know what I would do if you were still ill."

Erna heard the break in his voice. With her back still to her son, she said, "I saw Vera Balaban and your father in the yard."

Ernesta listened never interrupting while Stefan, full of emotion, told her what he had overheard. Finally, he said, "And, Ivan…Ivan is his son!"

All Erna said was, "Let's go downstairs."

Book II, Chapter 25

In the Vladislav house, the only rooms getting regular use were the kitchen, dining room and bedrooms, while a beautiful parlor and study were kept closed. There was also a library, a small room off the parlor, where Anton kept his books, furnished with a desk and a day bed. Occasionally when Father Lahdra came for dinner, the parlor was used for entertaining.

For years Ernesta tried to open the parlor, but whenever she suggested they retire to the parlor, Anton would remain at the dining table, as if she had not spoken. Finally, she gave up. For months at a time the furniture in the parlor would be covered with sheets and the drapes drawn. After a time the room had become a symbol of defeat for Ernesta. The closed off parlor was a daily reminder that she was not living the kind of life she had hoped for when she married the handsome Anton. They had even stopped going to the summer home in Riejeka. When Stefan went away to school, Anton found excuses for not leaving Vladezemla. Once, Ernesta and Sofie went alone to the beautiful white house in Riejeka. It was not the same without Anton and Stefan, so the two bored women, never very comfortable in each other's company anyway, shortened their trip.

Now in the parlor, Ernesta said to Stefan, "Pull the sheets away. Open the windows."

Klara heard sounds in the front part of the house and came out of her kitchen to investigate.

"My God, Erna, you have recovered. Should you be down here so soon?"

Ernesta's voice was cool. "I am fine, thank you." Motioning toward the sheets Stefan removed from the furniture, she said, "You can take these coverings away. We are going to use this room." Then, she added, "Find Anton and send him to me."

Klara stared long at Ernesta. Something was very wrong here. The quick recovery must have done something to Erna, for she was *really* not herself. She had always been somewhat rude and bossy, but there was something new about her. Something hard…something *mean*.

Mara, the young girl who had been eavesdropping at the kitchen door and was supposed to be of help to Klara was nowhere near the kitchen. Klara looked out the back door and did not see her. She went to the foot of the stairs and called to see if the girl had gone upstairs. There was no response.

Annoyed, Klara went down the three steps from her kitchen into the yard, grunting because her knees were hurting. She certainly did not enjoy walking around looking for Anton, when the young Mara could be doing it.

As Klara neared the barn door, she could hear whoops of laughter. The workers were gathered in the center of the barn listening to Mara tell what she had overheard. 'That Vera Balaban had come to Vladezemla to beg Anton's help, that Ivan was lovesick over Katya, that Ivan was going to America and lastly…that Ivan was Anton's son.' The men roared with laughter. Of course! What they had suspected for all these years was true.

Klara wanted to slap each and every one of them. Beat them with their rakes and shovels. Instead, she turned away feeling shame for the family she grew up with and loved. She felt sick hearing the laughter and knew the gossip would spread like a locust invasion.

She went to her kitchen and sat at the table, her head in her hands.

The truth was out. Mara, the young eavesdropper, had told the men in the barn and they would tell anyone else interested enough to listen.

In peasant huts, in the fields, on the open roads or at the river, wherever people starving for gossip gathered, it would be the same conversation.

"Sure, now we know how Marko got such a fine house, and the land, so much land, all because his wife slept with the landlord." There would be rough, coarse laughter and then someone clever would say, "If I knew how generous Vladislav could be, I would have given him my wife to sleep with."

Then surely someone would answer with, "Why would he want to sleep with your wife? YOU don't even want to sleep with her." There would be more crude comments and bawdy laughter.

Anton, still disturbed by Vera's visit, left the peace of the chapel and entered the kitchen to find Klara wiping her wet eyes with the corner of her apron.

"What's wrong?" His voice was full of concern. "Is Erna worse?"

Klara leaned her back against the wall sobbing, "They know. They all know. Everyone is laughing behind your back."

His hand was on her shoulder, "Know what? What are you talking about?"

"That little bitch Mara, the one who is supposed to be helping me, is in the barn telling the men what she overheard you and Vera talking about."

Anton's face drained of color. "I will throw them all off the land. I'll…"

Anton sank onto the wooden bench at the table, cradling his head in his hands. "Oh, God, This can't be! After all these years...It can't be! Oh, God!" he said again.

"Does Marko know?" He looked at Klara who only shook her head and shrugged her shoulders. "What will this do to Ivan...and to Stefan?" His mind was racing. How would he make things right? He never wanted Ernesta to be hurt or Stefan, who had been showing such maturity lately.

Anton needed air. He had to get out of the kitchen, out of this room that seemed to be sucking the air right out of him. Without another word to Klara, Anton rose and escaped through the doorway for some fresh air. At the entrance of the barn were several men talking intimately. Anton knew all of them. They had worked for him for years. He knew them from childhood. As if on cue, each man went into a different direction, without a greeting or acknowledgment. They dispersed out of a sense of shame or fear for their jobs.

Anton stopped walking. *Oh, God, they know.*

Anton never knew such humiliation was possible. He had grown up with the love and friendship of all the peasants around him. He was distantly related to some of them.

Long ago his family was no different from those who worked the lands around him and for him. During some long past invasion, a distant relative had gathered the serfs together to fight the marauding Turks. The reward had been a title and land. The serfs who were once peers became his ancestor's property. Anton, with his father before him and before him, the grandfather, all tried to make life better for those serfs and peasants who had once belonged to them. The Vladislav's efforts at kindness, fairness and generosity had been rewarded with love and devotion. But, now...it would change.

He had turned back toward the house, sickened by the behavior of the men and the thought of how Marko and Ivan would react to this revelation.

That was when he saw Stefan standing directly in front of him. Stefan's arms were straight at his side, hands balled into fists. His expression was cold, dark, and his body taut as if prepared to strike.

Anton opened his mouth to speak, but Stefan rudely interrupted. "Mama wants to speak with you. She is in the parlor." His voice had a triumphant edge to it when he had said, "She is in the parlor."

"She is in the parlor? She has recovered?"

Stefan gave no response, just led the way.

Ernesta sat on a comfortable settee with her feet resting on a petite, round footstool. A smug, tight little smile was on her thin lips. Stefan went to stand behind his mother near an open window. His handsome face hard, his eyes cold.

Anton bent to kiss Erna, but she turned away. He straightened and said, "Are you really recovered? Should you be down here so soon?"

With her voice cold as ice, she said, "Yes, I have recovered. And, it seems just in time to be publicly humiliated by the entire population of this area. Not only myself, but Stefan will also be the object of laughter."

"Erna...my Son...I...I," Anton stammered, looking from one to the other.

"Don't bother trying to explain. Sit down and listen to me," said Ernesta.

Anton wasn't ready for a verbal confrontation. He had too much to sort out, to try to explain, to make things right.

Back in the kitchen, Klara stepped into the enclosure where she slept. She took a long broom handle and did something she had not done since she and Sofie were children. She pounded her ceiling with the wooden handle to signal Sofie, whose room was directly above. As a child, it had been Klara's signal for Sofie to come downstairs.

Shortly, a laughing Sofie entered the kitchen, not having heard the signal for many years. "I am here Klara. Are you finished with your work so we can go out and play?"

She stopped her joking the moment she saw Klara's face. "What's the matter?" Sofie asked, concerned.

Klara sighed and said, "I have to tell you something...something that has been a secret for many years."

When Klara finished telling her of the night twenty-one years ago when Vera came looking for Anton, Sofie hurried into the parlor. She paused when she saw her brother seated on the divan looking beaten, while Ernesta and Stefan were poised for battle. Sofie seated herself next to her brother, concern written on her face.

In less than twenty-four hours, Destiny had taken charge of their lives in a way they never could have guessed.

Sofie gave Anton an encouraging smile and patted his hand. She could see how badly shaken he was and she was there for him. She would be his general, his ally. Just as when they were children playing games, she was and would always be alongside her brother.

Ernesta gave Sofie a cool look. "You don't need to be here. This is between my husband, my son and me."

"I will not leave my brother. I'm sure whatever you are planning to discuss has to do with property and I have a right to listen." There was a new strength to Sofie, which had not been seen before. She was taking command, but it weakened Ernesta's resolve only slightly.

Sofie continued, "I have just myself learned of Ivan Balaban's relationship to this family." She raised her hand to silence Anton, who started to speak. "I don't see why there need be any changes in our lives because of this exposé. After all it has been twenty years and Anton has never made any moves to claim

Ivan as an heir. We all know Stefan is to be the next heir of Vladezemlo."

"You both are ready to attack my brother," said Sofie looking hard at them waiting for a denial. When none came, she said, "What is this big commotion? All at once everyone is so critical. There is so much cross-breeding in this area that the church records are a joke." Sofie turned to her brother, who was listening to her intently. "You must stop behaving as if it is the end of the world. You may have kept a secret, but you have behaved honorably all these years. Have you been faithful to Ernesta?" she demanded of her brother.

"Yes...yes," he stammered.

Sofie stood up and looked into her nephew's face. "Has your father ever denied you as his son?" Not waiting for an answer she continued her interrogating, "Did he not have many of your clothes made in Venice...and your boots, fine Italian leather? How many times have you been to France and to England? You were sent to school. You did nothing there, but waste your time. You got a generous allowance which you drank up and gambled away." At the last remark, Stefan visibly flinched.

"What has your father given to Ivan?" demanded Sofie. "I'll tell you what, a few old books and some old riding clothes of his. No allowance. No schools...and certainly not the Vladislav name. What have you got to be angry about?"

Stefan was shaken by his aunt's outburst. He had never known her to speak in this manner...with such authority. She had always been the maiden aunt who made herself as invisible as possible. Now she was behaving as if she was the head of the house and with each sentence she uttered, Anton seemed to be regaining strength and his self-respect.

Erna interrupted, "He has shamed this family and the Vladislav name." She stood grandly, her back stiff as a board.

Sofie stared hard at her sister-in-law. Twenty-one years of hurtful words and actions came swirling in her memory. Sofie closed her eyes for a second before she said. "For twenty years we have all stayed respectfully out of your way, for you were the mistress of the house. I must tell you, that in all those years you have been a pain in the ass." Again Sofie's hand went up, keeping a red-faced Ernesta from speaking. "Nothing was ever good enough for you...or grand enough. We didn't live the kind of life you wanted. You knew what we were like, what our lifestyle was like. We aren't invited to Court. For that sort of a life, you should have gone to Russia and married one of the noble Romanovs."

Anton looked at his sister with newfound admiration. She was wonderful. She was protecting him, giving him strength when he needed it. He reached out and took her hand.

Seeing the gesture, Ernesta spat out, "Isn't that sweet. How touching, brother and sister, standing battle, side by side."

Anton stood up. He put his arm around Sofie, giving her shoulder an affectionate squeeze. "It seems I have handled things poorly, but I didn't mean to. No one was meant to be hurt. My father and your father arranged our marriage and I honored their wishes. I have been a good husband...as good as I knew how. I tried to be a good father." His voice caught as he said, "It was hard not to want to give to Ivan, but I didn't. If it seemed I was too generous with Marko, well, it is because he never knew who Vera was. Or, even that she and I knew each other before he met her. Marko thought she was a friend of Klara's, a friend who needed a place to stay. Marko has been kind and honorable. What I gave him I did perhaps out of a sense of guilt, for turning Vera away from our door on the night of my engagement to Ernesta."

At the word 'engagement' Ernesta flinched. Her hands were clasped tightly in her lap. Her face was no longer triumphant. Her eyes glistened as she asked "Did you love Vera when we were engaged?"

Anton, with his arm still around his sister's shoulder, looked from Ernesta to the crumbling face of his son.

"I suppose I have always loved her."

Book II, Chapter 26

Katya slowly rose from her bed. It was well past midnight and the room had the lingering smell of brandy and sex.

He was gone! He had come into her room, smelling of pear brandy, his face red from a combination of Krushkavac and anger. Stefan had been reeling from the encounter in the parlor between his mother, father and Sofie. Anton's open admission that Ivan was his son and that, yes, he had always loved Vera Balaban was too much for Stefan. Thinking his family was falling apart, alone in his room, Stefan drank several glasses of the sweet brandy. He didn't want to be here in the countryside. It was that damned Turk's fault, demanding more money. Stefan would have already been gone, gone far away from here if he didn't need money.

No, not really, he couldn't leave.

Now, he had to protect his future as the next master of Vladezemla. Oh, but he longed for the stimulating activity in Zagreb, the conversations, the company, the gambling and the women. Especially he missed the women! How he missed the warmth, the smell of them, the nights in bed with them.

From his bedroom door, it was only a few feet to the stairs leading to the attic room where the beautiful Katya lay sleeping. *Who the hell was this peasant playing at being a lady, anyway?* She was no better than that peasant Ivan who was playing at Lord of the Manor with his books, and wearing Anton's old riding clothes, instead of his peasant pantaloons. However, peasant or not, Katya was a stunning beauty with those green eyes and that glorious red hair. And then, there were those breasts and that slim waist.

Stefan carried a kerosene lamp with him and though he stumbled drunkenly on the steps, miraculously the lamp stayed in his hand. Katya had heard him fumbling with the door and watched as he staggered into the room, a foolish grin on his face.

She sat up. "Stefan, you had better leave."

He mimicked her, "Stefan. You had better leave."

"Please, Stefan," she tried to sound calm. "Please go. I won't tell anyone you were here."

He put the kerosene lamp on the top of the small chest, without spilling it.

"You won't tell anyone anything. My mother is ready to throw you out," he lied, falling across her, pushing her down on the mattress.

"Don't do this," she pleaded. "Come back when you aren't drunk," she suggested, hoping he believed it to be an invitation.

"I'm here now!" His weight was heavy on her body, his hands feeling her firm breasts through her linen nightgown. He tried to kiss her, but she moved her face from side to side evading him, an action that angered him. *Just who did she think she was, not letting him kiss her?*

The overly sweet smell of the pear brandy sickened her. She wanted to fight him, to kick him, to beat him off the way she could her brother-in-law, Elia, back in Selna. But she was afraid the noise would waken the others. Would they believe her if she said he forced himself on her? Probably not. Ernesta would surely think Katya had seduced him. And what would Sofie think? Would Sofie still be as fond of her if she accused Stefan of this attack? Katya didn't know.

She stopped struggling. She wanted to weep. She really liked Stefan and thought he liked her, also. But, drunk like this, it just wasn't right. This wasn't courtship. If she were to admit the truth, she found Stefan very attractive. She loved the way he took her arm when they sometimes walked in the yard. She loved his nearness when he helped her with her reading lessons. She loved the smell of him as he bent his head near, to look at a page in a book, when she didn't pronounce a word properly.

She didn't want this. Not this way. She wanted to hold hands, to look into each other's eyes, to feel something more than this, more than what Stefan was doing now.

Katya stifled a cry for his entry into her had hurt. She did what her poor sister Anka had always done, so long ago in Selna...just waited for it to end.

Stefan wasn't mean or overly rough. He just wasn't gentle and loving. He came quickly and dropped his weight on Katya. She waited a bit. "Please, get off me," she said, near tears. He rolled off of her, lying next to her. Katya lay quietly waiting for

him to say something, to do something. After a bit, she realized he
might fall asleep and she shook him furiously.

"What? What do you want?" he mumbled drunkenly.

Getting off the bed, she said, "For you to leave." She shook
him again. "Go to your own room. You know your mother will be
unhappy that you were here." Katya was sure this statement was
true for it seemed to reach Stefan's sodden brain.

"Oh, alright…" He muttered, as she pulled him to his feet. He
stumbled as he got up and Katya held her breath hoping no one
heard the noise.

He was leaning against her as she opened the door and helped
him down the stairs and across the narrow hall to his own room.
To Katya, each thump and bump sounded like a thunderclap to her
frightened ears. She led him to his bed with only the glow of the
moonlight showing her the way. Stefan fell on his bed making
another loud noise, or so Katya imagined.

She ran back to her room, fetched the kerosene lamp and
returned it to Stefan's room.

Back in her own room, with the door closed, she sat on the
bed trembling.

After a while she rose and went to the chest where a pitcher
stood. Katya poured water onto a cloth and cleaned herself. Were
all men like this? Taking what they wanted, whenever they
wanted? Of course not, she decided. Milan back in Selna wasn't
cruel. He was gentle, kind, protective. She felt a pang of guilt,
remembering how cold she had been to him on the journey here,
from Selna. She almost missed Selna. Well, not really Selna…she
missed Milan and Eva, the kind-hearted woman who kept her alive
with her breast milk. She missed Eva's children, young Milan,
Marica and Evica. She smiled to herself as she thought of the dog,
Vuk. He was always near her, brushing against her leg when they
walked, leaning against her protectively. Did Vuk miss her, she
wondered?

For a brief moment Katya wondered what it would have been
like if she had married young Milan and became a part of that
sweet family.

Katya didn't want to go back to sleep. She needed to think, to
think about her future. Was this what it was going to be like?
Would other men attack her?

For some reason Valina, the Gypsy Queen, came to mind. Katya recalled the old woman holding her hand and saying, '*The danger is in the path that will take you where you should have been in the first place. For some reason you were put where you did not belong. It will fall into place...you are finding your way.*'

Earlier that day, in the afternoon, Katya had been lying on a pew in the family chapel. She did that sometime when she was alone. Just being in the beautiful little chapel gave her comfort.

She wouldn't have remained hidden if she hadn't noticed Anton crying. He fell to his knees before the statue of the Madonna who seemed to look down protectively, her wooden hands slightly outstretched at her sides. Katya was embarrassed to be there, a witness to Anton's grief. She pressed herself against the pew hoping to remain hidden.

After a while she heard a scraping sound. Curious, she slowly lifted her heard in time to see the statue of the Madonna turned, facing a different direction. Anton lifted something out of the well in the base holding the statue. Katya could hear the clinking of coins and see the sparkle as light played on them.

She watched as Anton dropped the coins back into the bag and into the safety of the pedestal. Flattening herself on the pew, so as not to be seen, she heard the scraping sound again as Anton repositioned the statue.

Anton had been placing coins in the bag for years. He really didn't need to hide them, but he wanted to. He wanted what he was putting aside for Ivan, never to be found. Someday when the time was right and Anton could find a reason that wouldn't draw suspicion, he planned to give the money to Ivan. Now certainly wasn't the time for such a gift.

In her room, finished with her washing, Katya softly opened her door. She didn't hear so much as a snore as she cautiously felt her way down the hall, then down the stairs. At the kitchen she was the most careful knowing that Klara didn't have a door, but only a curtain as privacy for her sleeping area.

Barefooted, Katya took one tiny soundless step at a time, determined to get out the door without being heard. Just when she was about to go out the kitchen door, she remembered that the hinge squealed when pushed open. She turned and with more deliberate tiny steps…one at time…pausing to see if she had been heard, she headed for the dining room. There were no screens on the windows. Katya pushed back the curtain and lifted herself over the windowsill with ease. Once outside she looked about and seeing no one and praying the dogs wouldn't bark, made her way in the moonlit night to the chapel.

The door made a slight groan as she opened it. She left it open and still using the moonlight's glow shining through the windows she made her way to the statue of the Madonna. She gave it a twist, just as she had seen Anton do that day.

That had been earlier in the day. It was *now*, *now* in the middle of the night. *Now*, when Katya realized she must take care of herself. She was unsure of her future. She loved Sofie, but couldn't be sure how long she and Sofie would be together.

Katya reached into the well of the pedestal and took the heavy velvet bag of coins feeling only the smallest bit of guilt. Pushing the statue back into place, she scurried across the yard, slipped back into the house holding her breath with each step, praying no one would find her wandering about in the night.

Back in her attic room with her door latched, she was able to breath once more. She was perspiring. She poured a little more water from the pitcher and dampened her warm face and wiped the back of her neck. Again, as quietly as possible, she opened the door leading to the attic storage area. With a small candle in one hand and the velvet pouch in the other, she crawled into the attic. She knew which box she wanted. It was the one with the painted tea set that was to have been part of Sofie's trousseau. There, in the semi-darkness, Katya found and un-wrapped a large soup tureen. The money pouch fit securely in the bowl. Carefully, Katya re-wrapped the tureen putting it back with the rest of the set. Slowly, so as not to bump anything to make noise, she backed her way out of the attic. She closed the door and blew out the candle. In the darkness she found her bed. Her heart was thumping.

If she had to leave she would not be penniless. She would be able to take care of herself for a while.

By nine o'clock the following morning, no one had come down for breakfast. Klara was more than a little annoyed. After all, she had things to do, all more pressing than sitting in the kitchen waiting to serve a breakfast no one seemed to want. However, she was feeling a little smug, for she had sent away Mara the spy, by blocking the kitchen door when the girl came to report for duty.

"Good morning, Klara. I am here to work," said the eavesdropper innocently.

"Well, the family doesn't want you here," replied Klara. The young girl's cheeks reddened. "We don't like gossiping girls, and Master Anton just might let your father go. What will your father do to you when he finds out he lost his job because you listen to private conversations?"

Klara watched Mara, as she ran for home. Klara knew she had over-stepped herself. What if someday Ernesta, in her anger could persuade Anton to send Klara away? Would they do that? she wondered. Vladezemla had been her home all of her life. She would have to talk with Vera and Marko, to see if they would take her in should she be sent away. Klara suddenly felt very old and very sad. Nothing was the same.

Stefan was still asleep, the pear brandy not yet worn off.

Katya didn't want to meet any of the family, not just yet. Most of all, she didn't want to see Stefan. Would he remember coming to her room?

Ernesta had tossed and turned all night trying to think of what to do next. Perhaps she had over reacted to the news that Anton was Ivan's father. After all, she had always wondered about Anton's affection for Ivan. She was being too dramatic and it was interfering with her plan. This was the plan to rid herself of Sofie and that red-haired companion of hers. However, she didn't have a detailed plan...yet.

Sofie was in her room carefully dressing for the visitor she was expecting, taking extra care with her appearance. She was eagerly looking forward to meeting with him.

Alexie Lukas was waiting for Sofie in the parlor. Bemused, he looked around. In all the years of legal work he had done for the family, he had never before seen this room. Alexie was a short, compactly built man with a thick head of shiny black hair combed straight back. His round face sported a full mustache and thick black brows over brown eyes. His was a pleasant face, a friendly face, for he was a jovial man who enjoyed the work he did and as a rule he enjoyed the people he worked for. He brushed imaginary lint from his navy blue suit and wondered if Sofie Vladislav would think his red and yellow cravat a bit too flashy. He cared very much what the unmarried sister of Anton Vladislav thought of him. He was flattered and delighted that she had sent Yura with a message that she wanted to see him.

For twenty years or so, Alexie Lukas had been smitten with Sofie Vladislav. As a young man he would accompany his father, who had been the family's lawyer, to Vladezemla with hopes of seeing Sofie. He had been ashamed of himself for feeling a sense of relief when news of her fiancé's death reached him. After a while he ran out of excuses to visit Vladezemla, and when he heard she was in permanent mourning, he no longer listened to his heart, choosing to stay away.

He was admiring a large piece of Czechoslovakian crystal, ornately cut so that the clear crystal was visible under the garnet-red exterior of the vase depicting a running stag, when Sofie entered.

"Alexie, how kind of you to respond so quickly." She extended her hand and his lips barely touched her fingers as he greeted her in the continental manner.

"It is an honor to be here and to serve you," he said, aware of her cologne, hoping she wore it for him. She was a bit older, a bit rounder than he remembered, but she could still stir the passionate feelings of his youth.

"Please, be seated," she motioned to the velvet sofa, while she seated herself on a chair opposite him. "How have you been?" she asked smiling warmly, for she was genuinely glad to see Alexie.

"Thank you for asking. I am fine. It's a pleasure to be in your company once more."

"You must have left Karlovac very early this morning. Would you care to join me for breakfast?"

"It would be a pleasure. You are too kind." Did he sound like an idiot? Was he fawning over her he wondered, as he followed her into the familiar dining room?

Over a breakfast of steaming, just baked, poppy seed bread with currant jam, Sofie explained what she wanted Alexie to do for her. He listened thoughtfully as he drank his bowl of coffee and hot milk. At times he would interject an opinion or some advice. By the time they had finished their meal, Alexie was almost ready to draw up the papers.

"We will need witnesses to sign the documents." It was at that moment, Alexie realized he had not seen any members of the household, other than Klara. "Is there anyone in the house or near-by who is able to witness for you?"

"Oh, yes! Klara can write her name." Then Sofie thought about Ernesta and Stefan. They might not be pleased with what she was planning, so she couldn't count on them to sign. "If my brother is about, he will sign," she said. Now, she too was wondering at the absence of the family members.

Katya had just finished dressing when a tiny bell summoned her. The bell had been installed years earlier for the short time Sofie and Anton had a governess. It was attached to a pull on the main floor of the house to announce when it was time to come down to dine.

Katya walked down the hallway passed Stefan's bedroom door and prayed she wouldn't see him. The door to Ernesta's room was open and Katya could see the woman sitting in her rocker, looking out her window. "Dobro Yutro," said Katya. When the 'Good Morning' was not returned, Katya hurried on to the dining room.

Alexie Lukas nearly lost his voice when he saw Katya. She wore a collarless brown silk dress, long sleeved and tight at the waist. Her red hair was rolled into a bun at the back and smooth at the temples. The emerald green eyes looked questioningly at him, then at Sofie.

"Alexie Lukas, this is the girl we have been discussing. Katya Balich."

"It...it is a pleasure." He was aware that he stammered. He took her hand and barely brushed the back of her hand with his lips. Alexie hadn't planned to do that, to kiss the girl's hand, but she was stunning. She looked so sophisticated! How could this girl be the same girl of whom Sofie had told him? The one who had a brutal brother-in-law and had escaped a possible white slaver? The girl, who less than a month ago was barefoot and unschooled? There, before him stood a sophisticated young woman.

Katya felt the color come into her cheeks. She remembered that Zoltan had kissed her hand when they parted in the forest. It seemed such an elegant gesture. She nodded a greeting, not sure what to say or why she had been summoned.

"Sit down Katya," said Sofie. "Eat a little something." Katya saw the plate of poppy seed bread amid the papers and ink bottle. A couple of steel tipped pens lay on the table.

After Katya was seated, Alexie returned to his chair and resumed writing. Before him were several sheets of paper. Some blank, some showing writing. "We will need several copies," he said to Sofie.

Katya remained quiet not wanting to disturb what seemed to be a serious undertaking. She would have preferred to be in the kitchen with Klara.

"What if this is challenged?" asked Sofie.

"The way we have drawn this up, I doubt anyone can undo it." Alexie was holding one of the papers up, re-reading a clause. "You see," he was saying, "you are of sound mind and legal age. I don't see how anyone could over turn this."

"Good...good. I have made up my mind to do this. I only wish my brother were here. I wanted to tell him what I was doing. But," she shrugged her shoulders, "It is done."

"Not yet," said the advokat "Not until we have all the signatures."

Katya listened as she ate her breakfast. Alexie Lukas and Sofie were studiously bent over the documents, reading and re-reading, making changes whenever they found a more appropriate word, paying no mind of her presence there.

Finally, Alexie leaned back in his chair and said, "I think it is done. Here," he offered the papers to Sofie. "Do you want to read them?"

"No! I want them signed." Sofie went into the kitchen to fetch Klara.

"We need another witness," Alexie called after her.

"I can sign my name," said Katya, wanting to be of help.

"That is why you are here. We will need your signature, also," said Alexie, smiling warmly at Katya.

Katya spent several uncomfortable minutes waiting for Sofie to return. She smiled at the Advokat when he glanced her way, but wished she were anywhere but here. Here, alone with a stranger, however kind and pleasant he might be.

Sensing Katya's uneasiness, Alexie tried to make conversation.

"I have heard that there is a machine that writes. It has places for your fingers and when you press down a letter appears on paper. I should like to see such a machine."

Katya was relieved when she heard commotion from the kitchen, for it meant Sofie was returning and Katya didn't have to offer an opinion on the writing machine. Noisily, Sophie herded Klara and Yura, the eavesdropper's father, into the dining room.

"Yura can sign his name," said Sofie. "Will he do?"

"As long as he sees you sign the papers, it will be fine."

Sofie was visibly excited, her eyes shining. "Give me the papers."

Alexie placed four sheets of paper, with identical writing on all of them, before her. Sofie looked up at Katya, smiling. Then she took the pen, dipped it in the ink and signed the first sheet. After all four were signed, she gave the pen to Katya. When Katya looked at her bewildered, Alexie said, "Sign below Sofie Vladislava's signature."

"It's alright," encouraged Sofie. "Sign it!"

Katya did as she was told, careful that her signature was one she could be proud of.

Then Klara signed, not thinking much of it, for she had witnessed documents before. Yura took the longest to sign the four documents. It was evident that farm tools were more comfortable in his hands than a pen. On one paper he dropped a blob of ink, on another his signature wandered downward, but eventually he finished smiling proudly at his accomplishment. Yura was rewarded with a glass of fine old brandy before he was sent back to the barn, where he would brag to his friends that he "had been on important business in the house".

The lawyer was the last to sign. He signed with a practiced flourish and dated the documents. Klara returned to the comfort of her kitchen. Only Katya remained, still perplexed at her need to be there, sitting quietly watching Sofie and Alexie at their task.

Alexie gathered the papers, placed them neatly in a pile before him and exchanged a smile of satisfaction with Sofie.

Katya looked from Sofie to Alexie, for there was a sense of self-satisfaction in their attitudes.

"Shall I tell her, or do you want to?" asked Alexie.

Sofie was so moved with emotion she could not speak, so she nodded for Alexie to explain. "Sofie Vladislava has made you, Katya Balich, her legal heir, in other words, her daughter."

Katya said nothing. She didn't understand. How could she be someone's daughter? Her mother was dead. Katya was told that she had died giving Katya life.

Sofie took Katya's hand. "Katya, Dearest. Do you remember the conversation we had? The one where you said you were only a guest in this house and the time would come when you would have to leave?"

Katya nodded dumbly.

"Well," went on Sofie. "You are no longer a guest. Those papers," she pointed to them, "make you my legal heir. We can even go before the magistrate and have you take the Vladislav name if you like. No one can turn you out of this house."

"Can a piece of paper do that?" Katya looked wide-eyed at Alexie.

"Yes, it is called a legal document. One can accomplish many things with legal documents. One can buy and sell property, or change a name, or leave property to someone, as in a will. Or legally become part of someone's family, as in this case."

The reality that she was wanted enough to be legally adopted, made Katya's hands tremble. What did this mean? Was she now Stefan's cousin? Were Anton and Ernesta now her aunt and uncle?

"What does everyone think about this?" wondered Katya, aloud.

"No one knows. I didn't want anyone's opinion." Seeing the troubled look in Katya's eyes, Sofie said, "Katya, Dear Katya. I love you. I now know what it must feel like to have a daughter, to want to care for and protect someone. I never thought I would know what it felt like to be a mother, but I believe you have brought that feeling to me."

Sofie's eyes were brimming with tears and so were Katya's. Katya rose from her chair and went to Sofie. The two women clung to each other and Alexie Lukas had to get a handkerchief from his pocket to wipe his own eyes.

Katya and Sofie laughed nervously when they stopped hugging.

Alexie, feeling comfortable with Sofie and Katya, took it upon himself to pour three brandies. They drank in silence, smiling at one another each time their eyes met.

After a while Katya broke the silence. "Is it possible for me to have a legal paper written?"

"What sort of legal paper?" asked Alexie.

When she told them what she wanted, both Sofie and the attorney smiled their approval.

"That's a lovely idea," said Sofie, smiling.

Book II, Chapter 27

"Get up, Stefan! I must talk with you!" Ernesta was shaking her son vigorously.

Stefan tried to shrug off his mother's insistent hands pulling at him.

"All right!" he was annoyed. He pulled himself up, waving her away. "What do you want?" His question was tinged with anger. His vision was a little blurred and he had an awful taste in his mouth. He ran his fingers through his matted hair and rubbed his hands over his eyes, trying to focus.

"Your Aunt Sofie has lost her mind. Yes, lost her mind." Ernesta was nervously pacing in front of him. "I heard it all. I had to sneak down to the dining room when I realized no one let me know we had a guest in the house."

"What guest? What are you babbling about?" Stefan's head felt heavy and he had to relieve himself.

"Alexie Lukas was here." Her hands were on her hips and she waited for some response from Stefan. He had no idea what she wanted him to say. Lukas was the family advocate. That was all Stefan knew. She was waiting for his response.

He shrugged his shoulders. "So...?"

"That's it! That's all you have to say?"

"What do you want me to say?" Stefan was exasperated. He was not finding this conversation amusing and he still needed to relieve himself. "I have not seen Alexie Lukas in many years. I have no business with him," he said dully.

"Well..." Ernesta's voice was low and conspiratorial. "Your Aunt Sofie had business with him this morning." She nodded smugly at her son who wanted desperately for her to leave, so he could reach for the chamber pot resting under the bed. "Oh, yes, she had business with him!" Ernesta repeated.

When Stefan didn't respond, she went on. "That red-haired peasant is now your crazy Aunt's legal ward." Ernesta was shaking now, a combination of anger and of fright. Anger at Sofie for doing such a thing without consulting the family and fear...fear of losing what little control she had of life at Vladezemla.

She seated herself next to Stefan on the bed. "We must make our plans. We must decide how to handle this problem. Listen, my son, I won't let anyone take what belongs to you." Then her face became twisted and her eyes glittered icily, "I will kill Sofie and that ward of hers if I have to."

Stefan stood up pushing his mother's hand away. He turned his back to her, not wanting to see her face or hear her voice anymore. "Please leave me alone. I want to dress." His voice was cool.

Ernesta paused, a little taken aback. Why wasn't Stefan angry? Why didn't he want to form a plan to keep all the assets in his hands? Before she could speak, Stefan said, "Please leave me alone for a while. I need to wash and dress." He leaned down, taking his mother by the elbow raising her from where she sat on the bed and led her to the door. "We will talk as soon as I come down. I need to absorb all you have told me."

Ernesta's face brightened. She smiled broadly as she said, "I knew you wouldn't let anyone take what is yours." Then she paused at the door, her voice low and husky. "We could kill them, you know."

Stefan pushed her gently through the doorway and closed it behind her. He leaned against the door, closed his eyes and let out a long sigh.

Her voice came through the closed door. "I'll be waiting in the parlor for you, Son."

Stefan didn't answer her. *What the hell was happening in this house?* Was everyone mad? Ivan was now his brother, Katya has become his adopted cousin and his mother is talking about murder! God! How he hated being here in the countryside. He wanted to go to the city...to Zagreb. He wanted to sit at the outdoor cafes late into the night discussing world events. Yes! The world! Not all this idiotic intrigue about money. He was tired of his mother's constant worry about his inheritance.

He didn't care. Give the whole damn place to Ivan. He was sick of it all.

What the hell! He wanted the company of his charming, clever friends, and of beautiful sophisticated women. The kind of women who knew how to look at a man, signal with their eyes, tease with their eyes, and tantalize with their lips.

There were important things going on in the world and he
hadn't seen a newspaper since he came home. He wanted to see a
newspaper! He wanted to know what was happening in England
and America and everywhere else. Anywhere other than here with
the petty things he had put up with since he came home. At this
moment the events within his family were of no interest to him.
Every argument or disagreement had to do with money. Would
Ivan get the money? Will Sofie hang on to her share?

He didn't care. He had enough of them all!

He wasn't going to stay here. He would leave...leave and not
let anyone know where he had gone. Let them do what they will
with the whole damn place and to hell with everyone on it. Hell,
he could get money! He would get money, lots of it. He had been
stupid to come home when he needed to pay the gambling debt.
He had acted like a child, coming home to Mama and Tata. He
should have gone to the coast, to Sarajevo or Dubrovnik. Rich
Americans were there on vacations, with their plain daughters,
looking for husbands with royal connections. Anton could pass
himself off as a young Count. He could do very well for himself,
very well indeed.

Stefan looked at his reflection in the mirror above the
washstand. He smiled at the handsome face in need of a shave.
Yes, he would do very well on his own. The hell with all of them
and their games, he had games of his own to play. Games he
would enjoy much more than any his mother could come up with.
He would be a Count in Venice, entertaining vacationing
heiresses. *Now, that was a game worth playing.*

When he finished dressing, he looked in the mirror once
more. He was pleased with his reflection, especially the curly dark
hair and brows shading those sensuous eyes. He wore a gray riding
outfit and carried a carpetbag with his other clothing.

Stefan was not coming back.

At the Balaban farm, Ivan was seated on the ground in the
horse stall. Earlier he had been on his way home from his visit
with the Gypsies, when a wagon passed him on the road. He
recognized Vanjo, the musician from the wedding with the painful
boil Katya had cured with a soap and sugar poultice. Before Ivan

could greet Vanjo, the man stood up in the wagon and made an exaggeration of doffing his hat.

"How are you, Young Master?" The thin man asked, throwing back his bird-like head, laughing uproariously. Vanjo didn't stop, but kept the wagon moving.

Bewildered by such unusual behavior, Ivan leapt onto his horse to catch up with Vanjo's wagon. Ivan pulled at the horse's bridle to make it stop. "Hey, what are you doing?" cried Vanjo, more than a little frightened.

"Why did you call me the Young Master? What's going on?" demanded Ivan, more confused than angry.

Vanjo wasn't very brave now, especially with Ivan right there challenging him. He whipped his horse to escape and as he got further away from Ivan, called back, "Ask your Mother!"

Confused, Ivan had hurried home and ran into the house to find his mother busily dusting the dining room.

"Vanjo just called me the Young Master. He told me to ask you about it."

Her face paled. She started to say something, then turned away from her son and slowly slipped into her room, latching the door softly behind her.

Ivan didn't remember coming into the barn and putting up his horse. But now he was sitting on the floor of the stall.

His father, Marko, passing the barn door was surprised to see Ivan sitting there looking so devastated.

"Son, what's the matter?" Marko's weathered face was full of concern. "Why are you sitting there?"

Ivan looked up at his father and then shaking his head, unable to speak, dropped his chin heavily onto his chest.

Marko studied Ivan for several moments then sat on the ground beside him.

"So, you have heard what they are saying. Is that it?"

"Is it true? Can it be...I am not your son?" Ivan's eyes were pleading for it not to be so.

The old blacksmith let out a long sigh. "I have suspected it for a very long time."

Ivan's strangled voice disclosed his hurt and anger. "How could she betray you this way?" He said "she", not his usual endearing "Mamitza."

Marko placed his strong hand on Ivan's shoulder. "Oh, no, you mustn't think Veritza has been unfaithful to me. Never! Get the thought out of your mind."

Ivan watched his father's face as the old man searched for the right words.

"I remember the night Klara sent for me, as if it were yesterday," Marko began. "Klara told me she had a friend who had nowhere to stay and asked if I could bring her home for awhile. The house was only one room back then and not very clean as I recall, for I was living alone."

As Marko spoke, his face became softer with each sentence. It glowed with the love he had for Vera. "She was a young, frightened girl, alone. I fell in love with her the moment I walked through the door of Anton's chapel and saw your mother sitting alone on the pew, a tiny, lonely, lost little thing. I gave her the bed and the house, while I slept in this barn. Then, after she had been there about a month, she told me to come back into the house." The memory of that first night of lovemaking transformed him, for a moment, into the young man, he had been.

"But," protested Ivan, "Were does Anton come into this picture?"

"Does it matter?" said Marko, sitting alongside Ivan, on the straw-covered ground.

"What do you mean?"

"I mean that I don't care! God or Destiny, or maybe it is the same thing, brought your mother to me. Those first few months, I couldn't believe that I could be so happy." Marko looked at Ivan. "Then, you came. You were born late at night and I was alone with her. I didn't want to leave your mother for a minute, so I didn't go for the Baba to help with the birth. I helped your mother. I was the first person on earth to see you, to hold you." His face glowed with the memory of that night and the love he had for Vera and Ivan. "Don't you see?" Marko insisted, "You are MY son. Some things are just meant to be! I believe with all my heart that Vera was meant to be with me. How she got here doesn't matter."

Then Marko shifted his stocky body into a more comfortable position. Smiling he spoke intimately to Ivan, "I have never told anyone, but I shall tell you. Over the years, as I have watched Anton, I have felt sorry for him. Yes! I would look at the happiness I had with you and your mother, and then with Nikola and I felt I would burst with pride, all the while feeling sorry for Anton because you and Vera were mine!"

"But, people will talk and say hurtful things," said Ivan.

"It doesn't matter," Marko waived it away with his huge paw of a hand. "They have whispered it for a while. Now they say it out loud. It will be only a matter of time and someone's wife will sneak into a barn with someone else's husband, or some girl will get pregnant, or a two-headed calf will be born. Then, we will no longer be interesting."

"How can we ever be friends with the Kum Anton, again?" asked Ivan.

"We will never stop being friends with him," said Marko, patting his son's shoulder. "I believe he is suffering greatly from this gossip. Who knows what goes on in another person's mind or why they choose to do the things they do? I have loved Anton from the time we were small children playing together. I will always love him and Sofie. You must remember it is because of him that I have your mother and you. In truth, it is the greatest gift I have ever received."

Luba, the young bride looked at the closed door to Vera and Marko's bedroom. Her mother-in-law had retreated to that room and not come out since Ivan told her Vanjo had called him, 'the Young Master.'

Luba gently knocked on the door. There was no reply. She knocked again. Slowly she opened the door, no longer latched.

"Maika," The girl called tentatively, using her own special word for Mother. "Maika, is there anything I can get for you?"

Vera sat on her bed, her back to the door. She didn't turn, only waived the girl away.

Luba wanted to cry. She was terribly fond of her new family and the cruel gossip hurt her. Her father, in his coarse manner, had made a crude remark while drunk. "I suppose you'll be sleeping with young Stefan, so that your Nikola can get more land...just

like your mother-in-law did with the old land lord." When Luba
dared to defend her mother-in-law, the old man slapped her.

Poor little Luba, she ran all the way home sobbing. How
could people change like this, seemingly over night?

Desperately the girl wanted to show Vera that she loved and
respected her. Luba went into the kitchen and placed more wood
in the clay stove. While she waited for the fire to heat up the water
in the kettle, she set about getting out a cup and saucer, along with
the tea things. She adjusted her badge of marriage, the ever-
present babushka, more closely to her head.

At the back of the house, Marko entered the kitchen. He had
left Ivan sitting and thinking in the barn. "Hello, Lubitza."

"Hello, Tata," she greeted her father-in-law. "I'm making
some chai for Maika, would you like some?"

"She asked for chai?"

The girl looked grave. "No," she whispered. "I just thought
she might like some tea, since she hasn't had any breakfast."

"Still, she sits there?" Marko motioned with his head towards
the bedroom removing his leather smithy apron.

Luba nodded, scooping some tea between her fingers and
dropping a bit into each cup.

"This will pass," he said as if praying. "Sooner or later,
everything passes."

Marko glanced at Luba in time to see her wipe away tears. He
put his arm around the girl's thin shoulders. "There, there," he
soothed. "Did you hear something? Have people been saying
things about us?"

Leaning into his shoulder with her face hidden, he felt her
nod, yes.

"Well, then," he let out a sigh. "There are kind people and
cruel people. I think we shall find out who our friends are."

The boiling water started to rumble in the kettle and Luba
pulled away from Marko, to fill the cups.

He watched her as she poured. "Are you alright?"

Luba looked at Marko, smiled bravely and said, "As long as I
am in this family, I am fine."

When the tea was ready Marko said, "I'll take my chai with
Vera. Would you go find Nikola? We need to decide how many
pigs to give to the Gypsies when they camp in our pasture."

Impulsively Luba gave Marko a quick kiss on the cheek and ran out the door in search of her husband.

Marko smiled watching her run, like the child she was. How nice it was to have a daughter. Marko picked up the two cups, leaving the saucers behind. He wasn't sure his clumsy fingers could handle them. He walked to the bedroom he shared with Vera and stood in front of her. She turned her head away, ashamed to face him.

"It's a blessing I have a good memory, since you are determined not to let me see your face," he said, holding a cup in each hand. "Lubitza made tea for us. Have some chai, my love. I shall sit next to you and not look at you if you don't want me to."

He placed the cup of tea in her hand. "Careful, don't spill it. I forgot the saucers," he lied.

Vera sipped the tea in silence, keeping her face forward not able to look into Marko's eyes. He turned and looked at her for a long time, ignoring his promise to not look. She felt his eyes on her, but did not return his gaze.

"Oh, Veritza," he said, his voice trembling with emotion. "Don't you think I guessed? It doesn't matter! It never mattered!"

Book II, Chapter 28

At Magda's the popular gambling house in Zagreb one couldn't just wander in. An established patron might bring a friend who had never been there before and introduce him to Magda. If Magda approved, she would say nothing to the doorman. If she didn't approve, which wasn't very often, a word to the doorman and that person was not allowed to enter.

Tonight Magda sat alone in the tiny living space at the back of the house. It was a very tidy little room. Her bed was piled high with lots of fancy embroidered pillows. Her curtains had embroidered flowers of all colors and were hemmed with long knotted fringes. Tonight she wore a bright red caftan, which clashed terribly with her henna colored hair. On her table sat the moneybox with the receipts of the night's business.

The plump woman once had a very nice business and enjoyed the friendship of many men from the finest families. Of course, she was never invited to their homes, but that was understood. It did not mean she did not have affection for them, for many certainly called her friend.

This night it was very late. The last customer had left, and soon it would be morning. There was money to count and bookkeeping to attend to. She never had to worry about doing the count every night before she had a partner. In the past, she would go to bed and count the money in the morning. Sometimes a couple of days would go by before she did her bookkeeping. When she needed to pay someone, she would just reach into the box and pay. Now she needed to write everything down in a ledger. She needed to know which games brought in the most money and which lost the most.

Magda no longer just reached into the box and paid money to a winning gambler or an employee. Now she needed a signature when she paid money to someone. And she needed to make reports each week on every aspect of the business. The expenses of feeding the girls working upstairs had to be recorded. Magda never did this before she had a partner.

She was very tired. She was getting too old to stand on her feet all night mingling with her guests, greeting them and then seeing them off. Most of all, it wasn't a pleasure anymore. Since Abuh had become her partner, she discovered that she could never relax. She was always tense, aware that she was being watched.

Tonight was the worst night! Abuh called her to his office. It was more of a storage room for his merchandise than an office.

He was standing in front of the large desk, which was covered with an assortment of porcelain statues.

"Has the Vladislav boy come in to pay his debt?" Abuh asked abruptly, not asking her to sit.

"No," said Magda, "I have not seen him since the night he came here with Blaz Sukich. The night you told him he had seven days to pay the debt."

"What a stupid, foolish, rich boy!" Abuh snarled. "Does he think he can toy with me? He was supposed to have been here two days ago."

"He will pay," said Magda. "He never left me with a debt for very long."

"You stupid, fat woman," said Abuh, with disgust. "That is why you couldn't pay your own bills and I had to come in and settle your debts."

Magda shrank from his words. No one had ever spoken to her that way. She was used to friendly laughter, some shared confidences even some occasional token gifts. She knew her looks were gone, but no one...no one ever called her stupid or fat to her face before. She fought back the tears which stung her eyes.

"Don't start to cry," Abuh said sarcastically. "Women's tears do nothing to me...especially a stupid woman's tears."

He moved to the back of the desk, pulled the chair close and sat down, still leaving Magda standing like a naughty child.

"You take care of things for the next few days. I am going to find Vladislav and deal with him in a way he will not forget."

"What are you going to do?" she asked trying to hide her concern.

"You don't want to know!"

Magda shivered when she heard these words. She was sure that Abuh could be cruel...very cruel. Now she was afraid of him.

Yes, she was very tired tonight. But, she had too much on her mind to sleep.

First, she went behind a draped doorway to a small room that served as a place to wash. She poured water into a large bowl from a pitcher painted with red roses. With the pins out of her hair, she shook her thinning hair loose with her fingers and bent over the bowl. Magda then lathered her hair several times with scented soap, cupping the water from the bowl with her hands to rinse the soap. With several washings the water became rust colored. The henna was washing out. She emptied the bowl and with clean water from a pitcher gave her hair a final rinse.

Much of the soapsuds had slid down her forehead and cheeks, so that when Magda wiped her face of make-up and towel dried her hair, she no long looked like the Magda of Magda's Gambling House.

The reflection she saw in the mirror could have been a plump, gray haired grandmother. With her hair still wet, she smoothed it back and coiled it into a tight bun at the back of her head. This was the face she didn't like. It was a face without any powder or pencil drawn eyebrows or khol-lined eyes. It was the face of an old, plain woman.

She poured herself a Slivovica, the popular plum brandy. Magda sat down at her round table and looked about her little room, slowly sipping the drink. Her heart was pounding. Was she doing the right thing? It didn't matter. She couldn't stay here anymore. She couldn't face her old customers anymore. Nothing was the same. The warm ambiance was gone from the establishment known as Magda's.

Most of all, she was afraid of Abuh. He only kept her because for the time being he needed her. She was sure of that. It was just a matter of time before he would find a younger, beautiful woman to be the hostess of Magda's. What would happen to her then? Would he buy her out of her share of the business? She doubted it. Most of all she feared how he might end their partnership.

Magda found a plain gray skirt that came to her ankles. She put on a white blouse with ruffles at the neck, in the continental style. Her gray leather shoes laced up to the ankles.

Before she finished dressing, she took a carpetbag with wooden handles and laid it open on her bed. Magda only owned a few 'simple' pieces of clothing and these she rolled up and placed in the bag. Most of her wardrobe consisted of colorful evening caftans. She spread out a handkerchief and gathered up what jewelry she had, which was a surprisingly nice collection. After all, she hadn't always been old and fat. In her youth she had acquired gifts of jewelry from admirers. She tied the handkerchief into a ball and it also went into the carpetbag.

The last thing she put in the bag was the box from her table, full of last night's cash receipts. She gathered up the bag and hefted it. It wasn't as heavy as she thought it might be. Good, it would be easy to carry.

Over her white blouse with the ruffled neckline, came a gray jacket with tiny gray mother of pearl buttons down the front and at the wrists. Her hat was a wide brim gray felt with a flat crown. A large black hatpin finished her ensemble. She looked every bit the nanny or governess.

Magda took one look about the room. She went into the entry hall and looked around. She felt a twinge of regret. Not the regret of leaving this place, but the regret of getting older, the regret at not getting married when she could have, the regret of not having children, and most of all…of being alone.

Earlier she had given the girls who worked upstairs some money to go out on the town. This was a rare treat for them and they eagerly took the money and hurried out.

Magda had made sure no one would be in the house while she prepared to leave.

She went back to her room and slipped out the back way, so that anyone passing by would not see her. She didn't call a carriage. Instead she walked away briskly. Her parents were both gone and her sister died years ago. She had no family home to go to.

Magda bought a ticket for the Orient Express. She considered the money in the cashbox as payment for her share of the business. Magda would have a new life, a new start.

The Orient Express began its famous life on Oct. 4, 1884. Today it was on its way from Paris, stopping in Zagreb to go on to Istanbul. Magda knew that kings and princes often traveled on the Orient Express. She doubted she would see any of them, but it gave her a certain air of satisfaction to know she could be in close proximity to royalty.

Magda settled in her luxurious first-class car. The accommodations were costly but she didn't care. She was on a grand adventure.

As the train slowly steamed its way out of the lovely city of Zagreb, Magda never looked back.

Also leaving Zagreb, but in a different direction was Abuh. He was disgusted with that Vladislav boy. Did that young, spoiled boy think he could get away with not paying his debt? It didn't matter that the diamond and amethyst earrings were very old and valuable. That wasn't the point! Abuh didn't want these rich people to think they could play him the way they had played that stupid Magda. *Stupid Magda, always fawning over the rich customers as if they were special.* Abuh knew rich people weren't special. They didn't know what it meant to suffer in order to survive. To wonder where each meal would come from, to wonder where one would sleep at night, to be in fear that someone would take away what little money one had.

Abuh had suffered and survived. No one would owe him money for any length of time and no one would ever take what was his without paying the price. He had been alone on the streets since he was nine years old.

Abuh did not remember his mother or father. He didn't know where he originally came from or who his people were. His earliest recollection was of living with a shopkeeper on the outskirts of Istanbul. Abuh remembered sleeping on the floor of the shop. Maybe the man had been his father but he doubted it. Surely his father would have been kinder to him, he thought. This man was not kind. He thought nothing of beating Abuh and making him work long hours in the shop. It was his job to carry and move the rolled up carpets and rugs, a hard job for a skinny little boy.

Abuh couldn't recall how old he had been when he had been sold to the dark-eyed woman dressed in heavy, pleated skirts with much geometric embroidery on the trim. On her head was a white veil with colorful trim all along the edges. The woman took him to a place near Plovidiv, Bulgaria, where he had been dressed nicely, but treated poorly.

The woman was pretty with black hair and dark eyes set in a very round face. She was less pretty when she smiled, for she had uneven teeth that lapped over one another.

Again, just as he had done in Turkey, he slept on the floor on a mat. Kali, the woman who bought him was a whore. His duties were that of a houseboy who swept, kept the small house tidy and served refreshments when Kali entertained. Kali's male guests found little Abuh amusing, often teasing him, making fun of him, and sometimes tossing him a coin to keep. Even though Kali occasionally beat him for some infraction, Abuh was happy to have a roof over his head and food to eat. He had seen the street boys wearing filthy rags, with sores on their bodies, begging and stealing to survive. Abuh had been terrified of living like those boys, sleeping with the rats in the streets.

Abuh often wondered what course his life would have taken had it not been for that disgusting night, when one of Kali's guests requested that, "The boy take off his pants."

He could still remember with some pain how Kali had laughed that night so long ago, as if it had been a delightful suggestion. She was wearing a sheer yellow caftan and looked rather nice, even enticing.

How old could he have been, eight, nine? Abuh had been embarrassed and frightened. He cried, not wanting to undress and Kali slapped him into silence. Frightened, he removed his pants. The old man, also wearing a caftan, fondled Abuh's little penis. His bony fingers were tipped with yellowed fingernails. Abuh could not remember the man's face, but to this day he remembered those yellow fingernails stained from years of smoking Turkish tobacco.

Little Abuh tried to back away, but Kali pushed him closer to the man who was undoing his own sash, preparing to disrobe. Little Abuh had heard all the moans and cries many nights made by Kali. To his child's mind, he could only imagine the pain she was enduring. He couldn't equate such cries with pleasure. Crying and moaning meant pain. God! He didn't want to be hurt. He didn't want to be hurt so that he would scream and cry out. Kali stepped in front of Abuh to help the man undo his clothes.

Young Abuh saw his chance. With only a long shirt on his body, Abuh ran out of the room knocking over a low brass table, sending wine bottles and glasses scattering about. He heard Kali curse as she tripped over the upturned table. Abuh never looked back. He ran out the door, down the street and hid under a bridge, terrified of the rats scurrying past his feet.

Later that night when he was cold, hungry and frightened, Abuh crept back to Kali's house. She was in a deep sleep aided by much sweet wine. Abuh was so terrified that he held his breath as he slipped through a window and past her bed. He went to a cabinet. The key was in the lock and it sounded a loud 'click' when Abuh turned it. Kali didn't stir. By the gleam of moonlight that shined through the windows, he took some money and found his clothes. Quietly, he took some goat cheese and hard bread. He waited until he was outside to put on his pants and at his waist he tied the money pouch. It was on that night the little boy who had no one, swore never to trust anyone again - especially a woman. His greatest vow, as he tied the money pouch at his waist, was that it would always be full of coins.

That little frightened boy, now a man, had kept the vow he made so long ago. His money pouch was always full of coins.

His mind floated back and forth from the past to the present. That Magda, he would get rid of her when he got back. She was too softhearted. She gave away drinks and food when she should have charged the customers. She was still behaving as if it all belonged to her and she could do whatever she wanted with the money. Well, that was going to change. He would find someone else, someone beautiful. Someone who understood how Abuh wanted the business to operate.

Abuh thought about Stefan. How would he handle the boy? First, he would like to humiliate him in front of his family. But, what if they defended him? After all Abuh was only one man. Well, not really. He was supposed to meet Mustafa, the Gypsy.

Abuh had to be careful. He couldn't be part of any violence where he could be recognized. He had to get Stefan alone, away from his family if he were to give him a lesson the young man wouldn't forget. He really disliked Stefan. The young man was far too handsome and spoiled. Abuh would teach Stefan some respect, and perhaps make him not so handsome. Abuh liked that idea. He wondered how handsome Stefan would be with an ugly scar on his pretty face.

Anton hadn't come home for the past two nights. The first night Ernesta ranted and raved, the second night she was openly worried that some harm may have befallen him.

It had never occurred to any of them that he was at Father Lahdra's home, his closest friend and confessor.

After Anton finally told his friend the long humiliating story of his love for Vera and his rejection of her so long ago, Father Lahdra said, "How have you kept this secret so long? Did you confess it?"

"Of course not," said Anton. "I know priests are supposed to keep confessions sacred. I couldn't be sure. And I was ashamed."

After a long silence Lahdra asked, "What are you going to do? Will you claim Ivan as your heir?"

Anton's bent head jerked up, "Of course not!" Then, embarrassed at his prompt answer, he said, "I can't. I owe that much to Stefan. Erna and Stefan would both suffer if I legally acknowledged Ivan."

"And, Ivan, don't you think he will suffer?" asked Lahdra.

Anton dropped his head in his hands moving it back and forth in a negative gesture.

"I don't know if Ivan will want to speak with me ever again. Stefan hates me. Ivan probably does, too."

Lahdra reached a hand to Anton, pulling at his hand, so that Anton looked up at the priest. Lahdra said, "Anton. It is only human to make mistakes. Those you love will in time forgive you, when they see how much you are suffering. You must talk with Erna and Stefan...calmly. You must let them know how much you care for them. They need to know they are first and always your family." Lahdra waited for some reply from Anton, and when none came, he went on, "You must also go to Marko and talk with him. He has been like a brother to you. Don't you think he is in pain with all the gossip that is surely spreading? Reach out to him and Ivan, and what about Vera?"

"Oh, Vera, well I know where I stand with her. She has been cool to me ever since the night I turned her away from the house. Haven't you noticed she never speaks to me, conversationally?

She greets me politely and says 'Good-bye' politely and that is the extent of our speaking. It never varies, except for the other day when she came to the house. What a shock that was!"

Anton stood up and moved about the tastefully furnished room, with most of the furniture lent from his own family's things.

He went on, "Once she started talking there was no stopping her. It was as if she didn't care who knew. She only wanted me to try and keep Ivan from leaving. Vera thinks he wants to go to America."

"He is upset over the change in Katya," said Anton. "Who would suspect that a kind act by Sofie, bringing the girl to our home and teaching her to read, could do all this?"

"Anton,' said his friend, "I think you should go home. You are welcome to stay here as long as you wish, but I think you need to go home. The longer you stay away the harder it will be to make things right. Well…" he paused, "as right as you can make them, considering."

Book II, Chapter 29

Anton decided Father Lahdra's advice was correct. He had to talk with Erna and Stefan. He had to let them know that they were first and always his family. Later, he would talk with Ivan and Marko. He felt more trepidation about that encounter then with facing Ernesta and Stefan.

Anton's ride home was a nervous trip. He felt uncomfortable seeing the villagers who normally would wave a greeting. But today some turned as if they did not see him, or worse others just openly stared.

His head ached from thinking about it all. However wrongly he may have handled the situation, at the time he thought he was doing the right thing. He married the girl his father chose for him. He was as generous as he could be with Marko and Vera, trying never to overstep his concern for Ivan, and out of guilt, he had spoiled Stefan outrageously.

None of that mattered now. He had to find a way to let Stefan know how much he loved him.

As he rode slowly through the gate and into the yard, Anton could see a large man wearing a fez, speaking with Ernesta. The man wore black pants and a white shirt with a colorful sash around his waist. His hand held the reins of a large brown horse, beautifully saddled. Klara stood a few feet away, watching suspiciously. *What was going on? Who was this man and what did he have to do with the agitated Ernesta?*

As Anton rode within hearing range, he heard Ernesta say, "He is gone. No you cannot wait for him, he is gone!"

"What is it, Ernesta? What does this man want?" demanded Anton as he quickly dismounted, slapping his horse on the rump, a signal for the mare to head for the barn.

Ernesta turned to Anton, relief showing on her face. "This person wants to see Stefan."

"So...why don't you call him?" Anton was becoming annoyed. He wanted to talk with Stefan, to set things straight. This stranger was interfering.

Ernesta on the verge of tears, her lower lip trembling as she whispered to Anton, "I don't know where he is." Glancing sideways at the stranger she added, "Some of his clothes are gone!"

Alarmed, Anton wanted to ask questions, but checked himself. Turning to the Turk he asked, "Why do you wish to see my son?"

"It is of a personal nature."

"Since I am head of this house, I politely request you tell me the reason for this visit." Anton's words were cool.

The Turk looked from Anton to the nervous Ernesta. "Your son owes me some money and it is long overdue."

"A lie, we paid it!" Ernesta's voice could be heard all the way to the road.

Anton turned to Ernesta, in obvious surprise. What debt he wondered? And how was it paid? He would deal with Ernesta, later. Now he wanted to rid himself of this man who made him feel uneasy. "My wife says the debt was paid. Why are you here?"

"She is mistaken," Abuh said politely, giving a bow, which was not meant as a sign of courtesy, but more of sarcasm.

"I am not!" Ernesta's face was red with anger. "You already have my earrings."

Her earrings? Her mother's diamond and amethyst earrings? What other secrets did Ernesta and Stefan share! Anton needed to get rid of this menacing person, this person who spoke politely but mocked them with his eyes.

"You have already been paid enough. You won't get anymore from us, so you may as well leave," said Anton with calm authority.

Abuh looked at Anton, his eyes narrowing. "There will come a time when the rich will no longer take advantage of those less fortunate."

"You do not look as if you have ever been taken advantage of. And you do not look needy." Anton was angry. "If we owed you anything, we would pay it, but it seems we do not. Please leave and do not return. As far as I am concerned, you have no more business with my son or with any of us."

The Turk fought to maintain his calm. How dare this landowner, this user of the poor peasant, speak to him so rudely. "Because you are a man of position, I am to forget your son is in my debt? I think not."

"Was that a threat?" Anton's face reddened. "What is your name? Where are you from?" It was a demand.

The Turk gave Anton a menacing smile, turned away slowly, and mounted his horse, then leisurely rode towards the gate not looking back.

Once the Turk was out of sight, Anton gripped Ernesta's arm.

"You said Stefan's clothes are missing. Did you say something to upset him? What has been going on?"

"Why would I upset my son?" cried Ernesta, wiping away tears.

"Then, why did he leave?" Anton held onto Ernesta's arm.

"Perhaps he didn't like having Ivan for a brother." She managed to sting Anton with those words. "And, perhaps he wasn't delighted to have our house guest," she nearly spat out the words, "become his legal cousin."

Anton let go her arm and she rubbed the pained spot caused by his grip.

"What are you saying? I don't understand."

"Of course, you don't understand." Ernesta was becoming her old sarcastic self. "You never seem to be around long enough to know what is going on."

"Alright, Erna, let's go in the house and talk. Tell me everything and try not to be hysterical. I can't help it if I don't know exactly what has been said and done."

In an uncharacteristic move Anton put his arm protectively around Ernesta's shoulder, his anger melting into worry, "Together we will try and make things right again." It was both a wish and a prayer.

Katya and Sofie were seated on the heavily carved settee in the priest's sitting room. The women sipped chamomile tea, while Alexie Lukas and Lahdra held glasses of some homemade wine, a gift from a parishioner.

Lahdra never mentioned Anton's stay, nor did his guests mention any of the family's problems. The three had no way of knowing that Anton had already told the priest everything.

"We were hoping you could arrange for the local priest near Selna to accompany one of my assistants." Alexie was explaining the reason for their visit. "You see," he went on, "according to

Katya, no one in the village can read. Also we were concerned that they might be suspicious of a stranger, where as, if a priest came along, they would believe what my assistant had to say."

"May I know what message your assistant is taking?" asked Lahdra, his curiosity growing. He offered to pour more wine in Alexei's glass, but the advocate covered the glass with his hand, indicating he had enough.

Before Alexie could answer, Katya, her green eyes dancing with excitement, proudly stated, "I have had a legal document drawn up." She paused waiting to see the priest's expression, which was one of mild surprise.

"What sort of document?" he asked, looking to Alexie for a fuller explanation.

Alexie paused and looked to Katya. When she nodded, he spoke.

"Katya was given a house by a woman known as Old Julia."

Lahdra nodded. He remembered the old woman well, for she always made him feel uncomfortable.

"Katya assumes the house has been left unoccupied in her absence. She is sure that her friend Milan and his family are taking care of the property. Then," Alexie went on, "there is the home Katya grew up in, the one which belonged to her sister, Anka. There is a brother in law who lives there now."

In her excitement Katya jumped up, almost spilling her tea. "I want Milan and his family to get Old Julia's house." Her face shone with pleasure. "I wish I could give them the house I grew up in, but it is Elia's house now."

Katya's wish that her childhood home would also go to Milan and his family was as good as done. No one but Milan, his wife Eva, their children, and of course, the old man Stevo, who helped bury Elia, knew Elia was dead. Eva Kosich lived constantly in fear, worried someone would find out, and the authorities would come knocking at her door. She never meant to kill Elia. Eva barely remembered hitting him that rainy night when he grabbed her daughter.

Alexie interrupted, "We have made a provision in the deed that should Elia die unmarried, the house will go to Milan, also."

"You are sure that you will never return? You may want the house for yourself," said Lahdra.

Sofie spoke up, "She doesn't have to. Katya is now my legal ward and heir."

"Oh," said Lahdra surprised. "Oh, my, I mean how very nice." Then quickly he asked, "Were there any contradictory opinions on this decision?"

"This is a private matter between Katya and me. I discussed it with no one, but Alexie," said Sofie, smiling at her lawyer.

"Oh, my..." Lahdra repeated.

"So, Father," Alexie took control of the conversation again. "Do you think you could contact the local priest to accompany the man I will be sending with the legal papers?"

"Why...yes, of course, I can," Lahdra was thinking of Anton. He wondered how Anton was going to deal with this when Ernesta found out. He wondered. Oh, Dear!

Alexie broke into Lahdra's thoughts. "We were wondering if a monetary gift for the priest would be appropriate."

"Yes...that would be fine," he murmured. Lahdra's thoughts were still with Anton and Anton's reunion with Ernesta.

Leaving the priest's home, Katya and Sofie sat in the back of the open carriage, while Alexie drove.

It had been a lovely visit with Father Lahdra, though the priest did seem a little distracted later in the visit. Katya felt wonderful. She was elated that she could do something to repay Milan and Eva for watching over her as she was growing up. And, she was now ashamed for being so cool to Milan when he left her with Marko's family. She was sorry she didn't hug and kiss him. Instead she had been rude and ungrateful. Katya hoped with all her heart that her gift of Old Julia's house would make up for her bad behavior, and that it would show Milan that she still loved and thought about him and his family.

Katya felt very comfortable with Alexie Lukas. She liked him very much. He was a confident man who had a quiet strength about him that was reassuring to her. And she liked the way he looked at Sofie, who didn't seem to mind the attention he gave her.

On the ride home Katya felt warm and happy as the carriage bounced on the dirt road close to Vladezemla. How perfect her life was at this moment. She belonged to Sofie, as if she were Sofie's own daughter. It really didn't matter anymore that Ernesta didn't like her. Katya could deal with that. Just knowing that Sofie was now her guardian was like a miracle. And Anton was so good to her. When she thought of Stefan, it was with disappointment. She cared less for him now, remembering his drunken visit to her room. She knew he did not come to her out a feeling of love. She had seen enough of that sort of lovemaking when Elia had been drunk and forced himself on her sister Anka.

Katya's thoughts drifted to Ivan. He would never have abused her so. Katya remembered the first day she met Ivan at the wedding. How wonderful he made her feel. He was such a good man, such a handsome man. She would go visit him. Yes, that's what she would do.

She was probably the only person unaware of the fact that Ivan was Anton's son.

"Teta Sofie," she said. "I have not visited the Balabans in a long time. Do you think we could go tomorrow?"

Abuh was furious as he rode away from Vladezemla. He would fix them. He told their spoiled son that the debt would double if not paid on time. As far as he was concerned he was owed the money and one way or another, he would get satisfaction.

He guided his horse to the side of the road so that an on-coming carriage could pass by.

Katya *saw him* long before the carriage passed him on the road. She recognized him instantly. She couldn't breath. She felt herself go cold. She grabbed at Sofie's hand with icy fingers. Sofie, taken aback, turned to look into Katya's white face, which stared straight ahead.

The Turk bowed courteously, as he always did when passing a carriage, glancing only briefly at the well-dressed driver and the two sophisticated women. *Probably part of the Vladislav household,* thought Abuh.

Abuh stopped his horse and turned to look after the carriage. One of the finely dressed women had red hair. He watched the receding carriage for a long time, then shrugged his shoulders, and proceeded down the dusty road towards the woods looking for the Gypsy camp.

Klara didn't follow Anton and Ernesta into the house. Instead she went into the chapel to pray. Her life had been spent in the kitchen of the house, her bed in an alcove behind a curtain. She had never had a proper home or a proper room. Her life was in that kitchen. Today, her life seemed to be unraveling like a ball of yarn rolling across the floor. There had always been some discord in the household, but never anything that Klara thought threatened their way of living until recently. Ernesta might lose her mind if Stefan didn't return. She was becoming devious and demanding. In the past she had just been bossy and rude. If Stefan didn't come home, who would eventually take over the duties of running the farm?

Klara's prayers and thoughts were interrupted by the sound of an approaching carriage. She rose stiffly and stepped through the chapel door just in time to see the carriage driven by Alexie, pull up before the house. Klara could tell that something was wrong for Sofie was hugging a sobbing Katya, trying to comfort her.

Klara hurried to the kitchen door and shouted to Anton. "Come out here, quickly. Something has happened."

She called so loudly Anton heard her all the way into the dining room. The sound of urgency in her voice only made him wonder what more could happen. Klara stayed a respectful distance away, as Anton hurried to the carriage with a curious Ernesta fast behind him.

Katya was crying repeatedly, "Boze Moi, My God, it's him." An exasperated, Alexie Lukas, was standing at the driver's seat, trying to make sense of the hysteria. "Who, what are you talking about?"

Under the circumstances, Alexie dispensed with polite greetings only giving Anton a quick nod. "What has happened?" demanded Anton. "Is she hurt?"

"I don't know," said an upset Sofie. "We passed a man on horseback on the road and Katya turned to ice and has been crying and shaking ever since."

"Come, get down from there," ordered Anton. "Let's sit in the shade where we can talk."

Sofie was the first to the ground, while Anton and Alexie helped the crying Katya from the carriage. She was weak with fear, "I thought I was safe here," she sobbed. "I thought I was safe."

"Safe from what?" demanded Anton, as he guided her to the bench under an apple tree. *Was his life never going to know peace and quiet again?*

Klara hurried to the well, pulled up the bucket and carried it back to the group gathered under the tree. She handed Katya a dipper of cold water. They all stood watching in a semi-circle while Katya sipped the water, waiting for her to regain her composure.

Anton looked at Sofie for some comment, but she only shrugged her shoulders.

When Katya's sobs slowed and her breathing seemed normal, Anton asked again, "Safe from what?"

In a voice so small and low, they could barely hear her, "That Man!"

Anton asked, "The man that just left, the one wearing a fez?"

Her face wet with tears and her eyes swollen, Katya nodded.

"Why would he have any business with you? He owns a gambling house."

Sofie gasped, her hand flew to her mouth. It was as if she didn't want to say the words. Then, in a low voice she asked, "Is he the one? The one your brother-in-law brought to Selna?"

Again, Katya only nodded.

"Oh, Anton," Sofie said. "That's the man who tried to buy her. The one she is hiding from."

"Are you sure?" This news sent a shiver through Anton making him fear for Stefan's safety. "Could you be mistaken?" He looked to Katya hoping she was uncertain.

Katya shuddered as if a cold breeze had passed over her. "No, I am not mistaken. That is the man."

Throughout this drama Ernesta had stayed silently in the background. She had found the information very interesting and useful.

At last, she had her PLAN.

That night Anton never undressed or thought of going to bed. Instead, he wandered aimlessly through the house, fearing for his son's safety and wishing he could turn back time. As dawn was breaking he was seated outdoors beneath the wide spreading apple tree.

Anton watched as the workers from the cottages came in ones and twos to work on Vladazemla. News of Stefan's leaving had already spread through the village and the mood of the people was already changing. Now they respectfully doffed their hats in greeting. Gone were the smirks about the blacksmith's wife and Anton having a love child, like Klara, they too sensed all was not well. Vladazemla was the center of their lives. Anton was a good landlord, a generous man. What did the future hold if there was a change of hands? Was the young Stefan coming back? Would he be generous? And if he didn't return was there a chance it would go to Ivan? There were many regrets. Too much teasing, too many rude remarks directed at Ivan and his family. If he were to take over Vladazemla, would there be repercussions?

Alexie Lukas had spent the night sleeping in the small reading room off the parlor. Sofie invited Alexie without consulting Ernesta. *Well, that was fine, just fine*, Erna thought. Ernesta would let this pass. Soon she would be the only mistress in charge of the house.

In the morning, Alexie, with his shirt collar undone and shirttail hanging out over his trousers, joined Anton beneath the tree. His thick black hair was combed straight back from his face and he had already shaved. He handed Anton a glass of tea, wrapped with a cloth napkin to protect his fingers from the heat. Alexie sipped his own tea waiting for Anton to say something. They sat in silence for a time before Anton spoke.

"You are a polite man, Alexie. I appreciate that."

"Thank you."

"Is it really done? I mean… did my sister really make Katya her ward?"

"Yes, it's done." Then after a pause, Alexie asked, "Do you mind?"

"I mind if it was the reason for my son leaving, yet I don't mind if it makes my sister happy."

"Sofie is very happy. She feels she has someone to care for at last...someone of her own," added the lawyer.

"I suppose women have that need. That need for someone to care for," said Anton, thinking of his love for Stefan.

"I think we all have that need," Alexie said. "I know I do."

Anton glanced at Alexie, who kept his gaze straight ahead. Anton had known Alexie Lukas for most of his life. Today, for the first time, he discovered that he liked the man very much. He wondered what his sister thought of Alexie.

Book II, Chapter 30

The Gypsy caravan was settling on Marko and Vera's field. For the past twenty years the Gypsies made camp here on their way to France. There was much activity: women spreading blankets on the ground to display wares for sale, small children gathering sticks and branches for fires, and girls going to the stream for fresh water. For many it was an old familiar pattern. They would camp for two days having a festival of sorts with the villagers, do some buying, a little trading and take advantage of the stream to get the washing done and water the horses. There might be a horse traded, many fortunes told, amulets sold and even some late night visits by lustful men from the village to a caravan a little away from the rest, where a seductive Gypsy woman might earn some coins.

Ivan was keeping to himself, not wanting another encounter such as he had with Vanjo, when the musician had called him 'The Young Master.' Even when friends didn't say anything, Ivan could feel their eyes on him. He was sure they snickered behind his back and it made him feel a stranger, an outsider. And he hated what was happening to them all. The loss of respect, being the object of jokes and ridicule, was too much for him. He wished he could be like his father, Marko, and brother, Nikola, ignoring it all, holding their heads up high, but like a coward, he wanted to hide.

That was what he was doing now, hiding in the forest, keeping to himself as much as possible. When it was dark, he would make his way home, careful not to meet anyone on the way.

Ivan found that he wasn't bored, seated up on the hill among the berry bushes, hidden from view. He had his horse tethered near-by on a grassy spot and he could hear if anyone approached. Yesterday he had heard someone on the trail. At first Ivan stayed hidden, not wanting to be seen. He could tell by the sounds of footsteps, that a horse was being led and not ridden. Ivan looked through the branches at the approaching man and horse. When he recognized who was coming, something within him made him step out onto the trail.

Leading his horse, Stefan lost in thought stared at the ground. He was startled by the sudden appearance of Ivan on the trail.

They stood not speaking, each looking the other full in the face, searching for something...for what? All their lives there had been a distance between them. They looked at one another for what seemed a long time. There was now something different about each of them.

Gone was their arrogance, an arrogance they had never recognized in themselves: Stefan's for being the wastrel and Ivan's for being a favored companion. They had each lost something important, their identities. Stefan was no longer the firstborn. Now Ivan was. And, Ivan was not the blacksmith's son, but the bastard son of Anton. They were both floundering with the strangers they had become overnight, just as if they had fallen off a boat into water. Stefan looked away and Ivan stepped aside, letting him pass. Ivan knew Stefan was going away, knew that Stefan also was hiding in the hills and using the old trail so no one would see his departure.

Ivan was surprised to find he was sad as he watched Stefan, who never looked back, disappear into the forest. He wondered if Stefan also felt sad. If things had been in the open long ago, could he and Stefan have been as close as he was with his brother Nikola? Probably not, he decided.

That brief encounter with Stefan was yesterday. Today, Ivan spent most of the time watching the activities of the Gypsy camp below and if he stood, he could see his own home behind the encampment.

In two or three days the Gypsies would leave, so that meant there would be much more activity in the camp this day.

He watched as peasants on foot came with baskets of food to sell or trade or as payment for a fortune told or for a magical charm. Father Lahdra was nearly driven crazy by the peasant's belief in the magical charms. He would see scraps of knotted cloth pinned to someone's clothing to ward off evil, or a carving, usually phallic in nature, dangling from a string around a man's neck, for virility. Even women wore love charms, though usually hidden in their clothing.

From his hillside vantage point, Ivan could identify nearly everyone coming and going from the camp. He easily recognized his father Marko and brother Nikola when they came in a wagon carrying two young pigs. Every year his father gifted Valina's people with something to cook on the spit. Ivan felt a touch of sadness, for this was the first time he was not riding in the wagon alongside his father and brother. His mother wasn't with them, either. He knew she couldn't face the embarrassment. The pitying or mocking eyes of everyone and the hushed whispers would humiliate her. It broke his heart to think of her hiding in their home. She had always been so proud of her family. His mother had been admired and envied, but now she was the butt of jokes. It was too much for his dear, sweet Mother.

Ivan could see the excitement and the rush of Gypsies gathering around his father's wagon. He could hear snatches of the loud laughter and delighted squeals from the children. Though the Gypsies were adept at hunting and gathering food, the pigs were a welcomed luxury. Ivan could never get used to the fact that the Gypsies dined regularly on thorny hedgehogs.

Ivan saw Valina come from behind her caravan to speak with Marko no doubt thanking him for the pigs. At one point Valina turned from the group and looked upward into the hills. It seemed to Ivan he could feel her eyes on him through the cover of the dense berry bushes.

"This is only half the family," Valina said to Marko. "Usually you come with your wife, and I see that Ivan is missing."

"Perhaps my wife will join us this evening," Marko doubted his own words, but he said them anyway.

"I have a wife and we will come to see you tonight," said a proud Nikola.

Queen Valina looked at the stocky, handsome Nikola, sturdy like his father, and so unlike Ivan.

"I will look forward to telling your fortunes and as a wedding gift for the bride, I will have a special charm," said Valina, once again turning to look up into the hills.

"That will make Luba happy," said Nikola.

As the men turned to leave, Valina took hold of Marko's hard, leathery hand. She looked down into the palm scarred over the years by hot metal from the forge. She stared a long moment then said, "Too many scars and blisters. I can't see enough between them to tell your fortune."

"Thank you, Valina," said Marko, softly. "I don't think I want my palm read."

As Marko and Nikola rode away in their now empty wagon, they waved and promised to return that evening.

The old Gypsy Queen felt sad. She agreed with Marko. It was better he didn't know the future.

At his place on the hillside Ivan must have dozed, for the sun was no longer overhead, it was starting its westward descent. From the high point on the hill, Ivan noticed one of the Gypsies furtively slip away from the camp. The dark figure cautiously looked about before heading for the side of the hill where he began to climb. Ivan watched the Gypsy and wondered why he was being so secretive. His curiosity aroused, Ivan rose from under the bushes and found a better viewing spot several feet away.

Ivan nearly lost his footing when he noticed a man sitting on a rock looking down at the camp. The man wore black pants, a white shirt and a black vest and wore a black fez. Ivan didn't think the man heard him, for he seemed to be deep in thought. The stranger only stirred when the Gypsy appeared at the top of the hill. "Ah, you are already here. Have you been waiting long?" Ivan saw the homely Gypsy squat next to the stranger.

"No, not long. I'll need you tonight. We're going to Vladezemla. Meet me here when it is dark."

Ivan saw the Gypsy nod. "Will I need anything?" Ivan's heart froze when he heard the stranger say to the Gypsy, "Maybe your knife."

Ivan was in terror as he watched the Gypsy descend the hill and slip back into the camp. The Gypsy's disappearance from the camp had apparently gone unnoticed. Ivan watched scarcely breathing as the stranger, he assumed to be a Turk, slowly got up. Ivan was sure he had not been seen for the Turk glanced casually about the forest, walked to his horse, untied the reins, and slowly ambled down the same path Stefan had used the day before.

Whatever these two strangers had in mind, Ivan knew it could only be bad. What business could they have that had to be done at night? And the memory of the words '*your knife*' was disturbing. Should he tell his father or should he warn Anton? Did Stefan know about this and that was his reason for leaving? What about

Queen Valina? It was one of her people plotting with the stranger. Surely she couldn't be a party to this, never in all the years of the Gypsy's trips here had there ever been a serious problem. Nothing more than a few missing chickens, an occasional dog, or some disappearing laundry left drying on the bushes might be blamed on the Gypsies.

Then he thought of Katya. Surely she would be safe since she didn't have anything worth stealing. But, what if she would see the thieves? That would put her in danger, wouldn't it? He had to go to her, to be sure she would be safe. It never occurred to Ivan that this stranger could be the same man that Cousin Milan had told Marko about when he brought Katya asking if she could stay with them.

Ivan scrambled from his hiding place and hurried to where his horse was grazing. Tree branches hung low, growing over this seldom-used trail, so Ivan led his horse instead of mounting it.

Ivan tried to hurry as he went up the trail, back in the direction of his godfather's home. He had gone only a short distance when his horse gave a low whinny.

"Shuti, Bara," scolded Ivan. "Be quiet."

Ivan should have heeded the horse's warning, for the Turk had seen him in the bushes and was not sure how much of his conversation with Mustafa, Ivan had overheard.

Abuh had circled stealthily through the brush until he was behind Ivan. Instead of going down the trail, Abuh headed back up towards Vladezemla.

In his eagerness to get to Anton's house to protect Katja and to warn Anton, Ivan didn't hear the Turk as the man stepped from behind a tree. The blow he gave Ivan with the thick branch, the size of a log, sent Ivan tumbling unconscious down the side of the hill, bouncing off of bushes and scraping against protruding branches in his fall.

As dusk approached the merriment at the Gypsy camp could have rivaled any festival or Saint's Day. The villagers were in their best and most colorful clothes. The young single girls had bright red or yellow ribbons at the ends of their braids, while all the married women, young and old wore babushkas, tied at the back of their heads, or neatly knotted under their chins. Widows were all in black, the mandatory color for the rest of their lives, while widowers did not have the same tradition of wearing only black.

Blankets were spread in the out-lying area of the camp where baskets of food, bottles of wine and slivovica were brought by the villagers in anticipation of a picnic.

Some of the local musicians had gathered with the Gypsies to supply music for the circle or kolo dances. Later in the night the Gypsy women would dance their own wild steps accompanied with tambourines.

Queen Valina's caravan was in the center of the semi-circle of house-wagons. She was seated on a stool looking every inch the Queen. Her slightly gray hair was tied at the back with a satin ribbon. On her small frame she wore a loose blouse of purple silk, over a red and purple skirt. At her ears dangled gold coins, while around her neck were more coins. From her waist, resembling a long watch chain, were more coins from various countries. On each wrist was a wide gold band, set with various semiprecious stones from India. On her feet were simple leather sandals.

Valina's daughter Kaja was nearby as she had been when Katya first came to their camp during the trip from Selna. Kaja resembled her mother, with her dark skin and dark eyes and slender build. She carried herself proudly, though it looked as if she were a servant to her mother, for she attended to all her mother's needs. Kaja prepared her mother's meals and saw to Valina's comforts. Kaja was happy to do these tasks for she was destined to be the next Queen of the Gypsies.

Her great regret was that her only child was Zolton. She loved her handsome young son, but wished she also had a daughter. Kaja could not see Roha, Zolton's intended bride, as an attentive daughter-in-law, someday attending to Kaja's needs as Kaja willingly did for Valina. Roha was young, a little selfish and very aware of her dark beauty.

Kaja watched as Roha, barefooted, dressed in a red skirt and blouse, moved among the villagers. Roha teased and flirted, convincing man or woman that they needed their fortune told. Kaja would not have chosen Roha as a bride for Zoltan. It had been Valina's doing. The young Roha enjoyed the company of men too much for Kaja's liking. Too often Kaja had seen the girl allow her self to be fondled by strangers and more than once the girl would disappear, giving some feeble excuse for her absence when questioned. Now she watched as Roha pressed her body against a young man. She would have to speak to her mother about Roha's behavior and it should be soon.

Sofie, along with Alexie Lukas, who was still a guest at Vladezemla, talked Klara into going to the Gypsy camp with them. Katya would have no part of it as much as she longed to see Queen Valina and Zolton. Her fear of running into the Turk was so great, that she refused to leave her room. Ever since she had seen Abuh ride past their carriage, she had been sick with worry. Her sense of being safe was gone. That was why she ran away from Selna...to be safe, but now she realized she wasn't.

If the Turk found her, what would he do to her? Katya didn't know of such things as white slavery, if she had, she would have been more terrified than she already was.

She knew the Turk would take her away from Sofie, if he ever found her again. Katya had grown to love and trust Sofie. The thought of leaving her was painful. And Ivan, she thought of Ivan. It had been a while since she had seen him last. Katya realized she missed him terribly. Even if she had not seen him for some time, she knew that he was nearby, down the hill in the valley on his father's farm.

Book II, Chapter 31

Alone in her room wearing a blue night gown, hair coiled high on her head, Katya sat on the floor with the contents of the hand-painted tea set from Teta Sofie's unused trousseau spread around her. It was early evening and Alexie, Sofie and Klara had already left for the Gypsy camp for an evening of fortune-telling and visiting. They took with them corn meal, poppy seeds, hard cheese, some bread and smoked sausages. These were all gifts for the Gypsies.

No amount of coaxing could lure Katya from her room. She still shuddered at the thought of the Turk.

"He didn't recognize you," Sofie had argued.

"He came to see Stefan. The man doesn't even know you are here," said Anton.

"I don't care. I am not leaving the house. I am not leaving my room," she said. "I just want to stay here. Ernesta is staying home. I won't be alone."

None of their arguments convinced Katya. She was not going to leave the house or for that matter, her room.

Now with the others gone, she sat on the floor playing with the tea set, the way a child might. She set the cup on the saucer and pretended to pour tea. Katya held the colorful sugar bowl in her hand and studied the painted picture on its side. It was a village scene with thatched roof houses in the background. One house depicted a woman on a balcony airing the bedding, while in the foreground, a young girl cried on her lover's shoulder. The picture on the milk pitcher showed the same lovers in a garden, under a tree with a church in the far background. The lovers dressed in their Sunday best were embracing.

Looking at the painting of the lovers made Katya think of Ivan. He had been so nice to her! Remembering her time with him at the wedding gave her a warm feeling. It seemed such a long time since she had seen him last. She wondered if he was with the Gypsies, possibly dancing with one of the girls. Katya remembered how his face beamed when he had looked at her. Could he be smiling that wonderful smile at someone else tonight?

Or was he gone too, leaving the way Stephan did? She sighed deeply. She would not know since she wasn't leaving the house.

Carefully Katya rose, stepping over the dishes so as not to break any. She opened the door of the wardrobe. She took out the beautiful embroidered skirt and blouse she had borrowed from Ivan's mother to wear at the wedding, that first night when she and Milan had arrived from Selna. Wearing Sofie's stylish European fashions had put the ethnic outfit out of her mind. Katya felt embarrassed. She should have returned it to Vera Balaban long ago.

The pictures on the tea set of the happy couple each in peasant dress stirred something in Katya. She wanted to feel the homespun cloth against her skin once again, to feel the weight of the heavy cloth with all its embroidery. She wanted to feel happy the way she had when dancing with Ivan at the wedding. Katya pulled the nightgown over her head tossing it onto the floor.

She slipped her arms into the heavily laced sleeves and buttoned the blouse against her bare breasts. The skirt slipped easily over her bare hips. She wrapped the coarse cord tightly around her waist, finishing off the outfit with the apron, a riotous garden of embroidered flowers. Katya looked approvingly at herself.

In her attic room, she could hear sounds of the happy music carried on the wind. The music reminded her even more of how much she had really enjoyed herself at Nikola and Luba's wedding. She reached up and removed the pins holding her red hair, letting it cascade around her shoulders. Katya ran her fingers through her hair to loosen it giving her head a shake, sending the wild curls up and around her head.

Catching a glimpse of herself in the wardrobe mirror, she studied herself. She was back! She had found the old Katya and was pleased to find she was not altogether changed. For some unknown reason it was relief to realize that she could be both Katyas: the Katya, the old women of Selna had called Gypsy, and the one who could read and wear European clothes with ease. It pleased her to feel and know that she could embrace the peasant side of herself, knowing she would never have to live that life again.

Outside the house, under the protection of darkness, Abuh and the Gypsy, Mustafa, slipped quietly past the chapel and stealthily made their way to the kitchen door at Vladezemla.

Both men froze as the door sounded with a squeal when opened. After a few moments when no one responded to the sound, they entered. An oil lamp on the kitchen table with the wick turned low, gave off a soft glow, with only enough light to keep one from bumping into the furniture or the wall. A similar lamp glowed on the dining room table, making it easy for the two thieves to slip past the stairway, then onto the door leading to the parlor. No light shone there, so Mustafa took the lamp from the dining room and led the way into the parlor.

Abuh's eyes became accustomed to the low light and he made a quick appraisal of what the room held.

His eyes found the Czechoslovakian glass vase with the etching of a prancing deer on the face of it. "Take that," he whispered, "and the silver candlesticks on each side of it. And this." From the wall above the fireplace Abuh removed a gilt-handled silver sword.

Setting down the lamp, Mustafa found a shawl resting on a side table and in it, wrapped the vase and candlesticks quickly and expertly.

The Gypsy felt uneasy. He wanted to leave. "We should go," he said.

"I didn't come all this way for these few things," Abuh growled. "I'm going to make it worth my while."

Mustafa slid his eyes about the room and nervously licked his dry lips. He had lived by intuition all his life, listening to the unspoken messages within his being. Now he felt a strong silent urge to leave this place.

Abuh was feeling behind pictures on the wall, hoping to find something of value hidden there.

"We should leave," Mustafa whispered again.

"Why are you behaving like a frightened girl?" demanded Abuh. "Here, take this." He shoved a small oval painting into Mustafa's hand.

From the doorway they heard a voice. "I knew you would return." The sound of Ernesta's voice startled both men. Mustafa already wary spun around toward the sound of the voice and nearly fell over a small table. Ernesta stood in the shadows, the dim light not reaching her. "Put my things down and let us talk business," she said, as if she were bargaining the price of a cow at market. She had made a plan. She hadn't known if she would ever have the opportunity to use the plan she had formed in her mind should the Turk ever return. But here he was, sooner than she expected. This was perfect!

"It's too late for that," said Abuh. "Your son has lost me much time and money."

Mustafa didn't like that the mistress of the house had appeared. It made no difference to the little man that Abuh and Ernesta spoke calmly to one another. He wanted to leave, now more than ever. He didn't want to get involved in anything physical. Taking a few things was fine with him, but not confrontations. No, this wasn't going right, he could feel it.

"I have something you want very much," Ernesta said smugly. "If I give it to you, you must promise to leave my son and this family alone."

Abuh's curiosity was piqued. He didn't have a clue as to what she could possibly have that he wanted. "Let me see what you have."

Ernesta stepped forward, the glow of the lamp casting dark shadows on her face.

"First you promise," she said.

"That's bad business," said Abuh, facing Ernesta. "I never make a deal without seeing what I'm getting."

Mustafa hid behind the Turk watching Ernesta and Abuh stare at one another.

Finally, she looked away. "Follow me upstairs. Raise the wick on the lamp so we can see where we are going."

Abuh picked up the lamp, did as he was told, and a bright light flooded the room. Ernesta led the way up the stairs. Abuh followed while Mustafa glumly brought up the rear, still carrying the loot.

As the trio made their way to the attic room, Abuh made note of the rooms they passed, with the possibility of plundering them later.

The Gypsy knew that Ernesta would have to be killed. She could identify them. What if Abuh wanted Mustafa to do it? He couldn't! He wouldn't! This was the first year that he, his wife, Gulja and their beautiful daughter Fikria were traveling with Valina's tribe. A little taking of 'this and that' the tribe would understand, but not murder, especially to a family that had for years befriended the nomads.

Once upstairs, Ernesta climbed the three steps to the attic room. She knocked gently, a self-satisfied smile on her lips. "Please open the door. It is Ernesta."

Ernesta stepped down from the doorway pushing Abuh in front of the closed door, while taking the oil lamp out of his hand,

He was suspicious for he didn't know what she was up to. He and Mustafa might be attacked. Abuh was about to turn and leave when he heard someone at the other side pull the door open.

There before Abuh stood the beautiful Katya, the peasant girl from Selna, the one who ran away from him and was probably an accomplice with Elia. Her emerald green eyes grew large, as she realized who was standing before her.

Both Katya and Abuh had the same startled look of amazement on their faces. The shock of unexpectedly facing one another left each momentarily speechless.

Katya turned looking for somewhere to run and seeing no escape, let go the most terrifying anguished scream Mustafa had ever heard. He couldn't see Katya, for he was still in the hallway. There was no room for him on the narrow passage to the attic room.

Katya slumped to the floor in a faint. There was no running this time, no sliding down a ravine and dashing across a field, or hiding under a bush. There was nowhere to go!

Abuh stepped into the room and pulled a large pillowcase from the bed, freeing it of its feather cargo. He slipped the pillowcase over Katya's head. A red spot grew on the pillowcase from a gash on Katya's head, caused by hitting her head on a table corner when she fainted. Abuh gathered Katya with her upper body hidden in the pillowcase, flinging her over his shoulder like a sack of flour.

Still holding the items from the parlor, Mustafa had to head down the narrow hallway first. Ernesta and Abuh carrying Katya, were coming towards him.

Ernesta was excited. She spoke rapidly as they hurried toward the stairs. "Now, leave the things from the parlor. We had a deal."

Ignoring Erna, Abuh grabbed the oil lamp from her with his free hand, still holding Katya with the other. He stepped into Ernesta's bedroom and glanced about.

"No!" she cried, standing in the narrow hall. "We had an agreement! You mustn't take anything else."

Abuh raised his foot and gave Ernesta a kick in the legs that sent her sprawling onto the floor.

A frightened Mustafa touched Abuh's shoulder. "We should go. Someone might have heard the scream."

Abuh thought for a second. "Yes, you are right."

As the men descended the stairs, a crazed Ernesta rose from the floor and leapt at Abuh. "Give me my things. Do you hear? I'll have you imprisoned or hanged."

Stepping sideways, Abuh gave Ernesta a shove. Instead of falling back into the hallway, she spun around and fell tumbling down the staircase, nearly knocking Mustafa off his feet.

Both men stood silent staring at the crumpled figure of Ernesta. They waited to hear a moan, or see a movement. When there was nothing, Abuh ran hurriedly down the stairs, with a frightened Mustafa looking for an exit.

While Sofie, Alexie and Klara had gone to the Gypsy camp, Anton chose to stay behind. He promised to join them later. He had been thinking and praying in the chapel, praying for his son Stefan, gone, God knows where. He prayed for Ivan, hoping the young man would come to terms with what could not be changed. Then, he prayed for himself, asking for the strength to make correct decisions in the future. He wanted peace of mind.

"Please, God, guide me." Did God listen to him, he wondered?

When he left the chapel walking toward the house, he thought he heard a scream. Anton couldn't decide if it came from the woods or from the Gypsies. Surely it wasn't from his house! He stood a moment waiting to hear more, to get his bearings, but all was quiet.

He entered the house as usual, through the kitchen door, the oil lamp giving off a faint light. He opened the door to the dining room and was surprised to see it dark. For a low light usually burned on the tabletop until the last person went to bed. He could see no light reflecting from where the stairs should be. Why was the house in darkness? Did Ernesta go to have her fortune told? And Katya, had she changed her mind, had she gone also?

"Ernesta," he called. "Are you home? Katya?"

Silence.

Anton returned to the kitchen for the oil lamp. He lengthened the wick for a brighter flame and went back into the dining room.

He stumbled over her body before he saw her! Ernesta's body, crumpled like a rag doll lay at the foot of the stairs. Was she dead?

"Maika Boze! Mother of God! Erna, Erna! Speak to me." He gently raised her head, but she seemed lifeless. "Oh, no, this can't be! My God, it can't be. What has happened?"

He heard the whinny of a horse. It sounded as if it came from the barn. Lamp in hand, Anton ran out the kitchen door looking toward the barn. He heard movement: footsteps, wheels. Someone was taking the carriage or the wagon.

Anton ran back into the house, past the body of Ernesta, to the parlor for a weapon.

His sword was gone! Where was it?

Running back outside he dropped the lantern on the porch steps and guided by moonlight grabbed a log from the woodpile beside the steps. With haste he made his way to the barn.

The wagon was rolling! The thief, the murderer was getting away!

"Stop!" demanded Anton, as he stood in the middle of the road leading to the main exit. "Stop, I say."

The wagon didn't slow down as it came fast toward Anton. In the moonlight he recognized the Turk, who had come the day before demanding to see Stefan.

Anton moved quickly. As the wagon rattled past him, he made a jump for the driver. Abuh kicked Anton in the chest, sending him rolling on the ground.

Mustafa was in the back of the wagon holding onto Katya, who was beginning to stir. Mustafa pushed her down into the bed of the wagon. One of her hands managed to slip free of the pillowcase. Something bright and shiny sparkled in the moonlight grabbing Mustafa's attention. He took her wrist pulling it closer for a better look. He removed the lit lantern from the nail hanging at the side of the bouncing wagon and placed it next to Katya's wrist for a better look. Through the pillowcase, Katya was aware of the bright light, but she was still dazed by the blow to her head.

It was SHE! Mustafa had heard the story of the girl who was under the protection of the Gypsies. He knew the description of the bracelet with its half-moons and stars.

This had to be the girl with Queen Valina's bracelet. Now that he was a member of the tribe, he was honor-bound to protect Katya. His clever mind, quickly calculated his risk. The woman in the house was surely dead. The girl in the wagon had never seen him. The man lying on the road had not seen Mustafa, for he had been hidden in the bed of the wagon.

From his sash he pulled out a thin knife, the blade glinting in the light. It was sharp and deadly as Mustafa plunged it into the Abuh's back.

Book II, Chapter 32

The entire countryside was ablaze with light. Father Lahdra had never seen anything like this before. Lamps and candles glowed in the windows of every house he passed, while bonfires illuminated each yard. The news had spread quickly that there could be a murderer in their midst and he feared the worst for his dear friend, Anton.

Mustafa had come charging into the Gypsy camp with the horses at full gallop. In the bed of the wagon was the dead Turk, the badly bruised Anton and the dazed and bleeding Katya.

With shocked fascination, the Gypsies and peasants listened as Mustafa, told how while dozing on the hillside, near the main road, he thought he heard a scream.

"I followed the road thinking the sound had come from that direction. Then I heard fighting," he lied. "I saw this man." He pointed to the Anton, now cradled in his sobbing sister Sofie's arms, "Lying on the ground and that man," he pointed to the body of Abuh, "was going to bash him in the head with a log." Mustafa waited for the shocked murmurings of the crowd to cease. "You see how much larger he is than I am," indicating Abuh. His audience murmured agreement. "I had no choice but to put my knife in his back...to keep him from killing this man." He pointed to Anton as the crowd once again agreed that indeed, he had no other choice.

Katya now lay on the ground with blood on her forehead. It was what Valina had 'seen' in a vision a few days earlier during her talk with Ivan. Valina knelt beside Katya cleaning the girl's bloodied forehead, with cloths handed to her by her daughter, Kaja.

"I am so happy she is alive," said Valina to Mustafa.

"He must have struck her," said Mustafa, indicating Katya's wound.

Valina never looked up as she said, "You have saved her, Mustafa. I shall not forget this."

Mustafa smiled. This was good. Valina's gratitude was better than any amount the Turk would have paid him. "I saw the bracelet," he said. "I knew she was under your protection. That is why I brought them all here."

Valina stood up and peered into the darkness, past the caravans. "Why won't those dogs stop barking?"

Sofie watched as Anton struggled to a seated position. Had he been younger, his body might not have been so sore and bruised.

"What about Ernesta? Where is Ernesta?" asked Sofie.

Quickly Mustafa said, "I didn't see anyone else." He lied. "The house looked dark, so I came here for help."

Marko and Nikola came pushing through the crowd. "We just heard. My God! Anton, are you alright?" Marko asked, kneeling beside Anton, looking at the wound on his friend's head.

"Ernesta..." said Anton, "Ernesta. I...think he killed her."

A ripple of shock passed through the crowd. Someone said, "My God, there could be more of them. Maybe he wasn't the only killer." Another voice said, "My wife, she is home alone." Several people left hastily for their homes to see that their families were safe and if necessary, to protect them.

Nikola said to his father, "Let's go, Ta. Let's go to Vladezemla."

"I'd like to go, also," said Alexie Lukas, who had been standing quietly near-by.

Sofie gave Alexie a grateful smile.

Marko, Nikola and the lawyer Alexie were anxious as they rode into the yard of Vladezemla. In the moonlight they could see something lying on the ground. When Nikola pulled the wagon to a stop, Alexie jumped down and went to inspect what was there.

"Things from the house," he called to them. "He was robbing the house."

Alexie gathered the stolen items, quickly joining the others entering the kitchen. The lamp was still burning on the kitchen steps where Anton had put it when he thought he could stop the wagon.

"The house is dark," said Nikola. "Do you suppose someone is in here, someone who shouldn't be?"

Marko paused, "We don't have any weapons. What if we need to protect ourselves?"

"I found a sword on the ground," said Alexie, holding it up for the others to see.

"I'll take the sword," said Nikola.

"We'll find knives in the kitchen," said Marko.

Alexie had a long, sharp knife and Marko grabbed a broad butcher knife. The three men looked at one other, weapons in hand. Anton nodded and Marko led the way, butcher knife in one hand and the oil lamp in the other. Slowly, cautiously, he pushed the door open and the three men walked hesitantly into the dark dining room.

They saw her immediately,

Alexie bent down and tentatively took one of her hands. "It's warm," he said. "Madam, are you alright?"

Ernesta didn't answer. Nor did she acknowledge them. She stared straight ahead.

Marko tried to get a response from her. "Ernesta, please tell us what happened."

No amount of coaxing could get any response from her. She stared ahead aware of nothing. This time there was no acting on Ernesta's part. Some part of her body had been badly damaged during the tumble down the stairs. When the three men tried to lift her, her arms and legs dangled. After several unsuccessful attempts to get her up and out of the house, Alexie said. "There is a padded arm chair in the parlor. I have an idea."

The armchair was brought into the dining room and placed near Ernesta. With a little effort, Marko and Nikola lifted her and placed her in the chair. From the kitchen Alexie took the shawl Mustafa used to carry the vase and silver. Alexie wrapped it around the back of the chair and tied Ernesta into a sitting position.

"There!" Alexie said. "Now, let's put her in the wagon and take her to Marko's house. We need to send someone for a doctor."

"Aren't we going to search the house?" asked a disappointed Nikola, his blood racing with excitement.

"Do you want to take a chance on being the next casualty?" Alexie looked directly into Nikola's eyes.

Nikola held Alexie's gaze for a moment, "I guess not. We can come back in the morning light."

The moon was high above, casting a shimmering silver light on the countryside.

Only some children were asleep. All others, Gypsy or peasant were anxiously watching and waiting for the comfort of daylight.

Father Lahdra was with the injured Anton, who stayed behind at the Gypsy camp, while the men went to search the house.

Someone close to the road called out, "There's a wagon coming. I hear a wagon." Those still at the Gypsy camp, strained for a better look in the darkness. As the wagon neared, rattling loudly as it came closer, a lookout called, "They are bringing Mistress Vladislava." The sentence was passed on from person to person, until some even stood up and moved closer to the road for a better look.

What a strange and eerie sight to see the proud Ernesta Vladislava, tied to a chair as it bounced in the wagon. The on-lookers stared in awed silence. Someone or something had put a terrible curse on their peaceful countryside. The Vladislavs owned almost all the land, except for some small portions. Could this curse striking the Vladislav's family filter down to others? Who would be next? When did bad things start to happen? This can't be because of the Gypsies, they have been coming for twenty years and nothing terrible ever happened before. Could it be the red haired cousin? It was peaceful before she arrived. Did you hear that the Stefan has disappeared? Could he be dead, also? Who could have put this hex upon the Family Vladislav? The superstitious villagers all wondered about their futures.

Normally the cool and damp night would not have halted the festivities, but tonight almost everyone went home to protect their families. Marko suggested that, "Since no one was returning to Vladezemla, they should all go to his house for hot tea and some coffee." No one was going to sleep tonight.

Sofie, Klara, and Katya, with Ernesta still tied to the chair, along with Father Lahdra and Anton rode in the wagon to Marko and Vera's home. Alexie walked with Marko and Nikola across the field to the yard, where only a month earlier had been Nikola and Luba's wedding celebration. That was the first time Katya had come to the Vladeslavian countryside, the first time she had met Ivan and Sofie and all those who had come to mean so much to her.

Vera had stayed home since the gossip about her and Anton had spread through the village. She had no idea what was happening, only that someone had come to the house and told Marko that Anton had been injured and that he was at the Gypsy camp.

Standing in her doorway, she could make out a wagon and several people on foot coming towards her house. What did they want? Why were they coming to her house when she had no desire to meet with anyone?

Her desire to retreat to her bedroom halted when she saw several men struggling to lift from the wagon, Ernesta, tied to a chair. It was such a bizarre sight that she forgot her humiliation. She watched with awe, as Anton, his arm around Father Lahdra's shoulder was being helped into the house. Behind them came Sofie fussing over Katya who had strips of torn cloth wrapped around her forehead, her red hair billowing from beneath.

Klara's eyes were red-rimmed from crying. Marko and Nikola, the strongest men, carried the blank-staring Ernesta into the room. They placed her in the corner, like a plant, out of the way.

Luba the child bride of only a month appeared bringing a couple of chairs from her house and Nikola found chairs in other rooms and placed them about for seating. There was the usual scraping of chairs as people seated themselves. Some gave Vera a quick nod, but no one made conversation out of embarrassment or fear, for they all knew she had been in seclusion. That is, everyone knew except Alexie Lukas. He approached Vera. He took her hand and made a continental bow, put her fingers to his lips and said, "Alexie Lukas, Madam. I thank you for your kind hospitality under these unusual circumstances."

It seemed everyone in the room held their breath, even Marko, for no one knew how Vera would behave.

Vera bowed her head to the impeccably groomed man before her. "It is a pleasure to have such distinguished guests in my home."

With a huge sigh of relief everyone started talking at once, trying to make sense of the recent events. Someone struck a match lighting candles on the table and the lamp of red glass above the table was also lit, giving the room a warm, bright glow.

Vera tried to piece together what had happened from the snatches of conversation she heard. She understood that a man, killed by the Gypsy, had struck and tried to kidnap Katya. Then, he tried to kill Anton and somehow had attacked and left Ernesta in this mute state. Vera was surprised how awful she felt for Ernesta. With a feeling of great compassion towards the woman, Vera said, "Please, let's put Gospa, she used the respectful term, on the bed." She motioned to the bedroom she shared with Marko. Marko and Nikola carried the chair with Ernesta tied to it into the room. Once untied, Ernesta was placed on the bed and covered with a sheet. *My god,* thought Vera looking at the waxen face of the woman, *Ernesta looks dead.*

Vera started for the kitchen, but her happy daughter-in-law Luba, motioned for her to stay with her guests, while she, along with old Klara, went into the kitchen to prepare refreshments.

Marko placed glasses on the table and started pouring slivovica for the men.

The convivial chatter hushed when Alexie asked Anton, "How far are the authorities. Don't you think we should send for them?"

Nikola interrupted. He looked to his father with concern. "Ta, it will mean the Gypsy will be arrested."

Everyone at the table knew what that meant. The authorities considered the Gypsies to be worthless thieves, liars, swindlers and murderers. Any bad or illegal event that happened with a Gypsy nearby needed no investigation, for the Gypsy was always deemed the guilty party.

Marko paused with his pouring. "It could mean trouble for all of Valina's tribe."

"Yes..." Alexie said thoughtfully. "You seem very fond of the Gypsies."

Vera was standing at the opposite side of the table from Marko, waiting for everyone to be settled and for Luba to begin serving.

"We are fond of them," Vera said, looking affectionately at Marko as she spoke. "They came here the first year of our marriage and have returned every year since. They have been good to us. And," she added, "lucky for us."

Seated at the rectangular table was first Father Lahdra at one end, Marko at the other. Down one side were Alexie, Sofie, with Nikola next to his father. At Father Lahdra's left, on the other side of the table, sat Anton and Katya, with two more chairs waiting for Klara and Vera.

"It's because of the Gypsies that I am here and not with the Turk," said Katya, in a soft voice. All eyes turned to her. "This bracelet," she held up her arm for all to see the stones set in moon, star and ankh shapes.

"Valina gave this to me on my journey from Selna. Milan had gone looking for food. When I awoke, I began looking for him when I met Zolton, Valina's grandson. He took me to meet Valina in the forest where the Gypsies camped."

Everyone was looking at Katya and listening. Even Klara and Luba, standing in the kitchen doorway, listened with interest.

"Valina told me I was in danger. She said something strange."

"What did she say?" Sofie leaned forward eager to hear more.

"She said, '*The danger is in the path that will take you where you should have been in the first place.*' She also said, '*It will fall into place...you are finding your way.*'"

"That makes no sense. What does it mean?" asked Anton. He looked at Lahdra, "Does it make any sense to you?"
Lahdra hated fortune telling, the tarot cards, and the palm reading. He thought all of it so much rubbish.

"No, it doesn't make any sense to me."

"We must help them," Katya was almost pleading. She turned to Anton. "We are both here because of Mustafa."

"Yes," said Anton, "but how can we help Mustafa?"

Alexie swallowed his brandy and put down his glass, which Marko filled once more. "We must tell the authorities a story that will not involve Mustafa or the other Gypsies."

"But, almost the entire village was there. They all heard the same story we did," said Marko.

Alexie, now the lawyer, thinking as a lawyer, said. "Facts and details can be re-arranged to sound the same, but have a different meaning."

"What are you saying?" asked Anton. "That we can tell the authorities what happened, but not who killed the Turk?"

"We'll tell them who killed the Turk, but not who *really* killed the Turk."

Father Lahdra sat up straight in his chair. "You want us all to lie. Is that it? We are all to be party to a lie?"

"This would be a good lie. It would protect Mustafa and the Gypsies."

A good lie, thought Father Lahdra. Was there such a thing as a good lie?

"My thought," continued Alexie, now out of his chair and pacing as he thought out loud, "was that we could say that Madam Vladislava stabbed the Turk as he was about to kill Anton."

The group stared open-mouthed as he went on, "There would be no witnesses to the event, except for Anton. He would say that his wife saved his life."

"What about Katya?" asked Marko.

"Anton could say she was unconscious, that all this took place in the house instead of the yard."

"I didn't see anything," said Katya. "I think I fainted."

Anton asked, "How do I explain what happened to Ernesta? That she is this way, in a trance."

"You don't explain. Think of it. The shock of the attack was too much for her. Wasn't she ill in a similar fashion recently?"

Anton nodded that she had been, but certainly not as bad as now.

"Well then," said Alexie satisfied, sounding every bit the fine lawyer he was. "There we are. She was recently ill and the events of the evening were too much for her, and she retreated from reality in a world of her own." When he saw all the faces staring at him, he said, "I have read about mental illness. Dr. Sigmund Freud of Vienna has written many papers on why some people appear to be blind or paralyzed. It is a form of mental illness known as hysteria."

Father Lahdra said, "I've heard of Freud. Not everyone agrees with him. In fact there are some who think his theories invalid."

"Invalid or not, it seems to be all we have to work with." Alexie returned to his seat and looked around the table. "All right then, what other suggestions do we have?"

When no one ventured a suggestion, Anton said, "What do we say when someone claims they heard Mustafa say he put the knife in the Turk's back?"

"We say that Mustafa lied about saving your life in the hopes of getting a reward from you."

"Very good, Alexie…" said Anton, impressed, "very good indeed." Then, he added, "And I shall give him a reward. He deserves it!"

Young Luba came in from the kitchen carrying a wooden tray holding glasses wrapped in colorful napkins containing hot tea. Behind her came Klara with plates holding slices of nut roll and poppy seed cake.

With the story for the authorities decided upon and the arrival of tea and pastries, the gathering took on an air of festivity. Glasses were clinked and "Nazdrovlje," to your health, repeated many times, as the cakes were distributed.

Katya hadn't seen Ivan all evening. Was he gone? Did he go away like Stefan? She was about to ask where he was, when an abrupt knock sounded at the door.

Book II, Chapter 33

Earlier in the evening, before the robbery at Vladezemla, the constant barking of the dogs at the Gypsy camp had become annoying, so the dogs were tied to trees on the outer perimeter of the camp near a hill.

Throughout the evening, even when Mustafa had come with the wagon bearing Anton, Katya and the dead Turk, the dogs continued their irritating barking.

There was no more fortune telling and no dancing, for everyone was fearful that the Turk had not been alone. Not knowing the facts, many believed there could be more thieves and murderers in the woods, possibly in groups of twos or threes or more. The peasants made their way home using whatever they could for illumination, even bundles of straw tied to the end of a stick and set ablaze.

The Turk had been hauled out of the wagon, placed on the ground and covered with a blanket until the authorities could be notified.

"I don't like that we will have to deal with the authorities," Valina told her daughter, Kaja. "They will find a way to blame Mustafa and possibly keep us all here. Possibly even arrest some of the other men as accomplices."

"I've been thinking the same," said Kaja, no longer concerned about the flirtatious Roha, or the talk she wanted to have with Valina about the girl's behavior.

Valina studied the distant darkness and listened to the barking dogs. "Tell Zoltan to go see what has the dogs barking so much. Maybe wild pigs are nearby."

At Marko and Vera's home, it was the daughter in law, Luba, who answered the heavy knock at the door. Could it be the authorities so soon? Thank God, they had all agreed upon a story to tell them.

Instead of the authorities, a small Gypsy boy, dirty and barefoot stood on the stoop. His hair was dark and curly, his face very tanned with dark brown eyes. Katya recognized him as one of

Zolton's younger brothers. She rose from her seat and went to the door.

"Hello, Varol. Do you remember me?" she asked the little boy who had been so suspicious of her when he and his brother first saw her in the woods, back during her travels with Milan.

Shyly he nodded yes, staring at the bandage on her forehead.

"What do you want?" Katya asked, "Did Valina send you?"

He pointed behind him, into the darkness. "They are bringing the Scholar."

The words cut through the room like a blade. Why were they *"bringing the Scholar"? Where had he been all day? Dear God, was he injured or worse?*

"Boze Moy!" cried Vera, her hands to her face. "Not, my Ivan. My God! Not my Ivan."

Every face in the room registered disbelief. This couldn't be! What was happening to their tranquil village...their peaceful way of life?

Marko and Nikola ran out the door into the darkness with the other men following. The women were left behind, sick with shock and fear of what they might see.

Katya slid back into her chair. She folded her hands on the table. She was cold. She had never felt this way before. Not when her beloved sister, Anka had died, not when Old Julia had died, not when she left Selna. Not even when her wonderful friend Milan left her for safety with Marko and Vera, to return to his home.

Now in retrospect, it all seemed like a waste of time. She could have had that time with Ivan. The sense of loss was so great, she felt numb. She remembered how Ivan had looked at her, his face so full of love. She had let that go, why? Was the time lost with Ivan worth the dresses and the life she had with Teta Sofie? She felt a twinge of guilt. She loved being with Sofie, loved being at the Vladislav house. Couldn't she have had them both? She realized that she loved them both almost equally. Sobs came from deep within her. Katya could hardly catch her breath as the sobs overtook her, shaking her shoulders. The terrible events were catching up with her. The thought of Ivan...hurt...or worse made her lose control.

Teta Sofie, her face etched with concern, knelt beside Katya, arms around the girl, rocking her, trying to calm her.

A pale Vera at the doorway stepped aside as her second son Nikola came rushing into the room pushing chairs away from the table. "Clear the table," he ordered, as he grabbed plates and handed them to whomever was close by. "He's ALIVE!"

Katya, her face tear-stained looked dazed, as everyone assisted in clearing the table. "Alive? He's alive?" She whispered softly, for she had feared the worst.

Marko entered first, followed by the handsome Zolton and another dark Gypsy carrying a litter made of twigs.

"Here! Here on the table," ordered Nikola. "It's too far to go upstairs."

Someone tried to place a comforter on the table, but it was pushed aside.

"Majka Boze! Mother of God," cried Vera, as she gazed upon the pale, almost bloodless face of her son. His face was covered with deep scratches from rolling through the brush. The blow on the back of his head was no longer bleeding, evidenced by the congealing red mass at the top of his head. The tan riding pants and vest were shredded and blood stained from the down hill tumble.

Luba and Klara appeared from the kitchen with pans of water and towels. Father Lahdra made the sign of the cross and started praying. Katya prayed with him. She had never prayed this hard for anything before. "Please, please, let him get well. Please, let him live." She repeated the prayer over and over.

When the priest finished his prayer, Vera said, "Should we send for a Doctor?"

Katya rose pushing the chair away as she leaned over Ivan's battered body.

"Let me look at him," she said purposefully wiping at her tears with the back of her hand. "We had to do our own healing in Selna. The nearest doctor was in Petrinja." Gently, she ran her fingers over his head getting blood on her fingers. Ignoring the blood, she continued her examination, expertly feeling his neck and shoulders.

"We must take his clothes off," she said. "Luba, will you get sick if you wash the blood from his head?"

"No! I'll be fine," said Luba.

Alexie, with his own pocketknife, made a cut in the cloth of the riding pants on each leg, while Sofie tore at the cloth leaving Ivan's legs exposed. Then they did the same with the shirt and vest, leaving only his underpants.

Anton and Marko, with Vera standing between them, watched in hopeful silence, as others took over the task of caring for their son. The trio, their hurt and disappointments behind them, now stood in numbed silence, each in a daze of sorrow and fear unable to be of any use.

Katya, still with the white bandage wrapped around her head, studied every inch of Ivan's torn body with serious deliberation.

"Nikola, get a lantern and come out to the barn with me." To Luba, she said, "Wash the rest of him. We're going out for herbs to make medicine."

When Nikola and Katya were gone, Alexie Lukas turned to Zolton, who was standing in the background. "Where did you find him?"

"At the base of the hill," he said. "The dogs were barking all evening and into the night. We thought some animal was near them. When we went to see what had them so agitated, we heard a groan. When we let one of the dogs loose it went right to the Scholar."

"Could his horse have thrown him?" Father Lahdra wondered out loud.

"Not old Bara!" insisted Marko.

"Something could have startled her," said Anton. "Perhaps some animal, there are still wild pigs in the hills."

"Why didn't Bara come home?" wondered Marko aloud, for the horse should have returned to the barn.

"One of our tribe found her. He was going to wait till morning to look for the owner. But, when we found Ivan, we were sure it was his horse," said Zolton.

The truth was that the Gypsy who found the horse had no intention of looking for the owner. When the caravan would pack up and leave in the morning, the horse would have been tied to the back of his wagon-house. But, when it was determined that the horse belonged to Ivan, the Gypsy horse-trader had no choice but to return the beast or answer to Queen Valina.

Zolton moved across the room next to Anton. "This may not be the right time to talk of this, but my Grandmother is worried about the authorities. They may detain us."

"We have discussed that possibility and we think we have a solution," Anton indicated with a nod of his head towards Alexie. "Our lawyer and good friend has volunteered to handle the matter on our behalf when the authorities come."

After Alexie explained the plan of claiming that Ernesta had killed the Turk, he cautioned, "Now, you must tell Mustafa that he has to say he lied about saving Anton. That he fabricated the story hoping for a reward. Which by the way, we plan to give him before you leave."

Zolton smiled broadly. "This is wonderful. My Grandmother will be so happy! And so will Mustafa! I'll go now to tell them. We will come back in the morning to see how the Scholar is doing."

Zolton politely shook hands with everyone in the room and then disappeared into the night with his young brother Varol, who had been patiently waiting on the stoop.

Back from the barn with her arms loaded, Katya came briskly through the kitchen door. With her arms full of roots, she had tucked her apron up into the waste band forming a pouch in which to carry more greenery. Katya dumped her armful onto a chair then pulled at her apron emptying it of herbs. Her beautiful embroidered apron was stained with soil from the plants pulled out of the ground.

Nikola made a strange sight following Katya, with both arms extended outward in front of him, carefully holding a large spider-web. Surprise registered on all the on-looker's faces. Father Lahdra scowled for he was sure this was some sort of witchcraft.

"Come here, Nikola," said Katya. "Here...on this badly bruised shoulder. Carefully lay the spider web over it." She watched as Nikola placed the intricately woven web over his brother's wounded shoulder. "Wonderful. That is just how I would have placed it," she said.

Then turning to Klara, she said, "I need a pan of clean water for this moss. Someone take this curled dock and mash the roots. Bring it back as soon as it is soft enough to spread. Do the same with this comfrey. Beat it until it is mush." Sofie and the young Luba obediently took the greenery and disappeared into the kitchen.

When Klara brought a pan of water,   Katya dipped the moss into the water and squeezed out the excess, then gently laid the moss onto Ivan's wounds. When all the moss was gone, she took the mashed dock root Luba handed to her and with her fingers dabbed the mash with as little pressure as possible onto more bruises and scratches. Then she did the same with the softened comfrey, until most of Ivan's body was covered with some healing substance. Lastly, Katya made a tent over his head with a cloth and nearby placed a pot of boiled water into which she dropped the herb verbena, hoping the scented water would soothe him as he inhaled it.

"I'll need some chamomile tea with lots of honey," she said. Luba was running towards the kitchen before Katya finished the sentence. Katya turned to look at the assembly about her. "I think this is all I can do for now. We'll try to give him spoonfuls of tea throughout the night."

She finally sat down and realized just how tired she was.

Also looking tired Father Lahdra, in his black cassock, frowned. Displeased, he said, "This is too much like witchcraft."

Katya looked at the priest. In a very tired voice, she said, "I called on no spirits for assistance. I did what I know will work. The woman who taught me was the only person we could call upon. She was our doctor. When she prayed, she prayed to God, not to the wind, or the moon or whatever it is that witches pray to."

Vera moved behind Katya's chair protectively. "We thank you," she said, putting her hand on the girl's shoulder. "I'm so frightened I wouldn't have been able to do anything for my son."

"Yes, yes," agreed Marko, "We thank you."

Anton, with tears in his eyes said, "I shall never forget this. I shall always be grateful." His sister Sofia came to him and wrapped her arms around him. They cried as they held one another. Their fear for Stefan, not knowing where or how he was, and now their fear for the injured Ivan released their tears. At this moment it may be that Ivan was all that Sofia and Anton had left of their family. They weren't sure Erna would live and they didn't know of Stefan's whereabouts.

Katya, seated at the table dropped her head in her folded arms wanting only to rest her eyes for a moment. She was exhausted.

Alexie Lukas observed the sleeping Katya from his seat in a corner, trying to stay out of the way.

He said, not to anyone in particular, "I find Katya terribly interesting. Quite intelligent I'd say. Not at all like your average village girl."

Father Lahdra was seated against the wall. He closed his eyes, leaning his head back.

Lahdra briefly opened his eyes and looked at the red curls on the head of the sleeping Katya. He remembered Ernesta had once said something like, 'All our trouble started when that girl came here.' It seemed true enough. Since Katya came, the truth about Ivan's parentage was out. Stefan was gone…no one knew where. No one said it, but they all wondered if he were alive. Who knew if Ernesta would live through the night? A man tried to murder Anton, and now Ivan lay on the table, scratched, bruised and unconscious.

Was it possible Katya was to blame for these events? Lhadra shook his head as if to rid him of such thoughts. Still…evil could come in many forms. The devil never sleeps.

Throughout the long night Katya never awoke once. The others dozed in their chairs for short spans of time. Young Luba and Vera kept vigil all night. Vera fed Ivan a spoonful at a time of the chamomile tea, though she was a bit hampered by the steam tent made for the verbena infusion. Whenever the water for the infusion became cool, Luba had more hot water ready. Ivan stirred a few times, moaning but nothing more.

Handsome Anton seemed to have aged greatly in the course of twenty-four hours. His once clear gray eyes seemed dull and lifeless. His complexion was almost colorless and his face was drawn with worry.

His pleasant life in the country was over. Whatever happiness he thought he had was now replaced by sadness. Once he had a sense of contentedness. Now he only had worry. He had been proud of his heritage and his accomplishments and yes, proud of his power as the landowner. Now he was humbled. It seemed to him looking at Ernesta, who had not moved since being placed on Vera's bed, and battered Ivan on the twig litter, that he, Anton, had no power at all. He was at God's mercy. Whatever happened now was up to God. Anton was helpless.

Anton looked about the small room. Vera and Luba were attending to Ivan, spooning him tea, wiping his chin when he didn't swallow it. Klara was somewhere in the kitchen, probably dozing. Marko was somewhere outside with his son, Nikola. Katya was asleep at the table out of Luba and Vera's way. His sister Sofie and Alexie were seated away from the table deep in conversation. Father Lahdra's head leaned back against the wall. He appeared to be sleeping.

Anton rose from his chair and went into Marko and Vera's room where Ernesta had been placed upon their arrival. The loom where Vera wove her beautiful fabrics stood away from the bed, as if waiting for winter and the strum of Vera's talented fingers.

He looked down at the sleeping face of Ernesta. "Well, Erna," he said, "I guess things aren't going so well for us." He touched her pale face. "I'll send for the best doctors I can get from Zagreb for you. I promise we will try to make you well. And I promise to try and find Stefan." He patted her unresponsive hand. "It will all work out. I promise." He wasn't sure he could keep that promise.

Then for the first time in many years, he lay down alongside his wife.

After a bit, Sofie and Alexie escaped to the stoop for the cool night air. Sofie shivered more from nerves than the night air. Alexie slipped off his coat and put it around Sofie's shoulders. "Thank you, Alexie," she said softly. He pulled her closer to him, giving her more warmth.

"Thank you," she said again, "for being here with me, for being so helpful."

Alexie said, "I like being with you and doing things for you."

They were both silent for some time, just looking at the moon, savoring the comfortable closeness of each other.

"Alexie…"

"Yes?"

"I am somewhat surprised at how comfortable I feel with you. How much I like having you near."

"I feel the same," he said.

Sofie looked at Alexie's pleasant face in the moonlight. She liked what she saw. To her it was an honest face, a strong face. She especially liked his brown mischievous eyes, twinkling as if he knew a secret or a good joke. His black hair and mustache were always perfectly groomed. She marveled at his attire. Everyone else was a bit disheveled, a bit mussed from the day's events, but not Alexie. His shirt and pants looked as good as when he had dressed that morning.

"How long can you stay?" asked Sofie.

"As long as you want me to."

Book II, Chapter 34

With the first signs of morning light, Nikola, Marko, Anton and Alexie rode in a wagon to Vladezemla to search the house. For weapons they had only an old flint-lock pistol Marko had taken in trade for smithy work, a sword, a hatchet from the barn and a couple of cleavers taken from the kitchen.

Following the wagon walked several on-lookers, being sure to stay far enough behind should there be any danger, but close enough to see what was going on.

The quartet found no one. A thorough search of each room only disturbed a covey of doves nesting in the attic and annoyed the mice residing in the cellar. The barn and shed were combed, as was the chapel, but there were no intruders.

Relieved at finding no more murderers, Marko and Anton still wondered if someone dangerous might be lurking near...perhaps in the woods.

From his makeshift hospital bed, which was the dining table, Ivan could hear his mother's voice. Then he thought he heard Katya's voice and wondered how it was he could hear her voice, since he hadn't seen her in such a long time.

There! He heard his mother's voice again! Why couldn't he see her?

"Mamitza," he said it so softly it could barely be heard, then again, "Mamitza."

Seated at the table Katya thought she heard something. Pulling aside the steam-tent, she stood above Ivan looking into his gold-flecked eyes. Those wonderful eyes she first saw on the day of Nikola and Luba's wedding.

Ivan couldn't believe his own eyes. Just inches from his face, looking at him with emerald green eyes shining full of affection was Katya. He was sure it was a dream. This couldn't be real. And that white cloth wound around her head. What was that?

Mamitza, now he was seeing Mamitza. She stood in front of him crying. Why was she crying? He heard other voices. Voices he knew like Klara's and Sofie's. Now Teta Sofie's face was in front of him. No, now it was Klara's. Was that his sister-in-law Luba smiling at him?

He tried to turn his head to see where he was, but the pain stopped him. A sharp stabbing pain that made his head hurt. His shoulder ached. He felt as if someone had beaten him with a staff...*Mustn't move*!

He could hear the murmur of excitement. Everyone sounded so happy. Why wasn't he happy too? Where was he?

Someone was talking to him, but he wasn't listening. What was that red thing above him? Vera's face was above his, she was talking to him, but he kept looking past his mother, to the red thing above. She followed his eyes and looking up she moved out of his line of vision.

What was Mamitza's oil lamp doing there? He was sure it was the lamp that hung in their dining room, the red lamp with the dangling red crystals.

"The lamp, why is the lamp here?" His voice was weak.

His mother's happy face appeared above his, "It has always been there, don't you remember?"

"Where am I?"

"You're home, Dusho. You're home, My Soul. You're home," Vera sobbed.

"Why is the lamp there? When did you move it*?" Why had they moved it to his room, upstairs?*

Katya realized Ivan's confusion. "You are on the dining table, not in your bed."

"Why am I on the table?" he asked confused. "I want to see. I want to lift my head, but it hurts."

Katya slipped her arm ever so gently under Ivan's head, so that it was slightly raised. He didn't cry out, only winced a little from the pain. From this new vantage point, he let his eyes roam about the familiar room. He saw the tear-stained faces of all the women he loved. Still, he was somewhat confused. Then he slowly lowered his chin and looked down at his body. He discovered that his body was green with slime and moss, like some water creature in one of his geography books.

Katya would have given anything to have her stock of dried herbs and medicinals she had left behind in Selna. There were rare herbal combinations that Old Julia had prepared which Katya now realized, she probably couldn't duplicate.

She had picked every violet she saw in Vera's garden that morning knowing there was no time to properly dry them. Still, she simmered them to make a healing solution for Ivan's abrasions. Katya would have preferred marigolds, but didn't see any.

Pretty Luba was a marvel. Gone was the shy bride. Instead the young girl showed unflagging energy and seemed to appear wherever and whenever help was needed. She assisted Katya in any way she could, while still preparing coffee and tea for the family. Vera was so shaken by her son's condition that she seemed to only flutter nervously about fearing the worst.

Marko needed to know what had happened. The stocky man now sitting beside his wounded son asked. "Did Bara throw you while you were riding?"

"No, I don't think so." Ivan had trouble focusing. It was so hard to remember. All he could remember was waking up hearing the voices of Katya and his mother. Luba's face came into his memory, as did Klara's and Sofie's.

Exhausted and frustrated he said, "I don't know, Ta. I don't know what happened to me."

Once it was determined that Ivan was better, Father Lahdra left promising to return as soon as he could. Sofie and Alexie rode with Lahdra as far as Vladezemla so as not to crowd Anton's wagon.

Ernesta was placed once again onto the soft armchair and lifted onto the wagon. Her condition had not changed. She occasionally opened her eyes, but it was obvious she did not see. Or if she did see, it wasn't registering in her brain.

For the first time ever, Anton was seen giving Vera a hug. Vera and Marko were standing side-by-side bidding Anton and the others good-bye. Before climbing into the wagon, Anton full of emotion hugged and kissed his childhood friend Marko. When Marko stepped back, Anton wrapped his arms around Vera and she, too, returned the hug holding on to him. Such was their shared pain that past hurts or resentments no longer mattered. The twenty years of coldness Vera had felt for Anton were gone. What did it matter now?

When Anton's wagon left the barnyard, Katya, no longer in the fancy embroidered clothes, but in a plain homespun skirt and blouse, said "Ivan should be bathed."

Nikola and Marko, never questioning Katya's instructions, carried Ivan outdoors still on the litter made of twigs tied together. Ivan's moss covered body was no longer bright green, but a dull gray as the herbs and moss dried. The litter with Ivan on it was placed resting one end on a tree stump and the other on a milking stool up off the ground.

Father and brother took turns gently pouring from a bucket of Katya's healing potions. She brewed the potion in a huge caldron used for soap making. With each bucket full poured on him, his body became clean of the herbs.

The last three buckets of potion poured on him made Ivan cry out. He was being rinsed with a mild solution of salt water which stung his wounds.

"I'm sorry. I'm so sorry," Katya said several times. "I know it stings, but also makes you heal faster." Then she pleaded, "Ivan, forgive me."

Then they left him to dry in the sun, like a ball of homemade cheese.

Throughout the day, curious and concerned friends and neighbors came by to ask about Ivan. Children laughed and giggled, then were sent away by the adults. Ivan made quite a sight, naked except for his underwear, lying there in the open air for all to see, his skin drying white from the salt bath.

None of the onlookers came near. All kept a respectful distance standing in a line like birds resting on a fence.

"Will Ivan be alright?" asked an old man, his gray mustache so long it turned down at the corners of his mouth past his chin. His coarsely woven white pantaloons and shirt hung loose on his thin body.

"He's better, already," Marko answered. "Last night we thought he was dead."

"Why is he so white?" The old man, pointed at Ivan.

"It's the salt. We poured salted water over his wounds. It's a miracle how quickly he is healing."

The old man leaned toward Marko saying in a conspiratorial tone, "I heard that cousin of yours, the red-haired girl, is a witch."

"Where did you hear such foolishness?" Marko scowled, his face darkening with anger.

The old man didn't seem affected by Marko's outburst. "That's what I hear. More than one is saying it. I heard she does things with spider webs. You know witches use spiders in their spells."

"I don't know what witches use, you old fool," snapped Marko. "I know Katya learned her herbal healing from a very old woman in her village."

"The young witches usually learn from the old ones."

"Go home old man," demanded Marko. "I have better things to do than listen to your foolishness." Red-faced with anger, Marko turned his back on the old man and the other curious onlookers.

"There she is!" a hushed voice said, as Katya was seen walking out into the yard. She was near Ivan's litter. "There is the witch."

Katya stopped in her tracks. She heard, 'There is the witch.' Annoyed at being called a witch, she slowly turned toward the nosey villagers clustered together. With a threatening look on her face, she slowly raised her arm. The Gypsy bracelet, as if a mischievous accomplice, sparked and gleamed in the sunlight. Katya pointed her index finger straight at the group before her. She slowly swung her finger from left to right, to encompass all of them.

"My God!" A voice from the crowd cried out. "She's putting a curse on us."

Making the sign of the cross the peasants ran. They scattered in different directions, trying to get out her sight, fearful of what her powers would do to them.

Watching the peasants scatter like chickens, with a fox in their midst, made Katya throw back her head in laughter.

Greatly displeased, Marko frowned, "You shouldn't have done that, Katya. It only makes them believe it more."

Katya thought a moment. "I suppose you're right. I just got angry when I heard them call me a witch. I'm not a witch. I don't know anything about witches."

Marko put his strong arm around Katya's shoulder, comforting her. "These are simple people. Anything they don't understand is magic to them. The improvement in Ivan's condition from last night could be considered a miracle or magic. They choose to believe it is magic." Marko knew this foolish act of Katya's had given his superstitious neighbors even more reason to believe she was a sorceress.

"Marko," said Katya, "what I did was not so unusual. I knew the spider web would clot his blood. I knew the moss would heal his sores. There was no magic in it. I knew the verbena would sooth and calm him. These cures would work for anyone, not just for me. It takes no special powers to make them work. The reason Old Julia made such a secret of her knowledge was so that people would pay her. She always had plenty of food and fire wood." Looking into Marko's weatherworn face, she said, "Old Julia told me that I could always take care of myself...that I would never be hungry. She said that people would pay me well for what I knew."

Marko took hold both of Katya's small hands with his rough, calloused ones. "I think Old Julia may have been right. When I see how quickly Ivan's wounds are healing, I want to give you something in payment. Anything I have is yours."

Katya squeezed Marko's hands and blushed. "Careful what you say. I just might want something of yours."

Marko's ruddy face brightened, "What? Name it! What do I have that you want?"

With her cheeks pink, Katya ran towards the house, embarrassed that she almost told Marko she wanted Ivan.

That evening while Katya napped at the table, her head cradled in her arms, Ivan was put in his mother and father's bed, just as Ernesta had been the night before. Marko gently lifted his son, who was still in pain, and placed him onto a soft cloud of goose down. His skin looked pale against the white bedding, but he improved with each passing hour. Ivan was covered with scratches and bruises, but his eyes were brighter, more alert. He still couldn't remember what had happened. He would exhaust himself trying to remember what happened.

"I think I remember Stefan was on the old hill trail," said Ivan aloud still trying to sort things out in his mind.

His mother stopped fussing with the pillows. "Stefan did this to you?" She became more excited. "Are you saying Stefan attacked you?"

"No, no," Ivan struggled with his thoughts. "I just remember seeing him walking his horse on the trail. Maybe not...Maybe I didn't see him, after all. The thought just came to me. I can't be sure."

Vera spun around to face her husband, who had just come back into the room. "It might have been Stefan. Ivan thinks he saw Stefan on the trail." Her voice was harsh, accusing.

"No, Mamitza...no, don't say that." Ivan became agitated. He couldn't remember. He wanted to remember. In pain and frustration he rolled his head from side to side on the large lace-trimmed pillowcases, the ones his mother had woven on the loom sitting idle in the room.

"Don't, Son." Marko held Ivan's bruised face between his strong, blacksmith's hands. "Don't become so excited. It is all right. It doesn't matter, just get well. That's all you have to think about...getting well."

Seeing his son calmed, Marko gently steered Vera out of the room leaving Ivan alone. "I know you want desperately to blame someone," he said to his wife, "but don't be so quick to blame Anton's son, because you have a grudge of your own."

Vera gave Marko a defiant look. She knew this could lead to an argument, one she wasn't ready to have Ivan and Katya witness. She pulled her shoulder out of Marko's grasp and stomped into the kitchen.

Katya was awakening from a disturbing dream, when she heard Marko and Vera's harsh words. "Is Ivan alright?" She asked.

Marko still looking toward the kitchen hearing Vera making unnecessary noises with bowls and pots said, "He seems better. Maybe you could keep him company."

Katya rose from the table, smoothed her skirt and went into the bedroom.

When Katya pulled a chair next to the bed, Ivan said, "You look tired. Are you alright?"

"I napped a little. How about you? Do you feel any stronger?"

"I do. I really do." Then somewhat shyly he said, "You make me feel better, just being around."

"I'm glad." Katya gave him a warm smile. "I feel good when I'm near you, too."

"Katya,"

"Yes?"

"I want to try and sit up."

Katya stood. "I'll get your father."

"No. You help me."

She paused. "I don't know if I can."

"Try." He said softly, looking deep into her eyes.

Katya looked down at his bruised body. Afraid of hurting him, she thought the best way to help lift him, was to slip both her arms under his armpits and around his back. Her hair brushed against his face as she wrapped her arms about him. His heart skipped a beat as he inhaled the clean scent of herbs and flowers that clung to her. He braced his hands onto the bed and pushed down as Katya pulled his body up to a seated position. Before she could let go, Ivan gently kissed her cheek. She was so soft... so sweet smelling.

Katya pulled her face away and looked deep into Ivan's eyes. She looked passed the purple bruise above his eye and the scratches on his face, deep into those gold-flecked eyes. It was as if she were sinking into them. She leaned forward kissing him on the mouth. Both their hearts pounded, both pulses raced. He slipped his arms around her, forgetting any pain. It was a long kiss, neither wanting to let go of the other. It was the kind of kiss that could erase the past and make promises for the future.

When they parted, both overwhelmed and trembling, they were not the same. Not wanting to let go of each other, they kissed again...this time a softer kiss, each savoring the moment. Then Katya gently pulled away. She slipped down onto the chair beside the bed and laid her head on the bed near Ivan's lap, her arm across his body. He stroked her hair and admired the way it glowed in the sunlight streaming from the window.

Katya had never had this feeling before. For the first time in her life she felt as if she really belonged to someone. As a child growing up in Selna, she felt remote, like an observer, not a part of the pattern there. With Sofie, she was pleased to be at Vladezemla, yet never felt truly comfortable. Katya had been happy when Sofie had the guardianship papers drawn up, but that feeling was nothing to match the happiness she now felt. Today she felt complete. For the first time, in Ivan's arms, she felt part of something, of someone. Best of all, she felt safe with him. She never wanted to leave him. She always wanted him near, to make her feel forever the way she felt now, safe and complete.

"Tell me something," he said. "Tell me anything and everything about yourself. I want to know all I can about you."

Katya raised her head from his lap and looked at him. Her forehead wrinkled in a frown.

"Can I tell you about the dream I had while napping at the table?"

"I want to hear about your dream," he smiled lovingly.

She straightened herself in the chair and stared ahead. "I was outside, going to the well. It was late afternoon, the sun glowed strangely red, making everything look red…the barn, the trees, the ground. I was carrying a bucket and as I got to the well, people appeared. They hadn't been there before, but now they were grouped behind the well. So many I couldn't count them, all wearing black, even the children. It was eerie with the red sun casting red light and the people all in black against the red.

I was frightened. Yes, I remember being frightened. I didn't see the rocks in their hands. Then slowly, as if all their arms were connected to the same string, they raised their arms in unison and threw the rocks at me. The rocks came slowly. It was slowly raining rocks."

Alarmed at the look of fear on Katya's face, Ivan said, "Don't tell me anymore."

But, she went on. "I was on the ground and the rocks were piling on top of me. It got dark and I couldn't see anything. I was trapped under the rocks, my arms and legs pinned down. I couldn't move." She stopped talking for a moment, as if trying to remember more. After a moment she said, "I think I woke up then."

"It was just a dream," Ivan soothed. "Dreams can't hurt you."

"They can if they're true," she said simply. "Dreams can tell the future."

"Don't let anyone hear you say that," admonished Ivan, "You must know how superstitious people are."

"Ivan," she sighed deeply. "They already think I'm a witch. I heard them."

"No. No," he said. "You must be mistaken."

"I wish we could go away." Katya looked worried, her forehead creased. "I wish we could go somewhere far away...someplace where no one knows us." She took both his hands in hers, "Someplace where people won't call me a witch."

Ivan gently pulled Katya closer. He wrapped his arms around her and buried his face in her soft hair. "We'll go," he promised. "We'll start a new life somewhere, together."

Outside the bedroom door Ivan's mother overheard what they said. Vera felt no shame at listening to their conversation. After all, she was his mother and it was her duty to protect him, if she could.

Hearing her son say those words to Katya made Vera Balaban's eyes burn with hot tears. She turned away from the doorway, her heart aching from what she had heard. Vera was a strong woman, a fighter. She had traveled on foot from Zagreb to Vladezemla to find the young Anton, to tell him she was pregnant.

When Ivan was three years old, she had gone without sleep for three days when he was sick with fever, bathing him with snow to cool his fever.

There was the time he fell out of the wagon. Ivan must have been six or seven then. With the child unconscious, Vera never left his side for two days, talking continuously, urging him to get well.

Vera turned from the doorway and went teary-eyed out onto the stoop. She leaned against the house for support. Deep in her soul, she had known that someday Ivan would leave. She just refused to accept it. As recently as yesterday, she saw Anton's concern for Ivan. She hoped her Ivan forgot about going to America and would replace Stefan as manager of Vladezemla. She was sure that it would be only a matter of time for the gossip to die down and with a position of power no one would dare say anything to Ivan's face. It was already happening. The gossip was being replaced with talk of the attack on Anton and the murder of the Turk.

She thought of her neighbor Anda Maglich. Anda had a marriageable daughter. The girl must be fourteen now. Not a bad looking girl, except for the space between her teeth. She could be acceptable as a wife for Ivan. If he married someone from the village, he wouldn't want to leave. These thoughts whirled in her mind. Vera leaned her head back and squeezed her eyes. What was she thinking about? There wasn't one girl in all the surrounding area that could even come close to Katya's beauty. And, Katya wanted Ivan. So, that was that! All Vera could think of was that Katya wanted to take Ivan away from his Mother and his home!

Book II, Chapter 35

Katya sobbed all the way back to Vladezemla. Why did Ivan lie and say they would go away? She cried partly in sadness but mostly in anger. She didn't know if anyone saw her as she walked along the road. She kept her head down, wiping her tears with the sleeve of her borrowed blouse. At the kitchen door, she peeked in and saw no one. It appeared that everyone was in the parlor attending to Ernesta. Katya slipped unseen up to her little attic room to pack.

For twenty years Vera never came up to Vladezemla. Being stubborn she even missed her son Nikola's wedding held in the Vladislav family chapel. Then, a week ago she came to beg Anton to help stop Ivan from going to America, when Ivan announced he was leaving.

Today, the day after the attack on Erna and Anton, she didn't care if she was seen. There was no hiding among the trees or climbing over fences. She was a woman with a mission. The mission was to protect her son and keep him from leaving her. This time she marched boldly up the road to the fine house.

She knocked at the kitchen door. When no one responded, she knocked harder and called out, "Klara. Klara, it is Vera."

A startled Klara came bustling into the kitchen. "My God, don't tell me Ivan is worse."

"No. He is getting better," said Vera. "I need to speak with Anton.

"He is with Ernesta. She needs tending to." Klara pulled nervously at the waistband of her apron. "We have a woman coming to help and we sent for the Doctor in Zagreb." She was trying to let Vera know this wasn't a good time to come calling. The last time Vera appeared she upset the household and Klara feared this time it would be the same.

"Klara," said Vera, her voice firm. "Get Anton here or I shall go into the house and look for him, myself."

"Oh, Vera!" said Klara, shaking her head in disapproval. Without another word she left to fetch Anton.

A very tired Anton came quickly, his sister Sofie close behind him, but Sofie stayed at the door, not entering the kitchen.

"What is it, Vera? Is Ivan worse? What has happened?" It was evident he was agitated and not all together pleased with her visit.

"We need to do something about Ivan?" said Vera.

"Do what?" Anton's voice sounded annoyed.

"First of all, we need to get rid of Katya," she said.

At this Sofie practically flew into the room. "What do you mean...get rid of?" There was a touch of anger in her tone. She went on, "Get rid of the girl who very possibly saved Ivan's life. None of us knew about the herbs or the spider web."

"I think our neighbors are right," Vera avoided Sofie's eyes, looking only at Anton. "I, too, think she is a witch."

"Are you out of your mind?" Sofie nearly screamed the words.

"Oh, come now, Vera," said the tired Anton seating himself at the table on the bench. "This is nonsense. What has brought on this change of mood in you?"

Still standing, Vera said, "She has used her spell to convince my Ivan to go away with her."

Anton only shook his head at the absurdity of the remark.

"The boy is in love," Anton was disgusted. He went on, "Ivan has been in love since the first day he saw her. What is this nonsense about witchcraft?"

"I hear the neighbors. I know what they are saying. The truth is she has brought all the bad luck we are having here. Everything was fine before she came."

"Don't be foolish!" Sofie stood nose to nose with Vera. "This is stupid, superstitious talk."

"Of course, you want to protect her," said Vera sarcastically. "You don't know what it is to be a mother. With Katya you can pretend at being a mother. She is a plaything for you."

Sofie would have struck Vera, but Anton was on his feet between them.

"Listen to me, Vera." His voice was low, but firm. "I don't know what is going on with you, but don't bring it here. I am through feeling guilt at being Ivan's real father. I have done my penance. I have suffered pain. My wife is totally helpless. My son

Stefan is gone…I don't know if he is alive." His voice caught. "You come here talking nonsense." He let out a long sigh. "Vera, I am tired. I feel old. I need to take care of Erna. She deserved better than she got from me. I gave you and Marko things over the years out of guilt, when I should have showered Erna with the things a man gives his wife." He turned away from Vera with a wave of his hand. "Go away, Vera. I must take care of my family. We all have our own Destiny. If this be mine, to take care of Erna for the rest of her life, then I shall do it."

Concerned, Sofie demanded, "Where is Katya now?"

"She is gone," said Vera. "I told her we didn't want a witch in the house."

Unknown to the three in the kitchen, a very sad Marko had followed his wife and was listening outside the kitchen door.

Earlier, Luba overheard the mean words Vera said to Katya. She searched for Marko telling him that Vera was last seen walking on the road to the Vladislav house.

Now Marko stepped into the open doorway surprising them all. "It is time to go home." He said to Vera.

"Let's go home. This house has much sadness. We don't need to add to it." He went to her taking her by the arm and guided her out the door. Vera jerked her arm from his hold and stomped down the road ahead of him.

Marko walked slowly behind her. Where had his Veritza gone? He found her and fell in love with her twenty years ago, outside this very kitchen in the chapel. Now it seems he had lost her in the same place. Gone was the Veritza he had fallen in love with, shared a life with. Last night he thought there was peace between Vera and Anton. He didn't know who this angry woman had become. But he did know that nothing would ever be the same again.

A worried Sofie hurried upstairs and found Katya in her attic bedroom. "What is this?" she asked, seeing Katya gathering her things together on the bed. "It looks as if you are packing."

Katya was no longer crying. She was finished with tears. Somehow she knew all along that she would not be here for any length of time. Ernesta wanted her gone and now according to

Vera Balaban, the whole village wanted to see her leave. She was to leave, '*and take her witchcraft with her.*' That was how Ivan's mother had put it.

Sofie pushed aside the gathered things on the bed and sat down. She patted the place beside her and said, "Please sit, Katya. We must talk. I don't want you to leave."

Katya sat next to Sofie. "I must leave. People think I have brought unhappiness here," she said.

"Nonsense," scoffed Sofie. "You have brought me more happiness than I can tell you." She took Katya's small hand in hers. "You are part of this family. It is legal. No one can hurt you."

"I have to leave," she pulled her hand free from Sofie's and rose. "I need to get my things together. The Gypsies will be leaving soon."

"The Gypsies," Sofie's hand went to her mouth. "No! No, you can't mean to become a nomad. It is insane. You can't live that way. You can't run away from who you are."

"Who am I, Teta Sofie?" demanded Katya. "Tell me. I don't know who I am. All my life I have felt as if I don't belong, certainly not in Selna. For a while…" she looked at her reflection in the mirror on the wardrobe, "for a while, I thought I belonged here. But, now I don't think so."

"Please, don't go with the Gypsies. I will lose you forever if you do." Sofie started to sob. "Please don't let me lose you." She rose from the bed and wrapped her arms around Katya. The beautiful girl with the red hair and green eyes who reminded her so much of her beloved Vincent *couldn't* leave. *Mustn't* leave!

Tears welled in Katya's eyes as she held onto the sobbing Sofie. She didn't want to leave Sofie, but what choice did she have? Katya knew she couldn't bear the rude remarks and accusations that she was considered to be a witch. According to Vera, even Ivan thought Katya was a witch. Vera's words were, "My son thinks you have used your magic powers to make him love you and he doesn't want that kind of love." The words had cut deep into Katya's heart.

Weak from sobbing, Sofie again sat on the bed. She looked about helplessly, looking at the things Katya had gathered to take with her. The shawl she had come with, a simple peasant skirt and blouse. She was still wearing the white flaxen skirt and blouse borrowed from Vera yesterday, when she was tending Ivan.

Sofie noticed that the silver comb and brush with the initial "K" were on the table next to the washbowl. The comb and brush were part of her unused trousseau with the letter K representing Vincent's last name, Kurecka. Sofie got up and went to the table picking up the silver brush with the initial K.

Katya saw the look on her face and said, "What is it? I wasn't going to take your comb and brush. Really, I wouldn't take them."

"Katya!" cried Sofie. "I have just had the most wonderful idea." Sofie grabbed Katya and whirled her around the room.

"What?" a bewildered Katya said as she was spun around. "What wonderful idea?"

Sofie held up the brush so that Katya could see the initial. "So? I see the brush. What does the brush mean?" asked Katya.

"It means you are going to Trieste! You are going to Lucia Kurecka's house. She will be thrilled to have you. She adored you when we visited."

"I can't," protested Katya. "I can't just appear at her door." But, for a brief moment Katya did like the idea.

"I'll send a messenger ahead with a note from me telling Lucia that you will be staying with her for awhile and that I will be coming as soon as things are settled here. I mean," she went on, "as soon as I know what the doctor can do for Erna and that there is enough help for Anton and Klara."

Katya plopped onto her bed. It was a great idea! If she had to leave, Lucia Kurecka's home in Trieste was indeed nicer for Katya than living in a painted caravan.

"Are you sure I will be welcome?" Katya searched Sofie's face carefully for any trace of doubt.

"Of course you will be welcome. As much as I shall miss you, this is a blessing for Lucia. She is old and lonely. You remind her so much of Vincent. It gives her pleasure just to look at you."

Sofie noticed the bracelet from Queen Valina on Katya's wrist. She said, "I know that the Gypsies go through Trieste on their way to France. You could travel with them when they leave. Come to my room for my carpetbag. You will need more clothes than the few things you have on the bed. I will come to Trieste as soon as I can with more of your dresses."

With the carpetbag from Sofie's room, Katya was left to pack. Sofie dashed out to the barn and searched for Yura. It was Yura who drove Sofie and Katya to Trieste when they last visited the Signora.

"I need you to go to Trieste with a message," she told him. "Remember the house we last visited?"

"Yah, sure, I remember the house," he said. "When do you want me to go?"

"As soon as you can," she said. "Take the carriage or go on horseback, whichever you prefer."

"The carriage would be more comfortable," said Yura. "I need to get some food and feed for the horse."

"Fine," said Sofie. "When you are ready, come here and I will give you the message."

Book II, Chapter 36

Alexie Lukas was an interesting man. He was an educated man and a courteous man. Many lawyers felt they needed to be forceful to get their points across, but not Alexie. He was thoughtful, polite and almost never combative. He dressed well, but a bit understated. He was always well groomed and even after three days at Vladezemla without a change of clothes, he looked well turned out.

Alexie was a bit stocky in his build. He was not as handsome as Anton, or Ivan, still he looked pleasant enough. His thick, black hair combed straight back, was always in place. His mustache never appeared straggly. Even his thick eyebrows were the right proportion to his round face, as they framed his brown eyes.

He knew when to excuse himself during discussions that were no concern of his. That is what he did when Klara came to summon Anton, telling him that Vera was in the kitchen. He had excused himself. Alexie, one of the few people to use the proper front entrance of the house, and not the kitchen door, went out on the porch to smoke a cigarette.

Alexie was out there for quite a while. He saw Marko the blacksmith approach the house. Then later, he saw Vera leave stomping down the road with Marko slowly following behind. He wasn't curious about the visit. It was no concern of his.

During his stay on the porch, he thought about his own duties. He surely needed to return to Karlovac and his business. As much as he wished to stay with Sofie, he had to return to his office. There were papers to be filed and he needed to send Katya's document to Selna, the one deeding the house to Milan.

Sofie hurried past Alexie on her way to the barn with only a quick, "I'll be right back." He saw her speaking with one of the workers. On her return, she sat next to Alexie and said, "Katya is leaving."

Alexie raised his eyebrows. Sofie went on, "It seems I cannot talk her out of it. Vera has accused her of being a witch."

"Why that's ridiculous," said Alexie. "How can she say such a thing?"

"She will say anything that will keep Ivan from leaving her. According to Vera, Ivan and Katya were going away together."

"You said Katya is leaving. How can Ivan travel? He can't be well enough to travel," he said.

"Katya is leaving without him."

"Oh?"

"It seems he thinks of her as a witch, also."

"That's nonsense!" Alexie stood up, snuffing out his cigarette on the sole of his shoe, before tossing the butt out into the dirt yard. "It is obvious the young man is in love with her…and she is with him."

Sofie stood up. "I am sending a message to Vincent's mother in Trieste," said Sofie.

At the mention of Vincent, Alexie's eyes widened. He thought…that is, he had felt there was something warm happening between him and Sofie. He wanted to know why she was sending a message to Trieste, but dared not ask. He had hoped her ties to Trieste were over. Was he wrong? Could it be that Sofie did not care for him the way he cared for her? Perhaps she was still in love with the memory of the handsome Vincent. How could he compete with the memory of a ghost?

Gently taking her arm, he asked in a low voice, "May I ask why you are sending a message to Trieste, to Vincent's mother?"

"Why, to let her know that Katya is coming for a visit," said Sofie. "Didn't I tell you that?' With a wave of her hand she said, "How stupid of me. I didn't tell you that Katya was planning to travel with the Gypsies? I couldn't let her wander about like a nomad. Then, I thought of Signora Lucia and remembered how much she liked Katya. How much Katya reminded her of Vincent."

Relief spread over Alexie's face. "What a wonderful idea," he said. Just as quickly, he became concerned again. "Are you also going to Trieste?"

"Oh, no," said Sofie, entering the house, with Alexie behind her. "She will travel with the Gypsies. They go through Trieste on their way to France. Yura is leaving shortly to take a message to Signora Lucia so that she may expect Katya in a day or so."

In the house, Alexie again reached for Sofie, taking her hand. She turned, "What is it, Alexie?"

"Sofie, I must get back to Karlovac. I have been gone several days, now."

"Oh…" She was disappointed. "Of course you must go. I…" She looked at him, her eyes sad, "Oh, Alexie! I like having you here," she said. "How long will you be gone? I mean…will you be coming back?"

"I would like very much to come back, Sofie. I wouldn't leave if I didn't have to."

"Alexie…"

"Yes?"

"Are you able to leave your office for more than just a few days?"

"Why are you asking?"

"I would like you to go to Trieste with me." Seeing the look of surprise on his face she quickly added, "I want to take Katya the things she is leaving behind. Also…I want you to meet Signora Lucia…to know something of my past." She dropped her eyes, her cheeks reddening.

"Who else will be going?" he asked. When she shook her head, he said, "Do you mean we would be going alone?"

"Yes, it will be just the two of us. That is…if you agree."

Alexie drove Sofie and Katya to the Gypsy camp. No animals were grazing in the open field today. There was a practiced activity for breaking camp. Pulling up stakes was a way of life for these people. Packing up to leave almost had a rhythm to it. Each person knew what to do without being told. Food was stored and horses were hitched to the front of the caravans, while other animals, such as goats and cows were tethered to the back. Campfires were stomped out and watered. Everything that could be secured was put in its place.

Queen Valina stood waiting for Katya. Earlier that morning, when Vera turned Katya out, the crying girl came to the old Gypsy, asking if she could travel with them.

"Why would you want to leave a fine house to travel with us?" asked Valina.

"Because I am not wanted here," said Katya.

"And the Scholar," asked Valina. "Doesn't he want you?"

"He thinks I am a witch, just as his mother and the rest of the village."

Valina wanted to argue perhaps this wasn't true, but then, who was she to challenge Destiny. If Katya was meant to leave this place, Valina would not refuse her request to travel with them. Still, Queen Valina wasn't sure Katya was meant to live as a Gypsy.

When Alexie helped Sofie and Katya down from the small carriage, Sofie went immediately to the Gypsy Queen.

"Thank you, Valina. I am so grateful that you will look after Katya," she said.

Valina looked long at Sofie. "You are willing to let her travel with us? To live as we do, from day to day? She was not born to this sort of life." She said it almost as a reprimand.

"That is what she thought she wanted, but it is different now," said Sofie. "She will go only as far as Trieste with you. I have a very close friend there and Katya is most welcome to stay with her."

Valina nodded in agreement, as she watched her grandson take the packed carpetbag from Alexie and place it in his grandmother's caravan. "Perhaps that is good. Our way of life may be too hard for her. And it is not where she should be. She just hasn't found where it is she belongs."

Sofie and Katya both shed tears as they hugged one another, saying good-bye.

Alexie kissed Katya's hand, as he felt a hug would be too familiar, since he was not part of the family.

"We will come, just as soon as we can get away," said Sofie through her tears. "I will bring your things. Write to me if you need anything before we get there."

The two hugged again, clinging to one another.

"Say good-bye to Anton for me," said Katya. "I didn't see him when I said good-bye to Klara."

"It won't be long, my dear Katya," said Sofie again. "We will be together soon. I promise."

It was close to noon when the caravan slowly made its way out of the Vladeslavian valley. A few villagers waved as the houses on wheels rolled forward onto the main roads. The Gypsies would normally have left at daybreak, but Valina wanted to wait to know if Ivan was getting better and what the authorities had to say.

It had been just as Alexie planned. Once Anton told his story of the attack to the authorities that came to investigate, and when they saw the catatonic Erna, no more questions were asked. The Gypsies were not suspected of any wrongdoing. Anton, not wanting to leave Erna, asked Alexie to deliver several gold coins to the very happy Mustafa. It was the reward the Gypsy had been promised.

Earlier, before Sofie and Alexie were ready to take Katya to the Gypsy camp, Katya had gone to the chapel. She slipped in and looked around the beautiful holy place for possibly the last time. When she was sure she was alone, she moved the statue of the Madonna and replaced the pouch of money she had taken that night which now seemed so long ago. She turned the statue back into place and making the sign of the cross she left.

On the dusty road, as Valina's red and yellow caravan slowly jostled to and fro, Katya and Valina sat on thick pillows in a comfortable silence.

Katya thought she saw Valina looking at the sparkly bracelet she had given Katya for protection. The same bracelet Mustafa recognized, when he saved Katya from the Turk.

Katya started to undo the clasp. "I should return this bracelet to you," she said. "It has done its work. It has protected me."

Valina put her hand over Katya's, stopping her from opening the clasp.

"No, no," said the old Gypsy, softly, "Please don't remove it."

Book II, Chapter 37

Father Lahdra emotionally and physically tired from the previous night's events was not prepared for what awaited him when he entered the rectory.

His housekeeper Zlata, looking agitated, waved a note at him before he could take off his hat. "I was going to send someone to find you," she said. Zlata was short, round, pink-cheeked, and looked like a cherub wearing a babushka. "It is from the convent. I was told it is important."

Lahdra unfolded the paper.

"I heard all the awful news. I didn't stay here last night," Zlata said. "I went to my brother's home. I was afraid to be here alone."

Lahdra looked up. "What? What did you say?"

"I didn't stay here last night."

"That's good," he said barely listening. "Make me some coffee. I must change and leave at once."

"I hear that Mistress Vladislav is ill. Is that true? And what about Ivan, will he be alright?"

But Father Lahdra didn't answer her. He was already in his room removing his shoes.

He had to hurry. His cousin needed him. It had been months since he had seen her. How many months? Could it really be six months?

The note was only one sentence long. It read: Come quickly. Mother Superior is dying.

This time Father Lahdra went by carriage. Perhaps it would have been faster if he had ridden a horse. He was very tired from the vigil spent at Marko's cottage and he was getting a bit old for lengthy horse back travel.

When he arrived at dusk, the horse was in a lather and Lahdra was almost sick with nerves. He had no idea that Manda had been ill, much less dying. He tried to remember the last time they were together. He didn't recall her being ill or looking ill at their last visit. Though, perhaps she had been thinner. Yes, now he remembered she appeared a good deal thinner.

He was quickly ushered into Sister Manda's tiny candle-lit room. Lahdra could never get used to the austere simplicity of the nuns' cells. A candle flickered on a small writing table in the center of the room with only one straight-backed wooden chair beside it. Another candle glowed on a simple bedside table, its reflection making ghost-like shadows on the whitewashed wall.

A nun he recognized, dressed in the coarse cloth of homespun flax, knelt praying alongside the cot that held the skeletal frame of his beloved cousin. Another young nun bathed Manda's face with water. It was a face Lahdra could barely recognize.

His dying cousin caught the look of shock on his face and a look of contempt hardened on her pale face. With a weak wave, she signaled the attending nuns to leave the room. When Lahdra heard the door close behind them, he fell to his knees next to the bed. He took his cousin's hand into his. It was no longer the strong, soft hand he remembered holding when they ran together, or jumped hand in hand into the river as children. This hand was so small, dry...so frail.

"Manda," he whispered, on the verge of tears. He was hardly able to look at her pale, gray skin. She had once been so beautiful. "Oh, Manda," he repeated, choking back sobs as he rested his head on the cot, next to her shoulder.

In a flat voice with no emotion, Manda said, "I would like you to hear my last confession."

"What?" His head flew up from the cot. The cold tone of her voice and the request confounded him. She had stated long ago that she would never permit him to hear her confession. That he was *only* her little cousin. She had said it many times, over the years, though he was actually two years older than she.

"What did you say?"

Her voice was weak, but still unfriendly, "I want you to hear my last confession."

"My prayer book and oils are still in the carriage." Lahdra started to rise.

She held on with surprising strength. "Never mind the book. We don't have time."

A chill passed over him, as if a door had been opened to let in a cold wind.

He remained on his knees, unable to use his right hand to make the sign of the cross, because Manda held on firmly. He made the sign of the cross over her with his left hand and started to pray when Manda began her confession.

She dispensed with the formal prayer of confession, instead she said, "I have two things to confess, two sins. I don't know which is greater."

Lahdra started to say something, to refute that she could have great sins, after all she had given her life to the Church. But Manda stilled him with a stern look. "Just listen. I don't want your excuses."

Excuses! Excuses! What was she saying? What sort of confession was this?

"I did not become a nun out of love of God. I became a nun because the man I loved didn't love me. He left me. I have disliked my life here at the convent, even hated it."

This was a revelation to Lahdra. He had no idea Manda had been in love, for he had never heard of any suitors. He had to interrupt, "I don't believe that qualifies as a sin, I mean becoming a nun out of sadness."

"It does when it was done in spite!" She saw the quizzical look on his face. "You idiot. You left me to become a priest. Well, I married above you...I married God!"

Stunned, Lahdra fell back on his heels. He pulled his hand free of Manda's hold.

"We never talked of love!" He was trying to remember, to remember their childhood promises. No! Nothing about love and marriage could come to mind.

"I always loved you," she said. "When you left, I was angry that you didn't feel the same. When I became a nun, I thought the religious life would make a stronger bond between us."

He said nothing. There wasn't time to argue that he had always wanted to be a priest and that he was happy as a priest. And, didn't she remember in their childhood games, he always played a priest, pretending to give communion or pretending to perform the marriage ceremony. He couldn't count the times he had performed a pretend marriage ceremony with Manda and the tutor's son, Tomas.

"I hate it here," she went on. "We tend the sick. We clean. We tend the sick. We sew vestments. We tend to the sick," she repeated. "I'm dying because of it. Sooner or later every one of us catches something serious and we die of it."

Lahdra's feeling of grief was shifting into melancholy sadness. While Manda spoke, he slowly rose and reached for a nearby chair. He placed it beside her, sat down and no longer looked into her face as she went on with her confession. He stared ahead at the wall with only a simple crucifix on it. Lahdra fixed his eyes on the cross, listening to Manda's anger. Anger at him for not loving her the way she wished. Anger at God, for making her accept a life of sacrifice and anger at dying.

The dying woman's words drifted away as Lahdra realized the crucifix he was staring at seemed to glow. Were his tired eyes playing a trick on him?

As Manda went on venting her anger, Lahdra only half-listened, praying for her to lose her angry pain, when he heard her say the name 'Vladislav.'

"What did you say?" He asked.

"Aren't you listening?" She tried to sound annoyed, but her strength was slipping away. "I think I should have sent for Anton Vladislav and his sister, to tell them what I did, but I'm afraid they will take away their generous support of the convent."

"Why would they do that?" he asked. "They love this convent. Haven't they supported it for years?"

"That's why I was afraid to let them know the truth. They may never come back or help us pay our bills." The anger at Lahdra and God was gone now. Instead, her face reflected concern and contrition. "Oh, Lahdra, I thought I was doing the right thing."

Lahdra spoke calmly. "What is it you think you have done?"

Tears welled in her eyes as she stared at the ceiling. Tears of sadness for what she had done or perhaps tears for the punishment she thought awaited her soul. Lahdra couldn't tell which.

Lahdra sensed there wasn't much more time, so he urged, "Please go on with your confession."

Sister Manda never took her eyes from the ceiling. It was as if she couldn't look at him.

"It was that night...the night you first came here. Remember?"

"Yes, I remember."

"Mother Superior was dying."

"I remember," he said.

"It happened before you came." When Lahdra remained silent, she went on, her voice losing its strength. "Early in the afternoon, Vladislav arrived with the young Sofie very ill. Her gown was soiled and she was pale as death. She had been caring for her fiancé in Trieste, who had died. Anton Vladislav was sure Sofie had contracted the same illness and was also dying."

"I remember," he said again.

The sick nun paused to catch her breath. "Vladislav was so handsome back then, his face grave with concern, as he carried his unconscious sister into one of our rooms. I sent him out and then Sister Fillipa and Sister Eva removed young Sofie's clothing.

Then Sofie started to moan. We had an awful time trying to get her out of her clothes, because she started to thrash about."

Father Lhadra was concerned for his cousin, his Sekitza, the Croatian word for little sister or cousin. He could see her strength ebbing and couldn't understand why she was recounting this long past event. He wondered what tending to the sick Sofie had to do with Manda's last confession.

"Sister Fillipa came to the garden and motioned for me to come to the room where Sofie was." She continued, "I can remember the smell of her stained clothes and the odor in the room." Her voice trailed, she was silent for a moment, as if reliving that time once more. "She was pregnant. She was in labor too soon, too early."

Father Lahdra's eyes widened. He stared at his cousin, not sure he understood. Was Manda saying what he thought?

Manda caught the look on his face. "Oh, yes. It's what you think. I had sister Fillipa press on Sofie's stomach. We pulled the baby from her. It was a tiny thing, just fitting in both my hands. Sofie Vladislav kept calling for 'Vincent.'

No one came to assist us, for the other Sisters were needed to tend Mother Superior.

We cleaned the young girl's body and the bed beneath her. Then we covered her with cool, wet cloths trying to ease her fever.

'Well, Sister, asked Sister Fillipa. 'What do we do now?'

"Don't worry, Sister. I will take care of it. You are not to mention this to anyone. That goes for you, too, Sister Eva," I said.

Manda coughed. Lahdra took the filled water glass and gently raised her head so that she could take a sip of water.

It appeared she was finished talking, when she took a labored breath and continued. "I went out into the garden. Far in the back by the stone wall, I buried the baby."

Manda fell silent. She reached for Lahdra's hand. They sat in silence for a while. Lahdra felt a great sadness. *Poor Sofie.* What a wonderful mother she would have been!

"More water...please."

He raised her head and held the glass carefully to her parched lips, careful not to spill any.

When she lay back, Manda sighed deeply too weak to speak anymore.

Father Lahdra prayed as he had never prayed before. He prayed for Manda, beseeching God to accept her in His Heavenly Garden. He prayed for his own forgiveness, should he have in some way misled his cousin into thinking they would marry.

Throughout the night he held his cousin's hand. He didn't know when she left him. He didn't recall falling asleep until one of the nuns gently shook his shoulder, to let him know Manda's soul had left the earth.

His bag with his prayer book and holy water had been brought in sometime during the night. He opened the prayer book and prayed, his eyes filling with tears so that he couldn't see the words on the pages.

As he stepped out of the room, nuns entered ready to prepare the body for washing. Sister Fillipa stepped in front of him. He stopped surprised.

"Yes? What is it, Sister?"

"I am Sister Fillipa," she said. She had a long, thin face with large pores. Her skin was tan from working outdoors in the garden and groves.

"Yes, I remember you," said Lahdra.

"I would like you to hear my confession," she said.

"I am tired, Sister. Couldn't this confession wait for the priest who comes here to say Mass?" He was a bit irritated. His last living relative had just died and made a surprising confession to him. He was exhausted from the long night at Marko's. Couldn't this Nun see he was in personal pain?

"Please, Father. I beg you!"

Something in the sound of her voice and the desperate look in her eyes softened him. "All right," he said. "Must we go to the chapel or is there somewhere here that is private?"

"In the garden, Father, we can be alone there."

He followed her, carrying his bag with his stole and prayer book. Once out the door, the sunlight made his eyes water after being in the dim cell for such a long time.

"Here Father," Fillipa said indicating a bench under a tree away from the convent, in an area where anyone approaching could be seen.

Lahdra waited for the Nun to sit down and when he noticed she was waiting out of respect for him to be seated first, he quickly sat down. He snapped open his leather bag and removed his stole, placing it across the back of his neck so that it hung like a scarf.

He closed his eyes, waiting for her to begin.

"Bless me, Father, for I have sinned," was how she began.

When her prayer was finished she said, "I did a terrible thing Father."

She paused as if gathering strength to go on. "Years ago a young woman was brought to the convent, ill. Or so we thought. It turned out that she was not ill, she was pregnant."

Father Lahdra opened his eyes and looked into her face. She stammered a bit embarrassed at his stare, but went on. "The baby was pre-mature. Not breathing. No one knew the young woman was pregnant. She didn't seem to know it herself and certainly her family wasn't aware of it. So we said nothing."

Sister Fillipa had to turn away from Father Lahdra, for his stare was so intense.

Looking into the distance, she continued, "I remembered that the baby had not been baptized before it was buried. I hurried out to the wall where I knew it to be and with my hands dug a little to uncover it."

"I don't know how the madman got into the courtyard. He must have climbed over the wall. He came staggering towards me, calling 'Sister, Sister. I need a baby. I know you have babies here. I have money.' The man reached for me, frightening me. It was twilight and I could only make out that he was dark-skinned, thin, with lots of dark hair. 'I'll give you all my money for a baby.'

"I did a terrible thing. I took that man's money and gave him the dead baby. I didn't even baptize it! It is somewhere in limbo, because of me!"

A tear rolled down the Nun's cheek as she went on with her confession.

"He was insane. He knew nothing. I showed him the baby and he grabbed it out of my hands. It was wrapped in the soiled skirt we removed from the mother. He never noticed the baby was dead or the stained skirt. He shoved some bills in my hand, then, stumbled towards the wall, probably to the same spot where he had come in. Oh, yes...he said something strange...he said, 'that's all my America money. Now I have a baby for Mila.'"

Later, back in his house at his desk, the old journal he had looked at recently was again before him. In the Oct. 5, 1892 entry, he found what had been tugging at his mind ever since he left the convent. He read about his return to his parish and the caretaker's anxious report that Mato Balich had been there the night before behaving like a madman. Lahdra read the words: *He just kept wailing about a baby and being punished by God and America money.*

Dear God! Could it be true? How could it be true, if the baby was dead? But then, it must *not* have been dead!

Father Lahdra covered his face with his hands. Was God challenging him? Testing him to see if he could keep this *great secret* from his best friend, from the man he loved and considered a brother. He could never speak of it. He learned this secret through the Holy Sacrament of Confession. By the laws of the church he could never tell what he thought to be a miracle...that Katya *was* with her real mother.

He rose from his chair, walked around his desk to the lamp table where a carafe of wine and glass waited. He poured himself a glassful and walked to the window. He gazed out over the valley.

He looked at his beautiful church and the lovely green hills surrounding the countryside. How he loved it here. He loved his church. He loved the house and the furnishings provided by his friend and benefactor, Anton.

"Oh, Anton," he said aloud, thinking of his dear friend and now of the 'Secret' Lahdra was carrying within himself.

Lahdra turned from the window. He turned to see if his housekeeper was in the room. He felt a presence. It was as if someone was standing near-by. He looked about the room. He saw no one.

Then, he said softly, "Is that you, Manda?"

Book II, Chapter 38

From the second story balcony of her home, Signora Lucia scanned the road leading towards the south, the road the Gypsy caravan must use on their way through Trieste. Ever since the brief note from Sofie was delivered the day before, stating that Katya was on her way for a visit, Lucia was almost beside herself with excitement.

The note did not explain why Katya was traveling with the Gypsies. Furthermore, there was no explanation for her coming alone. Signora Lucia did remember some connection with the Gypsies...vaguely...the story of the beautiful and valuable bracelet came to mind.

As always, she was dressed in mourning, with a coral cameo pinned against her high black collar. Lucia left her lookout post on the balcony to speak with her servant, Mia. The pretty young girl was stripping the bed, preparing a room for Katya.

"Make sure the room has plenty of flowers," said Lucia. "I want the room to smell like a garden."

"Sí, Signora," said Mia, carrying the pillows to the balcony to freshen them in the sunlight and air.

Mia was a blond Italian for her family originated from the North of Italy, near the Italian Alps. She had worked for the Signora for almost three years, ever since she was fourteen years old. Mia was a good worker. She was trustworthy and as close to invisible as a person could be. In all the time she worked for Lucia Kurecka, Mia never made an attempt at personal conversation. She was there to work and that was what she did. At sometime during her three years with Signora Lucia, Mia had been entrusted with the task of dealing with any auxiliary help that was needed, such as a gardener, plumber, or handyman. At her young age it was remarkable how she could handle all the household decisions, leaving Signor Lucia to only worry about the Renaldi Trading Company.

And Signora Lucia did worry about the Trading Company her father had single-handedly made prosper. Her worry was that she was becoming old and had no blood heirs to take over the company when she was gone. She had tried to get Sofie interested.

Lucia had on several occasions asked Sofie to stay in Trieste to learn the business, but always, Sofie claimed she needed to be with her family.

Now Lucia's Cousin Carlo, the one who wanted to marry her when they were both young, worked for the Renaldi Trading Company. Also, his son Carlo, Jr., worked there. Lucia felt as if the two men were trying to push her out of her company. Recently Carlo the Father suggested, "That Lucia needn't come to pay her workers. After all," he had said, "I am here with the men. I can pay them."

Lucia personally paid each employee, including Cousin Carlo and Carlo Jr., each Saturday. Her father had handed the lira to each man and thanked him for his work. When her beloved Aleksy was in charge, he too paid each man and gave his thanks for work well done. Lucia kept up the tradition. She enjoyed speaking with the men who worked for her, asking about their families and thanking them for their work. But most of all, being there to hand out the pay, was a subtle way of reminding Carlo Senior and Junior that they worked for her.

Mia heard the arrival before Lucia. "Signora, I hear horses."

Together they hurried down the marble steps, across the large entry to the door.

When Mia opened the door, she and Lucia saw a once brightly painted caravan, showing signs of peeling red and yellow paint pulled by two brown rather thin horses. The driver of the team was a handsome, dark-skinned, young man seated up front with the reins in his hands.

He smiled at Lucia as he jumped to the ground. "Is this the house of Signora Kurecka?" he asked.

"Yes…Yes," said an excited Lucia.

Before he could get to the back of the caravan, the back door swung open with steps dropping to the ground. Katya burst out of the house on wheels, still wearing the plain homespun blouse and skirt borrowed from Vera. The last time Lucia had seen Katya, her hair was combed smooth with a bun at the back. Today it was wild with curls.

As Lucia rushed to hug Katya, she thought, *"My goodness. She could pass for a Gypsy if her skin was not so light."*

With tears in her eyes the older woman hugged Katya, saying, "Oh my dear girl. I am so happy you are here."

Katya felt safe in Lucia's embrace. It felt good to be held by her. The affection felt genuine. "Thank you for letting me come," said Katya.

"Stay as long as you want." Lucia stepped back to look at Katya. "You look so different in the peasant clothes."

"I was in a big hurry to leave," she explained. "I didn't take the time to change."

Zolton stood alongside his grandmother, who was now out of her rolling house.

Her arms were folded across her breasts and she studied Lucia and Katya greeting one another. There was a smile on the old Gypsy's face, as she searched for some resemblance between the two as they embraced. She didn't see any resemblance, but it didn't take away her smile.

Zolton carried Katya's carpetbag as far as the door, then set it down. With the agility of youth, he jumped up to the driver's seat of the caravan. Without speaking, Valina turned ready to retire to the comfort of her pillows, then onward to this night's campground.

Lucia, as if the two women were old friends, put her arm around Valina's waist. "You can't leave. You must dine with us. Stay the night if you wish."

Valina was genuinely surprised at this gesture of hospitality. She was used to wary and suspicious looks from people who were not part of the tribe. A flustered Valina stammered, "Oh...no...Signora, I couldn't impose."

"Oh, please stay, stay for a little while," pleaded Katya. "Have supper with us."

Valina looked from Katya then to Lucia. She felt the invitation was sincere and she was touched. "I will stay for a short while. That is if you allow me to sit in your lovely garden while I am here."

The old Gypsy felt she should not go into the house. Valina would do nothing to instill any doubt in the Signora's mind as to her honesty.

Lucia protested, "You are most welcome to come into the house and freshen up."

"No," said Valina, "I so seldom get to enjoy such a lovely enclosed flower garden, especially one with a fountain. I think I hear a fountain. It would be such a pleasure to sit there, if I may?"

Lucia, the wise old woman that she was, thought she understood. "Of course, you may sit in the garden. I will be only a moment getting Katya settled and it would be my pleasure to join you," she said. "Your driver is welcome to stay, also."

"My grandson will return to our camp. He can come for me later," said Valina.

"As you wish," nodded Lucia.

Zolton said nothing to his grandmother as he made his way back to the caravan.

"Zolton," Katya followed him. "Thank you for everything." She kissed him on the cheek and said, "Good-bye my friend."

He smiled warmly. "There are never good-byes with friends. Besides, I will see you again when I come back for Grandmother."

In a short while Lucia returned to the garden to join Valina. Quickly the women felt comfortable in one another's company. One a Gypsy nomad and the other a well-bred woman of means, yet each had an elegance all her own.

"I must thank you once more for bringing Katya safely to me," said Lucia. "I have no idea why she chose to come here. Do you know why?"

"I only know she appeared at our camp three mornings ago, her face red from crying, claiming she wanted to join us. When I asked her why she would want to leave the nice home she shared with Sofie, Katya only cried more, saying the Villagers accused her of being a witch."

Lucia's eyes widened. "How ridiculous, what could give them such an idea?"

"Partly because they are superstitious and partly because she has a remarkable knowledge of herbal healing. They mistake her knowledge for witchcraft."

"Couldn't Sofie's family protect Katya?" asked Lucia. "I understood them to be a family of some power."

"Signora," began Valina. "What is your Christian name? May I ask?"

"Of course you may," said Lucia. "It is Lucia…and your name? Is it Valina, as I have heard Katya call you?"

Valina nodded smiling, she felt warmth toward Lucia. "There is more to Katya's leaving than just having the villager's calling her a witch."

Lucia's eyes widened and Valina continued, "I think Katya was very fond of a young man called Ivan. As I understand it, he too, called her a witch."

"Oh, how sad for Katya!" said Lucia.

"And…" said Valina, "there was the murder of the man who tried to abduct her."

Lucia's mouth fell open. "Oh, my…" she said softly. "Oh…"

Valina told Lucia the story, that this was the same man who tried to buy her while she lived in Selna. She told how Mustafa saved her life by killing the Turk when he saw Katya's bracelet."

"Yes," said a stunned Lucia. "I remember Katya saying the bracelet was never to be removed. That it would protect her. Well, it certainly has!"

They sat in comfortable silence for a few minutes. The only sound was the gurgling of the mermaid water fountain in the very center of the garden.

Signora Lucia broke the silence by asking, "How well do you know Sofie?"

"Only that she is the sister of Anton Vladislav and unmarried," said Valina, taking a sip of tea.

"She was to marry my son, Vincent, but he died just before the priest arrived."

"Really?" said Valina, interested.

"Yes. Sofie would come and stay several times over the long period while my Vincent was ill. The doctors never determined what his illness was."

"I am so sorry," said Valina, almost feeling Lucia's heartache.

"Sofie's brother came here the morning after Vincent died. I begged him to let Sofie stay, but he nearly dragged her away."

Lucia's eyes were moist with the memory. "How different things might have been if Vincent had lived."

"Ah…Destiny," said Valina. "We cannot fight Destiny. It plays with us, as if we have no control of our lives." Noticing that

Lucia wore mourning clothes, Valina asked, "Have you been a widow long?"

"For a very long time," she said. "And you? Have you a husband?"

Valina smiled. "I too have been without a husband for many years. But you..." with a small wave of her hand, she said to Lucia, "you are a beautiful woman. Surely there were suitors."

Lucia frowned, "Only my cousin Carlo. He wanted the business my father built from nothing and if he could have married me, he thought it might be his. Finally, he married someone else but still thinks he can get his hands on my trading company." Then she asked Valina, "And you...do not Gypsy Queens remarry?"

Valina looked thoughtful for a moment. "Perhaps if I didn't have a daughter and perhaps if I had been younger, I might have considered marrying again. Nevertheless..." she had an impish grin, "That isn't to say, there were no opportunities."

The two women looked at one another. Lucia caught the meaning and both women giggled.

Lucia said, "I think you may have been very beautiful."

Another long pause and another impish grin from Valina, "I may have been."

And both women laughed again.

Katya joined the two women in the garden for a late supper of salad, steamed fish and fresh fruit. Katya marveled at how comfortable these two women from vastly different worlds were with one another. With the aid of some lovely Chianti, Valina and Sofia chatted all through dinner, every now and then giving one another a knowing look and laughing uproariously. There were times Katya had no idea what was so funny when they laughed the way they did.

When Zolton came to fetch his Grandmother, it was as if Valina and Lucia were long time friends. Mia the servant had made up a parcel of sausage, cheese and pastries for Valina to take on their journey.

"What can I give you?" asked Lucia. "I want to give you something to thank you. I want to give you something to remember this night, which has meant so much to me."

Valina took Lucia's hand in hers. "My friend, you have no idea what you have given me by having me in your garden and sharing your food with me. It was a lovely evening. One I shall not soon forget." She embraced Lucia, while Zolton and Katya looked on in surprised silence.

"Come back, Valina," said Lucia. "Whenever you are near, come and we will sit in the garden and talk, just as we have tonight. Promise me you will come."

"Of course," promised Valina.

And, she did come. She stopped to visit whenever the tribe was passing through or near Trieste. The bond of friendship grew between these two women. They were so very different and yet alike in many ways. Each was a strong woman, each a leader. The visits and friendship continued until 1910, the year Queen Valina died in her sleep.

Book II, Chapter 39

Anton Vladislav, the great landowner, should have had nothing in common with the uneducated, guilt ridden peasant Mato Balich of Selna. Anton had traveled throughout Europe, was University educated and a man of means. Mato had been poor and close to starving most of his life. He never learned to read and had never traveled more than few miles from his village. Yet, there was one strong similarity between the two men. Each at some point in their lives experienced the fear that God was punishing them. Mato was sure that God was taking away his wife Mila because he, Mato had deprived her of necessities by hoarding money to escape to America.

When Erna showed no improvement in her condition, after a series of doctors had come to examine her and Father Lahdra prayed devoutly night after night, Anton was sure God was punishing him, because he never loved Erna as a husband should. Often he would sit alone in the family chapel, surrounded by the lovely statues with glowing candles on the small altar. Above the altar was a glorious hand carved crucifix. Christ's half-closed eyes gazed with pity down at Anton, or so he thought. The chapel was the only place Anton felt any comfort.

There were times he fell to his knees fervently praying for Erna to recover. Other times he would pray for forgiveness, with tears streaming down his cheeks. He felt he needed to be forgiven for not loving Erna, as a husband should have. He prayed for forgiveness for the pain he caused Vera, the mother of Ivan, even though he felt he had no other options at the time she arrived at Klara's kitchen door. But, he prayed the hardest and the longest for Stefan, his handsome son. Ten days after his disappearance with no word from Stefan or about him, Anton contacted Alexie Lukas, asking him for help in searching for Stefan. Anton was embarrassed and surprised that he knew so little about Stefan's life. He didn't know who his son's friends were or where he went for entertainment.

Alexie promptly sent a trusted man to Zagreb to ask questions and hopefully find Stefan.

Ruda Klarich, Alexie's investigator returned after three days. Ruda, who later changed his name to Rudy when he went to America, was a small, slender man, only 5 feet 6 inches tall. His eyes were hazel, his hair brown, parted down the center. His face was smooth, so that with his short stature, nice eyes and wavy hair, he would have made a pretty girl. There was nothing feminine about Ruda. Because he was small, he felt he had to prove he was tough. And he was tough, in a pugilistic way.

"I don't think this Stefan is in Zagreb," said Ruda, once he was back in Alexie's office. "I've been to all the hotels, bars and gambling houses. By the way," he said, "that popular place, Magda's...is locked up. No one knows why. It hasn't been open for a couple of weeks. Even the janitor can't get in."

"Why so interested in Magda's?" asked Alexie, seated at his desk lighting a cigarette. He offered one to Ruda, who declined. Ruda slouched in a chair across from Alexie, one leg slung over the arm of the chair.

"Because," Ruda waved his hand in the air, "it seems Stefan was quite the gambler and the ladies man. It's been implied he accepted money from older women."

Alexie frowned. "That isn't the Stefan the family knows."

"Of course not," said Ruda, brushing lint from his pant leg. "I am sure he was the model son at home. Women and gambling are not topics one discusses at the family dinner table."

"Did you go to the University?" asked Alexie.

"First place I went," replied Ruda, as if the question was unnecessary. "His grades must have disappointed his father. It appears he missed more classes than he attended. The Vladislav money kept him from being dismissed. The father, it seems was a benefactor of the school. Not in a big way, but enough for the faculty to over-look Stefan's scholastic failures."

"So you don't have a clue where he could be," said Alexie, sighing deeply.

"He could show up dead." Seeing Alexie's startled look, Ruda went on. "Listen, the man was a scoundrel. It wouldn't surprise me if a husband killed Stefan or had someone kill him. I wasn't kidding when I said he liked women. Maybe he left the country." Ruda stood up, straightened his jacket. Seeing the disappointed look on Alexie's face, he said, "Listen. Stefan is a handsome man. For all we know he is on the coast, maybe Split, Rijeka or even Dubrovnik with an American heiress."

Alexie rose, stepped around his desk and extended his hand to Ruda. "I plan to go to Trieste for awhile. I am not sure how long I will be gone. Take care of things here, while I'm away."

"Sure thing," said Ruda. "I know what to do."

"By the way," said Alexie. "Be sure you go to Selna and deliver those documents. The name of the priest who will go with you is in the folder."

At their home in Selna, Milan Kosich and his wife Eva looked at the priest and the short handsome man who came to their door. The furious barking of their dog, Vuk heightened their wariness. They were frightened. The man in the brown suit holding a leather case looked very official. Officials usually meant trouble for the villagers.

Oh my God. They know about Elia. They know I killed him. Eva was terrified. Ever since that rainy night when she hit Elia killing him, she had been fearful that the authorities would come knocking at their door. Now it had happened!

Father Petra, the local priest, saw the worried looks on their faces. "May we come in?"

Milan and Eva stood mute, frightened.

"Please..." said the priest. He was round faced and round bodied, dressed in a black cassock. He always smelled of wine. "This gentleman has come all the way from Karlovac. He has some papers for you." Again he asked, "May we come in?"

Not waiting for an answer and seeing the fear in Milan and Eva's faces, Ruda gently pushed past the priest and into the house.

Both Milan and Eva stepped back, not knowing what to expect.

"May I sit down?" asked Ruda.

Neither Milan nor Eva replied.

"Relax," Ruda said. "You look as if I came here to arrest you."

Just then Eva's knees buckled, but Milan held her firmly by her arm and she remained upright.

"Hey," Ruda insisted, "I told you relax. I'm here with good news." Seeing no change in the looks on their faces he turned to the priest, "Tell them, Father."

The priest stepped forward, "My, yes," he said. "Father Lahdra sent word to me to come with this gentleman. So it is alright."

At the mention of Father Lahdra, Milan said, "The last time I saw Father Lahdra was at my cousin Nikola's wedding. Has someone died? Why has he sent you?"

Ruda spoke up, "I have a letter from Katya Balich and a couple of documents to read to you and leave with you."

"Is Katya alright?" Eva covered her mouth with her hand, fearing bad news.

"She's fine. She's fine…" Ruda was exasperated. "Can we *PLEASE* sit down so I can read these to you?"

"Yes. Yes, of course," said Milan, clearing some plates from the wooden table.

Eva wished she had used her pretty red and white tablecloth, the one she embroidered. It would look so nice for company, she thought.

Ruda and Father Petra sat down. Seeing that Ruda was not going to read until they sat down, Milan and Eva sat side by side, opposite their guests. Eva reached for Milan's hand.

Ruda cleared his throat. "My Dearest Eva and Milan," he read, "I am learning to read and write. I had help with this letter. I am not such a good speller yet. Please all be well and know that I think about you. I especially thank Milan for bringing me to Marko's home. I am now living with Teta Sofie at Vladezemla, so I will not be coming back to Selna."

Milan and Eva exchanged glances. *Why wasn't she with Marko?*

Ruda went on reading, "I hope Young Milan and the girls are well. I do miss them and think of them, often."

This last sentence wasn't completely true, but Sofie thought it was polite for Katya to put that in the letter. "I owe you both so very much. Eva nursed me and took care of me when Anka was too young to do so herself. And you, Milan, saved me from Elia and that horrible man. For this I thank you both with all my heart."

"I will write again sometime, though I don't know who will read the letter for you. I close now with love and affection. Katya Balich"

"I don't understand," said Milan. "Who is Sofie? Marko's wife's name is Vera." At the wedding Milan had a bit too much to drink and the people met so briefly, he now didn't remember. Sofie must have been one of them.

Ruda opened his brief case and drew out an official looking gold sealed document also stamped with a red wax seal. "I am not going to read all that is on these documents. I will tell you what they mean. This one," he held it high for all to see, "gives Milan Kosich the right to live in or give away or sell, as he wishes, the house left to Katya by Old Julia."

Milan's jaw dropped. "What? How can this be?"

"Because…" said Ruda, "this paper was drawn up by a lawyer, an advokat. It has been filed officially and the house is now legally yours. No one can take it away from you. Listen, there's more." He waved the second paper for them to see. "Now this document states that if Elia Sokach does not marry and have a family, Anka's house is to be yours when it is no longer occupied."

"Oh, God," murmured Eva, still thinking about that rainy night when her son helped bury Elia.

Milan stood up. "No one has seen or heard from Elia for almost two months. The house has been empty."

"Then," said Ruda, "take it. If he shows up, you can always give it back to him." Ruda slid a sheet of paper across the table in front of Eva. "I need each of you to sign this paper to show that I was here and that you received the documents."

Eva's face turned pink. She looked at Milan who looked nervous.

Ruda immediately realized they didn't know how to write. Not wanting to embarrass them he said, "Your names are already printed here. All you have to do is make your mark. Father Petra is the witness and he will sign also, that way when Katya sees this paper, she will know I gave you the deeds to the two houses."

The "X" Milan made was nicer than the one Eva drew. She was not used to holding a pen so her lines were uneven.

Book II, Chapter 40

At the Vladislav house Klara was now in charge of managing the household. She hired women to do what she, Erna and Sofie had done for years. The wife of one of the regular field workers came in to do the laundry and to clean. With Erna ill and unresponsive, there was a lot of sheet changing and laundering to be done. A full time cook was hired whose duties included caring for the garden planted outside the kitchen door.

There was an irony to Klara's new position in the household. As a young girl she had fantasized being the mistress of Vladezemla. There were times she pictured herself with the young, handsome Anton dining together and then he would read to her in the evening, while she mended or did some fancy handwork.

Now, twenty-one years later, Klara and Anton and Sofie shared their meals. In the evenings she would sit in the parlor which was now converted into Erna's room, for it was more convenient to care for her there, than to climb the stairs a hundred times a day. Klara listened as Anton read to Erna. He read or spoke to Erna continuously often his voice becoming hoarse.

Klara no longer slept in the curtained cubbyhole in the kitchen. The new cook now used it. Rooms on the second floor were available to Klara, but her bad knees kept her from choosing one. Instead she slept on a cot in the small library off the parlor.

One of the doctors had arranged for a nurse to stay with Erna. The nurse was a strong woman, tall as most men. Her light brown hair was braided in back and the braid coiled into a bun at the nape of her neck. She had pink round cheeks, bright eyes and always a smile. She wore a fresh, white, long-sleeved blouse each day. Her skirts were floor length, usually gray or black. Over this she wore a white bib apron.

She bathed Erna daily, changed her clothes and the bedding frequently. Feeding Erna was a challenge for Erna had trouble swallowing. She grew thinner with each passing day. A wooden wheel chair was acquired and with some effort, Erna was placed in it. Taking Erna out in the sunshine became a daily routine when the weather permitted.

If Anton noticed his sister's indifference to Erna's condition, he said nothing. In truth, Sofie's heart was broken for her brother's suffering. Each day she hoped Stefan would return to help with the maintenance of Vladezemla. Sofie herself was somewhat baffled by her lack of sympathy for the empty staring Erna. To Sofie, this body being cared for, lacking any emotion or response, was not Erna. To Sofie's way of thinking, Erna was gone. She certainly did not miss the often harsh or sarcastic remarks Erna could make, but at least that was a person. What was seated in the wheelchair now was a huge doll, not Erna.

Sofie did not sit with Erna or read to her. Instead Sofie thought of almost nothing but Alexie and Katya. She waited each day for word from Alexie to let her know when he could get away to accompany her to Trieste. She missed Katya very much and to her surprise, she found that she missed Alexie's comforting presence nearly as much. She wanted Signora Lucia to meet Alexie. It was very important for Sofie to know what Lucia thought of the lawyer.

Many an evening, in her after dinner walks through the grounds, Sofie wondered why she felt no guilt for her fondness of Alexie. For all the years since Vincent's death, Sofie thought to love someone else would be a betrayal of the love she shared with Vincent. But, now she didn't feel a betrayal to him. She had loved Vincent deeply with the heat and passion of her youth. She had kept him locked in her heart for sixteen years after his death. He was still in her heart...but no longer with sadness. Now there was a warm, sweet memory there. How had this change come about, she wondered? She had seen Alexie many times over the years and not felt for him the warmth she was now experiencing.

After Vincent's death, Sofie could not love. She had shut herself off from it. When she passed through the anger she had towards Anton for bringing her back to Vladezemla, she tried to be part of his family. She was sure she loved her nephew Stefan. Of course, she loved him...but *not in the way she loved Katya!* It was as if Katya opened up something in Sofie that allowed her to be herself, not the shadowy Aunt who shared in her brother's life...but a person with a life of her own...plans of her own.

She remembered the turning point in her life. It had been when she decided to make Katya her ward. She never discussed her plans with her brother, the head of the family. Sofie had some reservations about her decision right up to the morning that Alexie was to come. The moment she saw Alexie, someone she had known since she was a young girl, she felt safe in her decision. What an odd feeling to have. Safe! Yet, that is how she felt then and the feeling was stronger now. With Alexie she felt safe. In her heart she knew he would always advise her to do the right thing.

Sofie visited the chapel each morning. It was a peaceful place with beautiful statues and warm candlelight. Today the lingering scent of incense seemed more intense, as if someone had been in the chapel before her. This morning she prayed for her brother's peace of mind, for Stefan's return and God's protection for Katya and Alexie.

"There is a message for you on the dining room table," said Klara when Sofie returned from her morning prayers. "Sit and have some breakfast."

Sofie slid onto her usual seat at the table taking the envelope from a small tray where it had been placed. While she read the note, Klara, with a pot in each hand poured equal amounts of hot coffee and hot milk into a large cup for Sofie.

Klara saw Sofie break into a large smile. "Good news?" she asked.

"I will be leaving for Trieste in three days."

"Now?" Klara was disappointed. "You would go away now with Stefan gone and Erna...Erna the way she is?"

"I'm not needed here. You and Anton are taking care of things very well." Sofie was so happy that she overlooked Klara's reproachful tone.

Anton fresh from his morning shave was at the dining room door for breakfast, when he overheard the conversation between Sofie and Klara.

"Why are you leaving for Trieste?" asked Anton, finding his usual seat at the head of the table. As soon as he was seated, Klara started to pour coffee for him.

"I want to see Katya. I need to know that she is alright and that she is happy with Lucia."

Anton sipped his coffee from a large spoon. He looked tired. Lately he always looked tired. He no longer wore his lovely riding clothes with the cord trims. Today he wore loose woven wheat colored pantaloons and a large loose collarless shirt with the shirttail over of the trousers.

"I don't know that I can spare anyone to take you, at this time," he said.

"That's alright," said Sofie. "I am going with Alexie. He will bring his carriage."

Anton looked up from his coffee at Sofie, but said nothing.

Klara sitting opposite Sofie said sternly, "You can't go unchaperoned on a trip. What will people say?"

Both Sofie and Anton looked at Klara. She had never spoken her mind quite this strongly before. Then Sofie and Anton looked at one another and burst out laughing.

"I don't see what's so funny about an unmarried woman traveling with a man," Klara said, annoyed with the laughter. "After all, you have to guard your reputation."

Still laughing, Sofie said, "Oh, Klara. You sound like a governess or a maiden aunt."

"Anton," demanded Klara, "are you going to let her go alone with Alexie?"

"She is not a child." He stirred his coffee absentmindedly. "I can't tell her what to do."

"You are the head of the house. If you think it is wrong for her to go to Trieste, then you must say so." Klara looked at him, waiting for a reply.

He smiled at Klara…sweet Klara, their childhood playmate and then their loyal servant all these years. She still worried about the family and wanted to protect them.

"Sofie must do what she feels is right." He smiled warmly at his sister. "We have all been telling her what to do for a long time. I think it is time we each lived our own lives as best we can." Almost as an after thought, he added, "For whatever time we have left."

"Oh, Anton," Sofie rose from the table and went to her brother. She wrapped her arms around his shoulders and hugged him. "Oh Anton," she repeated, "thank you for understanding."

"Well," said Klara, shaking her head maternally, "I don't understand."

The young bride Luba, walking at the back of Vera and Marko's house near the kitchen, stopped when she heard Ivan's distressed voice. She was bringing fresh eggs to Vera. Hearing Ivan and Vera in what sounded like a seriously private conversation, Luba stayed out at the steps.

She heard Ivan say, "But, Mamica. How could she leave? Katya wouldn't leave without a reason."

Vera's tone was cool. Ivan had been asking the same question since the day Katya left. "I told you she couldn't take the accusations of being a witch."

"But it isn't true. In time, people would see they were wrong and talk would stop. Oh, why didn't you try to stop her?"

Vera's tone became harsh. Everyday the same questions to which she gave the same answers. She wished Ivan would stop the questions.

Losing her patience she said, "Why would I want to stop her from leaving? She wanted to take you away from me?" The moment Vera said 'She wanted to take you away from me.' Vera knew she had said too much.

Softly Ivan said, "What makes you think she wanted to take me away?"

Vera didn't answer.

"You were listening!" His voice rose, anger building. "You were listening when she came to my bedside and talked with me. Were you watching when we kissed?"

Luba only heard silence, no response from Vera.

"Then you know I love her." Ivan was trying to control his anger. His voice shook as he spoke. "We wanted to leave together. Together we could start a new life somewhere where no one knows Anton Vladislav or my connection to him. Somewhere where stupid people wouldn't call Katya a witch, but would appreciate the knowledge she has."

"Oh my son, listen to me." Vera sounded near hysteria. "Don't you see if you don't leave you could be the master of Vladezemla? Who knows where Stefan is? No word for nearly three weeks. Anton will need you! You are the true heir!"

After a moment Ivan said, "But, if Katya and I went away together, your dream of my being the Vladislav heir would vanish.

What did you do to make Katya leave? You did something or you said something. She wouldn't leave me without a good reason."

Luba moved closer to the window, glancing about hoping no one was passing near to see her as she eavesdropped.

"What did you do?" demanded Ivan.

"I didn't do anything. I only told her that the villagers thought she was a witch. She knows that people throw rocks at witches to ward off evil."

"That's nonsense." Luba could hear the anger in Ivan's voice. "Superstitious talk and you know it! It didn't mean anything. It was a temporary entertainment for our neighbors. It would have passed."

Luba thought she heard a struggle. Vera said, "Ivan, son…let go my wrist." There was a note of fear in her voice. "Stop. You are hurting me."

"There's more, isn't there?" demanded Ivan.

"Yes! Yes…let go my wrist."

"Not until you tell my why Katya left."

"I…I did it for your own good. I did it so you would get Vladezemla and not leave."

"What did you do?"

"I…I told her that you wanted her to leave. That you didn't want to see her anymore and that she would ruin your life if she stayed. That you didn't want anything to do with a witch."

There was silence. Luba strained to hear more. She tried standing on her tiptoes to look in the window, but she was too short.

Sobbing, Vera said, "I did it for you. I did it for you."

Luba left the basket of eggs on the top step leading into the kitchen. She ran as fast as she could to the shed used as a smithy where Nikola, along with his father and a couple of workers, were holding a metal wagon wheel to be repaired. The air was hot and smelled of molten metal and the strong scent of garlic, which was given off by the sweat of the men working in the unbearable heat.

Nikola was the first to see Luba at the door. Something about her made him drop his long-handled tongs and go to her. She wrapped her arms around his waist, tightly.

The men watching laughed and someone said, "Ah, the honeymoon is not over."

Embarrassed by this public show of affection from his shy bride, he said, "Luba, what is the matter?"

"Promise me. Promise me..." Her voice was muffled against his chest.

"What? What? Yes, I promise..."

She raised her head and said so no one could hear, "Promise me that you will believe that I love you. All of your life you will believe it. Even if someone else you love and trusts says I no longer love you...you will know that I do."

Book II, Chapter 41

Katya ran down the marble stairs barely holding on to the banister. "They are here! Nona, they are here." She flung open the door before Mia, the servant, could get to it.

Alexie was helping Sofie, dressed in a plain brown traveling dress, down from the carriage. Katya nearly knocked Sofie off her feet when she threw her arms around her dear friend.

"Oh, Katya, how we have missed you," said Sofie kissing her on both cheeks.

When Sofie let go of Katya, the girl threw her arms around Alexie and to his surprise she also gave him a hug and a kiss on the cheek. "How wonderful to see you, Alexie!" she said.

Lucia was close behind greeting Sofie, also with hugs and kisses.

"My dear, Sofie," she said. "I am always so happy when you come. Please don't be in a hurry to leave."

"Lucia," said Sofie, reaching her hand out to Alexie, "I want you to meet my attorney and my very good friend, Alexie Lukas.

Lucia looked at the compactly built man, with his dark hair combed straight back. His eyebrows and mustache were thick and his brown eyes were warm and sincere. She held out her hand. Alexie lifted her fingers to his lips.

In his usual polite manner, he said, "Thank you for allowing me the honor of being a guest in your home."

For a moment, Lucia didn't answer. She looked deep into Alexie's eyes. He was not as handsome as her beloved son Vincent had been, not at all.

Watching Alexie and Lucia, Sofie's heart stopped. Could it be that Lucia resented Alexie? Had she made a mistake bringing him to Lucia's home…the home that had once been Vincent's?

Lucia did not let go of Alexie's hand. Instead, she slipped her arm through his and started for the entry to the house.

Looking a bit bewildered Alexie looked back toward the carriage, "I should help with the bags."

"The girls can bring them in," said Lucia, leading him through the open door. Sofie stood staring open-mouthed.

Katya excitedly grabbed up Sofie and Alexie's bags, passing them on to Mia, the maid who took a bag in each hand, and easily carried them in to the house. Mia as usual was wearing her maid's attire: white blouse, black skirt with a white bib apron.

"Nona has each of your rooms overlooking the sea," said Katya, following Alexie and Lucia into the house.

Sofie stopped walking and took Katya's arm. "Nona? Why are you calling her Nona?"

"It means grandmother," said Katya.

"Yes," said Sofie, softly, "I know what it means. But, why are you calling her that?"

"She wants me to," said Katya. "Nona told me that she will never be a grandmother and that I make her feel like one. It gives her pleasure to have me call her that. "Is it alright?"

"Of course," said Sofie. "If it pleases her, then you should do it."

Sofie always felt she belonged in this grand house. It was so different from the dark wooden walled house she grew up in at Vladezemla. The cool marble floor and stone walls suited the climate of Trieste. Sofie loved the colorful Turkish rugs and never tired of the intricate designs woven into them. In contrast to the wildly colorful rugs were the subtle colors of the Flemish tapestries depicting large women with scarf draped coronets on their heads and cherubic children at their sides.

The marble Nubian statues still stood as sentinels in the foyer. The once empty large marble urns were now filled to overflowing with colorful flowers. *This is new*, thought Sofie, enjoying the fragrance of the blossoms.

Sofie wasn't listening to Katya as they walked through the large main room out to the garden. Alexie and Lucia had already disappeared into the garden.

"Teta Sofie!" Katya tugged at Sofie's arm. "Aren't you listening to me?"

Sofie stopped walking. Looking around she said, "I'm sorry. For all the years I have been coming here, I never saw flowers in the house only in the garden."

"Oh, that," dismissed Katya. "Nona thought flowers reminded her of death and dying, but now she says they remind her of rebirth…of living. We have them in every room. We go to the plaza every few days and bring home armloads of flowers.

Sofie stopped walking and stared open-mouthed at what she saw in the garden. Standing at the entry of the house and a bit to the side was a large iron cage on wheels. The cage was nearly as tall as Sofie who was a bit over five feet in height. The diameter was also probably five feet. Lining the inside of the cage was a fine screen to keep the assorted colorful twelve or so, canaries from escaping.

On the other side of the aviary Sofie could see Alexie and Lucia admiring the cluster of singing and chirping birds. Some were ordinary, small green, Italian canaries, while others were frilled with feathers, resembling a feather duster. One bird, the Belgian Hunchback, looked slightly deformed with a curve to its spine, which was natural to the breed.

"Isn't it wonderful?" said Katya. "That one is my favorite," she said, pointing to the Frilled Canary. "Doesn't it look as if he is wearing a preposterous hat?"

"When did all this happen?" asked Sofie, turning to Katya, just now noticing that Katya was wearing a new frock. It was emerald green, almost the color of her eyes, cinched at the waist with a full ruffled skirt. The bodice was form fitting with white lace around her throat and at the end of the long sleeves. Beneath the lace, Sofie could tell the Gypsy bracelet was still in place.

Before Katya could answer, Sofie said, "Isn't your beautiful dress new?"

Katya twirled around, her skirts brushing against the aviary, the movement scattering the birds. "I have a dressmaker," she announced.

Sofie looked across at Lucia, who was smiling proudly, like a mother showing off her child. She motioned with her hand for Sofie and Katya to follow.

"We will have lunch here in the garden. Mia!" She called and the girl appeared carrying a tray before Lucia could say more.

The metal table was covered with a blue cloth, set with white plates and drinking glasses from Murano. The garden was in full bloom with magnolias and roses.

Alexie politely pulled out Lucia's chair for her. Sofie and Katya seated themselves, not waiting for him to help with their chairs.

Seated Alexie looked around the garden approvingly. "Madam Kurecka, your house and garden reflect your good taste. It is such a pleasure to sit here, enjoying the surroundings and such good company. "

Lucia was charmed. "Please, call me Lucia," she said, as Mia set a platter of coarse bread and a dish of olive oil for dipping, on the table.

"Let me help," said Katya, as she rose and followed Mia into the kitchen.

"Lucia," said Sofie, "so much has changed. You never had flowers in the house and the birds…why the birds?" Then, she quickly added, "I like the birds. You never seemed to care for pets."

"We have a cat somewhere. It hides most of the time," said Lucia, spreading a blue cloth napkin onto her lap.

"A cat, too? Lucia…all these changes…"

"I know," said Lucia, offering Alexie some bread. "I have been having a wonderful time with Katya. It is as if life has become fun again. I no longer awake wondering what I will do to make the day pass wandering from room to room remembering the past." Her eyes shone with excitement. "Each day is an adventure now. I never know what I will see anew through Katya's excited eyes." She reached out and placed her hand on Sofie's. "Dear Sofie, I am alive again. Can you understand that?"

Sofie's eyes softened. She remembered how her own life had changed when Katya came to stay at Vladezemla. "Oh, yes, Lucia. I think I understand. Katya has changed my life, too. I, too, think I came alive." With that last remark she looked affectionately at Alexie, whose face reflected all the warmth and affection he felt for Sofie and the affection that was growing for Lucia. Lucia was a marvelous woman, strong and sensible. How did he know that? He just knew!

Lucia's attention abruptly turned to Alexie. "Tell me, Alexie, how long have you known Sofie?"

He put his piece of bread on his plate, folded his hands in his lap. "I think I have known her since we were very young. My father was the family lawyer back then and I would go with him when he had business." He smiled warmly at Sofie, remembering those days. "She was a thin, little girl who never noticed me."

"Oh, but I did," Sofie said.

"You are being kind," he said to Sofie, dismissing her remark. "You were seldom around when we came. I would see you briefly as we left, playing in the yard with the children, or later when you were older, reading under that large tree in the yard."

Lucia interrupted, "So now you are the family advokat. Are you a good one?"

"He is wonderful," announced Sofie, proudly. It was Alexie who drew up the papers for Katya to become my ward. I don't believe anyone can challenge the legality of the contract."

Lucia had been listening to Sofie, now she shifted her eyes back to Alexie, who was sitting quietly his hands still in his lap.

"Has Sofie told you that my husband's name was Aleksy?" Seeing the surprised look on Sofie's face she said. "No? Perhaps she didn't know it."

Mia and Katya appeared with plates of salad made up of lettuce, anchovies, onions and grated cheese. Katya slipped into her chair and picked up her napkin.

"Go ahead and eat," urged Lucia. "I want to tell you about my husband, Aleksy. Aleksander Kurecka was a thin, young man when he came to work for my father. He was a wonderful bookkeeper. My father came to trust him fully. Aleksy was quiet and always polite." She looked at Alexie, while he daintily put an anchovy to his mouth. "I see Aleksy in you." Seeing the surprised look on Alexie's round face, the wide eyes under the full eyebrows, she said, "No, not actually your build or your looks. In just the few minutes you have been here, I sense something in you. I feel it.

"Don't laugh…" she looked around at the faces staring at her, "I believe in Destiny. You three were meant to be here with me. And you," she nodded at Alexie, "I know there is a reason we have met."

She dropped her eyes, almost embarrassed. "I am sorry," she said softly, "Perhaps I am being a silly, old woman, maybe a bit emotional."

Katya was at the old woman's side immediately, her arms around Lucia's shoulders, with her young soft cheek against Lucia's wrinkled face. "Oh, my darling, you say whatever you feel. It is your right. Whatever you are thinking or feeling we respect."

Somewhat amazed, Sofie watched as Lucia affectionately patted Katya's arms still wrapped about her shoulders. Katya spoke to the old woman in a manner so familiar...in a way that Sofie would never have spoken to this lady she had loved for so many years.

"Are you alright?" Katya asked Lucia.

The old woman sighed, "Pour me some wine."

Alexie rose, took the wide mouth decanter and poured some of the deep red Chianti into her glass. She waved her hand around, indicating he pour the other glasses, too.

Lucia took a sip of the wine. Katya stood a moment, concern for Lucia evident on her face. Then she slipped into her chair. She asked again, "Are you alright?"

"I am fine. Just being a foolish old woman. Having you all here around my table has made me feel as if I once more have a family. Forgive me..." She smiled a bit embarrassed, "I didn't mean to make you feel uncomfortable."

Alexie took Lucia's hand, "We are honored that you could be so honest with us. Please don't feel embarrassed or think we are uncomfortable. For myself, I must tell you I have never found a garden so lovely, or the company so warm."

Sofie looked lovingly at Alexie. How wonderful he was. He said the right words and they were sincere. He had spoken for them all.

Mia's arrival with a platter of prociutto and cheeses brightened their moods.

"If you aren't too tired," said Lucia to Alexie, I would like to show you the trading company my father left me. At 2:00 the warehouse will be empty since the workers will be home for their afternoon naps.

"I would enjoy that very much," said Alexie, sincerely. "I have never been in a trading company before."

"Nona has a ship, too," said Katya. "It is capable of going to America."

"Well, maybe it could make it to America," said Lucia. "So far it has only been along the Adriatic and the Mediterranean."

As Mia set the last course of mixed fruit on the table, Katya jumped up and ran out of the room.

When she returned she wore an impish grin and winked at Lucia. This did not go unnoticed by Alexie and Sofie. Sofie gave Katya a quizzical look, but Katya pretended she did not see it.

The meal ended with relaxed conversation. Mia poured espresso into tiny delicate cups and, as always, withdrew silently.

Under the table from her lap Katya slipped something into Lucia's lap. The old woman's face registered from surprise to mirth as she recognized the object Katya had placed in her lap.

Looking at one another, like two naughty children, Lucia and Katya each, almost in unison, raised short carved bone cigarette holders with a cigarette in each, to their lips. Stunned Sofie watched as Katya struck a tiny match and held the flame to Lucia's cigarette. Lucia inhaled and let the smoke free from her mouth in a long stream. Katya struck another match and lit her own cigarette, inhaling and exhaling as Lucia had done.

The look of shock on Sofie's face had Alexie bursting into uncontrollable laughter. The tableau was a delight to him. Sofie had the look of a highly annoyed parent, while Katya and Lucia, one a girl, the other an old woman, looked every bit like two impish children enjoying Sofie's horrified reaction.

At last Sofie said, "Lucia! I am shocked!"

"I know," laughed the old woman. "You should see the look on your face."

Sofie rose from her chair, she flung her napkin on the seat of her chair. "I don't know which one of you to blame. Lucia, you should know better. A lady doesn't smoke. And you," she directed her annoyance at Katya, "I can see you are encouraging this behavior in Lucia."

"Oh, Sofie," soothed Lucia. "Don't be so annoyed. We have seen the women tourists, American and French, smoking in the plaza.

Sofie glared at Alexie who was beside himself with laughter. "You be quiet. This isn't funny. My God...what else has changed here in the last few weeks?"

At this Katya and Lucia exchanged another conspiratorial look.

"What? What!" Sofie couldn't believe there might be more.

Lucia with exaggerated elegance rose from her chair. She set her cigarette holder on the edge of her saucer. Alexie watched with tears streaming down his face, sensing there would be more disapproval coming from Sofie.

The old woman, dressed all in black, as she had since the death of her husband, never anything but black, walked a bit away from the table so that all could view her. Reaching behind the birdcage, she found a large bright red ostrich plume fan.

"Oh my God!" declared Sofie. This was too much. What Sofie saw was what amounted to a sin for a woman in mourning in the early 1900's, the end of the Victorian Age.

With a flick of her wrist, Lucia spread the plumes and made a grand show of fanning herself, while strutting about imitating a stage performer.

Sofie fell into her chair landing on her napkin. She shook her head in disbelief, while Alexie wiped the tears from his eyes, still laughing uncontrollably, never having seen such teasing behavior from women he knew.

Sofie looked at the two imps, Katya and Lucia smiling wickedly at her and the reaction they elicited from her. She looked over at Alexie, thoroughly enjoying himself. She had to smile for she knew they were playfully shocking her. Her smile grew larger. She threw a piece of bread at Alexie.

"Oh, be quiet!" she said.

Book II, Chapter 42

Sofie and Katya both watched Lucia and Alexie stroll down the cobblestone road to the bay, where the warehouse for the Renaldi Trading Company was located. Lucia wanted Alexie to go alone with her, so that gave Sofie and Katya some time alone. "I brought something for you."

"Oh, you brought me the dresses," said Katya, excited for she was quite pleased with her growing wardrobe and more dresses were welcomed.

"Yes," said Sofie, as they climbed the wide marble stairs, "I brought the dresses, but I brought you something more."

The sun glowed yellow on the white walls as the two walked to the room chosen for Sofie. The room was decorated with big pieces of heavy wooden furniture. The dresser drawers had an inlaid floral design of different colored woods. The curtains and bedspread were of thick rose-colored velvet trimmed with gathered satin ruffles. A small chair covered in dark maroon velvet matched a fainting couch near the window. On the bed was a box wrapped in plain white paper.

Katya could see the box was heavy when Sofie lifted it onto her lap.

"I brought this for you," she said, motioning for Katya to sit on the other side of the box.

When the wrapping was pushed aside, Sofie carefully lifted the lid from the box and Katya saw what the box held.

"Your painted dishes, oh, Sofie — the painted dishes. You brought them for me, but, why?"

Katya held a cup in her hand, looking at the lovers shown holding hands, while an annoyed mother looked on in the background. "I love these pieces," she said, now looking at a plate with a picture of a girl crying beneath a tree and her lover leaving through a wooden gate.

"It doesn't upset you to look at them?" asked Sofie. "I mean they don't remind you of the Turk and what almost happened to you, or of Ivan?"

Katya looked up from the plate she was holding and thought for a moment. "It is as if that happened to someone else." Seeing the confused look on Sofie's face, she went on. "You see, when I am here…it is as if I have always been here. As if…" she searched for the right words, "as if, the Katya that the Turk wanted, never was. Or that the girl Ivan called a witch, isn't me. Here I am Lucia Kurecka's granddaughter. I live in a beautiful house and I am *home*."

Sofie was quiet as she watched Katya take each cup or plate to admire the picture depicted on it. Katya *was* different here. Not only was she different here, but also she was almost totally different from the girl Sofie met at Nikola and Luba's wedding.

In such a brief time, only one summer, Katya learned to read, could do some writing and became such a lovely friend to both Sofie and Lucia. What a treasure this girl had become to the two women.

Katya broke the silence. "Why are you giving me these dishes? They were part of your trousseau."

"Because," said Sofie, "if Vincent and I had married and had children…especially a daughter, these would have been passed on to her. You are the closest to a daughter I will ever have." Tears glistened in Sofie's eyes. "I want you to have them. If you are a like a granddaughter to Lucia, then you can be like a daughter to me."

Katya put down the cup she was holding and wrapped her arms around Sofie. They held one another for a very long time.

Down at the docks, Alexie stood behind Lucia, as she struggled with the large lock on a door at the side of the building. This was the door used only by Carlo, Carlo Jr. and sometimes Lucia. Customers and traders used the large, front entrance with the large RENALDI TRADING CO sign painted over the door.

"Take the key, Alexie. You try. I am having trouble with it."

Alexie turned the key, but the lock held firm. "Is this the right key? It doesn't seem to work."

"It is the key I have always used," said Lucia. "Come, let's try the front door. I didn't want anyone to see us entering. That is why I wanted to use this side door."

The two hurried around the building to the front. No one was near as this was the time most workers had a two-hour lunch when they could nap.

The front door unlocked easily. Lucia and Alexie stepped quickly inside.

"Latch the door," said Lucia. "I don't want anyone coming in while we are here."

Once the door was latched, Alexie looked at the hundreds of cases, some of wood, but most of woven fibers, tied with crude rope. Shelves lined the walls displaying figurines, vases, bowls, cookware, woodcarvings and much more. Each item had a paper tag with a number identifying it, so that it could be located in the proper container in the warehouse. The warehouse was just that. Not a brightly lit display room, but a long building with container after container of goods. Each had a series of numbers printed or written on it. The building was alongside the water with large double doors opening onto the wharf where the cargo was unloaded and carried by men or pushed on wheeled carts into the building to be inventoried.

"I had no idea your trading company was so large," said Alexie, impressed. "It is good that you have a dependable manager."

Alexie thought he heard Lucia make a noise, something like a snort.

"Let's go up to the office." She pointed to the wooden stairs that led to a loft-like area. Lucia mounted the stairs slowly no longer able to skip up two at a time, as she had when she was a girl. Once upstairs they could see the warehouse from the windows surrounding the office.

Lucia lit a kerosene lamp for better light. "Help me look," she said to Alexie.

"What am I looking for?"

"I am not sure," she said, pulling open a drawer from a wooden file cabinet. "I don't know what I am looking for. I have this feeling." She looked at Alexie. "Do you ever get a feeling that you know something is not right, but you don't know what it is?"

"Yes, I think I know what you mean. But it doesn't help me much when I don't know what I am looking for."

Lucia sighed deeply. "Just look. If something seems wrong or out of place, show it to me."

Alexie felt they were wasting time. He wasn't sure what Lucia was looking for, but if it gave her comfort to have him help her go through drawers and boxes, he would do it. He riffled through some papers on the desk, thumbed through some notes impaled on a spindle not knowing if anything was out of order or not.

He pulled open the center drawer of the desk and saw a ledger. He opened it and couldn't tell if anything was amiss in it, since he wasn't a bookkeeper. He pulled the drawer out to its full length and *there it was*...another ledger. Later, when asked how he knew the other ledger was there, Alexie couldn't say. Perhaps it was something his assistant, Ruda Klarich mentioned during one of his searches for a client. Somewhere something had been planted in Alexie's subconscious about long drawers and it manifested itself at the right time.

"There are two ledgers in this drawer," said Alexie. "Do you keep two ledgers?" He asked.

Ignoring his question, she said, "Look at the dates. It could be that you found an old one. You read," said Lucia, "my eyes aren't that good anymore. I need a magnifying glass for these small numbers."

Alexie looked at the first ledger, the one that was at the front of the drawer. He saw the date, June 1907. He flipped open the second ledger, the one pushed way in the back of the drawer. There was the same date, June 1907.

"They both have the same date." He looked at Lucia who was deep in thought. Alexie could almost hear the wheels turning in her mind.

"Read the first entry," she ordered.

He ran his finger down to the first entry. "GR348." He read, watching her face for some reaction.

"Hmmm," she said. "Now look in the second ledger for the same entry."

He ran his finger down the page, then turned the page and searched. "I don't see it on these two pages.'

"Go to another one," she said, crisply. Lucia was all business now.

"SP448."

"Look again," she said. "Just like before."

"Here it is." Alexie was almost triumphant. He had no idea what it meant, but he could see Lucia seemed to know its meaning.

"What does it show after the entry in the second book?"

Alexie found the entry once more, moved his finger beyond the SP 448 and saw a dash 3.

When he told Lucia what he found, she asked him to go back to the first ledger. Alexie found SP 448 and said, "There is a dash 13 after it."

"Come let's go down to the floor," said Lucia. She scurried down the stairs, now surprisingly more agile than when they arrived. She was on a mission, Alexie didn't know what, but he sensed something was happening.

She started to read the labels on the crates. "Look for the row that has the SP numbers. They should be in order."

The two hurried from row to row, finding AF for Africa, GR for Greece, searching through the rows for SP indicating Spain. "Here it is," Alexie called to Lucia, who was two aisles away from him.

As she hurried to him, she called out, "Find all the SP 448 boxes."

"They are here," said Alex. "One, two, three…" He counted the stacks. There are thirteen of them."

She was at his side now. "Move them about."

Alexie looked at her. He wondered how heavy they would be. What if they were filled with woodcarvings or earthen pots? The boxes were stacked three high. Alexie grunted as he lowered one box and wondered if he was physically up to lowering them all. He lowered the second box, more than a little out of breath. He wasn't used to hauling crates of merchandise. His knee hit the last box, the one sitting on the floor. It moved. The box moved again, just from the nudge of his knee. The move didn't escape Lucia. She tore at the knotted cord tied to the box.

"Here, let me," said Alexie, using a small pocketknife to cut the cord.

When he finished cutting the cord, Lucia snatched open the lid. She dug through excelsior tossing it in the air and onto the floor. She looked up, triumphant. "It is empty!"

Alexie was catching on. With a burst of renewed strength he heaved at the second stack of three crates. Just as before, the first one was heavy, as was the second, but when they dug through the bottom box resting on the floor, they found another one empty of merchandise.

Alexie and Lucia performed this exercise a third time and found a third empty crate. Alexie silently thanked God that he started at the right end of the boxes and didn't have to lift more heavy boxes. He was tired, but with a feeling of satisfaction.

Cleverly the empty crates were placed under heavy full ones, so that it looked as if there were thirteen full crates, when really there were only ten.

"It's an old bookkeeping trick," explained Lucia. "I knew something was wrong, but didn't have the nerve to search on my own." She patted him on the arm. "I knew you came into my life for a reason. With you I accomplished what I suspected. I was sure my cousin Carlo was stealing from me." She sighed and shook her head, "I just didn't know how he was doing it."

She went on to explain. "The first ledger, the one meant for me to see, showed thirteen cases of SP 448. If I came on the floor and counted the cases, I would find thirteen. It would be impossible for me to move the stacked boxes to find the three empty ones. The second ledger, Carlo's own, showed SP 448 minus 3. That means they sold three cases and kept the money for themselves. We will need to go through both books and do a fresh inventory to find out how much swindling my dear cousin Carlo has done.

Just then they heard the creak of a door. Light shone in from the very door that Lucia and Alexie tried to unlock, but couldn't. Cousin Carlo obviously had the lock changed, for his key worked.

Cousin Carlo closed the door humming as he walked further into the warehouse. His brown suit coat was casually slung over his shoulder and he carried a small, leather briefcase. He stopped abruptly when he saw Alexie.

Alarmed he demanded, "What are you doing here?" Noticing the cases no longer stacked and the stuffing strewn about, he stammered, "Who...who are you? I will call the carbinieri, the police." His voice was not as confident as it should have been. Seeing the empty crates confused him.

Lucia stepped from behind a stack of cases, where she was hidden from view. "Yes, call the police, Carlo. I think they would be very interested in knowing how you cheat an old woman."

Carlo's round face was wet with perspiration and growing paler by the moment. He dropped his coat and briefcase on the floor. He pulled a handkerchief from his pants pocket and mopped his brow.

"Who...who is this?" he asked again, motioning toward Alexie.

"This is my Lawyer!" announced Lucia, triumphantly.

Book II, Chapter 43

The morning following Alexie and Lucia's raid on the warehouse, not wanting to disturb anyone, Alexie slipped quietly down the stairs and out to the garden. His shirttail hung out over his trousers and his sleeves were rolled twice, away from his wrists. As he passed the large cage of canaries, he heard only small chirps. It was too early for them to give full concerts of song, so they only blinked at Alexie as he passed by.

The morning presented itself gloriously. A few clouds drifted lazily across a pale blue sky and the panoramic view of the harbor from Lucia's garden almost took Alexie's breath away. The water appeared a calm turquoise blue waiting for ships with sails unfurled to glide over it for distant ports or perhaps to haul in fresh fish, clams, or eels. The combined scents of the sea and the garden were almost heady to Alexie.

The entryway of Lucia's house was level with the road, while the back, where the garden was, rested on the flat part of a stone hill. It was from the garden, that Alexie viewed the bay.

"Did you sleep well?" Alexie didn't hear Lucia approach. She was wearing a black silk Chinese floral embroidered kimono, flowing loosely over her body.

"Good morning, Lucia," he said, with a small bow. "I slept remarkably well."

"It is the sea air," said Lucia, as she stood next to him at wall. They looked at the view in comfortable silence.

After a few moments Lucia asked, "What do you think I should do about my Cousin Carlo and his son?"

"That depends."

"Depends on what?" Now she had her back to the wall and looked at his profile while he faced the bay.

"It depends if you only want revenge, or if you want to go on with your life."

"What is the difference?"

Alexie turned to Lucia. "Revenge is the satisfaction one gets from punishing the wrongdoer." He looked for some reaction to his statement. Seeing none he went on, "Getting on with your life is removing the problem, hoping that it doesn't happen again, and ridding yourself of any anger or resentment."

Lucia took a long moment to digest his remarks. "A part of me wants to punish Carlo and his son," she paused, "but then, another part of me feels that letting them go to find work elsewhere could be a form of punishment. Still, they could lie and say I cheated them. That way they would try to ruin my reputation. If I went to court everyone would know the truth and I wouldn't be judged as a greedy woman. People would know I was not tossing out men who helped make my business strong, but who stole from me."

More silence. After a while Lucia said, "Stay, Alexie. Stay here with Sofie and manage the trading company."

This was a surprise.

"Lucia..." Alexie had to collect his thoughts. He couldn't possibly do what she asked. "I have work back in Karlovac and clients there who depend on me. Oh, no, I think it is out of the question."

Lucia was not one to be denied. "What sort of clients? Are you defending someone from the gallows?"

"Oh, nothing that serious, I usually do contracts and wills."

She folded her arms across her chest and looked sternly at him. "Couldn't such challenging work be turned over to another advokat?" Did he hear a touch of sarcasm in her voice?

Before he could answer she asked, "What do you feel for Sofie? Are you in love with her?"

He didn't answer immediately, so she said, "Oh, don't think I am asking too personal a question. I have worried about Sofie ever since the day her brother took her away from this house, the very next morning after Vincent died." Her eyes were dry and clear. She had cried for years for the loss of Vincent and Sofie. There were no tears today. Now she needed to think of the future...hers and Katya's.

"If you love Sofie," she continued, "then don't let her be a widow any longer." His eyes widened at the word 'widow'. Lucia waved her hand dismissing his questioning look. "Haven't you seen that she has lived these last sixteen years as if she were a widow? Her loneliness has been the same as mine since I lost my husband, except that I had a child to live for. Sofie has pretended that her brother and his family would fill the emptiness, but it wasn't so." She looked hard at Alexie's face.

"You and Sofie could have a new life here in Trieste. Manage the trading company for me."

Alexie cleared his throat. "I am going to go for a walk."

"You haven't had any breakfast," said Lucia.

"I won't be long," he said, tucking his shirt in his trousers as he headed for the door.

"What am I going to do?" said, Lucia, as if asking the sea gulls circling overhead. She walked slowly to the table and sat down. Immediately Mia appeared and poured a creamy cup of cappuccino for Lucia.

"Mia, go see if Sofie is awake. Tell her I want to talk to her."

Alexie strolled along the cobblestone streets deep in thought. Could he leave Karlovac and move to Trieste? Were Sofie's feelings for him as strong as his were for her? Did Sofie want to marry him? They hadn't gotten that far in their courting. Have they even been courting, he wondered, or was he just a very good friend? He felt that Sofie cared for him, but he was almost afraid to find out how much she cared. Alexie thought he should have more time with Sofie before any commitments were broached.

His mind wandered to Ruda Klarich, his assistant back at the office in Karlovac. Would Ruda consider living in Trieste? Would he want to come and work with Alexie at the trading company? If Alexie decided to stay and manage the trading company, Ruda could easily close the office, passing pending work over to other lawyers. Alexie stopped walking and put his hands to his temples. He could not remember ever having so many thoughts crowd his brain at one time. He had no idea what he would do...what would be the right thing to do.

Katya sat at the table in the garden, alone with Lucia. Lucia was still in her robe, but Katya was dressed in a white scoop necked blouse with long sleeves. Her navy blue cotton skirt was long and simple.

"I will help you with the trading company," said Katya after Lucia told her of her conversation with Alexie and the similar conversation she had with Sofie. "I can learn, Nona. I will do whatever you ask of me."

Lucia patted Katya's hand. "We will see," she said.

"Do you think Sofie will want to stay?" asked Katya. "I wish she would stay."

Lucia said, "She gave me no indication that she wanted to stay. Pour me more coffee. I have asked her for years to stay, every time she visited, but she never wanted to leave her family. Maybe those ties are too strong to be broken."

Katya spread some jam on a roll and thought of the sarcastic Ernesta.

"I don't think it was a very happy family. Ernesta Vladeslav was not a very pleasant person, though I did like Anton very much and the cook, Klara. She remembered the handsome Stefan. Katya had liked him very much, remembering how he helped her learn to read, but the bitter memory of his drunken visit to her room, kept her from mentioning him.

Returning from his walk, Alexie did not see Sofie standing at the front of the house waiting for him. His head was down, his mind still wrestling with conflicting thoughts. When he looked up, he saw that she was wearing the same brown travel dress she wore when they arrived. *Could she be upset or angry? Is she ready to leave?* New thoughts assailed his already bursting brain.

She hurried to him and slipped her arm through his. "How are you?" she asked, noticing that he looked tired and troubled. "Come, you need some breakfast."

Alexie stopped walking, took Sofie's hand and turned her to face him. "What is it to be? Do we stay?"

Sofie's free hand fluttered to her face, trembling slightly like the wings of a butterfly. "I don't know," she sighed, shrugged her shoulders, "Lucia has asked me for years to stay. If I were meant to be here, I would have come as a bride. Not just as a friend."

"Then you are saying that we leave Lucia and Katya to handle the business alone? We are to leave an old woman and a young girl in charge of such a responsibility?"

"You could stay..." she said it softly, her eyes searching his face for understanding. "You could be in charge and I could come and visit you often."

Alexie let go of Sofie's hand. It was such an abrupt act that she looked bewildered. He said, "It is your decision, Sofie. I will not stay alone. We must stay together."

"But, but…this was Vincent's home," her voice was small.

"*Was*…was his home, Sofie. Vincent was your past. Are you going to continue living in the past?"

Sofie blinked. The corners of her mouth twitched. Alexie watched her for a long moment, when she didn't reply, he turned away entering the house, leaving her standing alone.

Both Katya and Lucia looked expectantly at Alexie as he sat at the table. He nodded to them both in a silent greeting and calmly reached for a roll. Katya and Lucia looked at one another, then again at Alexie, waiting for some response.

Sofie appeared looking very agitated, her face flushed with eyes glistening. She didn't look at anyone as she slipped into her chair with downcast eyes.

Alexie ignored Sofie, continuing to eat his breakfast. Katya looked at Lucia, questions fairly leaping out of her eyes, but the old woman only closed her eyes and gave an almost imperceptible shrug.

The breakfast continued in a strained silence, so strained a silence, that the sound of a fork clinking on a plate only emphasized the uncomfortable atmosphere.

Katya and Lucia didn't dare speak for they had never witnessed the indifference Alexie was exhibiting toward Sofie. All the warmth and love that seemed to flow from the man was apparently gone…or so it seemed. Lucia didn't like this at all. This was not good. She didn't know which it was, Sofie or Alexie, who didn't want to stay. It didn't matter. It was over. She knew it, could feel it. She just didn't want to hear it.

The only sound at the table was Alexie spreading jam on his roll, sipping his coffee, his gaze fixed somewhere beyond the table, seemingly ignoring the uncomfortable silence around him.

The awkward silence was broken by Mia's appearance. "Signora," she said to Lucia, "There are men outside to see you."

"What men? Who would come so early?" Lucia's brow wrinkled. *What now?* "Have them come in and get some coffee for them."

Mia dropped her head slightly, giving a quizzical look. "There are too many of them," she said. "I don't have a coffee pot large enough."

Lucia's mouth opened slightly. She looked at Katya, Sofie and Alexie. Each stared back as confused as she appeared to be. She said, "I am not dressed to receive guests."

"It doesn't matter," said Mia, concern written on her face. "I think you had better go out to see them."

They all rose from the table, Katya and Alexie with Sofie following Lucia, at the rear. Sofie was a little surprised that Alexie did not step aside and let her walk in front of him.

There, at the front of Lucia's house on the cobblestone patio, stood about fifteen or so men. Lucia recognized them as the men who worked in the warehouse.

A well-built man, his arms and shoulders firm from years of lifting heavy boxes, stepped forward. His pullover shirt was loose, coarse cloth with a v-neck collar. His brown stained work pants tied at the waist with rope.

Lucia recognized the tanned man, with dark thick hair, eyebrows to match. His nose was roman and his lips were thin. It was Guiseppi Sabo. Lucia knew why the men were at her door. But, she didn't know what she would say to them.

Guiseppi bowed to Lucia and looked nervously at the three behind her. "Signora, the doors are locked. We cannot go to work." He paused a moment, "We went to Signor Carlo's home, but no one came to the door. We know he is there. We could see him at the window. Please Signora, tell us what has happened." He was almost pleading now, "We all have families. We need to work. How can we feed our families if we do not work?"

Lucia wished she could be anywhere but here. She knew all these men by name, had handed them their pay week after week, had gone to some of their weddings, she knew their children's names.

"I...I," Lucia stammered, "I am sorry that I had to close the warehouse."

A distressed sound rose from the men. Someone called out, "How long will it be closed?" Another voice asked, "Should we look for other work?" More distressed questions were flung into the air.

Guiseppi, his hat twisting in his hands said, "Signora, I have worked for you for ten years. Is it right that you lock us out with no notice?"

Lucia found her voice. She sounded tired. "I have no one I can trust to manage the warehouse."

A young man in the crowd asked, "What about Signor Carlo? Why is he gone?"

Guiseppi turned toward the young man, giving him a stern look. "Be quiet." It was a warning.

Lucia stepped forward her eyes moving over the faces of the men. "You knew he was stealing from me! I see it in your faces!"

"Signora..." Guiseppi almost pleaded, "We thought we were working for Signor Carlo. He..." now the man was openly embarrassed, "He told us that because you were old, you only thought you owned the business. That it was really his. That he let you pass out the pay each week to humor you, out of respect for the memory of your father and husband."

The crowd of men almost all stepped back as one when they saw the look of anger on Lucia's face. Before she could speak, Guiseppi said, "We know now that it is not true. If it were true, we would be talking to him, not to you." Then he quickly added, "Please do not be angry with us...we didn't know. We believed him."

Sofie was alarmed when she saw Lucia's flushed face. Katya was behind Lucia, her hand on the woman's shoulder, a comforting, supportive gesture. It looked as if Lucia swayed slightly. The movement frightened Sofie even more. She had been standing behind Alexie, now she moved alongside him. She took his hand, causing him to look down at her, surprised by the action. Sofie looked into his eyes, searching, not saying anything.

No words passed between them. He looked deep into Sofie's eyes for a long moment. Then he said softly, "Alright, Sofie."

Alexie let go of Sofie's hand and moved alongside Lucia. He took her cold moist hand in his, smiled at the crowd and said to her, "I can't speak Italian...yet."

Her look of wonder transformed itself into a smile, when she comprehended the meaning of his words.

"Tell them," he said, "that today is a holiday for them...a paid holiday." He looked at Lucia, wondering if he had overstepped himself. When she smiled broadly, he went on, "Tell them to come to work tomorrow. That you and I will be there instead of Cousin Carlo and his son."

When Lucia translated Alexie's words to the men, they cheered. Each and every man stepped forward, bowing and shaking Alexie's hand, Lucia's and just to be safe, not taking the chance of offending someone of importance, they also shook, Katya and Sofie's hands. The crowd dispersed. The men with wide smiles waved good-byes with their caps.

When the last man was out of sight and the road was empty, a grateful Lucia turned to Alexie, who had stayed at her side. She leaned into his chest wrapping her arms around his sturdy body and sobbed. He held her gently wondering how it was that within 24 hours he could become so fond of someone.

Sofie stepped into view. She wore a contented smile, while tears of happiness trickled from her eyes. How could she not love this man, who within a day was willing to give up his way of life to help an old woman? This wonderful man who comforted her beloved Lucia?

Katya, too young to understand the enormity of the sacrifice being made by Alexie, was beaming with happiness. For Katya, everything was perfect. Just perfect!

Book II, Chapter 44

The following day Lucia, Alexie, along with Sofie, who knew just enough Italian to be of help to Alexie, walked together to the Renaldi Trading Company.

When they arrived, the happy workers were waiting. Guiseppi, the spokesman for the workers, gave Lucia an envelope, delivered earlier by one of Cousin Carlo's servants. In it was the key for the side door lock, the one she couldn't open the day before.

Katya didn't go to the warehouse. She was sure she would be in the way. Instead, she walked to the rocky shore where she found a comfortable place to sit and watch the curling of the frothy waves as they rolled into the shore.

The place she chose to sit was a favorite spot for Katya. It was the spot she always went to on her quiet walks. She loved looking at the sea. It gave her such comfort to watch the boats glide majestically through the waters. Someday she would take a trip on Lucia's ship the *Vincenti*. She wondered in which direction the ships turned to go to America. The thought excited Katya. She leaned back on her elbows, gazing at the clouds forming and reforming shapes in the sky. Katya thought she could make out a rabbit, a dog and then a woman's face in the ever-changing vapor.

Katya would never know that the spot she loved so much on the shore of the Adriatic Sea may very well have been the same spot that Signore Renaldi, Lucia's father and Katya's biological grandfather, loved so much. Perhaps it was the spot where he sat when he asked the sea if Aleksander Kurecka, the bookkeeper, would be a good husband for his Lucia.

The breeze blew Katya's copper curls about her face...the same color red Vincent Kurecka's hair had been. Katya didn't know now and would not for some time, that Vincent had been her father and that Sofie was her real mother and that the poor over-worked, starved peasant Mila Balich had *never* given birth to her.

What irony that Lucia, her real grandmother had asked Katya to call her Nona...grandmother.

Here was Katya, not knowing she was right where she had belonged in the first place. The Gypsy Valina, reading Katya's palm saw that the girl would find her *right place...the place where she belonged.*

Only one person knew the truth of Katya's parentage and that was Father Lahdra. For the remainder of his life, he kept the secrets of the confessions at the convent that revealed the truth of how Katya had come to Selna on that October night. Those were confessions by which the laws of the church forever forbade him from revealing Katya's true identity.

So, there it was...only Father Lahdra knew the truth of Katya's real heritage.

But...wait...another knew the truth...long before the priest did.

Her name was DESTINY.

THE END

CPSIA information can be obtained
at www.ICGtesting.com
Printed in the USA
BVHW030736190719
553892BV00005B/11/P